Agenda 22

JULIE VIGIL

PAGE PUBLISHING, INC.
New York, NY

First originally published by Page Publishing, Inc. 2019

ISBN 978-1-64544-576-0 (Paperback)
ISBN 978-1-64544-578-4 (Digital)

Printed in the United States of America

To my parents. In memory of my beautiful, amazing, creative mother, Christine Collier who has always loved me, supported me, and never judged me. To my beloved and talented father, Thomas Collier who has been there for me, especially when times were tough. You are my heroes. I love you both, always and forever.

> When I despair, I remember that all through history the way of truth and love have always won. There have been tyrants and murderers, and for a time, they can seem invincible, but in the end, they always fall. Think of it—always.
> —Mahatma Gandhi

> Those that are able to see beyond the shadows and lies of their culture will never be understood let alone believed by the masses.
> —Plato

Peace to all people, everywhere.

JD Vigil

CONTENTS

Part 1—First City
Chapter 1:   Life in First City: 2180...9
Chapter 2:   The Good Citizen Enhancement Facility (GCEF)....19
Chapter 3:   The Final Journey Ceremony 28
Chapter 4:   Assignment to the Badlands 33
Chapter 5:   Elite Watchers 1 50

Part 2—The Archa Compound
Chapter 6:   Malus and the Archa Revealed......................61
Chapter 7:   Screams in the Night................................74
Chapter 8:   Third City (The Farm)...............................87
Chapter 9:   Eighth City and the Yellow Eyes 97
Chapter 10: The Hunt of the Nahus..............................108
Chapter 11: Fourth City. The Obedience Reinforcement
               and Rehabilitation Center (ORRC)....................124
Chapter 12: Sixth City: Full Emergency Medical
               Assessment Center (FEMA) 131
Chapter 13: The Incident in the Gardens 137
Chapter 14: Nightmare Caverns 141

Part 3—The Quest
Chapter 15: The Long Trail 157
Chapter 16: Anna: The Keeper of the Words 172
Chapter 17: The Hive of Archon 178
Chapter 18: Living Wild...204
Chapter 19: The Taming of the Beasts 213
Chapter 20: Ninth City. The Hatchery 222
Chapter 21: Anna's Reunion 232

Part 4—The Revolution

Chapter 22: Return to First City..241
Chapter 23: Falling from the Sky..256
Chapter 24: Malus and the Archa 262
Chapter 25: Fern Point 266
Chapter 26: The Rescue of Boy 01 275
Chapter 27: Raiding the Training Area....................................281
Chapter 28: The Bombing of Ninth City 285
Chapter 29: Recon the Archa Compound................................291
Chapter 30: The Blue Cave..299
Chapter 31: Malus's Final Journey 306
Chapter 32: The Surrender of Eighth City..............................313
Chapter 33: Lyra's Story..318

Part 5—The Future

Chapter 34: Life under the New Earth Charter: 2183...............333
Chapter 35: The Sacred Hill of Golden Butterflies: 2238 337
Chapter 36: The Rising: 2272 345

PART 1

First City

"Welcome to the year 2030. I own nothing, I have no privacy, and life has never been better."

—Ida Auken

CHAPTER 1

∽✺✺∼

Life in First City: 2180

When the Eco-Charter of 2030 passed into law, the Archa (pronounced Arka) toasted themselves with crystal glasses of Gout de Diamants champagne, announcing, "Mission accomplished!" Their crushing defeat of the little straw-people was now permanently etched in history. The Archa had been planning this event for over two hundred years, waiting patiently for technology to become advanced enough for them to control the entire planet. Immediately the Archa ordered the destruction of all the towns, cities, factories, and majority of highways and byways. Specific technology and all forms of transportation suddenly became forbidden. Earth was deliberately taken back into the stone age under the guise of preserving the planet and her ecosystems. Within ten short years, only the Archa's domed cities remained standing.

In the year 2180, a massive translucent dome lay shimmering in a vast desert once known as the great American Southwest. An endless expanse of scrubby vegetation and a few gnarled cacti surrounded this premier icon of the Eco-Charter. Shiny black stinkbugs and iridescent geckos scuttled across the sandy soil. The air was dry and silent. Sometimes, whirling dust devils spiraled across the barren land. This great oasis was called First City, and it was the first of many sustainable cities built around the world. Populations did not exceed one hundred thousand people. Completed in 2040 and constructed to last two thousand years, it was an entirely self-contained system that needed little maintenance. The system provided everyone with everything they needed.

Deep inside the dome of First City, the Eco-citizens lived their lives precisely the same way as their ancestors had for the last hundred and forty years. Between each domed city, there were vast swaths of land referred to as the Forbidden Zones, where no humans were allowed. These regions were then surrounded by Protected Wildlife Corridors. Finally, there were Limited Zones, where a few selected bio-scientists were monitored the flora and fauna.

Under the one-world government and a single currency used, called tetchas (tokens), all citizens received equal credits of tetchas for whatever job they performed. First City, like every other domed city on the planet, was ruled at the local level by the Council of Twelve. They served in their positions for life and chose their own replacements.

In 2030, the Constitution was declared obsolete and outdated, primarily because it promoted individual human rights above and against those of Mother Earth. The Archa introduced a simple justice system called the Primary Eco-Persons Act (the PEPA Act). In the new judicial system, citizens had to represent themselves in all legal issues. The defendant would appear before the Council of Twelve, and there were no appeal processes. No one wanted to speak on another person's behalf at their trial because if the defendant was found guilty, all their character witnesses were also convicted. The condemned disappeared, never to be seen again.

Will 4523 was a citizen who lived inside the dome, in Sector 1, Skyline 6, the EEC (Eco-Enforcement Center), floor 3, unit 366. When the alarm went off, it howled like a shrieking monkey for a few seconds, and then there was a brief silence. The dawn's early rays filtered through the pale, louvered blinds, casting eerie shadows that danced across bleak white walls like sad and broken marionettes hanging from twisted strings.

The voice of MAMM (Medical and Mental Management) blasted from the tiny black-dot speakers that were attached to the wall above the narrow bed. There was also a small communication screen, about thirty-three inches wide, which was used for council announcements. Television no longer existed to entertain the people.

"Greetings, Will 4523. Today is day 15, month 4, the year 2180," announced MAMM cheerfully. She was a digital voice program.

Will's living space consisted of only 250 square feet. He was not permitted to have a kitchen, appliances, or even a tiny sink. In 2180, there was a meager standard of living for everybody, which meant the rationing of all food, water, and clothing.

Will had no carpets or curtains. On the floor were white ceramic tiles. His only piece of furniture was a steel-framed bed with its thin white sheets and worn cotton blankets. A compact, built-in closet held all his belongings. Hanging there were four black uniforms and one pair of black military boots. Will had three sets of gray tunics with matching pants. A single pair of black canvas shoes, size 13, and a few pairs of socks and underwear.

MAMM continued her morning commentary—the Council evidently believed that repetition led to the reinforcement of ideas— as indeed it does.

"Will 4523, it is time to wake up and prepare for the day with a positive attitude. Positive attitudes allow citizens to accomplish goals that are a benefit to our society."

Will opened his eyes while simultaneously stretching to the familiar voice of MAMM.

"It is time to follow protocol. You must proceed to the hygiene room to provide your daily urine sample," MAMM announced cheerfully.

Will complied, walking naked to the hygiene room, and yawned while providing his sample.

MAMM immediately gave the results of his urine analysis.

"Will 4523, your urine analysis is complete. Blood sugar is normal, no contraband foods or illegal drugs detected, and Vitalift levels are within normal parameters. No viruses or bacteria are present. For these reasons, you are deemed fit and healthy for duty."

MAMM issued her next orders. "Proceed to the steam shower for three minutes. Save water and save our planet. Remember, personal sacrifices always benefit society as a whole."

Will stepped into his steam shower and started to relax. A steamy cloud of vapor began at the top of his shaved head. Slowly it inched past the faint teardrop-shaped birthmark on the back of his neck and then moved all the way down his taut, muscular body to his feet—all in a smooth, methodical sweep. It felt like warm sweat beading on his skin. The steam shower lasted for precisely three minutes. It contained a chemical that neutralized his body odor and left a faint lemon scent.

MAMM spoke again. "Will 4523, eat your morning rations and then take your Vitalift pill. Remember, a healthy body creates a healthy mind."

All citizens had to take a mandatory Vitalift pill daily, which was provided free by the Council of Twelve. The Vitalift kept the citizens happy and healthy. Or at least that was their slogan. Both fluoride and lithium were deemed essential to an orderly society, and there was plenty of both in the water rations and tooth-cleaning paste.

Will walked toward the back wall of his living space, with a short white towel wrapped around his lean waist. There was a square metal food chute about twelve inches across. The flashing red light meant the food was incoming. Immediately, Will heard a rumble and clang, and a few seconds later, a small round steel container appeared. He opened it by breaking the wax seal. The steaming white paste smelled like soured milk; luckily, it tasted better than it smelled. For just a second, Will wondered what it would be like to have something different for his first meal of the day.

Will realized to his horror that he was having very negative and ungrateful thoughts. So he banished them from his mind. The Mental Health Facility required citizens to report such extreme feelings if they continued. Then the contaminated individual could be expected to undergo screening and, possibly, treatment. Will wasn't quite sure what the procedure included, because nobody ever spoke about it, but he assumed, although it was necessary, it probably wasn't something he ever wanted to experience.

As Will ate, he checked his rations card. Three more days, and it would be his Birthtime Remembrance Day. On this particular day, he was allowed to choose four ounces of real meat. He was dreaming of a perfectly grilled, juicy steak.

In 2180, there were significant restrictions on eating meat. The rest of the year, all the citizens ate bread, vegetables, and meat substitutes. The only exception was Celebration Day, which was held every year on the summer solstice. The ceremony honored the founding of First City and was the single community event where nobody went to work. The citizens would feast on fresh fruit and baked fish prepared the night before, while First City slowly ground to a halt.

Will's wandering thoughts were interrupted by MAMM. "Will 4523, it is time for your Vitalift pill." And on her command, he obediently swallowed the small bitter blue pill.

Then MAMM's voice bellowed again across the tiny living space.

"Put on your uniform, conduct remaining personal hygiene, and prepare to leave for your work unit in fifteen minutes. Remember, a productive citizen is always a valuable citizen."

After getting dressed in his black uniform, Will put on his combat boots and brushed his teeth with a thick white paste that he swallowed. He rubbed his hand over his shaved head, glancing into the mirror to ensure his uniform was crisp and professional. The insignia for the Eco-Enforcement Unit was a green triangle with EEU printed in black letters. There were two entwined green serpents placed on each side of the acronym.

Will took a final look into the mirror. His green eyes were bright and clear, and he had long black eyelashes. He looked remarkably healthy and active. Will was six feet, two inches tall and weighed 220 pounds. With a strong jaw and broad, even smile, he was a handsome man. But physical appearances weren't considered relevant in his society; efficiency and dedication to the community were the only attractive assets in 2180.

Will would be thirty-six years old in three days. He had spent twenty years serving the community as an Eco-Enforcement officer, and he was glad that he had been selected for that particular unit all those years ago. His duties included teaching classes at the Good Citizen Enhancement Facility, patrolling the streets of First City, and looking for Eco-violators (making sure nobody was trying to make or sell contraband goods). Naturally, alcohol, illicit drugs, and weapons were not allowed in First City. In fact, in the last 140 years, nothing illegal was ever detected.

Patrolling First City wasn't difficult because everyone was compliant. Also, the Cultural Enforcement Officers patrolled continuously, monitoring movement and social exchanges. Specific interactions were not allowed in First City, such as any physical touching or even eye contact between citizens. The only clothing deemed appropriate was government-issued. This social protocol was considered vital to ensure a well-run and efficient city.

Critical thinking was not encouraged. Nobody discussed or thought about anything important in life, due to the extraordinary properties of Vitalift and the education system. Gossiping was a destructive force that could potentially cause divisions in the city and was thus forbidden. In such a rigid society, people did not form any deep friendships—it was far too dangerous. A simple comment could cause a person a lot of unwanted attention from the authorities.

MAMM spoke her final instructions of the morning. "Will 4523, it is time to leave your quarters and go to your work unit. Every day it is your duty to help save our planet and preserve the human race. There is no higher calling than this. Have a productive Eco-day!"

Will closed the door to his living quarters—to his knowledge, there were no locks anywhere in First City—and he walked down the stairs toward the Eco-Enforcement Unit (EEU). He hesitated for a moment as he looked out of the large stairwell window and up to the cerulean sky visible through the transparent dome ceiling.

Will stared at his beloved city. The twelve tower buildings that dominated the dome were called Skylines and numbered consecutively. These ten-story towers housed the citizens, their workplaces, and all other facilities, such as the CDF (Central Dining Facility). The Skylines were gray, drab, and utilitarian. Similar to the old Russian Communist housing projects once called Khrushchyovkas, which were built during the 1960s.

First City was divided into four quadrants for easier control. All the sectors were identical and covered approximately five square miles. Except for the healing facility and the council chambers, which were both located in Quadrant 1.

From where Will was standing, he could see the Central Park, and it was beautiful. It was the only jewel of color in an overwhelmingly monochrome world. Located in the middle of the city, the park had soft, artificial grass and brightly colored solar flowers. The flowers had big velvety petals that glowed after dark, lighting the park with a mirage of exotic hues. The eight-foot-tall solar trees were gentle and feathery. At night, they shone and pulsed, illuminating the tightly packed city with ambient green light. Worn wooden benches appeared scattered across the park, marking designated meditation and retreat areas.

Close to the park was a library filled with about three hundred dusty old paperback books. Most were law books concerning the rules of the Eco-Charter. There were no fictional books, and long ago, all the classics had been burned. There were hundreds of hardback books about different ecosystems and animals. They were well-worn, and their pages fell out anytime somebody looked at them.

Other buildings included a museum dedicated to the madness of the Chaos Era (1964–2029). It contained many ancient artifacts, mostly vehicles, that were now considered a violation of an acceptable Eco-life. There were no personal phones, games, or computers. They had been destroyed a long time ago. Deemed as an unnecessary distraction.

There was a small fitness facility. Everybody had to sign up for a fitness program that depended on age and ability. Soccer was very popular, and there were four teams in the city, one from each quadrant, that played with one another. Nobody was ever declared a winner or a loser. The goals scored were points either for Mother Earth or its plants and animals, never for the team itself. All players were equally thanked for having participated in the games. Other sports activities included bike riding, yoga, and weekly running marathons around the city. As a powerful runner, Will regularly ran the gauntlet.

Entertainment in First City was limited. Movie theaters were obsolete, but there was a vast amphitheater made of stone and rock close to the park. Here actors and actresses, referred to as players, performed stories and plays, often about the infamous Chaos Era. The stories were predictable and always ended with a positive message about today's utopian society. All performances were eagerly anticipated and occurred about once every thirty days. Sometimes, story-makers would tell stories, or sounders would sing sad songs from the Chaos Era or happy songs about the Eco-Charter. There were no songs about passion, love, or emotion, because those things were forbidden in society.

The EEU was just three floors down from Will's living space. In this era, virtually no travel was necessary for everyday life; everybody either walked or rode the city bicycles. If a citizen needed transportation, they just took a bike, used it, and then returned it to the nearest Transit Center.

Will didn't know if life was different in other cities, but here, most people were born, grew up, worked, and died, never leaving First City for their entire lives. Travel passes in and out of the city were difficult to obtain, and First City was surrounded by miles of windswept, dusty desert. So there was nowhere to go. Even the most senior member of the Council of Twelve had never traveled anywhere outside the dome. Occasionally, people were selected for assignments located outside the city, but they usually returned after twenty years and they appeared to be unable to remember any of their previous experiences.

There was always a calm predictably and peacefulness that all Eco-citizens enjoyed in First City. Nothing ever changed; there were never any types of crisis or calamities from birth until death. Life was stable and orderly. Will understood that citizens' lives were so much better since the Eco-Charter had been implemented. For the last 140 years, the Council of Twelve and all the global laws controlled every aspect of a citizen's life. And rightly so, thought Will.

In 2180, cameras monitored everyone all the time. Each building had a walk-through RFID reader called a Relay Reader. At birth, each citizen had an RFID chip inserted into their forearm. The monitoring center was part of the transportation grid, which kept copious files on all the citizens living in First City, from their birth to their Final Journey. It was impossible to avoid being tracked, and Will believed it was a perfect system.

Arriving at the Eco-Enforcement Unit, Will walked in through the doorway and past the administration desk, greeting his fellow workers with a brief bow. Eye contact was discouraged to deter any potential altercation. The correct protocol was to keep one's eyes slightly downcast during any interaction with another person. The polite way to address an unknown individual was to say to them, "Greetings, Eco-citizen," or in parting, "Fare-well, Eco-citizen."

John 7863 was Will's over-leader. He was a small and slight man with dark-brown eyes and a large nose, but he was amazingly strong for his stature. John was capable and ran his department efficiently. He always followed correct procedures, as all good citizens did. John acknowledged Will. Even though they had worked together for twenty years, they were still socially correct when addressing each other.

"Greetings, Will 4523," said John.

"Greetings, John 7863," Will replied.

John continued his morning briefing. "This morning you must provide the daily informational block at the Good Citizen Enhancement Facility, and then you will attend a Final Journey ceremony. After you have eaten your second ration for the day, return here, and I will brief you on your new assignment."

Will was now at clearance level 20. On his Birthtime Remembrance Day, he would be at level 21, and that meant he was eligible for a special promotion. Will didn't have any idea what his new job would be. His type of assignment didn't matter to him because Will believed his only duty was to fulfill whatever placement the Council gave him.

Predictably, Will had no questions or any comments for John. Will merely nodded and stated, "I will comply."

Will left the building and walked to Skyline 3. A few Eco-citizens were striding with purpose along the street. Will did not greet anyone; he merely gave a slight nod of respect to others that were walking toward him.

In First City, humor was deemed offensive and forbidden, so people never made jokes. Citizens never smiled at one another because smiling at another person would be showing a preference to them above others. Being equal in every possible way was vital to society.

In a society where, microscopic surveillance was the norm, people usually made very superficial relationships with one another and held most thoughts to themselves. In such a rigid society, anyone could be reported at any time to the authorities for the mere suspicion that they might be saying or thinking something inappropriate. Predictably, this type of paranoia led to a very fragmented society that looked like a well-organized hive from the outside. But inside, like the ants, everybody was on automatic pilot.

CHAPTER 2

The Good Citizen Enhancement Facility (GCEF)

On the outside wall of Skyline 3, there was an old metal sign that read, "Good Citizen Enhancement Facility," and the mantra inscribed on the wall was one that every citizen had to learn:

1. *A healthy body creates a healthy mind.*
2. *A positive attitude creates a positive person.*
3. *To work is to live, because life must be productive.*
4. *Always accept less for the benefit of global conservation.*
5. *The common good supersedes personal needs.*
6. *Individualism causes division.*
7. *The sacrifice of the few is always necessary to save the many.*
8. *Choice leads to confusion.*
9. *Confusion leads to wrong decisions.*
10. *An obedient citizen is a valuable citizen.*

The Good Citizen Enhancement Facility (GCEF) was created in 2032 and cared for the masses of orphans who became dependent on the state during the Great Cleansing of the Dark Ages. Since the facility had produced obedient citizens consistently for many years, the New-Eco Charter was amended to mandate that all children be removed from their mothers for the benefit of society. The center trained children from six days old to sixteen years. The highly skilled and dedicated Guardians had trained in the art of teaching good citizenship and ran the facility efficiently. Since true equality meant no citizen could be smarter than another, the pace of education was always lowered to the weakest student, who set the standard for the whole class.

There was no individuality allowed. The sole purpose of the GCEF was to send compatible citizens to be assimilated into First City's society. Each class of children was a collective because they learned together and slept in neat rows of metal beds in the same large room.

The minor-citizens ate separately from the working adult population, in a massive food facility located in their Skyline.

The two sexes were completely equal, raised with identical conditions of discipline and opportunity. There were large communal bathrooms shared by all the students. Ethnicity or race wasn't important according to the Eco-Charter; compliance was a far more critical factor. First City was racially diverse, just as the incredible country of America had been.

Rarely would a child show a propensity for violence or question the regime in First City. Those that did were immediately classified as antisocial and segregated very early on from the remainder of the population. These troubled individuals were sent to the Obedience Reinforcement and Rehabilitation Center (ORRC) until they learned to obey the rules and the norms of their society. When the children returned, they were always very submissive, just like everybody else. A few children disappeared permanently because their mental illness was so severe that they were detained indefinitely in the rehabilitation center in Fourth City. Or at least those were the rumors. No one knew for sure. Protocol demanded that the names of those who were no longer part of First City never be spoken of again.

Will taught on almost every subject in the GCEF because humans had an impact on the environment in every aspect of their lives. As Will walked through the familiar, drab corridors, he could hear chanting coming from the various learning rooms. The facility currently housed five hundred children.

The minor-citizens were secretly monitored carefully for abilities, talents, and shortcomings. This information was compiled and used as a guide to select work units for them when they became adolescents. At the age of sixteen, the students were given a life-placement career, advised by their Guardians and ultimately approved by the Council of Twelve. It was essential to select the correct profession for each student because they remained in that job until death. In 2180, nobody ever retired.

Will had to give a lecture to the grade 5 minor-citizens about helping reinforce Eco-responsibilities. As he walked into the grade 5 training area, the children were sitting silently, their eyes downcast and their hands neatly folded on their laps. There were five rows of four children, making a total of twenty students in the learning class. They were wearing gray tunics, matching pants, and black canvas shoes. All their heads were shaved to conserve water, just like the adults.

The Guardian, referred to as G5, was teaching the minor-citizens about religion. Will settled in to listen, and he knew all the information she was lecturing by heart.

"What is the definition of *religion*?" the Guardian asked the minors. Immediately several little hands were clasped on top of their bald heads.

G5 nodded at the child in front of her.

The minor's tag read Ellen 2678. She stood up with her hands by her sides and spoke in a calm, controlled voice. "*Religion* is a primitive, barbaric reaction to the outside world by those who are too ignorant to understand scientific theories."

"Excellent," replied G5 primly.

Exactly how religion disappeared from society was never discussed, understood, or explained. Organized religion had been deemed divisive to the creation and cohesion of the Eco-Charter. In 2030, it became illegal to follow any religious beliefs at all. Every place of worship was ordered to be demolished by the New-Eco Charter. These new laws caused riots and violence all over the planet. To combat the civil disobedience, the Culture Enforcement Squad was formed and was assigned to rid Earth of all religion and its many zealots. The CES put bounties on religious people's heads and encouraged gangs of roving mercenaries to participate in the murders. These groups made millions, which the Eco-Charter confiscated before the mercenaries were exterminated.

Over an eight-year period, the Culture Enforcement Squads massacred millions of people without mercy. When all the religious dissidents were dead, the population of the world was reduced by 84 percent from nine billion to just over one billion. The Archa sighed with relief.

For many moons, the Earth was wet with the blood of her children. As the crematoriums worked day and night to destroy millions of dead bodies. They produced tons of ash that suffocated the Earth with smoky black skies, blocking out the sun and slightly cooling the planet for some years. Living through those times was like surviving Dante's Inferno. People walked around with respirators, masks, and long dark clothes to protect themselves from the falling ash and from being recognized. Huge bonfires burned twenty-four hours a day in this hellish twilight world packed with thousands of religious books along with the classics. The fires could be seen from space, dotting the Earth with ominous, glowing red blobs.

Eventually, the survivors stopped fighting, exhausted by all the devastation, death, and starvation. They surrendered to the new government laws. These people were immediately registered as the first Eco-citizens. This label meant that they were merely a citizen of the Earth and they had no assigned religion other than a belief in taking care of the planet. These obedient citizens were moved speedily out of the crumbling, stricken cities and were sent to clean, safe refugee camps. The new Eco-citizens became the first people allowed to move into the domed cities.

There were mandatory re-education camps for others, particularly the great minds of their time and, of course, those who refused to accept the New-Eco Charter. They were brutal torture camps, so most refugees did not survive them; those few that did became human husks.

G5 asked the class another question. "In what year were all the citizens finally free from all evil religious oppression?"

This time the Guardian chose a child two rows toward the back to answer. His tag was David 6790. David stood up and replied, "By 2040, society had finally succeeded in their mission, and citizens were officially united."

"Correct, David 6790," answered G5 with conviction.

"Last question, minor-citizens," the Guardian said while looking at the clock. It was exactly one minute before the hour. "What do we call this period in our history?" she asked.

Immediately all the small hands were gingerly balanced on their scalps.

The Guardian selected a child from the back of the room. Her tag read Susan 2312. She stood up and replied, "The Great Cleansing of the Dark Ages."

The Guardian merely nodded in response to the correct answer. She didn't explain to the class that this phrase sounded much better than globally-sanctioned religious genocide.

G5 motioned to Will, signaling that he could speak to the learning class. He stood up and scanned the room, cleared his throat, and introduced himself as an Eco-Enforcement Unit officer, as he always did, even though the students knew him. Will spoke for some minutes about how the fresh water shortage affected the whole of planet Earth and how conservation was vital to the human race's survival. That access to clean water was not a right but a privilege. Will talked about the environment and the necessary, strict population control that was critical to the sustainability of the Earth and her resources.

Will explained that back in history, around 2025, overpopulation became a significant problem, so a worldwide, one-child policy was introduced, but it wasn't very successful. Will stated that a virus appeared in 2027, which provided the perfect solution to the problem. This new type of waterborne illness originated in Africa, then spread to the Middle East and Asia. There was no cure for the resulting stillbirths, miscarriages, and sterility. Finally, live births plummeted all over the earth. The Archa viewed their piteous subjects via high tech surveillance while grinning like psychotic cats and, hissing mission accomplished.

Will continued his lecture. By 2040, he explained, the techno-logical and medical advances allowed the human reproductive sys-tem to be shut down on a temporary or permanent basis. Which was a positive step for humankind. Eventually, the birth procedure evolved into a lottery, called the Birthright Lottery. Will explained that today, the lottery only occurred when an Eco-citizen died. So it was an excellent system, allowing the population of the world to remain tightly controlled, thus becoming very stable for the first time in human history.

Will did not know that during this era, the punishment for trying to reverse infertility was death, or that a deliberate side effect of the virus was the destruction of sexual desire in 100 percent of the population, and so naturally there was no real incentive to procreate.

In 2180, genetically healthy citizens aged between sixteen and twenty-nine were forced to participate and undergo artificial insem-ination. Those chosen in the lottery were complete strangers. Most females were silently reluctant because of the problems of pregnancy and the danger of childbirth. After the birth, the relieved mother would never see her child again. Predictably, sixteen years later, the children and parents were unable to recognize one another on the street.

The minor-citizens were quiet and still as Will completed his speech. They had heard the same speech many times. He glanced across the learning space and saw nobody had raised their hands for questions that required further explanation. The Guardian thanked him politely, and he left.

Will walked back through the dull corridors to the next learning space, which was at the end of the facility. The most-senior students were in the sixteenth grade. These students would graduate at the end of the summer. Once these young citizens received their work assignments, they would begin as trainees immediately. The transi-tion from childhood to adult was considered critical and needed to progress smoothly and were no vacations in First City.

Will vaguely remembered when he first received his assigned career, which seemed so long ago. All citizens understood that they had to accept these life placements for the benefit of society. First

City had a hive mentality that relied on functional interactions necessary to run a thriving city. In 2180, the happiness of an individual was irrelevant.

As Will entered the sixteenth-grade learning room, the Guardian greeted him politely. Will immediately addressed the class and began his speech. When he had finished, the students remained as silent as those in the fifth grade. The Guardian, called G16, remarked that the minor-citizens had received their assignments, and she asked Will if he would like to observe the remainder of the career placements. Will gave a slight nod in agreement.

The Guardian opened a sealed white envelope; inside was a shiny, new, chipped ID card. This card held all the students' information for the last sixteen years. It would be downloaded by their over-leaders when they began their new assignments.

The Guardian spoke. "Jane 6543, you have been assigned to the Healing Center. You will be trained to become a healer."

Jane walked up to the Guardian to receive her new ID card. She nodded briefly and stated, "I am honored to become a new healer and serve other Eco-citizens," and with her eyes still downcast, she returned silently to her seat.

The Guardian opened the second envelope. "Derek 4512, you have been assigned to the Obedience Reinforcement Rehabilitation Center as an ORRC officer."

Derek's face appeared impassive while he gave the perfect and expected response. "I am grateful that I have an opportunity to serve First City." After the boy had returned to his seat, he turned his new ID card over and over on his lap.

The Guardian announced, "I have one final placement to read." She opened the last envelope and read the contents. "Joe 3421, your assignment is to the Central Dining Facility as a dish sterilizer."

Suddenly, Joe made a sound like a wounded animal and lunged forward, aiming for the door while shouting, "No! No!"

Immediately Will tackled him, threw him to the floor, and handcuffed him in less than ten seconds.

The boy continued to howl, and the Guardian was shocked but held her composure. "Joe 3421, why did you display this emotional outburst? You have never been anything but a compliant citizen."

Joe was sobbing, and his shoulders were heaving. It was like a dam had broken inside of him.

"I want to work on the Farm. I want to be a grower!" he cried.

The Guardian replied patiently, "But, Joe 3421, First City doesn't need any more growers at this time. First City needs a dish sterilizer. Therefore, you must comply."

"I don't want to!" yelled Joe. Now the room was visibly shocked by his continued tantrum.

"Very well," replied the Guardian quietly, "you leave me no choice." And she pressed a small red pendant that hung around her neck on a thin black cord.

Will had never seen an outburst like this before. He stood stunned, still holding the boy, who was no longer struggling, just sobbing and hiccupping, with tears streaming down his red cheeks.

Within five minutes, Will heard the boots of the Obedience Reinforcement and Rehabilitation Center officers. They came in, and without a word, they picked up the sobbing boy under the arms and dragged him down the corridor, taking him to the center for evaluation.

As Joe disappeared, he gave Will a look of total despair, and then suddenly his face became blank, as if he had resigned himself to his fate.

The Guardian spoke to the learning room about how the purpose of their lives was to serve First City and not themselves. She explained that Joe would receive the necessary rehabilitation to make him a better citizen and a compliant dish sterilizer.

Will was ready for his next appointment. He bade Fare-well to the Guardian, who nodded and replied, "As always."

As Will left, he glanced at the learning room. The minors were silent, and their eyes remained downcast. Will thought Joe's behavior showed a total lack of discipline that was not acceptable. Obedience was essential in First City, and he had never seen such an appalling display of emotion and wondered if G16 should reassign herself.

The moment Will stepped out of the dim building into the pale sunlight, he immediately forgot about Joe 3421, because it wasn't in his job description to worry about the behavior of minors. Will was already thinking about his next mission. Striding with purpose, he made his way to the Healing Center.

CHAPTER 3

The Final Journey Ceremony

As Will walked toward the Healing Center, he stared at the Skyline. Besides the Council of Twelve, eleven other principal agencies ran First City:

1. Skyline 1. The Council of Twelve: (CO12) headquarters. They controlled all judicial and legal oversights.
2. Skyline 2. Financial Credits and Housing: (FH). All living spaces were identical and were monitored by cameras, controlled and operated via MAMM.
3. Skyline 3. The Good Citizen Enhancement Facility (GCEF).
4. Skyline 4. The Obedience Reinforcement and Rehabilitation Center (ORRC).
5. Skyline 5. The Full Emergency, Medical, Assessment Center: (FEMA). Its primary purpose was for medical advancement and genetic testing.
6. Skyline 6. The Eco-Enforcement Unit (EEU).
7. Skyline 7. The Community Services (CS). Organized entertainment and sports activities.
8. Skyline 8. The Government Center of Power (GCP). Dealt with transportation: grid passes and the Monitoring Relay System (RFID), tracking movement and location.
9. Skyline 9. The Central Food Facility: (CFF). Provided meals for everyone, rations, and Vitalift.

10. Skyline 10. Managed Hygiene (MH). Water rations, waste recycling, the lithium and fluoride programs, and the processing of human waste products into digestible protein.
11. Skyline 11. The Healing Facility: (HF). Monitored health and the Last Journey Ceremonies.
12. Skyline 12. The Farming and Fauna Facility: (FFF). Provided eggs, goats milk, and cheese to the community. The Farm included an orchard, vegetable gardens and a small flower garden for Final Journey ceremonies.

The Final Journey ceremony was conducted for all citizens when they reached the age of sixty-five because it signaled the end of the human life span. In 2180, all persons expired on their sixty-fifth Birthtime.

The night before their demise, the citizen arrived at the Final Journey Ceremonial Wing at the Healing Center. Then they were put to bed, wearing a distinctive white cotton burial gown, and hooked up to an IV. That kept the patient alive long enough to say Fare-well to the citizens selected to witness the event. Will believed this to be an important and traditional ceremony.

Fresh, fragrant flowers were woven into a garland and placed around the neck of the dying person. So their final moments were filled with the scent, color, and beauty of real flowers. Death was just a part of the cycle of life, and everybody faced it with grace and dignity. There were no beliefs in an afterlife.

Will walked into the Ceremonial Room at the Healing Center in Skyline 11, where Steven 2381 was lying in his bed, looking remarkably healthy and alert for a dying man. But surprisingly, this was normal. Most dying patients appeared this way.

Steven stared at Will as he entered the room. The death ceremony allowed privileges and behavior not acceptable in ordinary, everyday life. The dying citizens were allowed to eat whatever they wished the day before their ceremony, and for breakfast too, even real meat.

The rest of the witnesses were waiting for Will, and they all gathered in a tight circle and chanted the Final Journey Ceremonial Words in unison at precisely 11:11 a.m.

"Good citizen, today it is time for your final journey. Steven 2381, you have served your community well, and your life has been one of productivity and sacrifice for Mother Earth. We stand with you as you take your last journey, where your body will return to the earth, from whence it came. We are thankful for your long and valuable service to First City and all its citizens."

Then each person broke from the circle to stand directly at the foot of Steven's bed. There they kneeled and bowed their heads in respect to the man's life accomplishments. It was an insult to turn their backs on a dying man, so each citizen stood and returned to their original place in the circle by walking backward with their head still bowed. When everybody present had performed the ritual, they began chanting again.

"It is now time, Steven 2381, faithful Eco-citizen, that we bid you Fare-well for one last time."

Then Steven spoke, as it was customary for the dying citizen to say the last words.

"Greetings, Eco-citizens. Thank you for being here to share my Final Journey. I return to Mother Earth knowing I have served her well and have sacrificed in my lifetime for the betterment of our splendid society. My heart is at peace. I am ready to return to the beautiful Earth."

At this moment, the healer put some medicine into Steven's IV to allow his expiration process to be painless. Steven closed his eyes, breathed two small breaths, and then exhaled loudly. The green line on the heart monitor stopped moving up and down and became a straight line while emitting a long monotone beep that filled the silent room.

Then the healer covered Steven's peaceful face with a white sheet, and she announced, "Our beloved citizen has returned to his mother, the Earth."

The witnesses clapped their hands in unison and began to leave the room quietly in single file. The group dispersed and went their separate ways. Not another word was spoken between them, because to speak the deceased's name was to bring dishonor to the whole ceremony and disturb the peace of the recently departed.

After a person had died in First City, their body went into a large composting pit, where microbes could decompose the body back into compost, which was then used to fertilize the soil. The disposal of bodies was the responsibility of the Final Journey overseer.

After leaving the Healing building, Will made his way to the Central Food Facility. The CFF was open twenty-four hours a day to accommodate those citizens working shifts. Everybody ate two hot meals there. Will stood in line while reaching for a metal tray and a bowl. A bland vegetable soup was usually served at midday with a slice of freshly baked bread and a tiny piece of goat cheese.

The Birthtime Celebration Room was separate from the central dining area so other citizens weren't envious or distracted while they ate their meals.

Will thought the third ration of the day was the best, as they served the green patty or the PP burger with potatoes and vegetables. For dessert, there was usually a piece of fruit or, occasionally, a slice of pie. Will thought the cherry pie was the most delicious, and his fantasy quickly faded into reality as he began to eat his warm bowl of watery soup.

The food was eaten in complete silence because it made the food facility less chaotic and more efficient. Everyone quietly ate their food, avoiding eye contact, and put their empty dishes into the disposal chute. Drinking water was rationed to two quarts (sixty-four ounces) per person daily.

In June 2011, a Japanese scientist called Mitsuyuki Ikeda developed a type of burger made from soya, steak sauce essence, and protein extracted from human feces. It was nicknamed the poop burger. Later its name was changed to the PP burger.

In 2013, there was a significant announcement by NASA. They invented a universal food synthesizer that used a 3D printer to produce food. The cartridges contained carbohydrate and protein powders, made from insects, grass, and algae. This magical powder, known as green replaced meat as the primary source of protein in most human diets. It was still eaten in First City.

In 2018, the eating of edible insects began to be promoted very aggressively by all the governments of the world because many mainstream scientists believed that insects were the perfect food for people, being low in fat and high in protein. By 2021, the insect industry created thousands of jobs while feeding billions of people across the world. Bugs were considered the solution to world hunger.

After he had eaten his food, Will sauntered back to the Eco-Enforcement Unit, continually watched by the eyes in the sky. The cameras glared everywhere, at everyone, with unforgiving and enormous red blinking lights. Will was idly wondering about his new assignment as he passed silently through the various RFID Relay Readers. He was blissfully unaware of the fact that society had rendered him into an indentured slave.

CHAPTER 4

Assignment to the Badlands

Will reported back to his over-leader to learn about his new assignment. As he walked through the Relay Reader, it acknowledged him with a loud ping. John 7853 was staring at the unit and finally said irritably, "Greetings, Eco-citizen. I have to get that Data Relay Machine adjusted," he remarked. "It is supposed to be silent."

"Is it recording correctly?" Will asked.

"Oh, yes," replied John tiredly. "It's still relaying data, but it keeps on pinging. It's been doing it all morning."

Will said nothing, because only facts were relevant to a conversation and his personal opinion had no value.

"No matter," John continued. "Enough about the Data Relay Machine. I have important instructions to discuss with you this day. We need to go to the Solo Room for our briefing."

The Solo Room was unique because it was only monitored by the Council of Twelve and did not have a standard Data Relay recorder. Will was surprised. In his entire career, he had never been inside the secret Solo Room, and for this reason, he had always thought it just a myth.

Will eagerly followed John as he opened a locked door next to the cleaning closet. Will had always thought this entry guarded large cleaning machines, and since he was not a cleaner, he had never tried to open it. Inside the tiny room was a locked metal door with a basic, luminous keypad. John was standing in front of the door, and Will heard six keys being pressed in rapid succession and a loud metallic click as the heavy door swung open, revealing a small sloping tunnel. At the end of the tunnel was yet another door with an equally anti-quated keypad. Although the dome itself was high-tech, the facilities within the dome were sadly primitive. The Archa did not want the Eco-citizens to be familiar with technology.

As Will and John walked toward the last door, the air smelled damp and felt slightly cooler compared to the temperature in the rooms above. Outside the room, John tapped out another code on the second keypad, and they entered the Solo Room. It was a small windowless white room. In the center of the Solo Room was a dark wooden table with six matching chairs, and a small mahogany desk that stood against the left wall. On the right wall was a large cup-board with its doors tightly locked with a big padlock.

Will was surprised, because the room looked so ordinary. A sin-gle camera was attached to a small blinking red light on the back wall. It glowed in the dark like the eye of Cyclops.

John pressed a small yellow dot by the door, and instantly the little room became illuminated by a glaring white spotlight.

"Sit," commanded John, taking the seat at the head of the table.

Will had said nothing throughout this whole process and merely obeyed. He noticed the second door in the back wall, beneath the blinking red light.

They sat in silence, and shortly they heard the sound of two pairs of boots walking along the concrete floor, and two Eco-officers walked in, so John and Will stood up to greet them.

"Greetings, Eco-citizens," announced John. "I am John 7853. I am the Eco-Enforcement over-leader for Quadrant 1. And this is Will 4523, selected for the Special Assignment."

The two unknown Eco-citizens identified themselves.

"Greetings, Eco-citizens. My tag and my number is Conrad 2343. I am the Eco-Enforcement over-Leader for Quadrant Four," replied a tall man with gray eyes and a stoic disposition. He had a large jagged scar on his right eyebrow. He had another on his left cheek that crossed from the corner of his left eye to the very edge of his mouth. The injuries appeared old. The man was about sixty. He seemed to have a perpetual frown because the scar twisted his mouth a little, and altogether, he looked very intimidating. Will wondered what had happened to Conrad; injuries like his were very unusual in First City.

Stepping from behind Conrad was a woman. She was lithe and fit and about five feet, ten inches tall. She had large blue eyes set in her heart-shaped face. She also had a prominent beauty mark on her left cheek, which she considered an unfortunate blemish, because it distinguished her from other citizens and made her memorable, which was not an asset in 2180. She looked vaguely familiar, and she spoke in a calm, clear voice.

"My tag and number are Mica 3432. I am an Eco-officer from Quadrant 4, selected for the Special Assignment." She spoke with almost a musical tone to her voice.

Suddenly, Will remembered that he and Mica had worked together one summer about twenty years ago. She had been a year older than him and was assisting with the training program for the new Eco-officers. Although they had barely known each other, he remembered her blemish. After completing his training, Mica returned to a different quadrant due to an unexpected death. Mica was chosen as the replacement officer in Quadrant 4. Will remembered her as an efficient and competent citizen.

Once the formalities were over with, Conrad and Mica sat down, and John closed the door with a loud clank. Then he took his seat.

"I am sure you are wondering why you are here in the Solo Room?" asked John rhetorically. He continued, "Will 4523 and Mica 3432, you have both been assigned to a unique unit, called the Elite Watchers 1. Selection for this particular assignment was due to your excellent characters, citizenship, and intelligence." John continued, "I believe that you are both capable of performing well in any mission you receive. I have great faith that you are both excellent choices and you will be very successful in your new assignments."

Will was somewhat confused about the statement John had made. Will had never heard of intelligence used as a deciding factor in anything concerning First City.

"Something else you both need to be aware of," said John. "At the end of your assignment, you will both be about fifty-six years old. At that time, you will return to First City and live the remainder of your lives here. However, before you return, both of you will have your memories of that period erased. Sometimes a few fragments of your memory may return. Unfortunately, memory erasure is not an exact science, and if you begin to remember things, you must report immediately to the Obedience Reinforcement and Rehabilitation Center for further treatment. Because your mission is highly classified, discussing it even with each other on your return to First City could result in both of you receiving the death penalty for treason. Do you understand?"

Will and Mica both nodded silently.

"Very well," said John. "Now, you must both sign paperwork stating you understand what I have just told you."

Will and Mica started signing several sheets of paper. Will realized that he was signing his life and memories away. He shivered, chilled by the thought. John's words were flowing over Will like a fast river, and he barely understood them because they were strange and fearful. Will was unaware they could erase citizens' memories, but he kept his expression blank and continually repeated the words with Mica.

"Yes, Over-Leader."

Then John told Will and Mica, "You will both leave this afternoon, after this meeting, and you will go immediately to your new destination."

Will wondered where their destination was. He had heard rumors of other cities, but he had no idea of their location or direction.

John continued, "Eco-citizens, Fare-well. Be successful in your new lives. Remember, only the very top 1 percent of citizens with the most excellent character traits are ever selected to serve as Elite Watchers 1. You both bring great honor to First City."

John finished his briefing and stood up. "You will follow Over-Leader Conrad 2343 right now. You will be given new uniforms and equipment at your new location. You are dismissed."

Conrad got up, and Will and Mica followed him out of the Solo Room, leaving John behind, deep in thought. John muttered under his breath to the empty room, "May Gaia give you both blessings."

The three Eco-officers walked back through the corridors and finally emerged into the light. Both Will and Mica wondered what lay ahead of them. This was the first time they had ever thought about anything except daily life.

The two new recruits marched behind Conrad to the beginning of Quadrant 4, which was about two miles away. It was a replica of Quadrant 1. They walked through that entire section until they came to First City's twenty-foot wall. Will and Mica wondered what they were doing there; there was no way to scale the wall. To their utter amazement, Conrad produced a tiny device that looked like a small black beetle, complete with miniature antennae. With one single press, a section of the painted wall slid back to reveal a steel door. Conrad used the tiny controller, and the steel door slid open sideways.

Will and Mica walked through the wall for the first time, realizing they were beginning a new chapter in their lives. The two Eco-Enforcement officers started staring at the expansive desert around them. A hot breeze was blowing the sand, and it was difficult to see much of anything through the stinging, dusty air. Conrad bent down and wiped away some small rocks and sand near their feet, and then he opened a trapdoor that had been invisible just a moment before.

Will and Mica walked down a steep set of stairs while Conrad carefully closed the trapdoor. They continued walking into a dimly lit concrete tunnel, where a slightly cooler air current was blowing through. There was a pungent and unfamiliar smell of fuel and oil. The three of them walked for about two minutes when the tunnel suddenly curved to the left. There appeared to be some checkpoint looming into view out of the darkness. It was a small desk, with a single light bulb shining on a lone man, who was sitting there, motionless.

"Wait here!" ordered Conrad, and he walked over to the guard on duty and handed him some papers. They greeted each other with the customary greeting. "Greetings, Eco-citizen." Then they lowered their voices and exchanged a few words that neither Mica nor Will could hear.

Conrad motioned for them to follow him, and as they walked through the checkpoint, the disinterested guard waved them through. Rounding another curve that snaked to the right, they could see there was daylight at the end of a long tunnel. They drew closer to the light until, finally, they emerged from the darkness. The bright sunlight dazzled their eyes.

Will and Mica, to their utter and complete amazement, saw a small Skybird in front of them, sitting on the runway. They couldn't believe their eyes. They were speechless. To their right, there was a significant rocky outcrop that shielded the tiny airport from the view of First City. Neither Will nor Mica had ever seen a working Skybird in real life before. To their knowledge, there were only a few of them left in the entire world, and to Mica's understanding, two of those were in First City's museum. Will thought all the Skybirds were evil, polluting machines that damaged the environment and sucked up gallons of precious fossil fuels that Earth had taken millions of years to accrue.

Will and Mica slowly walked toward the white Skybird. Mica noticed it had red wingtips with blue and red pinstripes along the sides.

Conrad stopped at the bottom of the boarding stairs and said, "I must return to Quadrant 4. Climb these stairs, and on board, you will receive further instructions."

He saw the guarded look in their eyes, as both the officers were still trying to recover their composure. He smiled weakly at them, saying, "You haven't seen anything yet. You are entering a different life." Then he whispered conspiratorially, "I still have some memories they couldn't purge. Just like my scars, they are mine, and I own them. The authorities will never know this, but those are the days I still long for." Conrad began to walk away, smiling sadly to himself.

Will and Mica did not understand a word that Conrad had spoken; they merely stared for a moment at his retreating figure and then followed his last order.

The two Eco-Enforcement officers climbed up the metal stairs and gingerly entered the Skybird. All their lives they had seen a strict, utilitarian world of black, white, and gray. Except, of course, for the Central Park. Inside the Skybird there was a thick, plush red carpet and eight pale, expensive cream leather seats.

Will and Mica were trying to absorb their new surroundings. Mica was on her knees, stroking the carpet, and Will was staring at the smooth leather seats. A tall woman approached them; she looked strange and alien. In a soft voice, the vision in red spoke. "Eco-citizens, follow me. I am Stella 642. I am your Skybird helper."

Stella was wearing a short red tunic that fitted tightly to her ample curves. On her dainty feet were bright-red shoes with long spiked heels. Her head was not bald like the rest of the Eco-citizens. The strange woman had a beautiful curtain of silky blond hair. Her face was painted with different colors.

Stella was wearing bright, metallic purple-and-brown eye-shadow around her big blue eyes. Her eyelashes were half an inch long and curled at the ends. Even her eyebrows were plucked into an exquisite design and embellished with jewels, making a trail of glittering tiny diamonds across the top of her brow bones. Stella's cheeks were pink, and she had bright-red lips. Her fingernails were incredibly long, painted red, and had little sparkles stuck on them.

Will thought she looked like an exotic butterfly he had once seen in a book in the library, and he was mesmerized by her. His eyes followed her every dainty move.

Mica stood up and felt uncomfortable being near another female for the first time in her life. She felt so dull and drab next to this strange, painted being. Mica wondered if Stella was even human; perhaps Stella was a metal creature that came with the Skybird. *Yes,* Mica said to herself, *that makes sense*. And she immediately began feeling less self-conscious.

The Eco-Enforcement officers followed Stella to their assigned seats. Both Will and Mica could smell a strong floral scent that wafted around her. They sat down, touching the soft leather, feeling luxury for the first time in their lives. Stella showed them how to secure their seat belts and asked them if they would like a drink, and Will and Mica nodded, unsure of what Stella meant; to them a drink was a cup half full of lukewarm water. Stella disappeared, walking toward the back of the Skybird, shortly returning with two glasses filled with sparkling water, ice, and a slice of lime.

Will and Mica sniffed their drinks, and the tiny bubbles tickled their noses. They had never seen ice before, and Mica kept poking at it with her index finger. The new watchers exchanged a glance, happy to embrace their new lives. Both felt optimistic, looking forward to their assignment in this wondrous, new world.

As the Skybird taxied down the runway, Will gripped the arms of his seat. Sweat started to bead on his forehead.

Stella smiled at him. "Do not have fear," she said. "I have flown in the sky many times."

Unconvinced, Will closed his eyes tightly, wishing it were time to land.

Will was sitting next to a window, and he noticed all the windows that lined the inside of the Skybird were blacked out with some dark, gel-like film. There appeared to be a tiny crack in the black gel, at the bottom of the left corner of the window, where a slither of light flickered.

Will and Mica had been flying for about half an hour when Will stared at the tiny crack in the film. For a long time, he could only glimpse the sandy desert below, and then nothing else for miles. About two hours later, Will glanced again, and he couldn't believe his eyes: miles below the Skybird lay a bright-green expanse that shouldn't exist. All the Earth was supposed to be a scorched desert. Slowly the chink of light faded as darkness fell, and he could not see anything else.

Finally, Stella told them they were preparing to land and took a seat across from them and fastened her seat belt. Will estimated they had been in the air at least four hours, heading northwest.

The Skybird landed smoothly, barely grazing the landing strip, then slowed and came to a complete stop. Stella undid her seat belt, motioning Will and Mica to do the same. Then she told them it was time to disembark. She walked down the aisle and opened the door of the craft, wishing them a pleasant evening. As Will and Mica walked down the steps to the runway, they felt an unfamiliar, damp breeze embrace them before they stepped into total darkness.

At the bottom of the stairs, sitting there and waiting for them was a small white vehicle with jet-black wheels. It was open, with no windows or proper doors. Inside the cart, Will and Mica saw a short man with sparse, straw-like hair. He was wearing huge sunglasses, even though it was dark outside. He was very overweight. They stared at him in disbelief; they had never seen such a round person before. Being overweight was forbidden in First City because it was not conducive to society to sabotage your body.

The strange, rotund man was sweating profusely despite the fresh breeze. Under his armpits, big patches of sweat soaked his khaki-colored shirt. He spoke, still panting while dabbing his forehead continuously with a large white rag.

"Good evening, Eco-citizens. I am the collector, and I am responsible for moving citizens to where they need to be. My tag and number are Roy 6345."

Will and Mica greeted him, giving him their information.

"Get in," demanded the collector stiffly. "We need to leave now." And the little vehicle sped off into the night with a whirring noise, the two tiny headlights barely lighting the runway.

As they veered to the left, they could see a massive glass building in the distance. It was filled with a myriad of lights sparkling like a thousand stars in a dark sky. As they drove closer to the building, Mica realized she could see thousands of small electric lights. The vision ahead seemed so beautiful and extravagant.

They pulled up to a small door located at the northeast corner of the glass building. The collector disembarked. "Follow me," he instructed, panting, as he struggled to get out of the tiny vehicle. It wobbled back and forth, unnerving his passengers.

Will and Mica followed the collector through the door into a brightly lit room full of padded, shiny black seats. The floor gleamed with white ceramic tiles just like the floors in their old living quarters.

"Take a seat, and your over-leader will meet you here in a moment and give you your next order's briefing," said Roy.

Will and Mica sat down, and the collector bade Fare-well to them while still puffing and panting. He left to return to his vehicle. Somehow he squeezed his massive bulk into the front seat and then whirred off into the night.

Will noticed there were no RFID Relay Machines or cameras in the waiting room.

Mica looked at Will and spoke for the first time since their meeting in First City. "There are no cameras or Relay Readers here," she remarked softly.

"Yes," replied Will. "I noticed that too."

Mica continued, "I wonder where we are."

"We are not supposed to question or discuss this, Mica 3432. We do not know who may be monitoring us. We should be silent," advised Will gently.

Mica suddenly became nervous and nodded in agreement.

At that moment, their new over-leader strode into the room. "Greetings, Eco-citizens! I am your over-leader for the Elite Watchers Force. My tag and number are Robert 6274," he said in a deep, booming voice.

Robert was taller than Will by at least an inch. He was a tremendous man; his arms bulged with muscles, and his thighs were as thick as the trunks of a solar tree. Robert had black hair, worn in a tight braid that almost reached his waist. His eyes were liquid brown, and he had a huge friendly smile, revealing perfectly white teeth. His skin was well-tanned, as if he had spent a lot of time outdoors. Robert exuded confidence.

Will and Mica quietly introduced themselves, feeling uncomfortable with Robert's high energy and multiple smiles. Robert continued, unabashed, "We are going to your new living spaces now. You will find everything you need there—new uniforms, boots, equipment, and food—and your first briefing will be tomorrow at dawn. We are leaving now since your day has been almost four quarters long. You must rest."

Robert opened the door, and Will and Mica silently followed him into the street. Parked there was a sleek long black vehicle. The same short sweaty collector was sitting in the driver's seat. All three got into the back seat of the car, which started to glide down the smooth blacktop road. On either side of the road were neat rows of long-necked streetlights.

In the streetlights, the watchers could still see lines of perfectly straight and tall green trees that were rustling in the gentle breeze. Mica wondered if they were real. The car was alone on the road, and after twenty minutes of driving, they pulled into a long row of squat white buildings with blue doors. Each door had a number etched on it.

Robert got out of the vehicle first and stopped between buildings 4 and 5. "Mica 3432, you are assigned to room 4, and Will 4523, you are in number 5." He gave them each a magnetic strip-key. "I will see you tomorrow at dawn."

Seeing them both hesitate, Robert held Will's strip-key against the small silver pad on the door. Will heard a dull click, and the door swung open. As the light flooded the living space, he was amazed. The room had a pale-blue carpet. The walls were painted eggshell, and there were fabric window covers that matched the quilt on the bed. All the furniture had been made from an exotic, pale-colored wood. There was a kitchenette with a cold box and some box that heated food, he assumed via the instructions on the door.

There was a hygiene room with a shower. Inside the shower curtain, there was an enormous oval white container that stood on clawed feet. It was large enough to sit in or even lie in it. Will wondered if they had problems with the steam showers flooding there.

Will opened the cold box and saw bread, meats, cheeses, butter, and other things in containers; some things he had only seen in picture books. There were tiny cucumbers in vinegar called pickles, some paste in a square tin called pâté, and a dozen other things he didn't recognize. On a small table, there was a decorative bowl filled with sweet, exotic fruit.

In the closet, there were seven uniforms, a pair of military boots, and a pile of equipment, neatly folded and wrapped in bright, translucent material. There was also a long white tunic for sleeping and several sets of soft black cotton pants with matching jackets. The laced canvas shoes had heavy rubber soles.

Will felt overwhelmed as he lay on his plush bed while eating a piece of pink salami. The mattress was full of downy feathers. His body sunk into the soft, warm depth, his eyelids fluttered, and exhaustion overcame him, and soon he was snoring loudly.

Next door, Mica was doing the same thing.

At dawn, a loud whining noise woke Will up. Then there was silence. MAMM was not there to keep him on track. Confused for a moment, he went into the hygiene room to provide his daily urine sample. He waited for analysis, but there was no report given.

Then Will went into the steam shower and turned it on. He immediately jumped back as powerful jets of warm water drenched him. He felt like he was drowning. The water kept spraying and streaming all over his body, and although Will waited full three minutes, water was still pouring out of the wall.

Unlike the steam shower, there was no chemical smell. Will saw a waxy white bar that had a familiar smell; he rubbed it all over his body, and after at least fifteen minutes, he turned the water off by himself.

Still, there was no voice of MAMM. It must be malfunctioning, thought Will as he dressed in his new uniform and boots. It was almost identical to his old uniform, but the insignia was different. It was a golden pyramid with an all-seeing eye perched on the top. On either side of the pyramid were two coiled golden cobras.

Will looked inside the cold box and decided to eat some bread with butter, meat, cheese, and little black pods that were salty and had hard pits in the middle of them. Will studied the container and saw the word *olives* printed on the label. The food was delicious. Will searched everywhere for the daily Vitalift pill, but he couldn't find it.

A few moments later, Robert knocked on the door, and when Will opened it, he saw Mica standing next to Robert, ready to start the day in her new uniform and boots. The three exchanged greetings.

"Are you rested?" asked Robert.

Mica and Will replied in unison, "Yes, Over-Leader."

"In front of the Archa or officials, we must use our tags and numbers, but between the three of us, we are just Will, Mica, and

Robert," informed Robert casually. "Today is your first day, Watchers. How are you faring?" asked Robert, with sincerity.

"Very well, Over-Leader," answered Mica.

Will hesitated.

"What's wrong?" asked Robert, looking at Will with concern.

"Over-Leader, I am just worried that I have consumed too many resources today. My shower was malfunctioning, and it did not turn off automatically. I used precious water that would have provided a month's worth of steam showers or many gallons of water rations. I am guilty of depleting the water supply on our planet. I have become an Eco-violator," Will said quietly, thoroughly ashamed of himself, wondering how harsh his punishment would be.

To his amazement, Robert began to laugh heartily. "Oh, Will," he said, "you have so much to learn. Your reality is not what you think it is. You have been living an illusion during your entire life."

Mica, forgetting protocol, stared at Will and then at Robert. Years of maintaining her composure with an expressionless face did not stop her eyes from narrowing.

"What in the name of Gaia are you saying, Robert?" she asked.

Robert stopped laughing and instantly became somber and professional. "It is always confusing for new recruits," he replied seriously. "The life you have lived in First City is merely an illusion. Will and Mica, you will not understand this until later. You must see and experience things to be fully aware."

Mica, briefly glancing at Robert, asked calmly, "Over-Leader, what exactly are we going to be doing here?"

"You will be working for the Archa, providing them protection and assisting them in whatever endeavors they choose to participate in," Robert replied evasively.

"The wise and fair Archa?" asked Mica, stunned.

The Eco-citizens didn't know much about the Archa. They believed the Archa were a benevolent group of elders who ruled the people with wisdom and fairness. If they were spoken of at all, it was always in hushed, respectful whispers. No one knew their real names or had ever seen them in pictures or in person.

"What an honor for First City!" remarked Will, astounded.

"They must be the perfection of humanity," Mica gasped, very proud she had been chosen to serve such worthy citizens.

"They are everything you are not," replied Robert cryptically. "It is time for your proper briefing. Follow me to the Zone."

The Zone was building number 1. Behind the blue door, there was a room filled with boxes of equipment and a small computer. There was a wooden table with four matching chairs, a couch, a small kitchenette, a machine to make coffee, and a cold box full of food.

"I know you have many questions," stated Robert as he motioned them to sit down.

"We don't know very much about the Archa," responded Mica excitedly.

Robert replied, "The Archa are citizens who are above the Council of Twelve. They control everything—all the cities on earth, all the citizens, and everything that determines your society and existence, from the food that you receive to the clothing that you wear."

"The Archa must be honorable and wise," interjected Mica.

"And very generous to provide us with so much," Will added gratefully.

Robert changed the subject. "I want to talk about your training program," he continued enthusiastically. "Will and Mica, you are going to learn how to use weapons: shooters, bangers, cutters, stunners, talkers, and combat defense. Among other things, there will also be classes to educate you on this new world."

Will cleared his throat. "Over-Leader, I didn't see any Vitalift. Where do we get some? I haven't had any since yesterday."

"We don't take Vitalift here," replied Robert very slowly. "Contradictory to what you understand, Vitalift is not a vitamin tablet, although this is unknown to the citizens that take it every day. It is, in fact, a very potent tranquilizer and antidepressant. So we have to detoxify your bodies for the first three weeks or so. Unfortunately, detoxing is very unpleasant. You will experience some severe withdrawal symptoms while you are withdrawing from the Vitalift."

Robert continued, "We will give you some medication to help counteract the side effects and pain. Unfortunately, this will be your first challenge, and the process will be excruciating for both of you.

We have no choice. You have to be fully aware and alert in this assignment to be able to respond rapidly, and you may have to make some crucial decisions concerning the Archa's safety."

Will asked quietly, "If Vitalift isn't vitamins and minerals to keep us healthy, why do they give it to us? I don't understand."

"It keeps the population happy and compliant, along with the fluoride you brush your teeth with and the lithium in the water that you drink. Sadly, your whole population isn't living—they are being suppressed from being human and from thinking, feeling, or reacting with any emotions," explained Robert sadly.

"Why do they do this to First City?" asked Will, still confused. Then he added indignantly, "Eco-citizens are already happy. We have a peaceful life in First City. Everybody is content, and everybody is equal."

"Precisely my point," replied Robert patiently. "Look, you will see things and feel things differently in time, but this day we need to go to the Healing Center, where the healers are already waiting for you."

"I can't believe this!" stated Mica. "You are saying we have been on drugs our whole lives?"

"Yes," replied Robert firmly.

"I still don't understand," persisted Mica.

"To keep you submissive," replied Robert. "You will understand soon. You have merely forgotten the call of the wild and become domestic stock," replied Robert cryptically. Putting his new recruits through detox was the hardest part of his job. "We need to leave now. The healers will explain all the side effects to you."

Mica looked confused after Robert's strange explanation but said nothing.

Will and Mica nervously followed Robert around the compound in an almost-trancelike state, still trying to make sense of the information they had just learned. Building 8 had a bright-red star on it. The sign read "EW Healing Facility."

The building, cooled by air-conditioning, made Will and Mica both shiver as they walked in, partly from the cold air and partly from the intense fear that was gnawing deep inside their guts.

The greeter gave them each a form to fill out. Then the healers took Will and Mica to rooms where they changed into cotton shifts. Then they were taken to a single room with two beds in it.

"Is that allowed?" asked Mica primly. "An adult male and female sharing the same living space?"

Robert replied slowly, "Within one more hour, you are both going on a journey that you might not survive. You may find some solace knowing that another citizen is going through the same experiences you are. This experience will strengthen your bond and make you a better team. I will be back soon, and remember, this is going to be the hardest thing you have ever done. Have the courage to know that this suffering is only temporary."

Robert turned and left the room while Will and Mica, standing in their white shifts, climbed into their beds while a healer started to hook up an IV for each of them.

Then she gave them each a red pill. "This will help with some of the symptoms," she said. "You may experience severe pain, nausea, vomiting, headaches, diarrhea, dizziness, and possibly strange dreams or night visions, which are experiences that occur while you sleep. They may feel real at the time. You could see frightening or bizarre things and find that the events in your dreams are not always linear or making sense. Do not fear, it is just your brain trying to sort out the jumble of information it processes every day. Plus, the Vitalift prevents any dreaming. In reality, we are bringing you back to life from being almost dead."

She turned and paused before leaving the room. "Fare-well," she whispered. "I will check on you shortly. May Gaia protect you and keep you strong."

Mica turned over in her bed to look at Will. "I have much fear," she said nervously.

"So do I," Will replied hesitantly.

"Is it too late to go home?" asked Mica, panicking for a moment.

"Yes," replied Will. "Things will never be the same again. We will wake up as different citizens. We are becoming elite watchers in this new world."

"We don't know who we are anymore," remarked Mica sadly. "Everything we believed in is not the truth." She paused. "Perhaps what we will become is who we were always supposed to be."

Will stared at her. He was beginning to sweat and shiver at the same time. "It's starting," he murmured.

Mica began to sweat too and tried to curl into a ball to stop the pains that racked her entire body.

Within four hours, terrible stomach cramps started, followed by violent vomiting and diarrhea. This lasted four agonizing days.

Then the excruciating headaches began; they couldn't bear any light, sound, or touch. These headaches continued for another four days.

Will continued to be plagued by night visions of a strange being. He saw a creature, a dark, shadowy figure, that whispered to him from the edges of his consciousness and repeated the same eight words. "Will 4532, I have been waiting for you." Then the image would evaporate like smoke, melting back into the dreamworld. Will would wake for a minute and wonder if he was in reality. Momentarily confused and afraid, Will would sink back into his foggy abyss.

Robert checked in on them periodically, and by the ninth day, he asked the senior healer, "Do you believe they will survive?"

The senior healer nodded solemnly and replied, "I have been performing this procedure for many years. I know they will survive, because they are both healthy, with strong hearts and great determination. In my experience, survival of this process seems to include a combination of things, having courage, wanting to survive, and having a strong willpower as well as good physical health and strength. These qualities are the key to a successful detox."

Then she smiled at Robert. "It is good news that they will both survive, and they have the abilities to make excellent watchers."

Robert nodded slightly. He was very relieved.

CHAPTER 5

Elite Watchers 1

The headaches began to lessen in severity, but vertigo and dizziness still lasted almost five more days before they gradually started to subside. Will and Mica were both fragile and slept practically solidly for another two days. They managed to eat a small meal on the seventeenth day. Both Will and Mica lost a considerable amount of weight.

By day 20, although Will and Mica were starting to heal, they had trouble controlling their moods. This overflow of emotions was overwhelming and the first time that either one of them had experienced anything other than dull contentment. They felt strange and unbalanced; a gamut of moods ran through them, ranging from mild anger to laughter and sobbing uncontrollably.

As time passed, they both gradually found it easier to control their emotions, and a lifetime of stoic training helped tremendously. They spent a further two weeks in the Healing Center, recovering their strength.

As they spent time healing, Will and Mica became closer to each other. They talked about the detoxing process and other things they had experienced since their new assignment began. Will and Mica discovered they loved the color red, pink salami, and olives, and as they learned new things about themselves, they also learned about each other. The hardest thing to cope with was the realization that they had lived in a tightly controlled, rigid society that drugged their citizens into a dull fog. Merely to control them. Will and Mica were both relieved that their old reality did not exist anymore.

Will and Mica were starting to become individual humans again—who they were destined to be.

What the new watchers didn't realize, until much later, was that this was just the beginning of their awakening. There were far more layers of reality to discover that were beyond their limited imaginations. No one told them that eventually they would, in time, explore their sexuality. It was far too complicated to teach, and Robert believed that they would figure it out in their own time. And it was not an important issue, because Will and Mica would remain sterile without fertility treatment.

By the end of those two weeks, they had both progressed enough to begin their training. Robert was very pleased with his new recruits. They learned quickly and efficiently; with clear minds and nutritious food, they were becoming stronger, their endurance was increasing, and they were both very articulate, intelligent, and learned the forgotten art of critical thinking.

Will and Mica had progressed socially, learning to smile, interact, and laugh heartily at Robert's famously bad jokes. They loved the freedom from prying eyes in this new world. Mica had blossomed into a vivacious person, and Will was a little more pragmatic. For both of them, life was different, because each day was joyful.

During the following months of training that followed, Will and Mica ran every day for a minimum of six miles. They learned to use several different weapons. Both were able to hit a target at three hundred meters, ride horses, practice survival skills and self-defense, and even learnt to swim. They had taken about a hundred hours of flying lessons in the Hopper (which was a tiny two-person type of helicopter), which took off vertically in a small area and could fly very low to the ground.

Will and Mica also learned the basics of how to operate a small Skybird so they were capable of flying the Archa to safety if the assigned pilot got killed or became incapacitated in any way. They learned to drive the MECAS (Mechanical Eco-Compatible Automobiles). Each one could seat four people and could drive about a hundred miles before needing recharging. Any MECA could hover above the ground to a total height of seven or eight feet, so traveling through dense forest was faster than walking.

Robert wanted to teach Will and Mica as many skills as possible. The continued success of his trainees was a mark of honor upon Robert's remarkable reputation and capabilities as a trainer. He had less than twelve months to get them ready for their big assignment.

Since Will and Mica were marked to serve the highest echelon of the Archa, any issues with them could come back to haunt him and could mean his extermination, along with theirs. He didn't tell them the whole truth, primarily because he did not want them distracted, and he wanted to ensure they became experts during their training program and not make mistakes due to fear of potential reprisal.

Will and Mica also took classes at the Zone with their teacher Melanity 2356. She explained the parallel reality that was their New society. Will and Mica learned during their sessions that First City was one of many domed cities throughout the globe and all the cities were designed to function precisely the same way but each city had its particular mission.

What surprised both of them was that there was plenty of water and Earth's many resources were abundant. Fossil fuels weren't the result of decaying plant and animal matter; they were abiotic and created within the Earth due to a simple chemistry involving pressure and heat that occurred naturally in the inner layers of the Earth, the process that generated hydrocarbon. Citizens had been scared into believing that the planet would run out of oil.

In 2009 Vladimir Kutcherov, a professor at the Division of Energy Technology at KTH in Sweden, had simulated the process and published the results.

Will and Mica realized it was not necessary for citizens to live such a grim and meaningless life inside the dome. Will believed that the new cities had become the zoos of the future and the human beings were now the ones in cages. Even the wild animals had more choice and control over their lives than the citizens did.

The Eco-citizens had sadly lost all their ancient knowledge of how to live off the land and since it was forbidden to live anywhere other than the sustainable cities.

The Archa needed all the citizens to be entirely compliant and dependent on them for everything they needed to survive. Most citizens had far less use and understanding of technology than their ancestors who had lived in the Chaos Era.

Melanity didn't know that most of the cities only had access to primitive technology, which the Archa controlled covetously. They wanted to prevent ordinary people from learning and finding discoveries, which could either threaten their power and their tight grip on the world's resources. Most of the scientists that worked for the Archa barely knew one another, and their work was compartmentalized. All information was on a strictly need-to-know basis. This system prevented the humans from sharing knowledge and possible inventions from being created.

According to Melanity, the Archa were a small group of individuals made up of twelve families. All Archa were descended from a unique ancient bloodline and controlled all the resources and riches of planet Earth. The Archa emerged from the shadows after the New Eco-Charter was established, but they had always been behind the scenes, orchestrating world events. Someone called Malus was the apex of the pyramid of power. He ruled over the Archa.

The Archa made their own set of laws (very different from those listed in the Patriot Person Act), and they were the most influential citizens of the planet. The Council of Twelve was once handpicked by the elite in each city many generations ago. The current Council was unaware that this parallel reality existed. The council members were not related to the Archa themselves, and since they had handpicked their replacements from First City for several decades, they knew no more about the world of the Archa than Mica and Will did when they lived in First City. The Archa lived in the Compound, which was not far from the training grounds.

Will and Mica were surprised to learn that planet Earth was home not only to humans (who were the lowest beings on the social scale) but also to another humanoid species called the Yellow Eyes, who exclusively lived in Eighth City, which was different from the domed cities. Apparently, the Yellow Eyes were a level above the humans in importance but below the Archa.

One day, while they were all training in a vast open field, miles from watchful eyes and listening ears, Robert, who rarely spoke about the Archa, told them that many people thought the Archa were immortal. Neither Will nor Mica was sure if that was a literal description or a metaphorical one.

Will listened to this new revelation, and he thought for a moment and asked, "How did they come to have so much power?"

"I don't know," replied Robert. "It has always been that way. Nobody can remember a time when it was different. They have been here controlling the planet since the beginning of time," remarked Robert stoically. "And maybe even before that."

"Someone somewhere knows the answer," concluded Mica quietly to herself. She now believed there was always an answer to everything.

Will was more accepting of the status quo, and he reasoned that sometimes things were just the way they were and that questioning things would not change them.

Mica asked Melanity privately why the Archa demanded the citizens to live such a harsh life. She couldn't answer that question to Mica's satisfaction and just kept saying that it was the way things were, and surprisingly, neither Melanity nor Robert seemed bothered by the misery suffered by the people in the domed cities. Both of them remarked that Will and Mica no longer lived in First City, so they should forget the past and be more concerned with the future.

Will's and Mica's days of training with Robert passed into a blur. Every day was exciting, and they became more accomplished, stronger, and more self-confident. Finally, they completed the grueling training program. Will and Mica were excited, proud, and eager to begin their new assignments.

In their last briefing, Robert explained to them the correct protocol to use when addressing the Archa. "Never look them in the eye," said Robert seriously. "Always keep your eyes downcast when they speak to you. Never address them first, unless it is a life-and-death situation. Never show emotion on your face. If a member of the Archa asks you a question, then answer them with lightning speed. Use brief sentences, and finish each sentence with 'my lord' or 'my lady.' Bow your head even lower after speaking to them."

Robert's voice dropped, and he sounded solemn. "It is critical for your survival to never, ever show your dislike or displeasure at anything you see or have to do. You must understand that failure to adhere to these instructions could cost you your life. Other watchers before you have been lost when they made that mistake. Never forget that the Archa hold immense power over you. If you displease them, they will terminate you permanently, and no one can stop them."

However, Robert said brightly, "Most watchers adapt and learn to enjoy the privileges that come with this assignment. In the past, our standards for the right candidates were lower, and some citizens burned out very quickly. Some even committed self-destruction. Presently, only excellent citizens are selected for this type of assignment and have to have at least twenty years of experience."

"Terminate us? Why would they do such a terrible thing?" asked Will, horrified. He had never heard of murder before and exchanged looks with Mica, who was feeling chilled at this new revelation.

Robert ignored Will's question and gave his final piece of advice on the subject of serving the Archa. "You are both going to Elite Watchers Force. Do not fail me. Remember everything I have taught you both, and you will excel. Elite Watchers 1 is one of the most prestigious positions that humans can hold in this society. You will receive further training on daily tasks and routines at the Compound from Gerald 4065. He has been a dedicated watcher for many years, but he is now becoming too old to perform his duties efficiently. It is his wish to return to First City within sixty days of your arrival. One last point: always be aware of what you say, because the Archa will see and hear everything. The monitoring you will be under in the Compound is far more intense than in First City."

Mica was disheartened to learn they would come under monitoring again; she had grown used to her freedom in the last year. Will was not surprised. He had expected that they would always be watched by someone.

JULIE VIGIL

Mica tried to question Robert more about the rules of the Archa, but he refused to discuss the matter any further, stating that he had told them everything they needed to know.

"Does Gerald have a partner?" asked Mica, changing the subject.

"Not anymore," replied Robert rather sharply, in a tone that meant no further discussion.

Mica wanted to ask more questions, but Will caught her eye and shook his head. So Mica deferred. She would save that question for Gerald.

When Graduation Day came one year after the day of their arrival, it was time for Mica and Will to say Fare-well to Robert. For the first time in their lives, they experienced a feeling of loss, realizing that he had become a great friend as well as a good over-leader, patiently teaching them so many new skills. They were grateful to him.

Later that evening, after packing their possessions, Will and Mica talked about the disturbing conversation they had earlier with Robert.

Mica wondered if it was like being charged with treason in First City—for example, when a citizen broke the rules and was judged by the Council of Twelve. Will agreed with her and stated that they would always honor the Archa and obey their orders so they would never face that problem. Satisfied with this explanation, they didn't discuss the subject any further.

Will's and Mica's hair had grown significantly during the year-long training program, but the Archa did not like hair on their watchers so staff members at the Compound were not confused with visiting guests. Somewhat sadly, Will and Mica carefully shaved their heads, not wanting to displease the mighty Archa.

The next afternoon, Will and Mica traveled toward their new assignment in a small Skybird. The windows were blacked out, and the interior was identical to that of the first Skybird, except for the pale-blue coloring in the interior. Even their Skybird helper, Sandy 634, looked like a carbon copy of Stella 632, only her hair was dark and her eyes were brown. She wore a tight electric-blue tunic, complete with matching high-heeled shoes and long white-painted fingernails. She gave the same speech and followed the procedures as flawlessly as Stella did. Even their voices seemed identical, as did their large toothy smiles. The Skybird helpers appeared to be mechanical. Both of the helpers seemed peculiar to Mica.

"They are robots," Mica concluded. Finally, she felt she had solved the puzzle.

It was merely a hint of what was to come.

Will was still transfixed by the lovely Sandy, watching her every move. He wondered what city she came from but was reluctant to ask.

As the Skybird took off, hurtling toward the clouds, Will felt more relaxed this time around. In fact, life in First City to him seemed an eternity ago. He never wanted to go back there. Although Will knew one day he would be returned there to die as an old man, with his mind and memory erased, waiting for his Final Journey in a drugged haze. He shivered and comforted himself with the thought that that was many years ahead, and the future was always subject to change.

Mica was deep in thought, staring at the bottom of her glass, shaking the ice and watching it melt. Even though her conversation with Will last night had calmed her frayed nerves, the words still replayed in her mind: "Disobedience means death." The phrase kept repeating itself. "Never refuse an order" was the other thing Robert had insisted they remember. Their primary job was to keep the Archa safe. That couldn't be too difficult. Mica comforted herself with that thought.

Their flight was short, barely ten minutes long. Will wondered why they hadn't been driven there by a collector, and he wasn't sure, but it felt like they had flown in a couple of circles. It seemed they took off and immediately landed. Will wondered if this was to disorientate them geographically. As their Skybird touched down, both Mica and Will were feeling reasonably confident and in control. They were both determined that, as a team, they would be an asset to the revered Archa.

On the runway, a thinner, less sweaty collector came to fetch Will and Mica and bring them to their new living spaces. The vehicle that was waiting for them was a very long dark car with blacked-out windows. Neither of them could believe the luxury of this incredible machine that purred along the streets. It had plush seats and a cold box filled with food and beverages. They drove for about ten minutes, very slowly. During that time, the collector, who was behind a glass screen that separated him from the watchers, had not said a word to either one of them. Both Will and Mica were silent and stared straight ahead during their journey, remembering that they might be being watched or listened to at any moment—and they were indeed correct.

PART 2

The Archa Compound

Not everyone who walks in the guise of a man is human.

—Aristotle

CHAPTER 6

Malus and the Archa Revealed

Like an iceberg in a prehistoric ocean, there were dark, twisted secrets far below the surface. Deep in the bottom of those icy, swirling waters, the Archa predators still lurked and hunted like their ancient ancestors.

The majority of the Archa were almost identical. They had been genetically engineered to be very tall and beautiful, with long muscular limbs, perfectly symmetrical faces, even white smiles, golden skin, and long manes of thick, golden-spun hair. Their eyes were mesmerizing and the color of liquid gold, which contrasted with their onyx-black pupils. As angelic as they looked, it didn't hide the fact that they were very dark spiritual entities.

By 2080, the Archa knew enough about genetics to be able to perfect the appearance, intelligence, and physical prowess of their species to produce perfect specimens. Although they still did not realize that some genes were locked, a safety feature that had been installed at their creation long ago, so they could never become smarter, faster, or evolve to a higher level than the Malus, the leader of the Archa.

The remaining Archa kept trying, but they could not even see the locked code, let alone break it. Malus believed that in the future, they would finally succeed, but they would still be millions of years behind the original technology of the Hive of Archon.

The Archa hated the physical restrictions of clothing. Most of the time, they wore a little more than multiple strings of colored beads and had intricate cosmic symbols temporarily tattooed on their skin. They particularly liked to place gems all over their bodies and glue them on until they looked like they were wearing some haute couture outfit.

Sometimes they wore toga-like white garments tied at the shoulders and decorated them with rich gold brocades, adding lots of carved golden jewelry, especially items that the Egyptian pharaohs had worn. They loved the glamor and power of gold and did not allow the rest of the planet to own one scrap of it.

On this particular day, some of the Archa had gathered in the dimly lit drawing room of their palatial mansion, which doubled as a communications room. It had various types of surveillance equipment, computers, and high-tech electronics.

The Archa were excited because now that the new watchers were on their way, their real hunting season could begin. They were all wearing huge thick black sunglasses, even inside the house, with all the curtains closed. Their golden eyes were extremely sensitive to light.

"Well, what do they look like?" asked the gorgeous Lustria lazily.

"I don't know," replied Ira, irritably. "They look like two bald watchers. It doesn't matter what they look like. They are both off-limits for you and Lucas. You can't play with the watchers. Remember what happened the last time and the incident before that?"

Ira was about seven feet tall, and he weighed around three hundred pounds. He had long golden hair and deeply set golden eyes and was very Nordic-looking and robust. He maintained the discipline and rules for the rest of the group via orders from Malus. Ira was always irritable and prone to outrageous and violent temper tantrums. He carried grudges for a very long time.

"What a shame," commented Lustria, laughing, mimicking Ira's scowl.

"Really," replied Ira crossly, "it just takes too long to train them, and in the meantime, we have no watchers, so we can't go hunting for months on end. So I am warning you, do not touch the watchers! Find other entertainment."

He stared harshly at all of them.

"That also applies to you too, Lucas, and especially Metus, Crudelis, and Gula. There are many play-toys brought here for all your pleasures. You have been through so many we have had to increase the number of birthers in Third City just to keep up with your mischief! Anyway, the order is not mine, it comes from Malus."

Lucas and Lustria exchanged a nervous look at that snippet of information.

"Malus said that?" asked Lucas nervously.

"Yes, indeed," replied Ira. "Be warned and confine your fun to hunting and such, or I will have to discipline you again, like last time."

"Oh no!" cried Lucas, shuddering at the memory. "That was no fun at all."

Lustria smiled. "It was unforgettable," she said, nodding and rolling her eyes at Lucas.

"Well, then, behave!" snapped Ira, now finished with the distasteful subject.

Ira's main vice was that he loved toes. The problem wasn't so much that he admired toes but that he liked to separate them from their owners. They were everywhere in his bedchamber, languishing in ancient canopic jars filled to the brim with formaldehyde. It was a gruesome sight.

"Yes, yes, you are right," replied Lucas, desperately trying to smooth things over by changing the subject. "I am so excited about going hunting again. I love to hunt those scavengers. They are always eating our crops, and they breed like rabbits. They are nasty, dirty little things, those Nahu, and the stench from them is deplorable."

Lucas had huge golden eyes, a perfectly symmetrical face, and very long golden hair, almost to his waist. He was about seven feet tall, with a perfect smile, like his identical twin sister, Lustria. They both had insatiable sexual appetites and were selfish, shallow, and childish. He was a coward. Lucas had a severe phobia about death, unlike his beloved sister, who was a wild and fiery dragon.

Lustria was the same height as her twin brother, strikingly beautiful, but behind all that beauty was a heart of stone. She was incredibly charismatic and liked to host parties and orgies so that she could toy with people. She would test her devoted followers, curious to see how far they would go. How many lines of deviance would they cross just for her nod of approval or a quick smile? She was powerful, untamable, and held the keys to the abyss for many lost souls.

Lucas and Lustria were inseparable. They shared a bed and were lovers, but they were also very competitive over almost everything, from hunting to running. The twins were both very fit and healthy, and they often competed for and shared sexual conquests—male or female, neither one cared, as it was all just a big game to them.

"Did they say anything?" asked Eva, who was tall at seven feet and very exotic-looking, with a mane of bright, unruly gold hair. It was always falling into her face and across her almond-shaped golden eyes. She squinted at the surveillance screen, which showed Will and Mica motionless, facing forward, and silent during their ride in the big black car.

"Not a word yet," replied Ira.

"Good," said Eva. "That's a promising start. Sometimes the watchers think they are too valuable to be eliminated, or even as important as us. Can you believe that?"

Eva, who was always wanting something that somebody else had, never had an original idea of her own. She was a follower, never pursuing her interests or path. She spied on the rest of the Archa all the time to see what they were doing, and the rest of the group feared she reported directly to Malus. So she wasn't included in very many group activities, and although she was beautiful, her demeanor made her less attractive. Three words described Eva: paranoid, spiteful, and bitter. She had a penchant for blond teenage boys, which she always denied vehemently.

"The audacity!" smirked Gula. "Everybody's replaceable except us." She laughed, patting down her unruly, frizzy golden hair. She was older than the rest of the Archa, and she and her twin brother, Desi, had not received the thin gene. Her eyes were a dull gold, barely visible under the fat of her eyelids. Gula's mouth was full of sharp white teeth that had been filed and capped with sharp titanium points. She was only six feet tall and weighed almost four hundred pounds, and her massive bulk quivered as she waddled to the table to ring the bell. She was always hungry, merciless, and vicious.

"I am hungry," she announced. "I think it is time for a little snack." The trouble was, Gula had an insatiable appetite. She liked to consume her food raw and made a grisly mess every time she ate.

"Gula, you will not eat here. Go and snack in the kitchen!" yelled Ira. He was becoming enraged by the thought of his expensive technological equipment being splattered and ruined by Gula's disgusting table manners.

"You are always hungry," grumbled Huber. "You should miss a few snacks, and then you could be as perfect a specimen as I am." He glanced at Gula briefly with disgust and remarked, "Well, not perfect like me, but certainly an improvement."

He flexed his enormous biceps. He had long golden hair and golden bedroom eyes. He was fit and healthy. He had a face of sheer beauty, chiseled, with perfect features and high cheekbones. He walked to the sizable gilt mirror on the wall, inspecting his face and hair.

"Damn, I am a handsome devil!" he boasted.

Huber was obsessive about his image, appearance, and always being right. He was very argumentative and known to be a compulsive liar. His particular vice involved the hybrids, which were kept locked away in some secret caverns.

"You are a demon, all right," replied Desi, laughing.

Desi, Gula's biological twin, was a dismal genetic failure also born without the thin gene. He was very pale and always sweated. He was lazy because his mounds of fat prevented him from moving too much. Desi's small beady gold eyes appeared buried in rolls of fat. His head was bald as a cue ball.

Something had gone wrong with his mental programming, and the intelligence genes, they became scrambled in Desi. He had been part of an experimental group where the fetuses were all given a genetic sequence that was supposed to enhance existing intelligence genes, as a type of booster. Some of the batches were accidentally contaminated by the scientist working on it, and he paid for that mistake with his life. Desi had been such a mistake. However, he was the child of one of the most prestigious Archa males, so he lived at the Compound, away from criticism.

Desi liked to do precisely nothing while beautiful female slavs (slaves) fed him and pampered him like a big baby. He even wore an enormous diaper and a ridiculous white lace sun hat that tied under his several chins. He suffered from a sexual deviancy called infantilism. Huber thought he looked like an enormous pale slug that had slithered out from beneath a dark rock.

Desi's nursery had a giant crib, changing table, and playpen. He had pacifiers, baby toys, and a mobile of smiling, singing stars over his adult-size crib. He even had wet nurses to feed him and rock him to sleep by singing nursery rhymes to him while cuddling him in his monstrous rocking chair.

Desi spent most of his time in his beloved nursery. He only went outside for his daily stroller walk, which he hated. Throughout his exercise, he continually cried and whined about the weather, which he insisted was too hot, too cold, or too windy. Desi was terrified of every single kind of bug and screamed whenever he saw one. He was covered from head to booties by a mosquito net, placed carefully over and around him. Desi only participated with the rest of the group when Malus ordered him to.

For some obscure reason, the whole room started giggling hysterically at Desi's bad joke, and they eventually spiraled into a nonsensical, guttural language filled with strange, dark energy vibrations.

Invedia walked into the room. "What is going on?" she snapped. "Why are you all laughing?"

She was attractive and about seven feet tall, with chin-length golden hair. Invedia had a beautiful face, but it was not quite as symmetrical as Lustria's or as exotic as Eva's, since only one of her features were exceptional. Her bright golden eyes were a fraction too small and close-set. Her nose was not prominent, but somehow it wasn't the correct proportion of her face. However, her lips were perfectly bow-shaped, and she had an incredible smile of perfect white teeth that lit up her face and made her beautiful.

Invedia was always comparing the lives of others to hers. She was bitter and angry, with a constant ugly scowl on her face. She was obsessed with Lucas and had tried for decades to gain his attention. Lucas had no interest in her and called her the bitter little mouse. She hated Lustria more than she hated life.

If she had just paid some more attention to her appearance, especially her hair, clothing, and attitude, she could have looked stunning, but most of the time she was busy scowling at Lustria. She was jealous of everyone prettier than her and hated all females except Gula.

Invedia loved to whip, beat, and burn beautiful young women until they were unrecognizable and permanently disfigured. Especially the ones that slept with Lucas. She was vicious to them—not even surgery could replace those poor faces she beat with such hatred and anger. She never killed them, because she wanted them to suffer by looking in the mirror every day, mourning their lost beauty.

Ava was sitting in the room, silent, poised, and beautiful. She was also seven feet tall and slim, with a blinding smile and long dark golden hair, enormous tawny eyes, and had a vivacious laugh. Ava worshiped material wealth and money. She owned hundreds of out-fits, shoes, and jewelry; she had the best of everything and considered herself to be superior to most other beings.

Ava always needed to be the center of attention, and most often, she was. She was famous for weaving a spell on others with her incredible wit and elegant charm. Ava was Malus's favorite and enjoyed many privileges above and beyond others. She was a charming, manipulative sociopath, like the rest of her so-called family. Her main vice was psychological torture; she was an expert, causing many souls to self-destruct in despair and madness.

Morus was the least intelligent of the group, but he was a brutal and efficient hunter. He rarely spoke because he was not eloquent like the rest of the Archa. He was very sensitive to any criticism, which would send him into a fit of rage. Morus was seven feet, four inches tall and robust. He was the physically strongest member of the group. He was attractive, with dark-gold eyes, light golden hair, and a strong square jaw, and had no patience for anybody. He liked to ride horses and hunt, drink, and womanize, in that order. He spent most of his time away from the rest of the group unless they were hunting or riding.

Crudelis glared at Invedia. "Why don't you ever shut up?" he snapped viciously.

Crudelis was cruel, devious, and spiteful and particularly enjoyed watching suffering and misery. He was a short man compared with the rest of the group, only about six feet tall, and suffered from the Napoleon syndrome and was very sensitive about his height. He was a slight man with long golden hair, pale gold eyes, a broad smile, and he looked like an angel. An illusion, because all he wanted was to orchestrate mayhem and chaos and then sit back and watch the results. He particularly liked pitting the Archa against one another. He teased Morus's social discomfort and laughed at Desi's misery outdoors. Another favorite vice he enjoyed was watching Metus work on torturing and dismembering his victims.

Metus was an incredibly handsome, wicked sadist. He was about seven feet tall and dressed elegantly, carrying himself with great poise. Metus had long dark golden hair, a well-toned body, and mesmerizing, molten-gold eyes that were slanted, like a cat's. He had a full mouth and even white teeth that glowed against his golden skin. He was like a siphon who fed on the fear of his victims. He loved to torture and murder and sincerely believed his skin was kept looking young and supple by moisturizing it with the melted whipped fat of the Yellow Eyes babies. He emitted charm and elegance that quickly manifested into abject terror for his unfortunate victims, who were often young and vulnerable.

Invedia turned around and snapped back at Crudelis. "Why don't you go out and hunt a mouse? It is about your size."

"Indeed, I will," replied Crudelis menacingly, "but next time it might be a bitter little mouse I kill." He glared at her.

"Bring it on. I will snap you like a twig, you sad, pathetic little sadist," retorted Invedia sharply.

"Ira, stop them arguing," ordered Connie, "before things get out of control."

Connie was tiny compared to the other Elite. She was barely five feet tall, but slim, beautiful, and looked like a delicate porcelain doll. She had big golden eyes and a cute, contagious smile. Connie had long golden hair that reached the back of her ankles. She moved gracefully like a butterfly, always alert and moving from place to place, looking for something. What exactly, she did not know. Her parents had bred her deliberately to be small and childlike on a whim. This child-woman was spoiled, bossy, and demanding, especially if people didn't obey her immediately. She liked to repeat herself continually in a high-pitched, grating voice. She would continue whining until the targeted individual complied. She enjoyed planning the most deviant entertainment.

"Ira, you must tell them to shut up!" wailed Connie, repeating herself.

"Stop it, both of you," ordered Ira as he raised an irritated eyebrow at Connie. "You will wake Malus."

At the mention of his name, the room suddenly became silent.

As if on cue, Malus swept into the chamber dressed all in black, including oversize black sunglasses. His long hooded cloak swished across the marble-tiled floor. His feet seemed to float above the ground. Malus emanated the air of fear and terror wherever he went. He was about seven feet tall.

Malus had an elongated skull, like the Paracas skulls found in Peru. He had brilliant gold eyes with reptilian black pupils. Malus had no visible nostrils, just three vertical slits where his nose should have been. Malus could smell by flicking his long reptilian tongue into the air. He could sense fear and terror and loved to feed on it.

Malus had two malformed, raspy sets of lips that did not look human, because one was the encased inside the other. The strange double lips surrounded a gaping mouth filled with two rows of sharp, pointed teeth. He was capable of tearing large prey apart in seconds. He could also dislocate his jaw for bigger meals. Malus's head was bald, and he didn't have any facial hair, eyebrows, eyelashes, and visible ears. His skin was a translucent black color. Gold symbols moved slowly beneath his outer layer of skin. Like the wax in a lava lamp, the symbols would move, merge, and separate continuously, depending on his mood and physical condition.

Malus's thin legs could lock backward and bend forward. He had wide flat feet with six toes. His arms were also long and thin, with six fingers on each hand, and long hard nails that looked like claws. Malus was terrifying to behold and as strong as a silverback gorilla. He had no visible genitalia. Malus had a strange odor around him—a bitter, metallic smell. He was pathologically insane, by human standards. Malus was able to predict what each one of the group was thinking, or doing, at any time by crawling into their minds. Malus was the most deviant in his vices. The Archa were terrified of him and obeyed his every order since he ruled ruthlessly, without pity or mercy.

He saw all humanoids as simple, useless eaters and pointless forms of life. He called them Dobos. Malus thought the Archa were foolish, egotistical, and genetically flawed and that their power, like their money, was merely an illusion. A small breath from his ancestors, the Hive of Archon, would blow their world into oblivion. He tolerated the Archa because even though he despised them, their various deviancies entertained him and merged with some of his own. But Malus had sinister plans for the parasitical Archa when the time was right.

The Compound itself, where Malus and the twelve Archa currently lived, appeared surprisingly ordinary. The Big White House and its estate had been built by a wealthy and eccentric recluse in the eighteenth century who had imported most of the house from Rome, piece by piece, using the finest Italian white marble. From the outside it looked like a priceless Roman villa. The estate had some fifty-five rooms and sat on a hundred acres of land. There was a movie theater, a golf course, tennis courts, a massive pool with a sauna, and various stables filled with Arabic thoroughbred horses.

The Big White House had been expensively decorated all in shades of white and gold. In addition to the typically expected rooms, like the kitchen, scullery, and mudroom (usually found in such a mansion), it had twenty bedrooms and twenty-three bathrooms. The first floor of the house also had a ballroom, a game room, smoking, sitting, and drawing room, a nursery wing, an extensive library, and a trophy room. In the basement, there were several cellars for wines, cheeses, meats, and even coal and wood.

The third floor was, of course, an attic, with slav quarters. At the back of the Big White House, there was an airstrip, complete with a hangar containing several Hoppers and two Skybirds. One of them could seat twelve people. The other Skybird was smaller and could seat six. There was also a second hangar, filled with various-terrain vehicles.

The grounds appeared beautifully manicured with lawns, flower gardens, and a fragrant rose garden. The rose garden lay between the Big White House and the watchers' cottage, and the air throughout the Compound carried their delicate perfume.

To the west of the Big White House, there was a vast orchard that contained many different and exotic fruit trees and bushes. Farther out there were various crops that covered acres of land. Most of the fruit in the orchard would lie spoiling and rotted beneath the trees.

To the east of the Big White House lay an intricately designed vast green maze built from tall thick green hedges. The maze covered about two and a half acres of land. Over the centuries, many brave souls had boldly attempted to defeat the infamous maze. Many who entered it would vanish, never to be seen again.

The stories of the maze had become legendary and were often recounted by the Yellow Eyes storytellers during the snowy winter months in Eighth City, which was the only open-air city. Families listened, spellbound, by the tales of the mysterious and sinister maze while they sipped fine brandy from crystal glasses or drank cups of hot, strong coffee beside their roaring fires on dark and frigid winter nights.

The remainder of the twelve Archa families officially lived in large houses on the estate, about five miles from the Big White House (which was in the center) in all directions, like numbers on a clock.

Most of the time, they banded together in a large rowdy group. They were the only citizens allowed to travel anywhere they wished. The Archa terrorized innocent people around the world while entertaining themselves lavishly, decadently, and as deviant as possible.

They rarely came home to the estate, which most of them considered boring and too rural. Perhaps, if they had spent more time there, they would have been astonished at what deviancies went on at the Compound. All instigated by Malus and their offspring while they were away.

Four times a year, the Archa held parties at the estate, and they invited some of the high-caste Yellow Eyes from Eighth City. The Yellow Eyes would kill, kidnap, bribe, or sabotage one another to get a precious golden invitation so they could be around the revered Archa.

The parties were huge and catered to about three hundred people. There was always some bloody entertainment provided; sometimes a fight to the death by human gladiators, who were kept isolated and trained fiercely from the age of eight on the estate to the north, in a secretive training compound.

The gladiators' visceral performances were madly popular because the Archa and the Yellow Eyes loved to bet on the outcomes of these type of events. Whether it was wild, starved animals that fought one another or wretched humans abducted and forced to fight exotic, wild animals that were flown in from the African continent or the old country of India. All these events occurred in the Pit, which was a real amphitheater imported from Rome literally stone by stone while constructing the original estate. The Pit was located to the north of the Big White House, near the gladiators' training ground, and could hold about three hundred spectators.

Other, more salacious and deviant entertainments were available at times, but only with carefully selected Yellow Eyes present, who enjoyed such deviances as much as the Archa did.

The rest of the household consisted of slavs (slaves), who maintained the various parts of the estate. There were chefs, cleaners, growers, several mechanics, two vets, two pilots, two collectors, and some clean-clothing maids. There were four butlers, a housekeeper, and five scullery maids who all lived permanently in quarters located in the attic of the Big White House. The one hundred ground maintenance crew maintained the farm and orchard. They lived in accommodation situated near the fields and rarely visited the Big White House.

All the slavs had shaved heads and wore tunic uniforms. White for the kitchen, red for the house staff, blue for maintenance, green for gardens, brown for the farm, gray tunics for the mechanics, and orange ones for the pilots. There was a single taxidermist highly prized by the Archa for his remarkable skills; he wore purple. And the watchers, of course, wore black and sometimes green camouflage. Occasionally, one or two of the staff just disappeared and had to be replaced. Only the watchers, the pilots, the taxidermist, and the two vets were relatively safe; the others were far too easy to replace.

Ira discouraged interfering with the house staff because he liked things to run smoothly on the Compound and didn't like unexpected hiccups. However, if any incident involved either Malus or Metus, he remained silent on the matter and irritably reorganized things so they would get back to normal as quickly as possible.

CHAPTER 7

Screams in the Night

Will and Mica finally arrived at their new living quarters, which was a small rectangular cottage located about an eighth of an acre southwest from the Big White House. Will noticed that the back wall faced the main house.

Will opened the thick steel-reinforced door. It squeaked and groaned, revealing a tired-looking man with pale gray eyes, a sad mouth, and a furrowed brow. Gerald ambled slowly toward them as if he had the weight of the world on his shoulders.

"Greetings, new Watchers. I welcome you both here. The Elite Watchers 1 helps guard and assist the twelve most influential families on the whole planet," said Gerald proudly as he gestured toward the main house. "There is no higher place for a human to serve."

Mica thought his little speech seemed somewhat contrived and insincere.

"Now you are here, I will be going back to paradise," Gerald announced happily.

"Where are you going?" asked Mica curiously.

"First City," replied Gerald happily.

"Won't you have your memory erased?" questioned Will, surprised at his answer.

"Yes," replied Gerald, "and even tomorrow won't be soon enough. I don't want to keep the memories from here, and you won't either. Trust me on that fact."

"But we are living in such a glorious and exciting world now," replied Mica naively. "Filled with new experiences, excellent food, and all the water we can use—you can drink as much as you want to and even swim in those big water tanks."

"There is a price to pay for everything you receive," replied Gerald sagely.

"What price is that?" questioned Mica, very curious about the innuendoes made by Gerald.

"Here, with these Lords of Chaos, it is your very soul you can lose and, at the very least, your sanity." Gerald stared out into the approaching dusk and locked the door firmly. A life of pain was etched into his face.

Then he spoke in a low, quiet voice. "Never refuse an order. Just remember this: no matter how horrible it gets, one day it will all be wiped away and erased from your mind. Live for that day, and you will survive as I have."

Mica felt fear snake up her spine and into every cell of her being. In the name of Gaia, what happened at this compound? she wondered.

Will, unnerved himself, decided to change the subject.

"Can you show us our new living space, Gerald?" he asked politely.

"Follow me," replied Gerald, and they walked through the massive doorway into an ample, open space that had a large living room with a kitchen behind it, complete with a big cold box full of delicious food and drinks. There were two spacious bedrooms with en suite bathrooms, brightly lit and very florally decorated. The white walls of the cottage contrasted with the pastel, rose-colored fabric of the bedcovers. The floor gleamed with polished Italian white marble tiles. Mica admired the hand-painted floral pictures that adorned the walls.

Will noticed none of the rooms had windows, except for a thin rectangular window set at least ten feet high above the massive steel door and ran the whole length of that wall. It had very thick glass. To look through the window, one of the watchers would need to stand on a chair.

Gerald told them that their new uniforms and equipment were in their closets.

He then pointed to an oval picture of a perfect white rose and revealed, "Behind that picture, there is a control panel." He removed the picture, and underneath was a small paneled door with several different buttons and switches. "This blue one here controls the air-conditioning, the red one manages the heating system, and these here are for all the lights and power. Any problems with the system, report it to maintenance, with the intercom," instructed Gerald, pointing at a small black box that sat on a sideboard against the wall of the living room.

He repeated his earlier instructions, "When you finish work for the day, come back here and lock the door immediately. Whatever you hear, or think you hear, do not go outside, *ever*!" said Gerald emphatically.

Then he murmured to himself, "They can't get you in here."

"Who can't get us, Gerald?" asked Mica nervously.

"You find out soon enough," said Gerald, looking at Mica with a strange, twisted smile.

"What happened to your partner?" asked Will, suddenly afraid.

"Which one?" replied Gerald. "I have had five in twenty years."

"The last one?" asked Mica softly, feeling her stomach spasm at this latest information.

"He didn't listen to me. He went out there one night, in the dark, and never came back," replied Gerald stiffly.

"Didn't you look for him?" asked Will, both confused and concerned.

"What they don't want you to find, you won't" was Gerald's ambiguous reply.

Again, Gerald insisted, "Never go out after dark unless it is in an official capacity. It is only then there is a guarantee of your safety. If you both mind what I say, you will both survive. Luckily for you, there are no more watchers available for training for three or five years. Perhaps even longer. If they lose you both, then the Archa can't hunt for many months."

"Isn't hunting the wildlife forbidden by law?" stated Mica primly.

"It is," replied Gerald caustically, "unless you are the ones that make the laws."

"What else should we know?" Will asked anxiously, transferring his weight from foot to foot, uncomfortable with the conversation they were having.

"You must observe certain things yourselves to understand this way of life. However, I will be here to teach you everything I know during the next sixty days. Then I leave." It was the first time they saw even a hint of a smile touch Gerald's lips. He was apparently dreaming of First City again.

"Well, back to business," announced Gerald sharply. "Your hot food will be delivered to you daily and left outside your door in a special red box. No other citizen is allowed in here at any time, except us, and eventually just the two of you. Is that clear?"

"Yes, Over-Leader," replied the new watchers in unison.

"Another thing. With the Archa or others, we must use our tags and numbers, but here in the cottage, we are Gerald, Mica, and Will."

Will and Mica didn't have a chance to reply as Gerald continued.

"I am tired," he said. "I have had a long day. More training tomorrow. Fare-well, Watchers, until the morning. Will, you and I have to share a bedchamber until I leave."

Will merely nodded, and all three went to bed exhausted. The watchers fell into the soft sheets, snuggling down into their warm, comfortable beds, and soon the sound of light snoring filled the small cottage.

At about three o'clock in the morning, the watchers were all violently awoken by high-pitched screams unlike anything Will or Mica had ever heard before; they heard banging, more screams, and growling. It sounded like a fight between two wild animals. Suddenly, there was a loud screech and then an eerie silence.

"What was that?" whispered Mica, who was standing in her sleep shift at the entrance of the men's bedchamber

"I don't know," replied Will, sounding very troubled.

"Go back to sleep, Watchers. It's just trouble with the local wildlife. It appears as if the problem has been taken care of. Go back to bed," ordered Gerald.

Mica left their room and climbed back into her warm, soft bed. She was puzzled but reassured by Gerald's apathy and straightforward explanation. Although Mica couldn't stop the uneasy feeling she was experiencing. Her instincts told her something was very wrong here at the Compound. Eventually, she fell fast asleep, and the little cottage remained silent until the morning.

The next morning, an hour before dawn, Gerald woke them and briefed them on the procedure for the hunt.

"Your primary purpose is to stay close to the Archa and make sure they don't get attacked by any predatory wildlife. If anything comes within fifty feet of them, shoot to kill, one shot, one kill. If they trap something that's sick or injured, you will exterminate it. Do not look at the Archa, don't speak to them first, unless you say, 'Drop…my lord or lady!' because they know that means you are shooting at something behind them. You are supposed to be invisible. Watchers, do you understand?"

Gerald paused a moment.

"Your other duties will include running errands in other cities and ensuring that you do anything else they wish you to do," he finished vaguely.

"Understood," replied Mica and Will, nodding.

"After we eat, we will drive to the hunting grounds in the MECA. We have eight MECAs. The MECAs will always be charged and waiting for you. Some of the good hunting sites are only within a few miles of the Big White House. The animals are attracted to the abundant food sources there, because of the orchards and the fields of crops."

Will and Mica smiled. They had driven the MECAs during training with Robert; they were exciting and lots of fun to drive.

"Here is a type of mechanical map we use," announced Gerald. He took a small silver rectangle from his pocket and opened it. Inside it was a foil map and a little white stick. "This is called a clicker," explained Gerald. "This is our cottage here." He pointed to a small white square on the shiny map. "Touch it with the clicker, Mica."

She complied and heard a small clicking noise. Gerald then spoke to the map. "Find hunting ground 1," he said, and immediately an area of the map lit up like a neon sign. "When you are ready to drive, hit the clicker again on the map and say, 'Route.' It will program the MECA with directions, or any other vehicle you use."

While Mica was engrossed, clicking on different areas of the map, Will asked Gerald, "What do they hunt out here in the woods?"

"Anything that moves," he replied. "Sometimes birds, sometimes beasts, like bears or wolves, but their favorite prey is the Nahu."

"Why is that?" asked Will.

"Because they are pests and do enormous damages to the crops, trees, and other wildlife, and they are fast and hard to track and even more problematic to catch. Hopefully, you will see some today."

Gerald then changed the subject abruptly. "I am hungry. Let's eat now."

They were all dressed in their new uniforms. They wore their black military boots and carried an arsenal of weapons, including smoke grenades (smokers) and stun guns (stunners). Laser weapons (shooters), plus two knives (cutters)—one in their boots and one on their belt—as well as two-way radios (talkers), helmets that had darkened visors, and night vision goggles (seers). The team of watchers was well equipped for any emergency that came along.

The watchers were starting to walk toward the terrain hangar when they heard a crackle and an unfamiliar voice on the talker state, "Watchers 1, speak now."

Gerald immediately spoke into his talker. "This is Watchers 1."

"Proceed to the hunting ground 1 immediately. The lords will connect with you there." The talker crackled and went silent.

"Copy," replied Gerald. "Watchers, go."

It was still early in the morning. The sun was starting to rise, and the dawn air felt fresh and crisp. The sky was painted with bands of electric pink, orange, and gold hues that stretched across the whole horizon.

The watchers left the central gardens and walked into the terrain hangar. They all climbed into a MECA, which looked like a snowmobile—long and black, with four seats, one behind the other. Gerald started the engine, which barely made any noise, just a quiet little hum.

They took a little trail through the woods. The MECA's small bright lights lit their way as they rode deeper into the dim, dark forest. The vehicle hovered about six feet above the ground, weaving in between the tall trees and thick bushes.

In a short time, the watchers had covered about five miles. They arrived at a small clearing where there were some wooden benches and a tall metal pole with two vicious-looking hooks. In a heap, there was a jumble of what appeared to be old nets. Gerald started to untangle and fold them; under the nets were long spears and several machetes.

"Sometimes you need those to cut through the undergrowth," remarked Gerald when he saw Mica staring at the blades. She nodded and continued to untangle the pile of nets.

There was a conical dense metal building behind the benches. Gerald opened it with a metal strip-key that hung around his neck.

One wall of the shed had racks of different types of weapons. On the other wall were various cutters (knives), a comprehensive healer kit, and a set of surgical tools. Stacked in one corner were boxes of latex gloves. In the center of the room was a long collapsible stainless steel table, a microscope, and some anatomy books, and on the back wall was a large working double sink.

In the distance, they could hear another vehicle approaching. "Haste," said Gerald. "We need to set up the table and put specific items on it before they get here."

Mica and Will quickly set up the stainless steel table outside while Gerald promptly grabbed an assortment of weapons and laid them out swiftly and methodically. By the time the other MECAs arrived, everything was in order, and all three watchers were standing to attention in front of the shed and behind the metal table.

Four males disembarked from the first MECA. Gerald whispered, "From left to right, that is Ira, Morus, Metus, and Crudelis."

Another MECA pulled up, and four more people alighted from this one. Gerald whispered again, "That's Lucas, Lustria, Huber, and Ava."

Two more vehicles arrived. Gula, Invedia, and Connie got out of one, and the last MECA held Desi, complete with his two birther nurses. Malus wasn't there. The watchers did not see the metallic shine of Gula's teeth or Desi's vast bulk because by now their heads were bowed deeply.

The watchers were able to peek at the Archa from behind their black visors as they straightened up to the position of attention. They were dressed almost identically to the watchers, but they had no helmets, just their big black wraparound sunglasses. Desi was wearing some camouflaged, willowy blanket draped around his vast bulk and was still wearing his little frilly white sun hat.

The watchers were shocked by the sight of Desi and Gula since they were so grossly overweight. They were fascinated by tiny Connie, who was like a delicate butterfly and was flitting alone around the forest. Will and Mica were overwhelmed by the remainder of the Archa, who made a stunning group portrait—they looked like ancient gods of the Earth, so tall, graceful, and incredibly beautiful.

Ira boomed out, "Greetings, Watchers. It is a good day to hunt." He was the only member of the Archa to address them.

The watchers bowed their heads in reply, remaining motionless, until Ira screamed excitedly, "Let the hunt begin!"

Morus started leading the Archa deep into the woods, slowly and quietly.

The netters had already gone ahead on horseback, carrying their flash-bang nets, which were compact and probably about the size and shape of a Frisbee. Once the net made contact with something, it immediately exploded with a deafening bang and a flash of blinding white light that was followed by clouds of billowing, noxious red smoke that the group could see for miles around. Then a tiny drone, about the size of a bee, separated itself from the unit. Then it flew back to the netter with GPS coordinates, reporting the approximate weight and shape of the prey caught in the net.

Once activated, the net automatically threw itself open and covered its intended prey. It wrapped itself around anything that moved. The more the animal struggled, the tighter the net became. The net would not release its catch until a netter disarmed it by remote control.

The watchers followed the Archa carefully, looking around for unexpected danger. They walked for about an hour, all except Desi, who had remained horizontally reclined at the main campsite, complaining loudly about various bugs to his two female slavs.

Suddenly, Morus signaled with a balled fist in the air. Everyone froze. There was total silence for almost a full minute, and then all hell broke loose. A herd of deer, spooked by something, came tearing through the underbrush at full speed, jumping in all directions.

Will could see that a huge buck was approaching from behind. The buck was preparing to jump over Ira, and a collision was imminent because Ira could not run fast enough to move out of its way. Mica was the closest to Ira and saw the same thing Will did, because she sprinted forward and slammed Ira to the ground, covering him with her body seconds before the buck jumped over both of them.

It all happened so quickly that initially Ira exploded with rage and threw Mica off him. "What the hell was that about?" Ira screamed, his face red, his beautiful golden hair full of debris and dead leaves.

Crudelis started to laugh. "That watcher just saved your arrogant self. You almost got trampled by a big buck!" He continued laughing, and the other Archa joined in as Mica jumped from the ground, brushing the dirt and twigs from her uniform.

Ira looked at her and said, "Take off that damn helmet, Watcher."

Mica removed her helmet but kept her eyes lowered.

"Damn fine job, Watcher," remarked Ira.

"Cute too," said Lucas, "if you had some hair. I despise bald females. Such a big turnoff."

Invedia scowled directly at Mica.

Instantly, Ira's manner changed when he suddenly realized that he wasn't being laughed with—he was being laughed at. Ridiculed, in fact, by the rest of the group. Instigated of course by Crudelis. A scowl grew on Ira's forehead. He was feeling indignant at his ungainly brush with the dirt, and he took his frustration out on Mica.

He bellowed, "What are you standing there for? Do you think you are on vacation? Put your damn helmet back on and start watching!" He thundered.

Mica quickly slipped on her helmet and immediately took her position.

The rest of the hunt was uneventful. They shot at a few birds that were lucky enough, or smart enough, to miss the hail of fire bombarded at them.

The Archa seemed to be looking for a particular type of animal, a bear or a Nahu perhaps. Whatever they were tracking, they kept losing the trail and gradually became louder and more abusive with one another. Each one blaming the others for the noise level.

Eventually, they returned to the main camp and piled into the MECAs, still insulting one another loudly as they headed toward the Big White House.

After they had left, the watchers removed their helmets, relieved to hear the peace and quiet of the forest.

"Good job, Mica," said Gerald proudly, beaming. "You saved Ira's life today."

Mica smiled. "If I knew he was going to yell at me so much, I might have just let him be trampled by that buck."

Will laughed heartily at Mica's animated face.

But Gerald's face was one of abject horror as he hissed at them. "They could be watching and listening to us. Say nothing more."

Mica's and Will's faces immediately became impassive, and they were silent all the way home.

After they had parked the MECA back into the terrain hangar, they went into their little white cottage. All three of them were hungry because while the Archa had eaten snacks, the watchers were not permitted to remove their helmets to eat or drink. Gerald had put a water-filled bladder inside their uniforms, with a small rubber hose that ran to their mouths so they could sip water slowly all day. This homemade ingenuity made life much more bearable.

It had been a long and noisy day. The watchers were exhausted but happy to see their little cottage. They picked up their red food bag, went inside, and immediately locked their door.

The three watchers sat down and ate their food, which was magnificent, some roast meat with vegetables, bread, and wedges of apple pie, complete with thick dairy cream.

While the sky was beginning to darken, the Big White House was lit up like a bonfire. Some weird music was screaming out over the loudspeakers, and the Archa were still yelling at one another in the midst of all the noise and mayhem.

"The Lords of Chaos," muttered Gerald. "It is going to be a long night tonight."

Gerald went to a drawer in the kitchen and came back with three sets of earplugs. "Put these in your ears," he said, shrugging. "It will help."

Will and Mica took the earplugs but ate silently, never quite sure of how much of the cottage was under surveillance.

Mica broke the silence. "What do the Nahus look like?" she asked. "I have never seen a picture of one, not even in the museum."

"They are filthy, vicious beasts," replied Gerald. He began wiping the crumbs of their roast beef dinner from his mouth in disgust. "You will see them soon enough," he said. "Don't worry."

Will had been looking around the little cottage and believed he had found one camera in each bedroom and even in the bathrooms. One was perched in the living room, but they were tiny, not like the vast glowing red eyes they had been used to everywhere at First City.

He also wondered why their little cottage was so well fortified. It could stand an attack from a small army. It had a massive metal door at least two inches thick, with titanium locks, and the long rectangular window was made of bulletproof, shatter-resistant glass. It appeared the cottage had been deliberately built preventing any view at all of the Big White House. Will thought that was odd, considering the watchers were there solely to protect and aid the Archa.

Will had noticed a lot of strange things since he had been here, but there was no one to trust except Mica. But he couldn't discuss anything with her because it was too dangerous. All his instincts were finely tuned and told him he was in danger. One wrong move and he wouldn't live long enough to have his mind erased.

The watchers were tired from their long day, showered, and went to bed as the noise outside the small cottage grew louder and louder. Gerald was right; the earplugs helped a lot.

As Mica went to bed, she thought about her first day. It didn't seem so bad, and she wondered if poor old Gerald had exaggerated the dangers at the Archa Compound. She decided to keep an open mind.

A few hours before dawn, the watchers were all woken by a sudden loud thud. It sounded like a big rock bouncing off the window. Will grabbed a chair and stood on it, trying to look out into the darkness. At first, he could barely see anything but the dark, but as his eyes adjusted, he could make out the shadow of a young female with long bright-red hair, strands falling everywhere from the tall pile upon the top of her head. He could sense the girl was terrified. Her dress was ripped to shreds, and she was covered in blood. She cried pitifully while looking up toward Will.

"Help me, O stars above, help me!" she begged.

Will immediately jumped down from the chair and walked toward the door, presumably to let the injured female in. Gerald started yelling, "No! No! No!" And like a flash, he jumped over the chair and beat Will to the door. Mica was startled and couldn't believe that Gerald had moved so fast.

"We must help her!" yelled Will, stunned by Gerald's callous attitude.

"No, we cannot," replied Gerald, now in a more-controlled tone. "The Archa are playing with their toys. It is not our business."

"That is not a toy, it is a woman out there needing help!" persisted Will, now outraged.

Gerald hissed at him, "They are watching us, our every move. Open that door, and we are all dead. You don't understand this world yet. Please, Will, just go back to bed and stay there until morning."

Will's years of training made him comply, and he wondered how very quickly paradise had turned into the worst nightmare imaginable. As he lay in his bed, the girl's screams became more and more guttural. It was a horrific sound. There were terrible growling and tearing noises, and suddenly, there was silence. A few minutes later, they heard Ira's voice admonishing someone.

"You have made a big mess out here."

Neither watcher could hear the garbled response.

Will wasn't sure what just happened outside, and he was glad he was safe in this little white sanctuary. But he could not get the sound of the young woman's screams out of his head. They haunted him.

Will hadn't told anyone about his continuing night visions. The dream was morphing over time. Now he was somewhere in the woods, and a strange being whose face was all blurred, like it had melted somehow, was staring at him, half-hidden in the brush. It said only seven words: "Will, I have been waiting for you." Then he would wake up, terrified and covered in sweat. The hideous face haunted his dreams almost every night.

CHAPTER 8

❧

Third City (The Farm)

The watchers ate their morning meal and got their equipment ready. The morning was quiet while the watchers got ready for work. One of the messengers had brought news that they had to go to Third City for some collections and deliveries. Surprisingly, Gerald did not mention the events of the previous night. Both Mica and Will wanted to ask questions, but Gerald seemed irritable, and there was no privacy in the little white cottage with the tiny blinking red lights everywhere.

Suddenly, Will felt suffocated and smothered. It was a strange, unnerving feeling, but with a clear mind and healthy body, he was becoming more and more disturbed by the insidious reality around him.

Then they had to walk around and behind the Big White House to access the terrain hangar and collect the Heavy One.

Gerald reminded them as they walked beside the beautiful, fragrant rose gardens, "If you see one of the Archa, you must stop and bow your head as they walk past you. Say nothing unless you are spoken to. Remain silent and bowed until they have walked at least ten paces away from you."

Will and Mica nodded that they understood. They were almost to the hangar when a tall hooded figure suddenly appeared from around the corner. It was Malus, wearing his long flowing cloak and huge black sunglasses. Immediately all the watchers bowed their heads.

It was the first time Will and Mica had glimpsed him, because he did not attend the previous hunt. His appearance terrified them. However, his aura was much worse. They could sense the purity of his evil, which emanated from his pores in the form of a bitter metallic smell. The two watchers were frozen in place, staring down in horror at his six splayed toes that poked out from beneath his cloak.

"Greetings, Watchersss," hissed Malus, sounding very reptilian, his voice full of menace. He addressed Gerald, "I understand you are going to the Farm today. Is that correct, Watcher?"

"Yes, my lord," Gerald replied, remaining bowed.

"Here are my orders and the necessary paperwork," Malus announced while staring hard at the bowed watchers.

"Thank you, my lord," replied Gerald respectfully.

"Good, good, there are a couple of special requests on there." Malus's tone changed, "Make sure you do not come back without them," he remarked pointedly.

"Yes, my lord," replied Gerald, grabbing the paperwork while almost bent over to his knees.

"Good job, Watcher," replied Malus patronizingly as he strode away back toward the Big White House. As Malus disappeared, Gerald stood up, clutching a sheaf of papers in his hand and some keys.

The watchers continued to the terrain hangar, and all three climbed into an enormous shiny black vehicle. It was a big commercial truck. It could seat at least six people in the cab, three in the front and three behind them. Inside the large cargo hold, there were folding benches along both the sides and on the back wall of the vehicle that could seat about thirty people. Covering the floor was a pile of fresh straw. In the back left-hand corner, there was an old metal bucket; attached to the left and back walls with large rusty bolts.

The top of the cargo hold was aerated, with a thick metal mesh. Will could see there was a rolled-up canvas cover. Just in case of rain, it could be stretched over the mesh and fastened with metal clips to the back, where there were large hooks welded into the black mesh. The vehicle looked like a big black beast. "We call this the Heavy One," announced Gerald, like nothing had just happened.

As they boarded the vehicle, Will and Mica were still in shock. Their RFID chips beeped, and Mica realized there was a Relay Reader on board. Will noticed it too. "Are we being recorded?" he asked.

"No," replied Gerald, "but they do monitor our mileage and who enters and leaves the vehicle. Farm pickups are all about numbers, period."

Gerald started the engine, and the Heavy One roared out and away from the Big White House. He immediately began to relax, unaware Mica and Will were still in shock over the encounter with Malus.

Will turned to Gerald and said, "I have some questions."

Gerald looked at Will with a resigned, defeated look, and he barely nodded.

"Who is Malus? Why does he look so strange? And what is he?" asked Mica forcefully before Will could speak.

"What do you want to know?" replied Gerald slowly. "There is not very much to tell."

Will could see he was visibly uncomfortable.

"I don't know what he is!" Gerald suddenly yelled at the top of his lungs in a strange outburst. "All I know is Malus feeds off the suffering of the human race. He has occupied Earth since the beginning of time. Malus has more power and technology than you have ever dreamed of. He is immortal, and he owns the planet and all of us in it. Accept it, both of you. We are just slaves to Malus and the Archa. Do you get it now? We are disposable, replaceable, and immediately forgotten after our death. Do I wish the world were different? Of course I do! What is the point of understanding anything when it's all so irrelevant to our survival? Now, no more questions on Malus or the Archa."

Mica, surprised by Gerald's outburst, replied, "I think we need a better explanation—"

"Silence!" roared Gerald, cutting her off in midsentence.

"Oh, I wish it were time to have my mind erased," groaned Gerald and held the left side of his head, which felt like someone was stabbing his temple with an ice pick. He was still trying to drive with his right hand and one eye closed.

Gerald continued to shout at the dumbfounded watchers, "And if you don't toughen up, you will not make it! You don't understand that you will not survive to be my age, do you? Accept things how they are because we cannot change them. This job is your new life now for the next twenty years. Welcome to their world, suck it up, and drive on."

Gerald was violently shaking and was very pale. Will thought Gerald might have a heart attack and drop dead right there in the Heavy One. For once even Mica had nothing to say, so they all sat in silence, just watching the trees whisk past as they thundered down the highway, lamenting their plight.

"We are visiting Third City," announced Gerald quietly after several miles and about an hour of driving.

"How many cities are there?" asked Mica, trying to stay away from controversial topics. She did not want to risk upsetting Gerald again.

"Well," he replied calmly, "First City is where you came from. It is an education city. Citizens are educated and trained for jobs there.

"Second City is a manufacturing plant, where things are made and built. Third City is a reproduction center, nicknamed the Farm. Fourth City is the Obedience Reinforcement and Rehabilitation Center.

"Fifth City is a technology and science center. Sixth City is the Full Emergency Medical Assessment Center. Seventh City grows food on an enormous scale—it is the biggest of all the cities.

"Eighth City is where the Yellow Eyes live. Don't be confused, they are still considered royalty and the same protocols apply to them as to the Archa. Ninth City deals with military operations. No one has clearance to visit there, except for Malus. Tenth City is a very long way away. It is a cotton plantation, and it also weaves and manufactures all the cotton cloth and clothes we use."

Gerald finally took a breath and remarked, "As watchers, we deal primarily with Third, Fourth, Sixth, and Eighth Cities."

Gerald fell silent again, and it took almost another hour to reach their destination. The Heavy One drove very slowly, barely thirty miles an hour. Will estimated, if they were in a regular car, they could have driven there in half the time. He wondered why they needed such a big vehicle.

The countryside had expanded into tall colonnades of green trees that lined the highway. Beyond the trees were vivid green meadows filled with a kaleidoscope of wildflowers: bright pinks, deep purples, vibrant yellows, rich reds, and a multitude of flowering shrubs and bushes were blooming everywhere. They also spotted several different animals, raccoons, and wild boar. Several deer were roaming through the Wildlife Corridors, which had fences running parallel to the long straight road. Will and Mica saw no people or other vehicles throughout the whole journey.

Finally, the watchers arrived at Third City. The first thing they saw was the fifteen-foot walls that surrounded the compound. Attached to one of the gigantic metal gates was a large old sign covered with peeling paint. It announced that they were entering the Eco-Charter Reproductive Services. Once through the gates, they saw the right side of the compound had at least fifteen buildings standing in a row. Each one was numbered, from infant, age one, age two, age three, and so on until age fifteen.

Immediately in front and continuing to the left as far as the eye could see was a Healing Center, much bigger than the one in First City. They parked the Heavy One in a large parking area and made their way to the central building marked Administration.

As they entered the building, they opened the door and immediately walked through a Relay Reader, which flashed information onto a small screen in neon-red letters. It was some numeric code. Neither Will nor Mica could decipher it. Then followed what seemed to be a biometric sequence, and finally a photo identification of each of the watchers. Security appeared to be very tightly controlled.

There was an enormous flashing board covering almost the whole back wall of the security room, with hundreds of names all coded numerically, with different alphanumeric codes next to the names.

It appeared the Full Emergency Medical Assessment Center was electronically linked to the board, which relayed information in real time. The board automatically updated every five seconds and provided information on hundreds of patients, assumed Will correctly.

The second door buzzed, and they went through into the inner sanctum. There was a team of doctors or scientists all dressed in identical white coats. Many of them also wore heavy-rimmed black glasses, and they were all standing around, discussing something that was top secret, because all conversation stopped as the three watchers walked into the room.

A small man approached them, and by the deference the others were giving him, Mica assumed he was in charge. His tag and number read Dr. Orrow 003.

"Greetings, Watchers! Welcome to the finest genetic lab on the planet," announced Dr. Orrow, beaming proudly.

"We breed the best genetic specimens at our facility," continued Dr. Orrow, almost beside himself with pride, which was not an attractive trait. Will and Mica felt their disapproval increasing minute by minute with this boastful little doctor.

"What is the order of the day?" asked Dr. Orrow cheerfully. His beady little myopic eyes looked enormous due to the magnification of his quarter-inch-thick-lensed glasses. He looked like a small bald owl.

Gerald spoke respectfully. "Greetings, Dr. Orrow. These are our new watchers, Will 4523 and Mica 3432," he said as he handed over the paperwork.

"Greetings, new Watchers," replied Dr. Orrow pleasantly as he read the order out loud.

Order for Farm:

1. *2 x 6 months (1f, 1m) requested by Gula.*
2. *4 x 5 years old (2f, 2m) required by Malus.*
3. *5 x 10 years old (4m, 1f) sought by Metus.*
4. *16 x 13 years old (assorted, m/f ratio not relevant). Use your subgenetic groups. Deliver them to the House of Dreams in Eighth City.*

5. *2 x 15 years old (both must be attractive and top genetic breeders for 2nd wives in Eighth City). Delivery will be to the Marriage and Betrothal Center.*

Will could not believe his ears—they had just read a grocery list of children!

Mica was so appalled at this new revelation; she had difficulty holding her expression impassive. This farm was full of human beings. All of them were procured for sinister purposes. She doubted she was capable of hiding her real emotions from the rest of the group.

"Would you like to tour our facilities?" asked the little doctor politely. "Then we can have an excellent lunch while your order is being filled and packed for transport."

"We will be delighted," replied Gerald rather loudly. He made a crucial point. "A good working relationship is vital to keep all the programs running smoothly. Any problems here could cause problems for all of us." Gerald paused and looked directly at Will and Mica.

"Ah, yes, indeed," murmured Dr. Orrow. "First, we will visit the Birthing Wing."

As they walked toward the Birthing Wing, they entered the elevator on the ground floor. There were four levels. The elevator doors swished open on the top floor, and they accessed the large Birthing Wing, with row after row of beds filled with pregnant women.

What was most surprising to both Will and Mica was that the birthers were some of the most impressive specimens of physical beauty Will and Mica had ever seen. They scanned the room for the elusive Yellow Eyes, but neither one could see any because the Yellow Eyes were housed in a different section.

Mica approached a beautiful, bored, very pregnant human female.

"Greetings, Eco-citizen. What are your tag and your number?" she asked.

The female was lying in bed, looking very irritated, and a scowl formed on her beautiful face. "Breeder 463," she answered sulkily while staring rudely at Mica.

"Did you win the lottery?" asked Mica foolishly.

The woman stared at her viciously, as if she had lost her mind.

"Watcher, I am a breeder. I am having my eighth baby. There is no lottery here. There are no men here. This," she snapped as she pointed to her distended belly, "is all done by science and artificial insemination."

Mica continued to badger the unfortunate woman.

"At what age did you birth your first child?" Mica persisted, not noticing the disapproving looks from the rest of the group.

"Thirteen," snapped the woman. "I am trying to sleep right now, Watcher. All I do is grow them and push them out. If I can reach twelve healthy births, then I finally get to rest and maybe be a midwife to the others. If I live that long. Chances are, I will die before number 12. Not many make that magic number." The woman stared at Mica with a despising look. "Can you get rid of her? She is angering me, and I am tired of her foolishness." The pregnant woman directed her comments solely to Dr. Orrow.

Mica ignored Gerald's terrified look. "Please, one more question and I will leave you alone," begged Mica. "Where are all your babies?"

"I don't know where those parasites are, and I really don't care about them," she replied angrily, putting in her earplugs and turning over in her metal bed to face the wall.

Then Dr. Orrow said very stiffly, "It is time to go and leave her to rest. She is one of our best breeders, despite her temperament. It seems you have the same problem with one of your watchers too," he said, staring at Mica with venom.

Gerald apologized for Mica's rudeness. "I am full of profound regret by my watcher's ignorance. Please forgive her. She is new and unfamiliar with the correct protocol."

Then he admonished Mica very harshly, "In future, Mica 3432, you will address the breeders and thank them for their contribution to society, nothing else. Do you understand? Or you will be severely punished."

By the shocked faces around her, Mica realized she had just made some serious mistakes.

"A thousand apologies," she said quickly. "Dr. Orrow, my inexperience has embarrassed my over-leader. I spoke out of place. It will not happen again. I am just overwhelmed by all your incredibly valuable work here."

"Apology accepted," beamed Dr. Orrow at the compliment.

Then he leaned in toward her and said in a very insidious tone, "Everyone may make only *one* mistake."

Mica nodded in submission, realizing immediately this was not a Q and A but a silent tour, where one showed nothing but admiration for this little monster's horror show. She was here merely to observe while their order was being filled and not to comment unless requested to do so.

Leaving the Birthing Wing, they toured the Birthing Room, which contained about ten moaning women, all in various stages of labor.

Then they went down to the third floor and glimpsed into the Sorting Room. Dr. Orrow said this was where all the babies were taken immediately after birth. They were genetically tested and graded like eggs. The humans and Yellow Eyes were separated. Then they were sent to various sections as potential human birthers or possible wives to the Yellow Eyes or assigned to research.

The whole second floor was labeled Research and was the largest and the busiest level, filled with lots of cribs, equipment, and healers. It seemed the majority of the babies were housed here.

Dr. Orrow told them (while smiling, of course) that all the babies had multiple genetic anomalies; some were so diseased or deformed that Mica couldn't bear to look at them.

Will thought it was a place of horrific suffering and was glad to move on as the ever-cheerful Dr. Orrow happily explained, "These specimens help society as a whole by giving their lives to medical research. Their valuable contributions will one day provide cures for various diseases and genetic defects."

Mica realized in horror, via Dr. Orrow's words, that these babies had been specially bred to be terminally ill.

At last, Dr. Orrow announced it was lunchtime, and they all went to an extraordinary dining center on the first floor, which also housed the administration offices and the doctors' living quarters.

The food smelled delicious, and it was a buffet fit for the Archa. On the table were several roasted slices of meat cooked with roasted potatoes, baby carrots, tiny sweet peas, and lots of thick gravy, complete with crusty, freshly baked bread and lots of real butter.

Neither Will nor Mica had much of an appetite, but they forced themselves to eat and make appropriate small talk, most of it centering on the immense genius and success of Dr. Orrow and his monstrous center.

Finally, the watchers returned to the Heavy One. Luckily, most of their wretched cargo had been loaded while they were eating lunch, so they didn't have to see the faces of their victims. However, there was screaming and crying coming from the back of the cargo hold. The noises were disturbing and chaotic.

It was even worse because they had to sit and wait for a few minutes for the two Yellow Eyes breeders to arrive.

As Will and Mica waited in the Heavy One, they suddenly realized the value of their dull lives as ordinary Eco-citizens. In this new world, they wondered what other horrors they would have to endure.

"We must deliver the two second wife breeders to the Marriage and Betrothal Bureau in Eighth City, which is just a few miles away from here. Then the sixteen subgenetics have to be taken to the House of Dreams. Finally, we will transport the remainder of the cargo to the Big White House," ordered Gerald in a tone that meant no questions or comments.

Will and Mica remembered from their training that the Yellow Eyes were below the Archa in social status but above the humans. Gerald told them the Yellow Eyes had grown in numbers over the eons and they all lived in Eighth City.

CHAPTER 9

Eighth City and the Yellow Eyes

Will and Mica were curious about the Yellow Eyes. When the two breeders eventually came out of the building, they sat in the back seat of the cab, motionless, dressed in pure white cotton shifts and black canvas shoes. They looked extremely anxious, and neither one said a word throughout the whole journey. They had pale yellow-colored eyes with vertical black pupils. Their hair was sparse and straw-colored. They had luminous white skin that quickly burned and no eyebrows or eyelashes. They were quite bizarre to look at.

Gerald had previously explained that the girls were above them in social status and they could not speak to them unless they were addressed first by either girl.

Gerald had told Will and Mica that the Yellow Eyes came in all shapes and sizes. They could live the average human life span, but with replacement organs and various other medical procedures they had developed, they could live for up to 180 years old, if they were rich enough.

The Yellow Eyes were continually comparing themselves to the Archa. They felt self-conscious about their lack of hair, and to compensate, the females wore elaborate wigs made of human hair, which they dyed in bright and neon colors. They drew on or glued on to their white faces unique eyebrows and fluffy long feather eyelashes. However, they were forbidden to emulate the Archa by using real gold or golden colors.

When the Heavy One approached Eighth City, the watchers stopped at the checkpoint and had their papers thoroughly inspected and stamped by an officious-looking guard who refused to speak to them. They drove through the gates, toward the Marriage Bureau, which was only a few minutes away. Here the girls would be dressed and coiffed to Eighth City standards. Their future husbands would be anywhere from twenty to forty years older than them.

The two young Yellow Eyes had no idea of what lay ahead. They were very excited because they had escaped the Farm and were beginning the final preparations for their marriage debut. They were young and naive, believing they were starting a beautiful, magical life with a rich and handsome man.

The young women didn't realize that they would be under the complete control of a jealous first spouse who, for the first time in her submissive and restrictive married life, would now be able to exercise some real authority and power.

Unlike with both the humans and purebred Archa, who enjoyed equality between the sexes, Eighth City was strictly a patriarchal society. All females were considered, first, their father's property. When they married, the women became their husband's exclusive property, to treat and dispose of as he saw fit. They had security because divorce was not considered a socially acceptable option. Sadly, there was no equality or freedom for women in Eighth City.

Male children were horribly spoiled and pampered, while female children were taught from birth to be submissive and expected to always defer to male's authority, irrelevant of his young age. By the time they were two, these little man-monsters would wield power over anybody they could, and so they grew up to be deviant, terrifying demons.

Almost every wealthy male in Eighth City had a mistress (called a courtesan) and often more than one wife. In reality, a favored courtesan wielded enormous power, receiving many more privileges and liberties than the legal wives did. Wives always stayed at home with the children; they were allowed to shop, but any entertainment venues were closed to them, and they were forbidden to work.

When a man grew tired of his courtesan. He usually discarded them like trash. Very few of them lived long, happy lives unless they were able to receive enough gifts in their youth to retire upon in later life.

It was common knowledge that many second wives (concubines) in Eighth City met with accidents within months of marriage. For a second wife to live long enough to give birth was expected, but most of their babies were said to be "stillborn," or they were sent secretly to the Big White House as a gift. Many of these unfortunate young Yellow Eyes wives "died" in childbirth or met with accidents well before they became pregnant again.

Some became lucky. If the second wives bore a child with either gold hair or eyes, the child was revered and the other women dared not dispose of a golden child. Then and only then would the concubine have respect in the family and live a long life.

Sometimes, if the husband was a real tyrant (and many were in Eighth City), the women formed bonds, but most often the male would play one wife against the other for complete control.

The Yellow Eyes society followed a strict caste system, whereby the lighter their coloring, the lower their caste. Predictably, the pale lower ranks served the darker higher ones.

Occasionally, a genetic throwback would occur and a child was born with almost gold eyes or slightly thicker hair. These rare beings, either male or female, could command very high dowries on the breeding market. Families would pay vast sums to wed such prime specimens.

All breeding revolved around trying to produce a pureblood child with golden eyes and golden hair. Of course, no one was able to create that perfect child despite a lot of research and physical practice.

What the Yellow Eyes didn't know was that the twelve families of the Archa were purposefully and individually sterile, so their bloodline would be preserved for eternity and could never be accidentally contaminated.

The Yellow Eyes women that came to the Compound hoping to conceive a golden Archa child were sadly disappointed and usually became the night's entertainment, only to disappear when the Archa grew tired of them.

For the pureblood Archa to produce offspring, a gene sequence needed to be unlocked with a unique chemical key. The secret serum was guarded by the master of the ceremonies in the Archa family.

To Will and Mica, Eighth City was an incredible sight filled to capacity with bustling people dressed in brightly colored clothing, where there seemed to be every shade of scarlet, blue, green, and yellow. They looked like birds of paradise. They all wore neon-colored wigs made of real hair. Each style was more outrageous than the last. The wigs were shaped into animals, flowers, even seashells. Some styles were geometric and full of sharp angles, while others appeared soft and puffy like clouds and decorated with ornate, jeweled, hair accessories.

The wealthy women wore their nails long and painted to match their wigs and shoes. The females wore a gemstone ring if they were married. The type of stone indicated her owner's social status. Everyone in Eighth City was obsessed with appearance and wealth.

Everyone wore enormous dark sunglasses to shade light-sensitive eyes from the bright sun. Everything in Eighth City glittered, sparkled, and shone.

The males wore neon wigs too, but they were less elaborate than the females'. They also painted large black eyebrows upon their brow lines and used kohl to accentuate their eyes. The men wore brightly colored togas decorated with silver, copper, or brass and adorned with semiprecious jewels.

The city was full of beautiful ponds, where fat croaking frogs lounged on full lily pads as metallic colored fish swam silently beneath them. There were elaborate fountains, some as high as twenty feet, that glowed neon colors in the evening hours.

Everywhere in the city were beautiful pastel and tropical flowers and real fruit trees covered in spring's fragrant blossoms. There were outdoor cafés, where people sipped tall fruity drinks or hot, steaming coffee and ate small crumbly pastries and delicious layered fruit tarts while their exotic, hybrid pets snarled and hissed at one another at the end of their very expensive leashes.

This city wasn't like First City. Here there were little cars that speckled the landscape, and in the distance, large homes loomed on the horizon. Stores were open twenty-four hours a day, where a person could buy anything they could want, from clothing to exotic food.

There were bathhouses, separated by sex for men and women, although both bathhouses were staffed by women. The pools outside looked smoky and eerie with clouds of steam rising from the warm waters. The inside of each pool was made from hundreds of mosaic tiles that formed different-shaped flowers. There were saunas and massage rooms, where many soothing, fragrant oils eased tired and aching muscles.

The city was hypnotic, so alive and colorful, and the smells of spices and flowers mingled with the sounds of melodic music that drifted across the city, emanating from black-dot speakers hidden in tall fluttering trees. The iconic flowing city made First City seem very dull and monochromatic.

The watchers parked at the Marriage and Betrothal Bureau and escorted the two young girls into the center. Once they were inside, it was like discovering a hidden cave filled with priceless treasures.

There was one room with hundreds of beautiful dresses in every hue and another room full of brightly neon-colored wigs. On one wall, designer jewelry was displayed, and shoes of every style and shade.

The last room had several face-painting stations where females were busily painting red lips and fastening long fluffy eyelashes onto the eyelids of young brides. Other workers were painting semipermanent dye onto the girls' hands and feet and fixing tiny jewels to their intricate tattoos. Wigs were teased into incredible shapes, some even a foot tall. This was a place where brides were made.

The two breeders looked excited with all the glamor around them and were soon whisked away by different workers to be transformed themselves. Starting with the bathhouse, where they would be scrubbed thoroughly, then taken off to the massage center to be massaged with exotic oils that would make their skin soft and glowing. Finally, they would be returned to the Bureau, to be painted and dressed for their big day. Once coiffured to perfection, the young women were married to their new husbands, who would meet them in the marriage office, and their future would be signed away forever once they became the legal property of their new masters.

The director of the betrothal center was a tall Yellow Eyes female wearing a lemon-sorbet-colored silk dress. It was gathered and clasped at the top of each slim shoulder by giant carved metallic brooches. The fabric fell in soft, silky waves and was covered with tiny glittering yellow gems. Her wig was pale yellow with silver strands woven into it; it was expertly piled on top of her head and held in layers by decorative pins and bows. On her feet, she was wearing beautifully crafted lemon leather shoes that had pentagram-shaped heels.

Gerald bowed, so Will and Mica followed suit. Gerald stretched out his hand toward the director, and she snatched the papers from him with such force they almost ripped in half.

"Two, is that all today, Watcher?" she snapped as she glanced at the paperwork.

"Yes, my lady," replied Gerald, still bowing lower.

"Then leave my sight and return to the place you came from," she said spitefully, and then she twirled around on her pentagram heels and walked away very haughtily.

Gerald replied, "Yes, my lady," still bowing in respect well after she had gone.

As the watchers walked back to the Heavy One, they kept their eyes downcast. The sea of people that had gathered around the vehicle quickly parted as the watchers walked by. The Yellow Eyes turned their faces away in disgust. They mocked the humans by making pig noises, speaking very loudly about the foul stench in the air. All of them started pointing and laughing at the surprised watchers. One child even threw a rock, shouting "Leave, you ugly beasts!" Others dared to spit at them, and the watchers were forced to close their visors for safety.

Mica was fuming inside, wishing she could snap their necks in a second and throw their pitiful corpses into a pile. She had wondered how many she could kill before someone stopped her. Shocked by her own feelings of anger and hatred, Mica took a long, deep breath and switched off by zoning out into another place and time. A useful tool that she would often use in her new job.

Will was shocked by the feelings of such hatred shown toward them by the Yellow Eyes. He realized that whatever genetic breeding they had pursued was a complete failure since they had bred the humanity out of these twisted creatures.

The Yellow Eyes were just as vicious and intolerant to their own people. They were like the demons that were described in ancient times. Now Will understood why some people had believed in such ridiculous stories in the Chaos Era. The Yellow Eyes were standing around taunting, snarling, and spitting at them. It was disgraceful and primitive behavior. Some young boys were hitting the cargo hold with rocks and sticks while laughing at the terror-stricken screams coming from the captive humans.

Relieved to leave the cruel Yellow Eyes crowd behind them, the watchers quickly piled into the Heavy One and drove off. Their next stop was to drop off the sixteen thirteen-year-olds. There were nine females and seven males. This genetic subgroup looked physically no different from the rest of the Yellow Eyes—in fact, most were gorgeous.

Maybe they carry bad genes, thought Mica, but surely that would just exclude them from the breeding program.

Curiously she asked Gerald, "Why are they marked for eventual extermination?"

Gerald sighed. "I have never trained a watcher who has so many questions. Why does it matter?" he asked. "It doesn't affect your existence, does it? Whatever they do with them, it is not your concern."

Mica said nothing and just shrugged her shoulders.

Gerald, still shaking his head wearily, answered Mica's question nonetheless. "The subs carry genes for physical or mental diseases, which tend to manifest in five to ten years. So the subgenetics must go to the House of Dreams, which is in the middle of Eighth City."

"What is the House of Dreams?" asked Mica quietly. "Is it a place of beauty?"

Meanwhile, Will was silent. He was wondering how they decided who had mental disorders in an insane world.

"Not if you are a subgenetic," retorted Gerald sharply. He saw Mica's inquisitive look. He retorted, "Imagine horrors far worse than you have ever seen. Mica, are you sure you want me to describe in graphic detail what will happen to our cargo?"

"No," replied Mica quickly. "I understand. I do not wish to learn more about the House of Dreams."

They drove through the streets, watching the events that unfurled daily in the seemingly perfect world of Eighth City. Sadly, these beings were just as depraved as the Archa at the Big White House, but they were not as wealthy or powerful. Here their depravity was determined solely by budget.

Several blocks later, they arrived at the House of Dreams. The House of Dreams was a sizable, garish building covered in red and black metal masks. The main door was a big wooden one covered with elaborate carvings of gargoyles, completed by an ornate iron handle.

The watchers parked behind the building in the private parking area, where the customers' cars couldn't be seen or recognized. It was empty because no Yellow Eyes wanted to be seen in public in the House of Dreams parking area.

The watchers unloaded the cargo from the Heavy One. The children looked hot and sweaty as they filed silently, and defeated, inside the building, as if they knew their destiny was going to end in a nightmare here in this house of demented dreams.

The watchers stood in the shadows of the large pentagon-shaped entry hall. It was a pale room with a white marble floor, elegant marble columns, and hundreds of painted portraits hung from the white walls.

The room was dim and smoky. The smoke wafted from the burning incense and hundreds of long red tapered candles that were lit at the brightest time of the day. The sunshine was shut out by heavy brocade curtains.

The watchers were met by the hideous director, a female about a hundred years old. She was wearing an outlandish bright-red wig that was slightly crooked and a black toga dress covered in hand-sewn red silk poppies. She was wearing large flat black shoes that made her feet look like a pair of flippers.

Her face was red and blotchy—probably from an excess of drinking. Other than the Archa, the Yellow Eyes were the only beings allowed to consume any type of alcohol.

The director's face was smeared with white stage makeup, and she had drawn on her own eyebrows. They looked like squiggly little black tadpoles. The woman's bright-red lips revealed her yellowing teeth. She looked like a psychotic clown. The woman just stood there, assessing the cargo with her icy yellow eyes. She didn't speak a word and waved at them as they filed past her, shouting instructions to the invisible staff.

"Hurry! Hurry!" the director screamed to her staff, who finally scuttled out of the corners like hungry cockroaches. "Get the new stock ready now," she ordered.

The children marched to different rooms, one for the snuff room, two to the reactive room, three to the bondage room, one to the wrecking room, and two to the orgy room. After assigning the cargo, the director finally addressed the watchers without even looking at them. She merely screamed, "Papers!"

Gerald rushed forward with the orders in a strange bowing motion. She grabbed them, scribbled a signature, and tore off the bottom copy, throwing it at Gerald. He swiftly caught the receipt as it floated down toward the floor. Then the director turned her back on them, walked from the main hall, and continued up the long curved staircase, which led to the second floor of the House of Dreams.

The watchers left the House of Dreams and quickly walked toward the Heavy One, glad to escape Eighth City and return home to the relative peace and safety of their little white cottage.

Mica and Will had almost forgotten about their remaining cargo. When they started driving, they could hear the remaining children sobbing and crying.

"Can we give them some water?" asked Mica sadly.

"No," replied Gerald softly. "It is better if you don't."

"Why?" Mica asked, confused.

"Because you will prolong their suffering," replied Will unexpectedly. "The longer the children go without food and water, the quicker they will die. Am I right, Gerald?"

"Yes," replied Gerald happily. "Will, you are beginning to think like a real watcher."

"May the stars help me," whispered Will under his breath, "so that I won't become who they want me to be."

The watchers sat in silence for the rest of the journey home. When they arrived at the Big White House, it was late, and the house was quiet and dark. Gerald told them he would deliver the remainder of the orders. He instinctively knew that neither Will nor Mica could handle any more deliveries.

As Gerald unloaded the cargo, one small girl walked forward fearfully, still clutching her dirty pink stuffed bear. Her face was red, and her big eyes were swollen from crying. She was probably about five years old.

Some of the Big White House's staff came out to collect the cargo of children. One of them approached the little girl and snatched the bear from her hands and threw it into the bushes.

Mica's face remained impassive, but a single tear ran down her cheek. For the third time today, she wanted to kill someone, all of them, the whole corrupt, evil, pampered Archa. The demonic Yellow Eyes and the weak selfish humans who allowed this to happen. Mica wished she could raze them from the Earth, one by one.

Will remained silent. He was unable to watch the heart-wrenching scene, so he stared down at the floor and away into the darkness of the Heavy One. Neither watchers spoke a word.

Their list finally accomplished, Gerald parked the Heavy One and the watchers walked toward their cottage, emotionally drained by what they had witnessed throughout the day.

Mica whispered to Will, "I can't do this anymore."

"Yes, you can," replied Will.

Mica looked away into the darkness, shaking her head sadly.

Gerald walked up to them. "What are you two talking about?" he asked, immediately suspicious, and looked around him.

Will quickly intervened. "We were just wondering what was for dinner. It's been a long day, and we are hungry."

"Yes," replied Gerald. "A good day's work." He smiled at both of them and suggested, "Let's go home and eat."

"I hope dinner is roasted chicken tonight with mashed potatoes and gravy," remarked Mica innocently, wanting peace with Gerald. Even though her stomach had been sick and churning all day.

"Maybe cherry pie too," remarked Will, playing along.

"Oh, that's my favorite too," commented Gerald happily.

They all returned to the cottage to eat their dinner. Then the three watchers showered and went to bed. Will and Mica lay there in their rooms, hoping sleep would come and erase the visuals of that awful day.

Mica finally slept as sheer exhaustion overcame her.

Will was not so lucky. The murky face that continually haunted his dreams whispered, "I have been waiting for you, Will 4523. We will meet soon."

Just then, his predawn night vision was interrupted by the beeping of the morning wake-up alarm.

CHAPTER 10

The Hunt of the Nahus

Since Will and Mica had arrived at the Archa compound, they both wrestled with severe depression. Neither one smiled anymore or had any happy thoughts. If their duty days weren't bad enough, they both suffered from sleepless nights and were tormented by night terrors.

As time passed, one day melted into another. To Will and Mica, their new assignments seemed like an endless amount of picking up and delivering victims. They despised this new reality, and the heinous acts they were forced to participate in with the degenerate Archa.

Will and Mica felt like there was no escape from the waves of dark oblivion that were gradually consuming them. They were both afraid they would lose all their human empathy, becoming like the army of emotionally dead zombies who surrounded them. It seemed that nothing could raise their spirits.

Gerald was lying in bed one morning, thinking about Will and Mica. He knew they were having difficulties adjusting to their new duties. Gerald was becoming very concerned that he wouldn't be able to leave the Compound on time. Worse than that, Gerald also had the strangest feeling that he would never return to First City.

Will and Mica had no choice, thought Gerald angrily; they would have to assume the duties of a watcher or face elimination. Gerald wondered why the last three watchers he had to train were so different to him. They seemed very traumatized by their assignments. Perhaps the human race was changing, growing a conscience or something? He didn't understand these young people. After all, they did not have a choice in the matter. The faster Will and Mica would accept things as they were, the easier it would be for both of them.

Gerald decided that he would have to talk to them and set them straight on how this system worked. Will and Mica had only been there for about two weeks, so there was still time to assimilate them into the program.

In Gerald's humble opinion, no one could take on the Archa and win—they were simply too rich and powerful. So undoubtedly it was better to go along with the status quo. It was just a matter of survival. If it wasn't one of the subgenetics or others, it could just as easily be himself. Obeying orders was the only way to survive. He didn't agree with what most of the Archa did but didn't believe that one man could change the world. In his opinion, it was impossible.

Gerald's thoughts were interrupted by a message from Headquarters. Apparently, they were all going to the forest today. He hoped that hunting the Nahus would cheer up the young watchers.

After they had showered, dressed, and eaten their morning meal in dismal silence, Gerald announced cheerfully, "Today, Watchers, we are going to have the great privilege of hunting the Nahu. The trackers have reported to me that the Nahus were last seen in Sector 5. Hopefully, we shall have a good and profitable hunt."

Mica and Will nodded in assent, smiling weakly.

Don't they ever get tired of killing? thought Will.

Gerald seemed more energized than they had ever seen him before. He continued, "It is one of my favorite parts of being a watcher. Since it's such a long way to Sector 5, we will be spending the night in the forest. Our orders are, as usual, to catch some Nahus alive, especially the young ones, but we do get to shoot the old, diseased, or injured. The more we net, the better bonus we get."

"What type of bonus?" asked Mica.

"The best," replied Gerald. "A whole day of duty credit. We must make our quota, though, so let's make it count."

Will and Mica both instantly cheered up. The idea of spending a peaceful night in the gentle green forest, under the pale moonlight, without the spying, blinking red eyes watching them, would be pure bliss. Then to be spared from the terrors of this job, even for one day, would be worth almost anything.

"Are you expert snipers?" Gerald asked hopefully.

"Yes," replied Mica excitedly, "and grade 1 trappers and netters."

"This is going to be a wonderful day. I can feel it," Gerald said, smiling.

Will and Mica exchanged a raised eyebrow behind his back and out of the range of the surveillance cameras.

Every day their bond was becoming stronger. They were the only two humans they knew who had actually realized the madness around them.

"Gerald," Mica asked innocently, "you are a good over-leader. How long have you been a watcher?"

"Twenty years," he replied proudly.

"Do you enjoy the duties?" Mica asked. Will tried to signal her by shaking his head violently.

"It took some getting used to," Gerald commented, unsure what direction she was going with the conversation.

"Well," replied Mica, "one day, I want to be a good and dedicated watcher, just like you."

Gerald smiled again, relieved at Mica's answer. Perhaps the newcomers were finally coming around after all, he thought.

Happily he replied, "And so you shall. You just do everything I have taught you, and you will be here for twenty years too. Remember, never refuse an order. Enough of rules. Let's have some fun today, catch some Nahus, and earn a duty day off."

"Good," agreed Mica, smiling back. "Let's go and make it happen."

Will was confused by Mica's attitude, but he said nothing.

Mica was trying to put Gerald at ease so he wouldn't shadow them everywhere they went. She was hoping there might be a slim chance of escape at some time during the hunt.

The three watchers piled their equipment into the Heavy One, climbed in, and started the long drive to Sector 5. They headed deep into the forest, which took several hours, through some very rough terrain.

Will wondered why they didn't use the MECAs.

Eventually they arrived at the campsite in the late afternoon, as the mellow rays of the sun were streaming through the trees. They set up camp in the pale green light of the woodland foliage. Will and Mica felt immediately calmer in the peace and beauty of the ancient forest, where the only eyes in the sky belonged to the birds and the squirrels.

There was a concrete compound about five hundred feet away, where the Archa would stay. According to Gerald, it was a comfortable, self-contained accommodation unit, with a generator, hot showers, kitchen, bedrooms, a living room with a fireplace, and even a fully stocked bar.

The slavs were already airing out and cleaning the accommodation unit, busily preparing for the Archa's arrival. They were due to arrive early in the morning by Hoppers. The watchers would be sleeping in high-tech tents that night. It would be the first time in their lives that Will and Mica would sleep beneath the stars.

The evening air was surprisingly warm, with a gentle breeze blowing from the east, softly stirring the leaves. The night seemed perfect. Mica and Gerald were walking around, picking up kindling for their campfire and becoming familiar with their surroundings, when Mica noticed four metal sheds behind the Archa's concrete building.

"What are those buildings used for?" she asked Gerald.

"They are for storage," he retorted abruptly. "You'll find out soon enough. Right now we need to build our fire, eat some food, and get some sleep. It will be a long day tomorrow."

The three watchers had decided that they didn't need to put up their tent because the evening was so mild and dry. After eating his evening meal, Will lay by the fire, looking at the pitch-black sky, which was studded with billions of blinking stars.

He was wondering why they had brought the Heavy One instead of a MECA, which would have gotten there in a third of the time and still held all the equipment. They must be expecting to catch a lot of Nahus, he thought dismally. He hoped tomorrow would progress peacefully, with no horrible surprises.

It seemed every day was like stepping deeper and deeper into the dark abyss, and he didn't like any of it so far, except maybe Mica and the excellent food. The rewards from his job were not good enough to lose his sanity over. Will thought Mica felt the same way as him, but after the comments she had made earlier that morning, he was unsure.

Back in First City, people always maintained the same impassive face whether they were asking a question about what flavor soup was available at the Central Dining Facility or their participation in a Final Journey Ceremony. There was never any emotion displayed for any reason. The Vitalift had helped a lot. Life in the city was a pleasant, even experience that just continued monotonously until death.

He thought this situation was worse than the Chaos Era. Once, he remembered feeling so smug and happy that the society he had lived in was so calm and organized. Every day since they had come to the Archa compound, part of him wished he could take some Vitalift and just fade away back into the oblivion of ignorance. Without the Vitalift, everything was crystal clear, and clarity had a jagged edge.

Will was beginning to believe there was no purpose in his life anymore. Once he had thought he was helping save the planet, which at least seemed like a worthy existence. There was no community in this society; everyone was selfish and existed merely to service themselves.

Another part of Will felt alive and rebellious for the first time in his sheltered existence. As his mind expanded, Will could begin to comprehend things he had never thought or understood before.

That night, he slept fitfully, and once again he had the dream of the strange being, who said only three words: *You are here.* He woke up shouting, "No!"

"What is going on?" demanded Gerald irritably. "Why are you yelling and waking everyone up?"

"Oh, my deepest apologies," replied Will very calmly. "It is these night visions. I am still not used to them."

"Do you think you can get some control over these night visions? We have so much to do. We cannot lose sleep over your personal issues," grumbled Gerald, annoyed at being woken up so violently.

"Of course," replied Will quietly. "It's just a question of adjustment."

"Good," said Gerald, satisfied with Will's answer.

The three watchers were sitting peacefully around the last glowing embers of their campfire, finishing their breakfast while the dawn was breaking and the horizon was full of red and gold hues. The forest felt like paradise just for a few minutes—until they heard the Hoppers approaching. Then Will's stomach suddenly sank, and Mica felt that familiar cramping spasm that seemed to grip her body whenever something horrible was about to occur.

Immediately Gerald jumped up and threw dirt on the fire. "They are early," he remarked. "Perimeter search, right now, around the camp. The one-mile area to start with. Shoot anything that looks threatening. Spread out, Watchers, and remain in talker contact."

The three watchers stood up, put on their helmets, picked up their shooters, and started to walk the perimeter. Mica didn't see much of anything that was menacing. Mind you, she hadn't seen the vicious and notorious Nahus yet. Mica imagined they probably resembled some type of ferocious bear.

As she strode silently through the woods, Mica wondered what it would feel like to keep on walking and never come back again.

Then Gerald's voice crackled over the talker. "All clear?" dashing the slim sliver of hope for her freedom.

"All clear," replied Mica dismally, walking back toward the camp.

She didn't notice two small green eyes watching her from the undergrowth.

As the Archa were preparing themselves for the big hunt, the excitement was palpable. Slavs were striding back and forth with a purpose, with armfuls of various supplies and equipment.

The watchers had continued their perimeter sweeps, noticing nothing more significant than small forest animals like rabbits, birds, and squirrels, when, all of a sudden, their talkers crackled and shrieked, "Targets spotted!"

The netters, mounted on horseback, had been dragging an area to the east of the main camp and had apparently caught a Nahu, which was struggling in their net. The watchers ran toward the location of the netters to provide frontline defense for the Archa, in case the Nahu broke free.

The Archa were already on their way too. As the watchers reached the netters first, they could hear guttural screams and the netters shouting, "Stop moving! You are not getting away, you filthy Nahu."

They could see something struggling and tearing like a wild beast in the net.

"Got one early!" yelled Gerald excitedly, and he began aiming his shooter erratically.

"I hope you have a safety catch on that weapon, Gerald," asked Will, concerned.

"Of course it is," Gerald replied, bouncing around, acting like a crazy man. "I want to shoot me some Nahu."

Mica and Will both laughed at Gerald and walked away from him and toward the net.

"Finally, we get to see a real Nahu today," remarked Will, smiling.

As they reached the coiled and writhing net, they both stared down in abject horror. Trapped there was a wild, dirty, thin female with very long dark hair and brilliant green eyes. She wore a mixture of cotton and animal skins.

"Oh my stars, she is human!" gasped Mica.

"May Gaia have pity on her," whispered Will.

"No!" Gerald snapped furiously. He was right behind them and had heard every single word. "These creatures are Nahu, not animals, and definitely not humans. They are wild and diseased beasts. They can't talk, and they breed like rabbits. They are vermin of the World. The Nahu try to destroy all our crops. They don't contribute anything to society, they are just filthy parasites."

"Where do they come from?" asked Will, unable to stop staring at the struggling woman.

"When the Chaos Era ended, some humans went renegade and decided not to join our proper and civilized society. So now they have degenerated into wild beasts who must be exterminated, recycled, or retrained to be part of the system for the safety of the planet and all of us," Gerald replied self-righteously.

He continued, "Mostly, the very young ones go to the Obedience Reinforcement and Rehabilitation Center, where they become civilized and able to join our society. This one here can be transported." He pointed to the struggling woman. "She is active and healthy, so she will go to the Full Emergency Medical Assessment Center, for organ harvesting, cloning, or medical testing."

"Watchers, tie her up, muzzle her, and take her to metal storage shed 1," Gerald ordered loudly. He then lowered his voice, whispering, "Remember, Watchers, never refuse an order."

"Yes, Over-Leader," replied Will loudly. Mica just nodded as they dragged the poor, wretched creature out from under the flashbang net. They realized, hidden underneath her was a little child, maybe four years old. She had long dark wavy hair and enormous green eyes, just like her mother. She had small flowers made of colored bird feathers in each of her tiny pierced ears. Her eyes were wide with terror.

"This one," stated Gerald, pointing to the child, "goes to metal shed 2, for retraining."

"No! Put it in my toy box!" bellowed Malus, both interrupting and stepping forward at the same time. He was standing in front of shed 4. He was wearing a hooded black cloak that hid his face.

"Yes, my lord," replied Gerald, and he immediately picked up the child and carried her under his arm like a sack of potatoes. Mica and Will dragged the defiant, wild woman to the guards at shed 1. The little girl looked at her mother; something passed between the two of them, like an unspoken language, because the child instantly became silent and limp like a rag doll.

"What do the numbers on these sheds mean?" Mica asked one of the guards.

He replied respectfully, "Shed 1 is medical hold. FEMA, shed 2, is for retraining and rehabilitation. Shed three 3 is the dead box. We put the dead Nahus in there. Shed 4 is the toy box. We don't handle that one," replied the guard nervously. "His lordship, Malus, is in charge of it. No one ever goes in there." He paused. "Until afterward…for cleanup."

"Thank you," Mica replied, distraught and desperately trying not to show it.

She didn't notice Malus watching her and analyzing her distress with his empty, soulless eyes. His tongue flicked out to taste the sharp, bitter air of female empathy he seldom detected. Malus was excited and curious about the watcher. He wanted to see her face. He would play games with her, perhaps until the next watchers could be chosen and trained. By then her terror would be an elixir extraordinaire aged perfectly like an excellent wine. He had never waited so long to claim a victim; this would be a new and fascinating experience for him. Malus stepped silently back into the shadows of the trees.

The Archa decided that they wanted to take a lunch break, and so a large extravagant buffet was set up for them. The table was laden with roast beef, pork, and duck. There were piles of steaming vegetables and several delicious desserts. Expensive crystal glasses were filled with fragrant wines and stood upon the most delicate of linen tablecloths. The sumptuous feast was a picture of elegance and was entirely out of place, sitting in the middle of the fragrant and rustic woods.

It was like watching a bizarre tea party. Reality seemed upside down. There were starving human captives held in metal sheds just a few feet away from the grand buffet table. Meanwhile, the remaining 99 percent of the population lived on recycled human waste, soup, and Vitalift. Will was beside himself with rage as he bent down and picked up his weapon.

"Not now," whispered Mica wisely as she gently touched his arm. "We are outnumbered. If we die today, we cannot help anybody."

Their eyes met and locked. Will nodded. They both understood they could not be part of this empire anymore, but they had to keep their enemies close to learn how to destroy them.

Will and Mica stood up and took their positions. All the other slavs were allowed to eat the leftovers once the Archa had finished and walked away.

Gerald gave Will and Mica their orders. "Today the Archa will take a nap and resume hunting this evening and into the night." So for once, the watchers could also take turns eating, standing guard, and taking naps.

Mica went to the buffet table and took as much food as she could reasonably eat. "Come here, Will, and eat," she said.

Will walked to where Mica was standing. "I would vomit if I ate this food," he whispered.

"So would I," she replied, "but this food is not for us."

Will nodded and went over to the buffet and started to fill his plate. They had intended to smuggle the food to the captive woman and her child, but they were too well guarded. So they were forced to abandon the plan.

According to Gerald, all the action happened after dark, because if one Nahu was caught, it meant others were nearby, since the Nahu were tribal. Now they couldn't afford to rest since there were hunting parties searching for them. The Nahu had to move continuously to evade the hunters. Eventually they would be slowed down by their tired children, their aged, and their sick. So it was a just matter of time before they caught the rest of them.

Gerald told Will and Mica, if they were lucky, the hunters could encircle an area and find the village and burn it to the ground. They would then destroy their supplies and kill or capture as many Nahus as possible, thus leaving the remainder of the tribe to starve to death. They would not survive the oncoming winter without supplies and shelter. Gerald believed that the Nahus would be extinct within ten years. In his opinion, that was a good thing.

As dusk grew and the fires were lit, the hunting camp became very active. The Archa appeared, refreshed by their rest.

As Mica was bending down, attending to the weapons and preparing to put on her helmet, she suddenly felt an ominous presence next to her and smelled a strong, bitter metallic smell. She knew instinctively Malus was standing there and dropped her eyes immediately.

"Ssstand up!" hissed Malus.

Mica obeyed instantly, but he still grabbed her wrist and clenched it to him with his gloved hand.

"Look at me!" he ordered. "I demand it!"

Mica looked into his cold black eyes and suddenly realized that he was indeed evil incarnate.

He hissed in her ear with his monstrous face inches away from hers. "I smell your fear," he whispered. "It is sweet nectar to me."

He smiled, revealing his pointed double rows of teeth. Then without warning, he suddenly licked the side of Mica's face with his long reptilian tongue, which was cold, slimy, and terrifying.

"The scent of your fear is intoxicating to me," he said sinisterly while she shuddered.

"You felt empathy for the Nahus," Malus hissed and spat on the ground while still holding her wrist. "Your pity was bitter and vile-tasting to me," he snarled. Then his eyes turned completely black.

Mica felt like she was like staring into oblivion.

"I know what you are," Malus sneered.

Still close and holding her wrist tightly, Malus whispered viciously, "Understand something, my little seer, the roast beef and pork I eat is like cardboard to me. What I desire the most is fear. It is my elixir. The more terror and torture I inflict, the sweeter and stronger the fear, especially the very young. It has a purity that sadly diminishes after a certain age."

He paused.

"I could devour you now, right here." Malus smiled and removed one of his black gloves, revealing his long sharp nails that could slice through flesh, like a knife through melted butter. He slid his talon slowly down her neck, drawing a small trail of blood. He licked his claw while Mica stood transfixed with terror.

"I know how to inflict maximum fear and suffering. I am the master of the eternal darkness," he boasted. "You, my little watcher, will die very slowly and painfully. Think of my words before you sleep and remember them when you wake, until you become so afraid that even taking a breath will cause you fear." He laughed. "Once in a while, your species produces a challenge, one that can see through the veil. I like to entertain myself with your kind—so few of you are left. Although eventually, I shall tire of you and then your elixir will be even sweeter to me." He put his glove back on and vanished into the dark shadows, laughing at his discovery.

Mica was left stunned and shaken by the incident with Malus. She looked across the forest and stared at the little campfire's glowing warmth. The flickering, burning flames were engulfing the dead old wood.

An idea formed in her mind. It only took a tiny spark of light to chase away the darkness, just like the little campfire was lighting up the forest, chasing away the shadows as the fire grew stronger and brighter. She had seen darkness so thick and dense that one teaspoon full would weigh more than the Earth itself. Light could never shine from this being, but light could shine upon it.

Mica took a deep breath and began to fill her whole being with pure white light until it spun around her and she felt the power of all that was good and pure. Then she felt safe again. The enemy had revealed its weakness, and she had not spoken a word.

Will came running up to her, filled with dread. "Why was Malus talking to you? In the name of Gaia, what did you say to provoke him so?"

Mica stared intensely at Will, and then she whispered, "Will, I know who I am—I am a seer. And you, Will, are a changer, and Malus is a parasite from another realm entirely. We have to go and participate in this hunt tonight, but when they all leave tomorrow and we clean up the campsite, we must speak. If we do not obey every order, we will be shot." She hesitated. "Or worse."

Will nodded in agreement. They were definitely in a dangerous position.

For the rest of the night, they helped with the hunt. They rounded up about a hundred Nahus, which was apparently the target number and enabled them to earn a whole day off duty. Gerald was ecstatic.

However, the Archa were furious that their hunters didn't find the main village.

Will had noticed that the hunters had rounded up very few Nahus of breeding age. He wondered if the weak, sick, and old had sacrificed themselves to protect the others.

Another issue that surprised Will was that the prisoners could not speak and appeared to be very primitive. Intellectually, they seemed to be below the norm, unable to focus on anything or answer questions. That didn't make sense to him. How could these people build villages, hunt, and survive the harsh winters with no intelligence or language?

Most of the time, the captive Nahus were oddly silent or occasionally babbled like babies. Sometimes they would all scream in unison, with a weird, high-pitched noise that sounded like a siren. They refused to stop even when the guards tried to beat them into silence. Will believed it was entirely possible that their weird screaming was a warning and used to alert other Nahus in the area to danger.

Will thought there were many mysteries about the Nahus. Perhaps they were not what they appeared to be. He kept such thoughts to himself. The majority of Nahus had black hair or very dark hair, white to light-brown skin, and either brown or startling green eyes.

Will did not understand why the Nahu kept such wrinkled old humans who were almost bent over. Even their fingers were curled and crippled. Many shuffled along, barely moving. What was their purpose to the tribe? he wondered. It simply wasn't efficient to the tribe to keep those old ones alive for so long.

"Gerald, why do these creatures live so long when all humans die by their sixty-fifth Birthtime?" asked Will.

Gerald laughed loudly. "Hasn't anybody told you? Humans don't die at sixty-five! Sometimes they can live to a hundred, and the

Archa, well, they are immortal. That means they never die, they live forever."

"How can that be?" asked Will, shocked. "In First City, they have to use an IV to keep the citizens alive long enough to survive the Last Journey Ceremony."

"That's not to keep them alive," Gerald replied, laughing heartily. "That's to kill them. They kill the old ones on purpose, and why do you think they do that, Will?" asked Gerald sarcastically.

Will didn't get a chance to speak. Gerald continued animatedly, "Because it makes sense, doesn't it? Just look at these struggling bags of bones that we've caught. They are all wrinkled up, slow, and sick. They can't work, they consume too many resources, and they have no particular purpose. Don't you think that our way is so much neater, cleaner, and eco-friendly?"

"But why do the Nahus keep them alive?" asked Will, still trying to comprehend why perfectly healthy citizens continued to be murdered daily in First City.

"I don't know," replied Gerald, "why anyone would keep these sad, broken old Nahus."

"Yes, indeed," wondered Will out loud, "it's certainly a mystery to me."

"Why does anything do what it does? There are not always reasons for things," retorted Gerald as he walked away to put some more folded nets onto the Heavy One.

Will disagreed with Gerald; he thought there was always a reason for everything, even if it made no sense to most people.

The most significant problem was evident to Will. After being exposed to all the cruelty and brutality over the years, most slavs eventually became either numb to it (as a survival technique), or some secretly started to enjoy it vicariously. After many years of exposure, the bizarre became the norm, and then this norm was then supported by all those who participated in that particular society.

Will continued to think. There must be those who were awakened, like himself and Mica. Sadly, they were probably scattered across the tightly controlled globe, frozen with fear. The words "Never disobey an order" were repeated daily in training for a reason.

It was psychological warfare, purely to reinforce terror among the humans and thus maintain control over them by the Archa.

But the Nahus seemed different, thought Will. They refused to comply even when everything was against them. They seemed to sacrifice themselves for others in their group. They were the only ones who practiced service to others, and they hadn't destroyed the ecosystem. They must live in complete harmony with the planet, assumed Will, and they remained well hidden. The Nahu trails had to be tracked for weeks to even find them.

After Malus and the Archa had left and all the equipment had been packed up and put away, the watchers settled down for a few hours' sleep. Everyone was exhausted, and the few remaining slavs lay there with them, snoring noisily. The acrid black smoke from shed 3 curled upward into the inky sky and luckily was blown away from the camp by a slight breeze.

Will couldn't sleep; his mind was turning over and over. All this new knowledge and new ideas were streaming into his brain, and he couldn't stop it. He lay farthest from the fire, dozing with his eyes firmly shut, wishing for the dark, peaceful place of sleep.

Suddenly, Will felt an old dry hand across his mouth, and a familiar voice whispered in his ear, "Will, I must talk to you."

Will opened his eyes and nodded. The sun was beginning to rise. Dawn was breaking. He started to walk toward the woods, trying to see the face that had just spoken to him in his dream. Puzzled, he saw nothing but a few rabbits and a lone deer.

Mica was waking up as Will walked back to the camp. "Where did you go?" she asked sleepily.

"Oh," he replied, "I thought I heard something, but it was just a deer in the woods."

Gerald woke up and stretched lazily. "Today we have to deliver the cargo to the Obedience, Reinforcement, and Rehabilitation Center or the (ORRC) and the Full Emergency Medical Assessment Center."

The watchers walked in silence to the sheds to collect their cargo.

The cremators were still burning the bodies in the crematorium behind metal shed 3 (where the old, the dead, and the dying were held). There were others in contamination suits cleaning out shed 4 with some strong-smelling chemicals that made Will's eyes burn and water. They were scrubbing the walls, floor, and ceiling with small scrapers and big brushes because there were human remains still splattered everywhere.

As she was leaving, Mica saw a tiny ear with a little flower pinned to it. It lay by her foot among the leaves. With reverence, she gently moved it with her boot so it was hidden under the leaves, and with quiet determination, she secured the Heavy One for prisoner loading.

As they loaded the Nahus into the Heavy One, both Will and Mica kept their visors lowered. They were glad that Gerald had suggested it. He said it was necessary for safety reasons because the Nahus frequently spat, bit, and probably carried communicable diseases. Will and Mica didn't care about that aspect; they just couldn't bear to look at their victims' faces.

CHAPTER 11

Fourth City. The Obedience Reinforcement and Rehabilitation Center (ORRC)

After the Watchers left the forest, it was a relatively short drive to the ORRC (about two hours), where they delivered the youngest Nahus, who were mostly under the age of ten.

"Greetings, Watchers," said the Obedience Reinforcement officer. "I am Zeta 25, and I am the director here. Since you are both new to your assignments, I would consider it an honor to show you our facility. We are very gratified by the valuable work that we accomplish here."

"Greetings," Will and Mica replied politely and introduced themselves.

"We appreciate your invitation," answered Mica gracefully.

Will stated, "Today I must attend to the cargo with Gerald, but I am sure Mica 3432 would enjoy your tour. Farwell, Zeta 25." And he returned to the Heavy One to help Gerald.

As Mica and Zeta walked through the long gray corridors, it occurred to Mica that the center was a carbon copy of the Good Citizen Enhancement Facility at First City. There were many learning rooms and children wearing gray tunics and canvas shoes, with shaved heads, and their hands held folded on their laps. Mica felt repugnance at the situation because the children were being brain-washed right in front of her.

"We have an excellent recovery rate here," continued Zeta brightly, "about 99 percent."

"That is an excellent recovery rate, which shows your expertise in running this facility," replied Mica enthusiastically.

Mica continued, "I am very curious about what type of corrective training methods you have to implement in the more severe cases, when citizens do not comply with your program."

"Well, fortunately, that is usually a rare occurrence," replied Zeta somewhat hesitantly.

"That is why it is interesting," commented Mica. "How do you deal with the 1 percent?"

Zeta 25 replied stiffly, "It is a difficult assignment to deal with the insane. It takes lots of patience and many treatments to help them."

"I think it would be very challenging," agreed Mica. "In your expert opinion, do you believe these citizens are genetically defective, socially corrupt, or emotionally bankrupt?"

"There are many interesting theories," remarked Zeta, looking a little startled at Mica's apparent understanding of the human psyche.

"It appears to our finest experts that these brains are somehow defective, which prevents the citizens from becoming compliant and productive, although the actual precise cause is unknown," Zeta replied.

"Indeed," replied Mica. "What do you do with the citizens that have this condition?"

"The condition is, of course, incurable at this time," replied Zeta 25 carefully. "Our Level 1 program starts with education. Level 2 is medication and therapy. Level 3 consists of electric shock treatments, then various deprivation techniques. At Level 4, we sometimes induce extreme abuse to try to fracture the personality. Sometimes, as a last resort, we use Level 5, which is a form of brain surgery. Of course, surgery is still very experimental. Over the decades, we have tried many different methods. Usually, after surgery, patients become useless eaters, and so they are terminated, but there are a few we keep for study purposes."

"I would be very interested in observing your most complicated case," requested Mica.

"I don't know if I can authorize that particular request," replied Zeta nervously.

"Really?" Mica remarked casually. "I am one of the watchers to the elite, and I have the highest security clearance available. I could call the Big White House and check whether I am authorized to view all areas of your facility, but I wouldn't like to cause you problems with a little misunderstanding. We are going to have a long working relationship. I would like to report to Headquarters that this is an excellent facility with an extremely cooperative and informative director."

Mica, while still looking intently at Zeta, slowly pulled out her talker. It crackled loudly.

"Watcher, you may inspect any part of the facility that you wish," replied Zeta quickly. "I will be your guide. Please wait for a moment here in the reception area. I need to retrieve some strip-keys."

Mica nodded, relieved her bluff had worked, and very shortly Zeta returned and started showing her some more learning rooms.

Mica thought to herself, *Enough of this! You are wasting my time.*

"I wish to see your most interesting case, Zeta 25." Mica's voice had now become insistent, and she was no longer casual and friendly.

"Yes, Watcher," replied the RRC officer as she showed her room after room of electric shock and various deprivation techniques that she had expressed in her outline of the program there.

"What are the water tanks for?" asked Mica.

Zeta 25 replied, "When immersed in the dark, warmth, and silence in vats of water for days on end, the individual loses all sense of direction, time, and place. They lose their sense of reality altogether and begin to exist in a type of void." She paused. "Unfortunately," she continued, "we can't keep them in there very long, usually just a few days, or they go insane."

"What's the longest time anybody has survived total deprivation?" asked Mica curiously.

"Six months," replied the officer, somewhat hesitantly.

"And they are still alive?" remarked Mica incredulously.

"Yes," replied Zeta 25, showing obvious discomfort with the direction of their conversation.

"I wish to observe that very individual," demanded Mica.

"Very well. This way," Zeta 25 replied, defeated, realizing it was pointless to argue with Mica, "but there is nothing to observe. He just babbles nonsense and paints his walls with his own waste. He is quite insane and vicious."

"I wonder why," Mica murmured under her breath. "Nevertheless, I want to see him," insisted Mica firmly.

"As you wish," replied the reticent Zeta.

They passed other areas that were not being used, which held various forms of torture equipment. There were several surgical rooms with their doors tightly shut.

At the end of one of the dim gray corridors was an elevator door with a keypad. The director punched in a code: 625436. Mica noticed there was a choice of three floors. The elevator swished down to the second floor, where it stopped and the doors pinged open. They walked along another corridor. There were six rooms on each side, but they had no little glass windows one could look through. They were just solid gray doors with a number painted on each one.

"What is in these rooms?" asked Mica curiously.

"A couple of patients that need restraints and storage mostly," Zeta 25 replied evasively.

At the end of the hallway, there was a gray door on the left marked with the number 01.

Zeta 25 used a strip-key to open this door.

Mica could see there was a six-foot-by-eight-foot iron cage in the room, and inside that was a young boy aged about eight, completely naked and busily painting his walls with his own feces. The smell was unbearable.

"What are his tag and number?" Mica asked, trying not to choke on the stench.

"He is Boy 01," mumbled the director, covering her nose and mouth with her hand.

"Boy," called Mica softly as she approached the cage door. The boy looked up, not at Mica, but as if he heard something a long way away. "Boy," she whispered again, and then she started to hum one of the more pleasant tunes she had heard at the Big White House.

The humming caught Boy's attention; he froze and stopped his bizarre artwork and began crawling toward her on his hands and knees. Then he climbed like a monkey onto the bars of the cage door so he could see Mica eye to eye.

He put his finger through the bars as if to try to touch her. Mica put her finger out, and for an instant, they touched. She felt an incredible shock wave that tore through space and time. Mica could see the past, present, and future all at once.

The ether was full of incredible, indescribable harmonics. Atoms, quarks, and neutrinos flashed by in pure golden light that resonated with her whole being. It was the most intense and beautiful experience she had ever witnessed. She could see Boy's brown eyes shining in his thin pallid face. Mica sensed his essence was no longer here; only his body remained in the stinking cell.

"I am with the One," he whispered.

Suddenly the director slapped their fingers apart. "You cannot touch him! He bites and may carry diseases," snapped Zeta 25, terrified the prized watcher would return, minus a finger or two and it would be all her fault.

Instantly at the sound of the director's voice the boy jumped at the cage door like a chimpanzee, rattling it furiously, trying to spit and bite Zeta 25, who stayed well back. Then Boy 01 gave Mica a strange, crazy smile and went back to writing on his wall. Mica could see he was drawing the vision they had just shared. Faster and faster he painted with his fingers until his scribbling became frenzied.

"I told you he was insane," remarked the director indignantly while she still covered her nose with her hand.

You made him that way, thought Mica as she watched him draw the sun and musical notes. As she left, she turned to get the last look at him.

"Home," Boy 01 mouthed to her and pointed to his drawing of the sun. Then he smiled for the last time and turned his attention back to his scribbles, lost once again in his solitary world. Boy 01 seemed oblivious to the filth that surrounded him.

"Why don't you give him crayons or pencils and paper to draw with?" Mica asked. "It would surely be better than this." She pointed to all the fecal art.

The director studied Mica for a moment, making her feel very uncomfortable. "Because he eats the paper and the crayons and uses pencils to stab whoever comes near him," Zeta replied stiffly.

Zeta continued, "I have never seen the boy respond to anyone the way he did to you. Usually, if you try to touch him, he tries to bite the handler's fingers off. What did he say to you, Mica?"

"I don't know," replied Mica, lying. "I couldn't understand him."

Mica changed the subject, "What is below here?"

"Scientists on level 3 work on varied and classified projects. That is not my area of responsibility, and I know nothing of these projects," stated Zeta very coldly. She knew Mica had just lied to her.

Zeta continued, agitated, "I do not have access to that level, and I think it is time for you to leave this facility," she told Mica, looking deeply troubled. "If you became injured in any way, I would have been held responsible for the incident."

"I hope I will not be a source of concern," Mica replied quickly. "I am obviously in good health, with all my fingers," which she wiggled at Zeta 25, trying to lighten the mood of the very offended director.

"Putting others at risk is not correct or responsible," admonished Zeta. The director was solemn and official as she led the way very speedily to the main entrance.

"Fare-well, Watcher," said Zeta and then paused for a moment while staring at Mica for a full minute. Then she spoke pointedly. "Too much curiosity is not a good thing in this society. It may lead you down a dangerous path, where the result might not be what you expect.

"Fare-well, Director." Mica nodded, keeping her eyes downcast for a second. "I am sorry I offended you, and I will remember your words."

Mica walked briskly back to the waiting watchers, feeling the eyes of Zeta boring into her back, and she climbed into the Heavy One, where she felt safe for just a few minutes. Until she remembered they had to take the remaining Nahu cargo to the Full Emergency Medical Assessment Center.

Before the watchers drove away, Mica glanced back to the director, who was still standing outside and staring at the back of the moving vehicle, with her arms tightly folded.

CHAPTER 12

Sixth City: Full Emergency Medical Assessment Center (FEMA)

It was another two-hour journey from the woods, mostly on a high-way that stretched for miles. Huge fences, twenty feet high, lined each side of the road, and periodically there were signs in big red letters that read, "Warning: This fence is electrified and touching it will cause immediate death." It was impossible to see beyond or through the fences because the vegetation was so lush and thick that it formed an impenetrable green curtain.

As the Full Emergency Medical Assessment Center came into view, Will and Mica were amazed by its immense size. The gated compound seemed to expand forever.

Gerald pointed to the cracked old gray wooden map of the facility, which was standing next to the guarded entry gate. It listed the eight different sections:

> *Section 1: Administration*
> *Section 2: Workers Facilities and Amenities*
> *Section 3: Decontamination*
> *Section 4: Sorting*
> *Section 5: Medical Evaluation and Testing*
> *Section 6: Surgical and Transplant Unit*
> *Section 7: Research and Development Unit*
> *Section 8: Crematorium*

Gerald stated they had to go to Administration first. He pulled out several different sets of orders and handed them to the guard, who looked at each sheet thoroughly and gave them back to Gerald. He then waved them through the magnificent iron gates, shouting loudly, "Greetings, Watchers!"

Gerald replied, just as loudly, "Greetings," to the apparently deaf gatekeeper, who just smiled.

The Heavy One thundered to Section 1: Administration, which was a long linear building about eight hundred feet from the gate. As they parked, Will and Mica noticed there were no other vehicles parked there.

The three watchers walked into the building through a large wooden door. They approached the reception desk. Behind it, there were six separate workstations. A loud voice announced that the watchers were to proceed to Section 3 for processing. A soft blue light was blinking over a workstation marked number 3, and as they approached and sat down, the light changed to a pale amber color.

"Greetings, Watchers. I am Processor 3. Where are your orders?"

Gerald produced them from one of his uniform's many pockets and handed them to Processor 3.

The processor read some of the information out loud. "I understand you have fifty visibly healthy young Nahus to deliver, twenty females and thirty males. All the Nahus are about between the ages of twelve and fifty. Is that correct?"

"Yes," replied Gerald, nodding.

Mica wished she had been assigned a job like a processor and could just shuffle papers all day.

"Excellent work, Watchers. It is getting harder and harder to capture the young ones. Are they all muzzled and restrained?" the processor asked.

"Yes, Processor," replied Gerald cheerfully. He evidently appreciated the processor's compliment.

"Good," replied the processor. "Please drive your vehicle to Decontamination Bay 8. They will be expecting you."

"Thank you, Processor. Fare-well," replied Gerald cordially.

"Fare-well, Watchers. You are worthy citizens," added the processor respectfully.

After leaving the Administration building, the watchers climbed back into the Heavy One and headed for Section 3, Bay 8.

They came to a crossroads and continued straight ahead to a large building marked Section 3.

The decontamination bays were on the left side of the building, in numerical order, so they pulled into Bay 8. The watchers got out of the Heavy One, and two decontamination experts appeared from behind the truck, wearing white protective gear from head to toe. Their helmets had black visors, and each decontaminator carried a steaming hose and a tool belt full of various equipment.

"Okay, Watchers, one of you unlock the doors and then stand by, ready and armed. Shoot any Nahus that try to escape. Shoot only to wound in the foot or hand," ordered one of the deconners. The watchers nodded and took their positions.

Then the cargo doors were opened—the smell was terrible. The Nahus were all lying in a muddled heap at the very back of the Heavy One, in some squalid straw. All of them were muzzled and restrained. They seemed temporarily blinded as the bright sunlight blazed onto them, and they huddled tighter to one another, making pitiful bleating noises, like lambs at a slaughterhouse.

One of the deconners bellowed to the Nahus while another one used a sort of sign language showing them what to do. "All restraints will be taken off. Then you will remove all clothing and jewelry, including shoes—if you have any. Finally, you will come outside of the vehicle. Females must line up on the left, males on the right. Understood?"

The deconner continued his instructions, "If you try to escape, the watchers will only shoot you in your hand or foot so you will survive. There will be no kill shots, understood?" He looked at the watchers for confirmation; they all nodded and remained in their positions. The Nahus were eerily silent.

The deconners went in and removed both restraints and muzzles. Within minutes, they came out with a pile of dirty clothing and a few pairs of handmade shoes.

The Nahus filed out silently, naked and defeated. They didn't try to cover any parts of their bodies, but their heads hung low and their eyes were in a fixed stare to the ground. It seemed as if their minds were somewhere else entirely. Each of them was given a washcloth and told, in great detail, how to properly wash all parts of their bodies.

Then the deconners started spraying the Nahus with some warm, soapy chemical solution. Some of them coughed and sneezed while they vigorously used their washcloths. Then they were rinsed twice in a lemon-scented water. The smell reminded Will of the old days and his daily three-minute steam shower when life seemed good, clean, and wholesome—which seemed preferable to the life he was living now.

The Nahus, now soaking wet, naked, and shivering, were all herded to a vast drying area. The enormous fans dried them thoroughly within two minutes. The blasts of warm air were so powerful that the Nahus had trouble remaining standing. Some of the shorter ones were blown to the ground.

At the end of the bay were the dressers, who gave each Nahu some underwear, a gray tunic with matching pants, and a pair of black canvas shoes.

The dressers combed the long hair of both the males and females, and they carefully braided the hair, tying a band at the top and bottom of the braid. Then the braids were cut and put into a long metal container. There were about a hundred of them, all black and dark brown. The dressers then quickly shaved off the rest of the Nahus' hair until their heads were bald and shiny. In single file, they disappeared through the curtain at the back of the bay, without a word.

While they were walking back to the Heavy One, Mica asked Gerald, "What do the dressers do with all those Nahu braids?" She had to say something just to alleviate the misery she was feeling on behalf of the poor, wretched Nahus.

"I think they use most of the hair for wigs, worn by the Yellow Eyes in Eighth City," Gerald replied, sounding tired.

"Why do the Yellow Eyes do that?" wondered Mica out loud. "I mean, it seems an odd thing to do to put someone's dead hair on your head. I wonder if it is even hygienic?"

"I don't know, and I don't care," replied Gerald, getting irritated with her babbling. He said sharply, "Don't ask me why anyone would do that, because I don't know."

"What happens to the Nahus next?" asked Will, changing the conversation to a less-controversial one.

Gerald explained, "They go through a sorting process that records how many of each sex, their height and weight, their ages, and any visible health issues."

He paused.

"Then they go through a medical evaluation and DNA testing. They are tested for blood type and to ensure all their organs are fully functioning. Those selected for organ donations are well fed and taken care of until the day comes when their organs need to be harvested," Gerald said cheerfully, staring at Mica.

Gerald continued, "They will stay in quarters near the surgical transplant unit. If they are lucky and only one of their kidneys needs to be harvested, they complete the surgery and then return to the center until another one of their organs is needed.

"If they age much past thirty-five and haven't been a donor match, they are usually sent to Research and Development. Those who are not in prime health automatically go to the Research and Development Center.

"The noise there is so terrible you have to use special earplugs. Most of them only survive there for a few weeks, where they undergo new drug testing and innovative medical research. All this benefits our society," Gerald said pointedly, staring at Mica's impassive face.

"Why do they scream so loudly?" Mica asked, not really wanting to know the answer, but she had to know the whole truth.

"Well, it was explained to me this way," Gerald replied, annoyed by the question. "The healers can't effectively test new drugs on subjects if they already have pain medicines in their systems because of possible drug interactions. Therefore, they can't give them any pain medicine." Gerald continued in a matter-of-fact tone, "Or if they are researching a rare disease, it has to progress from beginning to end without any medical interference. That's how the healers learn about the symptoms and how the disease progresses. Then after studying the disease, they will infect some Nahu with the disease.

"The next step is to try experimental drugs or different medical treatments on the Nahus, hoping to discover a cure. However, it usually takes a long time to find the right treatment. When any of the Nahus die, they are all autopsied, humanely of course."

Gerald glanced at Mica briefly and, with no emotion, finished, "Then they are cremated over there, and that is the end of what I know."

Will wondered what the exact definition of *humane* was in this lunatic asylum.

Gerald took a deep breath. "Enough questions," he said, and he meant it. They stood silently for a minute, then one of the deconners signaled to Gerald.

"Aha!" Gerald chirped. "They have finished decontaminating the Heavy One. Now it is all shiny and clean, not even a twig or trace of those dirty, nasty Nahus. We shall now go back to our living space and eat and rest."

Will and Mica were deep in thought, so the journey home was silent, much to Gerald's relief.

CHAPTER 13

The Incident in the Gardens

It was both late and dark when they returned to the terrain hangar to put away the Heavy One.

The watchers had to walk past the rose gardens to get to their little white cottage. As they walked, they could hear lots of noise and commotion. Bizarre music was playing—if it could be called that. It was more like a strange, eerie, very low vibrational, whining, and howling that was emanating from the Big White House.

Gerald suddenly held up his finger to his mouth. "Ssshhh," warning the watchers to be quiet. He looked at Will and Mica and whispered urgently, "We need to get inside *now!*" Gerald's face had drained of all color, and there was an edge to his voice. It was pure, unadulterated fear.

Will and Mica were terrified because they had never seen Gerald act like this.

"Hurry," he whispered. "But whatever you do, do not run. It sets off their predatory instincts."

They caught glimpses of the Archa running and gyrating around the gardens, giggling and singing. Their bodies were carefully painted with strange, neon-colored symbols that glowed in the dark. They were wearing outlandish costumes made of only braided strings, luminescent beads, and flashing jewels that left little to the imagination.

They were apparently playing some bizarre game, running in and out of the sculptured shrubs and bushes.

They must have guests, thought Will. *Probably some of the Yellow Eyes from Eighth City.* Will wondered how many of them would survive until morning.

The air was smoky, and there was an odor coming from the barbecue pit. It smelled like pork cooking, but the animal was too long and thin to be a wild boar or pig.

Will stared harder as the cookers were busy, continually turning the meat around on the spit. The coals glowed and spat as the fat dripped into the fire. Then the full horror of what Will was watching hit him with such violence it was like a punch in the stomach. He could barely breathe. Mica paused and stared at the horror before her.

This decadent, indolent, wealthy group of Archa had lost all sense of their humanity and had become not only hunters of men, murderers, rapists, sadists, torturers, and child molesters, but cannibals too. They were parasitical miscreants that needed to be destroyed. If that meant giving his last breath to this cause, Will decided he would give it gladly, and with honor.

The watchers crept on in silence, barely breathing. Right before they reached the safety of their cottage, they were startled by Lustria popping her head over the bushes. She smiled at them with her huge mouth, and her large white teeth glistened in the pale moonlight. The look in her eyes was strange and predatory, and the watchers instinctively realized they were in serious trouble.

"Greetings, Watchers!" she yelled, her speech sounding very slurred. Then she turned and shouted to the others, "Come and look at our new watchers! Aren't they cute?"

The others began to approach slowly, silently creeping toward the watchers from all directions. Like a pack of wild, hungry animals.

Immediately, all three watchers bowed.

"Oh no," whispered Gerald under his breath. He sounded terrified. "We are in a very dire situation. Watchers, do not move an inch. Stay very still, no matter what."

Lustria emerged from the bushes naked, except for a few misplaced beads and jewels. She started to run her hands down Will's body. "Mmmmmmm," she said while all the others began walking toward her, wondering what she was doing.

Luckily, Ira had heard her calling, and he rushed over to the watchers. In a loud and commanding voice, he boomed, "Lustria, what did I tell you about the watchers? Malus said not to touch them."

"But he is sooo delicious," she murmured, still mauling poor Will. Then she began licking his face like a dog.

"Go and find your other play toys," commanded Ira sternly. "You do not want Malus angry with you, do you?"

"Ooh no," she said drunkenly, still holding on to Will. She stumbled and almost pulled both of them to the ground. She was incredibly powerful.

"Well, go back to the party, or I will summon him here right now," ordered Ira sharply.

"You are no fun, Ira," replied Lustria sulkily as she pulled a sad, animated face. Then she shrugged her magnificent shoulders and turned to walk away. She walked off, barefoot and naked, into the darkness, her long gold hair blowing in the breeze. Like a beautiful and vengeful Greek goddess.

"Watchers, immediately return to your living space," ordered Ira. "Then lock the door, and whatever you do, do not come out. Do you understand?"

"Yes, my lord," they all chorused, very relieved.

Still shaken by the encounter with Lustria, neither Will nor Mica noticed that standing in the dark shadows were four more very plump Yellow Eyes, tied, gagged, and bound to wooden stakes. They were wide-eyed and terrified, and Gerald looked away, saying nothing.

They hurried to their cottage and bolted the door. Now Will understood why this place was so fortified. Even with their superior strength, the Archa couldn't tear this cottage apart.

Gerald was sweating and shaking as he locked the door to the little cottage. He said, "We were fortunate that Ira was there. Things could have gone very differently."

"He wasn't protecting us," interrupted Will, feeling dirty and defiled by Lustria. "He just didn't want to make Malus angry at him."

"The reason doesn't matter," commented Mica, trying to soothe Will. "We have survived another day."

"For what purpose?" snapped Will. He was still furious and kept rubbing his face with a washcloth where Lustria had licked him. He rubbed his face so hard it began to turn red and raw. "That filthy parasite," he muttered under his breath.

Gerald was now enraged, and with his back to the camera, he hissed at Will, "Watcher, keep your mouth shut and go to bed. Do not say another word. We are being monitored. Do you want them to come back? Because they will if you continue this conversation. I have been a watcher for twenty years, and I have had five partners during those years. Do you know why I am still here?" Gerald was white with rage. "Because I keep my words to myself, and I don't ask too many questions," he growled while glaring at Mica. "Do you really want us to die tonight? If not, listen to me and go to bed and say no more. Now I am going to eat. Do either of you want any dinner?"

They both shook their heads silently.

"Suit yourselves," snapped Gerald.

Will and Mica went straight to bed as ordered and put in their earplugs immediately because it was going to be a long night again, and their dreams gave them no rest.

They were both haunted by what was on that spit turning over and over in the Archa's barbecue pit.

CHAPTER 14

Nightmare Caverns

The watchers tried to sleep that night and most of the following day. They did not dare go outside to see the aftermath of the party. Luckily, the Archa slept most of the morning.

In the late afternoon, Gerald announced they had been ordered to escort the Archa to one of their favorite outings, which they called playtime.

The place they had to prepare was in the woods not too far from the Big White House. *Whatever it is,* thought Mica, *I am sure it's disgusting and inhuman.* Mica's face dropped, and an aching pain filled the pit of her stomach.

It wasn't a long trip, but apparently, there were specific preparations watchers had to do after they arrived at the location.

Even Gerald looked grim. He barely spoke, and Will got a distinct feeling that even he didn't care for this particular type of debauchery they were about to witness.

As the three watchers walked to the hangar, they could see remnants from the barbecue strewn across the lawn. There were bones everywhere, gnawed and shattered for their marrow, and the grass was full of scrape and drag marks.

The posts were the Yellow Eyes had been tied were bare and empty. Tiny fragments of bloody ropes were softly swinging in the breeze, and the fire had almost burned itself out, leaving a few glowing embers that lay among the gray ashes.

Will turned his head away from the macabre scene, wishing he were somewhere else.

Mica couldn't help but stare at the carcasses, which were now being picked clean by shiny black ravens that were squawking at each other in delight at the sight of the massive feast laying in the grass in front of them. Gerald ignored the grisly scene, intent on his next task. He had seen the results of the Archa bbq's hundreds of times during the last twenty years, to Gerald, it was normal.

The watchers drove silently into the woods in a MECA, toward a large rocky area peppered with caves. A short hike took them up to one of the more extensive caves. The entrance had an ornate massive iron gate that was securely locked with an enormous steel chain. Gerald opened the padlock with the specially crafted key he carried around his neck. The big iron gate creaked and groaned as it was pushed open by the three watchers.

Gerald then closed and locked the iron gate behind them. He stopped and gave them some extra ammunition, a stunner, and some pepper spray. He saw Mica and Will exchange looks. "It is just a precaution," said Gerald.

"What is this place?" Mica shivered. She felt cold and damp, even though minutes ago they had been hiking in the glow of the afternoon sun and climbing among the hot, baked rocks at the front of the cave.

"I call it Nightmare Caverns," replied Gerald grimly.

"Why do you call it that?" asked a very nervous Mica.

"You shall see for yourself," Gerald replied sharply. "Follow me. Stay alert and stay alive."

The watchers walked through several long stone corridors. The caverns were like a maze. They had been walking for almost three minutes when they arrived at the last massive metal door, which had a small metal grill placed about eye level, but it was too dark to see what was inside.

As they got closer, the smell of excrement began to be overwhelming, and they could hear chirping, whining, snorting, and other animal noises. There was a loud rattling sound, like metal cage doors being climbed on and rocked back and forth.

Gerald produced another specially crafted key from the chain around his neck; it was slightly smaller and more ornate than the last one. As he turned the lock and the door swung open, Mica started to retch, and Will began to cough as their eyes began to adjust to the dim light. The pungent smell of ammonia burned their eyes. To their utter horror, through blurred and teary eyes, they saw cages after cages filled with weird creatures that terrified Will and Mica. They were apparently human-animal hybrids, seemingly composed of every kind of species imaginable and had been created in some diabolical laboratory

Some creatures were bizarre, with anywhere from six to eight appendages. Others were small, furry and had opposable thumbs, looking part human and part lemur. One animal seemed part rabbit, but it had a tiny baby-like pink face. It had curled itself into a tight, fluffy white ball and was crying softly like a child.

It was heartbreaking to watch.

Some of the other animals were tall and fierce and walked upright, part predators like a wolf, dog, or hyena.

Others were more sinister. One creature in particular looked like a cross between a praying mantis and a giant scaly lizard. It was standing still in its cage, barely visible, motionless, and silent, with its forearms bent, ready to strike.

Massive bearlike Minotaurs had short curved horns and stood eight feet tall on their hind legs. They growled ferociously while holding on to the steel bars and biting them with incredibly long sharp teeth.

In one large cage, there were six tall birdlike lizards. Each one had a sharp curved beak and bright-red eyes. They had strange, mottled green fur that was spiky and stood upright, and on each of their back feet, they had raptor claws. They were like velociraptors that had roamed the Earth millions of years ago. These creatures seemed to be communicating with one another by blinking their eyes and making little clicking noises.

Suddenly, they became quiet, and then all the raptors turned at once to stare at the watchers. They were insidious.

Some creatures tried to reach through the bars; some were even able to speak. From the back of the room, one poor creature kept saying, "Help me," over and over. Others made gentle cooing and trilling sounds.

Near Mica, in a cage, there was a being. It could only be described as a cat-man. He had pale cream fur with orange and black stripes and a catlike face, but his slanted, glowing eyes were beautiful and expressive. He was about five feet tall, standing on his back paws complete with a three-foot tail. Cat-man had strange, half-human-looking hands and feet. They were pale and without much fur.

The energy in Nightmare Caverns was one of the worst Mica and Will had ever experienced. All the sadness and the pain these creatures had suffered were reflected back in their haunted eyes. There were so many grotesque beings. This place was a hall of genetic nightmares. Both Mica's and Will's hearts were aching for the suffering of these beings. Even Gerald seemed affected by these tormented and abused spirits.

"In the name of Gaia, what is this place?" whispered Mica, distraught.

"I don't know the whole story," replied Gerald sadly. "I understand many of these types of beings were created during the Chaos Era. Scientists from DARPA were experimenting, trying to make supersoldiers by enhancing human DNA with animal DNA. To design and create a faster, stronger, more invincible army. They also mixed alien DNA from the Archa with some animal and human DNA. Most creatures from the original experiments died, and the rest of them had to be destroyed because they were so wild and savage they could not be tamed or learn to be obedient."

Gerald cleared his throat.

"In their infinite wisdom," he said with some sarcasm, "the Archa decided to resurrect the program, primarily for entertainment purposes. Mixing the DNA from various Earth creatures became a popular art form. The Archa had many competitions to create the most bizarre form of life. These beings here were created a long time ago and were the result of Project Resurrection. These are different from the originals. Somehow they seem more human, with parts of something else. I think they possess some form of consciousness. Some can talk. They have learned to make a type of sign language among themselves, so the ones that can't speak can still communicate collectively with one another."

Gerald sighed. "The Archa keep them here, locked up, because most of the creatures are very dangerous. The Archa like to play with them," he said wretchedly.

"Play with them how?" asked Will icily, disgusted by what he was seeing.

"Some are made to fight to the death in the pit at the Compound, over on the north side. Others are put in the maze and then hunted. Some are considered a delicacy and are eaten alive. Others are sexual toys," said Gerald, wrinkling his nose in disgust. "Many are tortured to death in competitions where the Archa make bets on which creature can survive the longest. Every way you can abuse and destroy something happens here. When I go back to First City, this is the memory I want to have erased. These caverns haunt my dreams and are in every nightmare I have ever had."

Feeling suddenly weak, Mica leaned toward the cat-man's cage without thinking. It hissed at her, showed his long canine teeth, and grabbed the bars with its fingers. The fingers suddenly twitched, and long sharp talons shot out of its strange, catlike hands and feet.

Gerald grabbed her quickly and pulled her away from the cat-man's reach.

"Don't go near it, Mica. That is one of Malus's favorite fighters. It has killed so much I can't believe it has any soul left. Feel pity for these abominations, but never, ever let your guard down. These creatures have been so abused and mistreated they are very vicious and will attack and kill you given half the chance. We have lost several Elite watchers in this place. Malus is the only one that has complete control over these beasts. They are all terrified of him, for a good reason."

Mica looked over at the cat-man, who was pacing in his dark, dirty cage. She whispered, "I am so sorry this happened to you." She locked eyes with his beautiful orange ones, and she gasped. For a microsecond, his eyes changed, and she could see there was a human in there somewhere. A tear ran down her cheek, and in that instant, he had turned away from her, hissing and growling while swishing his tail from side to side.

There was an enormous but silent creature next to the cat-man's cage. He was just sitting in the shadows of his fortified cage, with his back toward them. He was huge, probably weighing at least five hundred pounds. His skin was a mottled brown, and his entire body had scabby, bald spots and small patches of brown hair. His back and arms were covered with long ragged silver scars. His body showed years of blatant abuse. He looked like an ape-man.

Mica was overcome with grief but somehow managed to regain control of her emotions and said calmly, "Gerald, what preparations do we have to make here?"

"Assemble the equipment," replied Gerald. "Put the chosen beast in the slaughter room, set up the fight ring, prepare the bed-chambers, and restock the torture room with clean instruments, plastic sheets, and clean towels. Lastly, set up the weapons for the hunting maze."

He looked around.

"The Archa always view the creatures behind the two-way glass over there," he said, pointing to the only plain wall in the room, which held a huge pane of glass. "Then they choose the ones they want to play with," stated Gerald soberly.

"Today, it will be different." Gerald paused for a moment and then concluded, "Mica, you or Will must choose the beasts that will be involved in the games tonight. You must do this ceremony, or you will be selected instead, or the Archa may select your partner or all three of us."

Mica and Will exchanged horrified looks.

Gerald continued, ignoring Will's and Mica's faces. "It has always been done this way, to ensure that the beasts despise us more than the Archa. The watchers prepare everything in front of them, the theory being that if they ever escaped, they would target us first and not the Archa. What we do here is a way of protecting them. You cannot refuse this order, or we may die a horrible death," warned Gerald. He left the room for a minute so they could digest this information.

"I will not do this!" retorted Mica, enraged, her eyes filling with tears while staring at the ape-man's huge back, wondering if he understood anything she was saying. "We need to let these creatures go. I refuse to sentence any being in this room to death. In the name of Gaia, I will let them go. There will be no more death here," she said furiously, now shaking with anger.

Suddenly, all the beings in the room became quiet. They began signing to one another frantically while still staring at the two watchers.

The ape-man had now turned around and, while still sitting in the shadows, watched them intently. Mica glanced at him; his face filled her with horror. It was a human face, but it did not have human proportions because of his prominent eye ridges, flattened nose, gigantic jaw, and thin lips.

Small patches of coarse, dark hair covered his body. Except for his ears, face, hands, and feet. When his brown eyes met hers, Mica knew immediately he was different from the others. The ape-man was an entirely conscious being. It looked like the Archa had taken a man and tried to turn him into an ape and had failed miserably.

"I will not sentence any being to death either," stated Will passionately. "We have to escape this tyranny and insanity right now! It is worse than the Chaos Era. I refuse to live in this demented horror show anymore!" He, too, was shaking with anger. "I will die here tonight rather than kill any creature here."

"Agreed," replied Mica. "We should let all these poor creatures loose on the Archa when they arrive, so these beings never get abused again."

"Brilliant idea," said Will. "We do have extra weapons," he said, "but they are no match against the Archa, who are invincible and have powers we don't even understand."

"How exactly do you kill an immortal?" asked Mica worriedly.

"I don't know," replied Will, "but we need to cause a distraction and escape from here. The rest we can figure out later. However, nothing in this crazy world is what it seems. The Archa might not be who we think they are." Will murmured the last part to himself.

"Remember," said Will, "the arms the Archa need for protection are all here right now, and they will stay here."

"What about Gerald?" asked Mica, concerned.

"He will defend the Archa to the death. He has no other option. He is as damaged as these poor, wretched creatures. Years of seeing such abuse has almost destroyed him. Whoever he once was, he no longer is. Gerald has become what the Archa wanted him to be. Perhaps we should lock him somewhere safe, but I don't think we have time to save him."

"I will not kill him," stated Mica firmly.

"He would kill us without any qualms," replied Will. "Gerald would be just performing his duties, but I will not hurt him or anyone else. I will not live as a monster anymore. We are not part of this society. We must change it now, today, even if it means our deaths."

They stopped talking as Gerald walked in, carrying various supplies. Will and Mica continued to prepare for playtime as if nothing was wrong. The creatures, familiar with this routine, started to screech, whoop, and howl. Some were banging, and others were pacing in their cages. The noise was deafening. Others cried out, making strange, human-sounding words, but it was apparent they were all terrified.

Soon Will and Mica could hear the Hoppers arriving at the caverns. The creatures heard them too and became eerily silent. Judging by the noise coming from outside the room, Mica estimated most of the Archa, and possibly a few guests, had arrived. Which was not a good sign; it made things even more complicated, because they were outnumbered.

Gerald left the room to greet the incoming Archa and their guests after telling the watchers to continue with their preparations and make their choices as to which beasts would participate in playtime. He left the keys to the cages on the table.

Will and Mica looked at each other after he left; they agreed they must do it now or never, as they could already hear the Archa walking down the stone corridors.

Instantly they ran from each cage to cage, unlocking them with Gerald's slip-keys. They let all the grotesque creatures out of their miserable prison, praying they would not be the targets of the carnage about to occur.

As Mica opened one cage, she saw a tear trickle down the poor creature's gnarled face. Another lunged at her, screeching. She closed her eyes and felt something gently touch her face, and when she opened her eyes, it had gone. Will was opening the cages too, and the creatures were not trying to hurt him either.

Many of the beings possessed intelligence and language and were able to display some human emotions. It was apparent they understood precisely who their tormentors and murderers were.

As the creatures swarmed down the tunnels, Will and Mica could hear the Archa's shock and surprise as they were confronted. Ira's voice boomed through the tunnels, "You will die, for this watcher" he was talking to Gerald."

Then the screaming started, it was high pitched. What Will and Mica didn't realize is that the menagerie was taking its time, slowly exacting revenge upon the Archa and their guests, one small mouthful at a time. The Archa were strong and fought hard, but the sheer number of beasts overwhelmed them, tearing them to pieces.

Will thought to himself, *I see. They don't tolerate torture as well as they deliver it.*

Mica said under her breath, "For all those who have suffered, this is justice for you."

One of the biggest animals, the ape-man, which Mica had locked eyes with earlier, came barreling toward her. His huge gnarled hand grabbed Mica's arm. For an instant, she panicked and flinched as she looked at his grotesque features. Then he put a twisted old finger to his sad mouth, and when she looked into his sad, dark eyes, she was no longer afraid. He mumbled one word. "Come."

Mica grabbed Will's hand as they were led down a maze of tunnels while the frenzied screaming of the Archa continued. Eventually, they could see a small sliver of daylight in the distance, which got larger and larger.

The ape-man was even more grotesque in the fading sunlight. He gestured to stop and tried to speak. "More," he said. And again, with difficulty, he repeated in a hoarse, garbled voice, "More."

"More what?" asked Mica.

He nodded slightly and tried to speak again, "More them."

Will grasped what he was saying. "There are more of the Archa?"

The ape-man nodded.

"Where?" asked Will.

The creature gestured with wide open arms.

"Everywhere?" asked Will, and the ape-man nodded.

"Do you know about the Nahus?" Mica asked the ape-man, who nodded slowly.

"Where are they?" she asked. The creature pointed north. In the distance, there was a dark mountain range just visible in the early evening light.

Mica suddenly realized the ape-man was old. "How long have you been here?" she asked.

He held up his mangled digits to indicate twenty years. Will and Mica shuddered at the horrific memories this poor, wretched beast had survived.

"Where did you come from?" Mica asked.

He pointed to the smoky blue mountains. Suddenly, Mica understood and said, "Oh my Gaia, you were once a Nahu?"

The ape-man nodded sadly.

"Then they experimented on you," said Mica indignantly. The ape-man acknowledged this with a small nod.

"Why did they do this to you?" asked Will, horrified.

"Fun," replied the ape-man quietly. "They try to make man into ape for fun."

The ape-man motioned to them that he must go. "My people," he said slowly and distinctly.

Will and Mica suddenly realized that these poor, hybrid creations thought of themselves as people. They both nodded, and the last words the ape-man had said before he ambled back into the cave was, "Friend always." Then they heard a tremendous roar that echoed through the dark tunnels. It was a victory cry as he thundered his way back to his people.

Will and Mica hugged each other for the first time. They were free. Their plan had worked. They held each other for several moments, overcome by emotion and comforted by the human interaction.

But their joy soon turned to concern.

Mica broke the silence first. "We need supplies," she said.

"Yes," agreed Will. Then he continued, "We can go back to the Compound. I think most of the Archa are dead. Soon it will be dark. We should start now. Do you still have your weapons, Mica?"

"Yes," replied Mica. "Let's head back, although I am not sure they all died. Some could have either escaped or been late arriving."

Will made a wise suggestion. "First, we have to cut out our RFID chips so they can't track us."

Mica agreed. "Yes, a splendid idea. Let's do it now before it is too late and they come looking for us."

Will withdraw a large knife from his boot and heated it with his watch-laser-lighter until the tip was red-hot.

"This is going to hurt," he warned Mica. She nodded, held out her right arm, and turned her head away. She placed her other arm across her mouth as Will quickly cut out the RFID chip. Will was about to smash it with his heel on a nearby rock when she gasped out.

"No! We must put the chips back in the tunnels with pieces of our uniforms ripped to shreds. There is so much blood and gore back there it will take them a while before they figure out we are not really dead."

Will agreed. "A good idea," he said. He reheated the knife and handed it to Mica and watched as she cut out his RFID chip.

"I am glad it's gone," he said. "I feel free."

They bandaged their arms with fabric torn from their uniforms, making sure it was well-soaked in their blood.

Warily they looked at the entrance of the tunnel. It was silent now. Will and Mica carefully made their way back to the main massacre site. The floor was slippery with blood and strewn with body parts, long tufts of bloody gold hair, and pieces of colored wigs. Surgical tools littered the floor, along with machetes. It was undeniable that the weapons Will and Mica had prepared for the Archa were the ones that were used against them.

It was clear that the butchered Archa had been hacked into minuscule pieces while still alive. A karmic death, thought Mica. She hoped they were all killed, but in the darkness, and with blood everywhere, it was impossible to tell who was who.

Will wondered if Gerald had survived, he didn't see Gerald's head four feet behind him, still rolling back and forth with terror frozen into what was left of his face.

Will and Mica threw pieces of their torn uniforms into the bloody heap along with their RFID chips. Eventually, the authorities would discover the truth, but at least they might be considered dead long enough to buy them more time to escape.

They couldn't hear the hybrids anymore. The caverns were deathly quiet.

Will and Mica left the grisly scene and made their way quickly and silently back to the exit, hoping they didn't run into any of the hybrids on the way. Luckily, they didn't see a living soul.

Relieved, they made it back to where the ape-man had left them and walked out into the sweet, fresh, warm air.

"We must be cautious," warned Mica.

Will agreed. "We will stay in the shadows and the foliage. No speaking. Only use sign language."

Mica nodded in agreement.

With their weapons loaded, Will and Mica began to hike back with stealth and in silence back to the Compound to get supplies and equipment before the sky grew too dark. They were watching for any movement and listening to every sound coming from the darkening forest.

Wild animals had proliferated over the decades in the surrounding Wildlife Corridors and Forbidden Zones. Packs of wolves roamed these areas; mountain lions, bobcats, and black bears were all formidable predators. Especially if they came upon two lone humans who were on foot and splattered with blood.

When they finally reached the Compound, there were still lights on in the Big White House, and two figures were moving around the garden. It was Malus and Metus. Somehow they had survived and were raging and screaming furiously at each other.

Will and Mica immediately froze, melting into the trees and bushes, holding their breath and listening to the manic pair.

Malus suddenly snapped his body around, sensing something, and he was staring hard into the darkness and looking directly toward Will and Mica. They didn't make a sound.

Malus was suspicious and flicked his tongue into the air. "All I can smell is blood," he said to Metus.

Metus was irate. "I am not surprised you can smell blood. The family—they are all dead! All of them killed by your freak mutants in the caverns."

Malus hissed, "Those dumb, hybrid beasts, how did they escape and attack the family and the Yellow Eyes?"

"I really don't know," Metus kept repeating, evidently disturbed by the whole event.

"Where are the watchers?" suddenly screamed Malus.

"Dead with the others, I expect," replied Metus irritably. "Who cares?"

"Did you actually see their bodies?" demanded Malus.

"I am not sure. It was dark, and there was blood everywhere. I do remember seeing Gerald's head. I don't know where the rest of his body was, though," replied Metus, filling his crystal glass for the third time with very expensive cognac.

"The new watchers, you idiot, did you see them?" Malus demanded angrily.

Metus shrugged and drank the remainder of his cognac. "I don't know," he replied irritably.

"Well?" yelled Malus. "Did you see them or not?"

"I don't remember hearing them or seeing their bodies, but that doesn't mean they weren't dead," replied Metus, wondering why Malus was obsessing over the new watchers when most of his Archa family were dead and ripped to shreds. It would take days to sort out the gory mess.

"It was them," said Malus. "They are still alive, I feel it. They did this!"

Metus continued, wondering if Malus had lost his mind, "Morus is now preparing reinforcements to go back to the caverns.

He will kill anything left on site. When it is safe and cleaned up, we will look for the remains of the other two watchers."

"Very well," agreed Malus. "I will follow you."

Metus was visibly pale and shaken; he nodded and went to see Morus, who had begun to gather the black-eyed bio-hunters and arm them with various high-tech weapons. Malus followed a quarter of a mile behind with four hunters, who were evidently acting as his bodyguards.

As the two Archa finally disappeared into the darkness, Mica and Will ran to the equipment hangar, grabbed some weapons, and went toward the little white cottage to get food, clothing, and other supplies.

"Perhaps we shouldn't take anything. The Archa will know we have been here," wondered Will out loud.

"They already know," replied Mica sensibly. "It will make no difference. We can't take a MECA, though. They can track it too easily."

"Yes, I know," said Will. "We need as many weapons as we can carry. Plus a waterproof backpack, clothing, water holders, water purification dots, magic bags filled with food, and a pot to boil water in."

"Do you know what's ironic, Mica?" asked Will thoughtfully.

"What?" Mica replied, still full of adrenaline and distracted by all the packing. "Don't forget the map and Eco-blankets."

"Well, the worst murderers and torturers, Malus, Metus, and Morus, escaped death," said Will. "It seems ironic. Do you think Desi was there too?"

"I doubt it," she replied. "Desi probably stayed in his nursery the whole time." She stopped packing for a second. "I suppose this means we still have much work to do," Mica said wearily.

"I suppose so," repeated Will. "We must hurry, and we have a grueling path ahead. The Archa or the bio-hunters could return at any time."

They loaded as many supplies as possible in just a few minutes. Then Will and Mica ran into the chilly, dark night, trying to escape the evil that seemed intent on pursuing and destroying them. They headed north, toward the fabled land of the Nahus.

PART 3

The Quest

Be the change that you wish to see in the world.
—Mahatma Gandhi

CHAPTER 15

The Long Trail

It was a long quest to the smoky blue mountains. At least fifty miles, through the thickly forested terrain.

The first night, Will and Mica were fortunate to find a cave to rest in. They took turns wearily watching for wild animals that might discover them in the little cave. The first night, they were lucky.

The following morning, as soon as the earliest rays of the sun began peeking over the horizon, Will and Mica left the cave. They found a little stream nearby. It was fast flowing, with cold, sparkling water.

Will and Mica were dehydrated, so they filled up their water holders (adding a purification dot, which worked in five seconds), and they both drank two whole containers of water. Then they washed their grimy hands and faces in the stream. While sitting down on a couple of large warm rocks, Will and Mica ate some chunks of bread and some creamy cheese they had taken from the cottage as they tried to figure out their next plan.

Their food was held in thin metallic bags that resealed themselves and sensed the type of food that was in it. The bags kept the food at precisely the correct temperature to preserve it. Will and Mica called them magic bags. They had different ones for cheeses, crusty bread, smoked meats, smoked fish, and pickled eggs, cucumbers, and olives.

"Maybe we should try to follow a river," suggested Mica.

"I don't know," replied Will thoughtfully. "Rivers attract animals."

"But we have weapons," stated Mica.

"Yes," replied Will, "but you can hear a shot for miles out here in the forest, and you know they will be looking for us."

"Do you think they will track us swiftly?" Mica asked, concerned.

"I don't know," replied Will. "Supposedly, they have some technology that we don't know about. It's hard to say. Let's just keep going north and see what happens. We must keep undercover of the foliage and travel as many miles as we can until dark."

"Yes, it is the only plan we have. We have no choice but to continue north," agreed Mica.

"What about using the stunners?" asked Mica. "They work on the Nahus, who are much lighter than either bears or mountain lions, but perhaps they would stop wild boars, wild dogs, or wolves."

"Unfortunately, the stunners emit a heat signature," replied Will. "You know the Hoppers and the Skybirds have the technology to pick up the tiniest spark."

"Yes, indeed," agreed Mica. "Our weapons can only be used as a last resort."

Will and Mica packed up their supplies and began walking and stopped after only two miles. It was a challenging trail because the woods were so thick and overgrown. They hadn't been thinned out in over 150 years. Trees felled by lightning, old age, or disease just lay where they fell. It was a very slow trek, as there were no existing paths cut or used in many decades.

"I think I should climb a tree to see if there is an easier route we could take," suggested Will.

"Be careful," warned Mica nervously. "If you fall, you could break your bones, and then we won't be going anywhere."

"I will be safe," replied Will confidently. He deftly climbed the old tree, reaching the top in a few minutes. The air was crisp and clear, and Will could see for miles in all directions. He did spot a small Skybird flying to the far south and miles of woods to the north.

Will climbed down from the tree and shared his observations with Mica. "They might be looking for us in the south, but I only saw one small Skybird. It's hard to say. Somebody might just be traveling somewhere. Unfortunately, there is no clear path ahead toward the north. It will be an arduous journey."

"I expected this," replied Mica. "We have to continue."

They set off through the forest, being as careful as they could, trying not to disturb the environment and leave a trail behind them that could be easily tracked, and that was almost impossible.

An hour or two, before sunset they had only covered about eight miles. The day had been warm and humid, and they were both hot, dirty, severely scratched by briars, and utterly exhausted.

Will and Mica searched for somewhere safe to rest for the night. By sheer luck, they discovered a small pool of water about twenty-five feet in circumference. It was clear, fresh and deep, complete with a beautiful but miniature waterfall that cascaded down the rocks, splashing into the pool with a gentle, babbling sound.

"I think we have just found our little paradise," Mica remarked, smiling.

"Indeed," replied Will, smiling back. "We should wash in here so we don't smell so human."

Mica didn't need any encouragement. They took their boots off and left their weapons, clothes, and supplies on the edge of the bank. Then they both dived into the pool in their underwear. They lay there, floating for a few minutes, the cool water feeling refreshing on their clammy skin.

Suddenly, Mica dived down under the water. Will followed her, but he went deeper than Mica, and he could see something a few feet beneath the water. He surfaced, took a deep breath, and submerged again. Then Will saw a type of entrance to something in the water. When he resurfaced, he told Mica they should explore the possible tunnel.

"It could be dangerous," commented Mica. "I should go because I am smaller than you. If I get into trouble, I will jerk the rope hard, and you can drag me out."

"All right," said Will, agreeing with her.

Mica tied the rope around her waist. She took a deep breath and disappeared for a minute, then two, then nearly three. He was about to pull her back when she surfaced, gasping.

"Will, it's amazing! The pool leads to an underground cave, which is above the waterline," Mica said breathlessly, "and there is some tunnel beyond that. They cannot detect our heat signatures through rock. So we would be safe in there for the night."

"Good news," said Will, relieved.

They packed and tied their waterproof backpacks to ropes and dived into the water, swimming down through the tunnel for a few seconds. They quickly surfaced into the small cave system, both dragging their backpacks. Once everything was safely ashore, they used their flashlights to explore the dark and dusty cave. Immediately Will saw the remnants of an old fire.

"Do you think this is an Archa cave?" asked Mica, concerned. She quickly scanned the cave with her flashlight, lighting up the whole cave, which was about thirty feet wide and shaped like a semi-circle. A large tunnel to the left plunged into pitch darkness.

"No, I don't think so," replied Will, looking at the old fire meticulously. "This was made with primitive tools, twigs, and branches generations ago. It shows no signs of technology at all. This fire is not one the Archa would make. It looks more like a Nahu fire."

"I wonder where the tunnel leads to," Mica asked curiously.

"I don't know," replied Will. He felt exhausted. "But I think we should rest and find out in the morning."

Mica agreed but still continued to look around the cave. She spotted a pile of brittle old sticks and branches covered in dust and cobwebs.

"I agree with you, Will. Nobody has used this cave in a very long time," remarked Mica. "I am beginning to feel chilled. We should light a fire and get warm."

"I am starting to shiver too," agreed Will.

So they prepared a fire, hung their clothes on the rocks to dry, and placed their sleeping mats on the cave floor. Their mats were unique; they folded into a small square for storage, but once unwrapped, they self-inflated into a thin but incredibly comfortable mattress.

Will and Mica lay down on each side of the fire and began wrapping themselves in an Eco-blanket. (Which looked similar to a space blanket.) It was very high-tech. It was waterproof and adapted immediately to the body's shape, including the head. It even had a breathable face covering for severe weather. Somehow its sensors could calculate the body's temperature and that of the external environment. Then the blanket emitted precisely the right amount of heat and warmed the body efficiently and almost instantly. It could also cool the body down if it was overheating. It was a remarkable piece of technology.

Together, propped up on their elbows, Will and Mica ate some bread, cheese, sausages, and pickled eggs, washed down with some fresh, cold water from the pool. They were silent as they ate, both too hungry to talk. After their meal, they refilled their canteens with more water and lay down to rest for the night.

"I am curious to see where the tunnel leads," murmured Mica drowsily.

"We will explore the tunnel in the morning. It will not move," replied Will. "We are both exhausted. No one can track us here. For the first time since we escaped from the Archa, I feel safe."

Mica nodded, and they both drifted into a deep sleep as the fire shadows danced around them on the walls of the ancient cave.

Twelve hours later, they woke up. The fire had gone out, but Will and Mica were still warm under their blankets, and their clothes had dried while they slept and they smelled earthy and smoky. They got dressed and ate some of their food, drank a lot of water, and prepared to find out the secrets of the dark tunnel.

Will scanned the tunnel with a type of infrared reader that was on his watch, which also had a compass on it, a small laser to start fires, and a clock.

It showed him how long the tunnel was and displayed a map of it on its tiny screen. "It's about a mile long," stated Will. "It is low in some places, but we should be able to walk the whole distance without having to crawl on our hands and knees. Although the exit is much smaller and we may have to wriggle through the last five feet."

Mica listened carefully. "I am ready," she said, and with their flashlights on high beam, they disappeared into the darkness. There was nothing remarkable about the tunnel, but periodically they found homemade, burned-out old torches scattered along the cave floor and some strange writing and various symbols etched into the cave walls. This tunnel had been used regularly once, but somehow it had been forgotten and unused for many years.

Mica thought about all the people who had traveled through this tunnel. She wondered who they were and why they had stopped using it.

Halfway down the tunnel, Will noticed what looked like a massive stone door. He showed it to Mica. "The people must have blocked up a large hole to stop animals from coming into the cave system," she suggested thoughtfully.

Will agreed with Mica. It had been sealed shut for many decades. Caked all around it was dried old mud. Will tried to push it open without success. The massive stone appeared to be welded to the tunnel; its secrets would have to remain hidden.

Eventually, Will and Mica came to the end of the tunnel, and the ceiling began to drop lower and lower until they were both on their stomachs, dragging their supplies behind them.

Finally, Will and Mica crawled out into a dimly lit glade in the forest, breathing in the sweet air. The valley was scattered with fragrant flowers. Brightly colored butterflies fluttered everywhere, and fat bumblebees buzzed in this beautiful secret garden. It was gloriously silent, except for the birds singing and the occasional rustle of small creatures among the dead leaves.

As their eyes finally adjusted to the pale green light, Will and Mica could see this place had once been a thriving village with many dwellings made of wattle and daub. Now it was crumbling, vacant, and empty of life. There was a fire pit in the center of the village that had once roasted wild boar or deer.

Old animal pens were on one side of the village and lay broken and rotting, but they looked as if they had been deliberately destroyed or trampled by something or someone. There was even a tired old well complete with a cracked wooden bucket that once carried water, but now it was filled with dust, dead leaves, and cobwebs. As they walked through the deserted village, Mica noticed something peeking out underneath the piles of old leaves and debris.

"Will, come here," called Mica excitedly. "I have found something interesting." While kneeling down and moving armfuls of leaves, she revealed an old human skeleton. It was a young female. She had a deep depression in the back of her skull and had probably died from blunt force trauma to the back of her head.

"Look," said Will, "there are cut marks on the bones, more like a slaughtered animal."

They both started moving the leaves around them, finding more and more remains. Some skeletons had broken bones in almost every part of their bodies. Most had head wounds, but every one of the deceased had the curious blade marks on their bones. Will and Mica counted at least forty skeletons, including a few tiny skeletons of babies and young children.

"There was a terrible massacre here many years ago," stated Will sadly while poking around in the piles of leaves.

"It looks like the whole village was wiped out. Possibly more than fifty years ago," replied Mica.

"Here, Mica!" yelled Will excitedly. "I think I have just found an old sign. It says, 'Fern Point: Population, 60,' the year something." Then Will continued, "I think the writing has been carved into the sign, but it's difficult to read because of exposure to the elements. Does it look like 2130 to you, Mica?"

Mica nodded in agreement. "I wonder why these people were murdered," she said.

"I know whole towns and villages disappeared during the Chaos Era and the Cleansing of the Dark Ages. Billions of deaths occurred then, didn't they?" replied Will.

Mica was still not satisfied with Will's answer. "It doesn't make sense. Why would they be murdered almost fifty years later?"

"I don't know," replied Will, "I think the fate of Fern Point will have to remain a mystery." Mica nodded thoughtfully, even she couldn't solve this puzzle.

Will decided he was going to climb a tree to see where they were. As Will reached the top of the tree, he realized the tunnel in the cave had put them much closer to the smoky blue mountains, with perhaps only two or three days of walking left. He could see several smaller Skybirds and Hoppers searching the skies, still much farther south than they were.

Will climbed down from the tree and told Mica what he had seen.

"So do you think the Archa have realized we are not dead? I wonder why they assume we went south," Will asked, confused.

"Because they think we are trying to find our way back to civilization," replied Mica earnestly.

Suddenly, Will and Mica burst into uncontrollable laughter. Their tears left salty tracks down their dirty faces, and still, they laughed even more.

When they stopped laughing, Will said, "That was a good joke, Mica. Oh my stars, I don't think I have ever laughed so much in my life my sides are aching."

Will and Mica took a short break to eat and drink. Then they both stood up and continued to walk through the forest for several miles until the sun began to set. The sky was a palette of gold, yellow, and vermillion red. Finally, the golden orb of the sun sank, thankfully, beneath the horizon, and darkness fell across the forest.

Mica had an odd premonition something was wrong; she was unnerved and hyperalert. Then she suddenly stopped, looking around the shadowy forest.

"We still haven't found a cave yet," Will said nervously, "and it is almost dark now. I think we should climb a tall tree, tie ourselves to it, and sleep for a few hours."

Mica quickly agreed. She could see Will was just as concerned as she was.

Will and Mica climbed the nearest old oak tree that had large branches and a thick trunk the size of two large men. When they climbed toward the top of the tree, to their surprise, they found an old wooden platform that could comfortably accommodate four people lying down. Although it had been made years ago, it was still sturdy. Whoever had made it was ingenious, because they had thought to put an edge on three sides of the platform to prevent anybody from falling out.

Will and Mica got out their mats and blankets. They chatted a little as they ate some food, drank a little water, and lay down on the platform to settle down for a peaceful night's sleep. Both of them were feeling safe and well-hidden in the old tree.

They were just beginning to fall asleep to the sound of the owls hooting and the odd rustling on the forest floor when suddenly, out of the comfortable silence came the loud howls of a wolf pack out looking for prey.

"They sound hungry. I am glad we are up here," whispered Mica.

"Me too," whispered back Will. "I think they are getting closer."

The wolf pack's howls became louder and louder, and soon they were growling down on the forest floor, beneath the very tree where Will and Mica were resting.

The wolves started to try to climb the tree, even jumping against the trunk and falling back into the leaves. One wolf made it about a foot or so up by using his claws and trying to grip onto the bark. Luckily for Will and Mica, climbing a tree for the wolves seemed an impossible feat.

"They have picked up our scent. Now we have a problem," said Will seriously. "If we use any weapons, we could be tracked immediately and found very quickly. If we stay here, the wolves will somehow know that we will run out of food and water, and they will wait us out, knowing we will have to come down eventually."

"We cannot do anything about the wolves right now," Mica said. "It's too dark. We should rest, and maybe they will be gone by the morning."

"I don't think so," said Will. "They will just hide until we come down, and then they will stalk and kill us."

"No," said Mica forcefully, "we will figure something out. We haven't outwitted and escaped from the Archa to meet our demise in the jaws of wild animals."

"That's very true," agreed Will, smiling.

"We should stop talking, rest, and maybe they will find some other prey to stalk," whispered Mica, and they both lay there, listening to the wolves that howled and snarled beneath them.

When they awoke, the early light of dawn had illuminated the forest with warm, golden rays.

"Are the wolves still there?" whispered Mica.

"I don't think so. I can't hear them or see them," Will replied, peering down to the forest floor.

"Throw a stick down, just in case," insisted Mica.

Will threw a stick down to the ground. The watchers could hear nothing but the wood falling to the forest floor and landing with a dull thud. They waited a few more minutes. Still nothing.

"I don't know," said Mica. "I think they are still here somewhere. I feel their presence."

"I think you must be imagining things," replied Will, beginning to pack his things away and preparing to climb down the tree.

"Please, Will, do not do that. I have a bad feeling about this," whispered Mica.

Surprised by the intensity of her voice, Will stopped and turned around. For the first time, Mica realized how green his eyes were, a forest green, bright and shining in his dusty face. For a moment, she stared at him, noticing the line of his jaw, and she realized he was a handsome man.

Will's hair had started to grow back. It was very dark, almost black, and the stubble on his face was dark too. She had never felt an attraction to him before, and she suddenly realized that there was nowhere that she'd rather be.

Will noticed her staring at him in a way that made him feel uncomfortable.

"Please, Will, stay here. Something is not right," begged Mica as her thoughts immediately went to their situation, and Will, unnerved by her strange behavior, nodded and sat down.

They were both silent, listening intently to the slightest sounds coming from the forest floor.

Still hearing nothing, Mica dropped a whole sausage from the tree. Suddenly, from all around their tree, the wolves jumped out from their camouflaged hiding places and fought aggressively over the food.

Mica whispered, "See? I knew it."

"In the name of Gaia, why are they still here?" Will was shocked. "I can't believe they haven't gone."

"We are in their territory," said Mica. "They won't leave. We are in trouble. We must start rationing our supplies. We have four or five days of supplies left if we are careful."

"Well, in four days, they will be gone," replied Will brightly. "After all, they have to eat and drink too."

"Yes," said Mica. "We have supplies, they do not. I hope we can wait them out."

Mica stared hard at the wolves, suddenly noticing something different about the pack. "Oh my stars, Will, look at them," she whispered. "They are not ordinary wolves."

"Oh no, they are not," agreed Will. "Their eyes are a bright lemon-yellow, and their fur has a weird sheen to it. They are much bigger than regular wolves. Their legs are much longer, and they have two sets of teeth."

"They must be hybrid wolves," replied Mica. "Probably created by the Archa, used for protection and replaced a long time ago by something bigger and meaner, and then thrown out into the forest to survive. They will be smarter and more evolved than any normal wolf. We must be cautious."

As they rested throughout the day, Will and Mica fell asleep for a couple of hours and then woke up and talked some more. They talked about everything, all their feelings and experiences over the last year.

"Will?" said Mica thoughtfully while they were lying peacefully in the tree, looking at the azure-blue sky. "I am glad you have been my companion throughout everything. I wouldn't want to be with anyone else."

Will was silent, and then he whispered, "Me too."

Mica smiled and fell asleep, dreaming of things she had never dreamed of before. Will watched Mica while she slept, etching the shape of her face into his mind and replaying her words.

"Me too," he repeated to himself, smiling, and then he fell asleep.

When they woke up, Will noticed the wolves had started dragging wood over to their tree and were piling it on top of one another.

"What in the name of Gaia?" Will asked incredulously. "Are those wolves actually making a den?"

Suddenly, Mica put her hand over her mouth. "Oh my stars, Will, they are trying to build a ladder to get to us!"

"That's ridiculous!" retorted Will. "Wolves don't build ladders!"

"Hybrid ones do," replied Mica.

Mesmerized, she watched a few of the wolves drag more pieces of old wood to the bottom of their tree. One of the wolves jumped on and tried to climb the woodpile; he almost made it to the top, about five feet off the ground. Then suddenly, he fell back, and the pile collapsed. Will and Mica were about twenty feet up in the tree, just watching in disbelief as the wolves tried to stack the wood again.

"They might eventually figure it out." Mica stared at them in disbelief.

"But not before morning," replied Will.

Will and Mica lay quietly, listening to the monotonous falling and rebuilding of the woodpile by the wolf pack.

"It's a good job these wolves don't have opposable thumbs," commented Will.

"Where are the rest of the pack?" asked Mica, now very concerned.

"They must be hiding or sleeping," mumbled Will.

Both Will and Mica fell asleep and were woken up two hours later by the wolf pack yapping, barking, and snarling.

Mica peered down. It was now dark, but there was a bright, light full moon, so she could see the wolves feeding on the carcass of a freshly killed deer. The metallic smell of blood filled the night air.

"Will, I don't believe this. Some of the wolves left to hunt a meal, but the others stayed here guarding us. They must be very intelligent. I wonder what the Archa did to them."

"They have no intention of leaving," said Will. "Now I am convinced. The wolves will wait until we are too weak to stay up in the tree. Then they will kill us. We have to use the stunners, or we will die," suggested Will solemnly.

Mica agreed. "We have no choice but to stun them now. We can't wait until they have finished eating, because they will slip back into the shadows and we won't have them all together in a pack for another few days. We need to do it right now."

"Yes," replied Will. "They may not hunt for another few days, and that will be too late for us."

They quickly packed up their equipment, and when they had finished, they looked down at the ferocious wolves, who were still busily tearing the deer carcass apart.

Will whispered to Mica, "You take out the left side of the pack, and I will take out the right, on three. One…two…three!"

Quickly they took out the whole pack, stunning the wolves in seconds.

"We must go now," whispered Mica fearfully, "the smell of their kill will bring other predators."

Across the moonlit skies, several Skybirds were searching, and finally, one patient pilot found what he was looking for, the energy blinks of a stunner far to the north.

"Headquarters," he radioed, "I have just seen a stunner light far north. Repeat, Operation Predator, I have just seen stunners used far north."

"This is Headquarters. All planes return to Headquarters. We will brief you on your new mission, Headquarters out."

The pilot smiled; that bonus would buy him some delights he always wanted but never could afford. He turned back toward Headquarters, which was located near the old training grounds.

Will stared at the sky intently for a moment. There were a lot of Skybirds, all of which suddenly turned together, probably going back to Headquarters somewhere near to the Archa compound.

"I think the Skybirds and Hoppers have seen our stunners," he said to Mica, dismayed.

"Yes," she said sadly, agreeing with him. "I saw all those Skybirds turn too."

"We need to leave now, even though it is dark," said Will, who, by this time, was very apprehensive about their whole situation.

Will climbed down from the tree first, holding his stunner while looking for stray wolves hanging near the pack. All he saw was a couple of little cubs fighting over the most significant feast they had ever seen, and they paid no attention to him.

Will didn't see the alpha wolf raise one eyelid, staring at him with his big yellow eye. He curled his lips, revealing his double rows of very sharp teeth, but he was still too stunned to move. He couldn't fight the exhaustion and fell asleep with the rest of his pack. But he would not forget the smell of humans. Or how they had outsmarted him.

Once, humans were kind to him when he was just a cub; they fed him, petted him, and his family slept in a warm barn. One day the humans became tired of them and threw him, his mother, his brothers, and his sisters out in a raging snowstorm to die. When his mother had howled and scratched at the door, they shot her dead, and the cubs ran off in fear. While running away, they had fallen through the snow into a little cave, where they curled up together to stay warm. Later, the pack came back to drag their frozen mother to their new lair, for food. It was their only way to survive. The alpha wolf would not forgive or forget their cruelty.

Next, Mica hurried down the tree, and the two former watchers disappeared into the moonlit night, unaware they were being watched themselves.

Out of the forest, several shadows moved. Their skin was colored various shades of green and brown and blended into the foliage perfectly. They were the ghosts of the forest and used an herb that disguised their scent from predators. The wolves had not seen them, smelled them, or heard them as they moved silently through the trees. They were like a breath, disappearing in a second, their feet barely touching the ground. They followed Will and Mica calmly into the night.

Mica asked Will, "Are you sure that we stunned all the wolves? I feel like we are being watched."

"I feel it too," replied Will anxiously. "It is a strange feeling."

"Perhaps it is a mountain lion stalking us," suggested Mica, feeling panicked as they moved noisily through the undergrowth. "We are making too much noise," she whispered, looking around, trying to see if any eyes were glowing in the darkness. But there were none.

"We have to move," replied Will. "We don't have a choice. Those wolves will only be stunned for an hour or two." He, too, was feeling the same panic as Mica.

Will felt like the creatures were coming closer and closer, and he was right.

Suddenly, Will and Mica felt a sharp sting on the sides of their necks, followed by a sensation of falling into a deep, dark abyss.

CHAPTER 16

Anna: The Keeper of the Words

Somewhere in the vast forest, in a small hut made of grasses, mud, bark, and branches, Will and Mica lay unconscious on a warm, downy bed that was raised about two feet above the floor. The simple wooden frame supported a mattress made of fabric and stuffed with feathers, lavender flowers, cedar chips, and soft mosses.

Their bodies were clothed in clean cotton shifts and covered with sheets and blankets. On the floor was a large woven reed mat and two handmade wooden chairs with a small matching table. Tallow candles sat inside hollowed-out rocks. Their belongings were neatly piled at the bottom of the bed. Their clothing had been cleaned and dried, and all their equipment was present and correct.

The small woven window was cracked open, and the door was slightly ajar so that a fresh breeze blew through the little hut and cooled the interior.

"Where are we?" asked Mica sleepily. She felt so tired and disorientated her limbs appeared heavy and were unable to move properly, and her head ached.

A woman's face appeared in front of her, smiling and blurry, but she didn't recognize her. The woman kindly held a wooden bowl to her mouth, and the icy, fresh water soothed her parched throat. Then Mica gratefully sank back into the abyss.

Will barely opened his eyes, and he saw the strange face from his dreams. It was standing over him, speaking the words that had haunted him for so long. "I have been waiting for you, Will."

Will tried to reply, but his lips felt numb, his arms didn't want to move, and his eyes wouldn't stay open. He thought the Archa had found them, and as he slipped back into the darkness, where there was no pain or terror, he thought he was dying and felt an overwhelming sense of relief.

Will and Mica finally woke up properly about twelve hours later. They were alone in the hut, and there were several hand-carved wooden bowls on the table, filled with water, fruit, meat, cheese, and bread.

"Where are we?" asked Mica drowsily.

"I don't know?" replied Will, trying to focus his eyes on the ceiling of the little hut.

"Should we eat it?" Mica asked, looking at the delicious food with her mouth watering. "Do you think it could be poisoned?"

"It is unlikely," Will replied hazily, trying to get his bearings. "I believe that we are being treated as guests, not prisoners."

"True," agreed Mica. She was so hungry and thirsty at that moment she didn't care if the food was poisoned or not.

Will and Mica ate all their food and drank a lot of water.

Mica noticed there was a big bowl of warm water and a couple of white cloths next to it, with some fragrant liquid soap in a stone dish. Mica washed her face and hands; the soap smelled like wildflowers. "Oh, smell this, Will," she urged. "It's beautiful."

Will buried his face into the wet cloth and breathed deeply, smelling the sweet fragrance of wildflowers. Then he wiped his hands and the back of his neck. They were both feeling much better and more alert again.

"Who do you think captured us?" asked Mica, still feeling slightly disorientated.

"I would guess, judging from our surroundings, the Nahu have found us," replied Will.

Mica looked at the hut more carefully. "I think you are right," she said and breathed a sigh of relief.

"We are still being hunted by the Archa, and we are not welcome or safe anywhere else," remarked Will honestly.

"A traumatic event always precedes any form of change in life. One path is destroyed, yet another one appears. It is simply the way reality works," remarked Mica wisely.

"How did you come to be so insightful?" Will asked, impressed.

"I don't know?" replied Mica. "I just feel it," she continued. "We are home, yet we are not. I don't know where we belong anymore."

Will interrupted her. "Mica, why would you want to be oblivious to reality? I don't understand. You would still be working in the First City slavery camp for a minimum lifestyle with no way out. Death was the only way to leave there, and everybody was murdered at the age of sixty-five by a tyrannical and corrupt society who lied to us. Our reality and everything we knew to be the truth was all a lie. Our whole existence was a lie," retorted Will angrily. "How can you possibly miss that?"

Mica thought for a few seconds. "But it wasn't a bad life, was it? We did not know any different, and everybody seemed happy," replied Mica calmly.

"Of course they were happy—they were in a drug-induced bliss!" exploded Will. "Those citizens were not given any other choice. They were just trained puppets, performing in predictable patterns, following a script written by some of the most corrupt and evil beings in the entire universe!"

"I suppose you are right," agreed Mica, "but it is still very complicated…"

Their conversation was cut short by a woman walking into the hut. She was much older than them, but her age was hard to define because she walked with such grace and dignity. She was wearing her long gray hair tied at the base of her neck with a wooden clasp, a clean white shift and beautifully carved tribal wooden jewelry around both her neck and wrists. A cloud of lavender scent moved with her. Her voice was gentle and melodic. She looked directly at Will and spoke softly.

"I have been waiting for you, Will."

Then she smiled at both of them. She had a sincere and friendly smile that lit up her pale green eyes. Somehow she had a very calming presence.

She spoke again in a gentle voice. "I am Anna. I am the Keeper of the Words for my people, and they are not called the Nahu." At that word, she spat on the ground in disgust. "I must clean my mouth so the rest of my words are not bitter."

Will could not believe his eyes; he was looking directly at the strange woman from his dreams, but this time, she was clearly in focus.

"You are from my dreams," said Will, standing up far too quickly, feeling light-headed, dizzy, and confused all at the same time.

"Yes," Anna replied quietly.

"How is that possible?" asked Will.

Anna put her finger to his lips. "The answers will come in the order they were meant to be heard," she said firmly and didn't remove her finger until he nodded.

Anna continued, "I keep the history of our people alive. We are the tribe of Terranze, and we have always been here, in one form or another. The Terranze are wise and gracious people; who wish to live their lives in freedom."

Mica, unable to contain herself, interrupted rudely. "I did not know you can talk. The other Nahu—er, Terranze couldn't speak."

Anna explained patiently, "It is our protection, my dear child. If the Archa thought we could talk, they would torture us for information. They believe that we are babbling half-wits. It suits us well that they believe this."

Anna continued, "I am also a healer for my tribe. We, the Terranze, believe that we are all connected to the universe, every rock, tree, animal, and being. When you are connected to everything, there is no linear time. Everything is there, the past, the present, and the future, all in one space. It was how I was able to enter your dreams. I am sorry if you felt fear. It was not my intention."

"Who told you I was coming?" questioned Will, still not understanding her explanation.

"It is not easy to explain, to make the answer more straightforward. It was the universe who told me," replied Anna.

"How?" asked Will. "I don't understand."

"It is like the small communication devices you talk to one another with," she explained very patiently.

"Oh," replied Will. "Do you mean a talker?"

"Yes," replied Anna. "You speak words on a particular frequency, do you not?"

Will nodded.

"Well," she continued, "if one of you is on a different frequency, he will not hear the other. It is only when you share the same frequency you can talk."

"Yes," said Will with sudden clarity. "I think I understand. Anna, you are on the same frequency as the universe, I am not," he said, "because I could not talk back to you."

"That is so," replied Anna, "but you will be able to learn this, just as you learned to use the talker."

Will nodded in agreement.

"There are many things I must tell you," announced Anna.

"Why me?" asked Will, still perplexed and staring at Anna.

Anna looked at him and spoke very clearly. "You are the changer."

"The changer?" asked Will. "What is that?"

"You were chosen to balance things here on Earth," replied Anna quietly.

"How can I do that?" Will asked, now utterly bewildered.

"You will find a way," she replied, smiling, "because you are the changer."

"When do I have to change things?" he asked, still unsure of what precisely a changer did.

"When the time is right," replied Anna, "you will know. Will, you will feel it, not just in your mind, but in your heart and spirit too."

Anna spoke earnestly. "Tomorrow is the time that I will tell you the truths of the ancient ones. You will understand many things after you hear this story, but now it is time to rest your bodies and your minds. I will see you during the dawn hours."

Then she smiled at both of them and turned to leave the hut on her cloud of lavender scent. She walked through the doorway and disappeared.

Mica sat quietly, still amazed by everything that had just happened.

Will said, "I think we are where we are supposed to be."

"Yes," replied Mica with conviction, "we are."

Feeling suddenly weary, they rested for a few hours and woke up to a delicious smell.

"I am starving," announced Mica.

"Yes," replied Will.

As if on cue, a brown-eyed young woman, with sun-kissed skin and beautiful long black hair that reached her waist, walked into the hut. She was carrying two steaming wooden bowls filled to the brim with stew and a chunk of warm bread on a large wooden tray. They thanked the woman, who smiled at them.

"My name is Rayna," she said quietly and left as Will and Mica began to demolish the food.

"This is the best food I think I have ever eaten," remarked Mica, licking a wooden spoon that matched the bowls.

Will replied, "It is good, but I liked the food better at the Archa Compound."

"Ah, no," said Mica, smiling, "this food is made with love, I can taste it. And besides that, the company is so much better."

Will was unsure what to say to that particular comment. Somehow, the word *love* was uncomfortable to him; it was not a word he had ever used. *What is* love? Will wondered. *What does that word really mean? To each person, it probably means something different.*

After they had finished eating, Rayna came to collect their dishes and brought them more fresh water. Still feeling exhausted and still effected by the blow dart, they both fell asleep.

CHAPTER 17

~ ✿ ~

The Hive of Archon

The following day after breakfast, Anna returned to Will and Mica's hut to tell them the story about the Hive of Archon and the human race. Anna was accompanied by Rayna, who was holding a tray of tea, and a warrior carrying a tribal drum.

"First, we must drink some of this ceremonial tea," announced Anna, smiling. "It will help you see the vision that I see. It is made from a plant that has no name so others cannot find it and abuse it."

As Rayna began pouring the tea, the warrior started to beat his drum rhythmically, like a beating heart.

"Do not ask any questions until I have finished. This story was handed down to me with honor and respect, so you must listen to all my words," stated Anna firmly.

Will and Mica nodded, silently sipping the bittersweet red liquid. After they had finished their tea, they began to feel light-headed and relaxed. Everything seemed to look different to them, as if they could see beneath the very layers of existence while being mesmerized by the hypnotic drumming.

Then Anna began her story.

"Many eons ago, even before the birth of the stars and the universe, there was a place called the Void. It was a place of deliberate darkness, where the blackness oozed slowly within the confines of the bitterly icy void. Such coldness was neither measurable nor imaginable to humans."

Will and Mica both shivered; it seemed as if they were standing there on the edge of the black void; it was a terrible and desolate place, so different from their beautiful and vibrant Earth.

Anna continued, her voice entranced them, and they both could see what she saw. Somehow their bodies were still in the little hut, yet they were not. It felt like they were traveling in their minds. They were actually connected to the Akashic records of the universe, where all knowledge was held. A person just had to know how to communicate with them, and Anna did.

Anna continued her story while Will and Mica were mesmerized by the drumbeat in the distance.

"The beings that lived in the Void called themselves the Hive of Archon. They had no definite form. Their nanoparticles just drifted like long twisting wisps of smoke. They moved and swarmed together, working like a hive."

Will and Mica were able to see this strange black life-form swirling about them like dust particles.

Anna began to speak again. "The Hive wanted to evolve because, without light and form, they could only exist in the darkness of the Void. They wished to leave the Void and explore other universes and dimensions of space and time.

"So for millions of years, the Hive of Archon traveled together in a dense, dark cloud, roaming the icy void, desperately trying to find a way to escape out of it.

"Eventually, they encountered a young and primitive life-form that was just starting to become self-aware. The Gemins were just fragile filaments of dark matter strung together in colonies that looked like strands of black pearls. They floated along gently in the dark outer reaches of the Void—a peaceful and elementary race."

The Gemins appeared small, round, soft, and gentle to the watchers.

"Initially, the Hive approached the Gemins with idle curiosity, but as they came closer, the Hive detected something exotic emanating from the little life-forms. It was both new and intoxicating to them.

"Instinctively, the Hive began devouring the Gemins in a maniacal feeding frenzy, like a shoal of piranha fish furiously attacking their prey. However, they were actually absorbing the pheromones of intense terror that was evaporating from the dying little Gemins."

Mica had to look away as the poor little Gemins were eaten alive. She felt their terror, and suddenly, she smelled a bitter, metallic smell. It smelled just like Malus!

"The Hive of Archon had now discovered a new, compelling, and addictive elixir that they would never stop looking for. They had also found the ultimate form of power, which is the control over life and death. The Hive had now become gods in their dark, icy realm.

"The whole purpose of the Hive's existence changed. Now they existed only to conquer and consume. They hunted relentlessly. The more beings they consumed, the stronger the Hive of Archon became, and their consciousness expanded into darker and darker realms."

Both Will and Mica shivered because they could feel the Hive's evil realm. It was so dark that it had no beginning and no end. It was thick, filthy, and cloying.

"The Hive had learned during their predatory infestation of the Void that a very powerful and immortal light being existed in a different dimension and universe to theirs. It was the realm of light.

"The Hive of Archon tried to find a way to construct a stable portal between their dark realm and a new light realm, because, above all, the Hive craved this gift of immortality, but they could not achieve it in the Void because they were not created with a spirit or a soul. When an Archon expired, they faced permanent annihilation.

"So the Hive grew more driven and ruthless, desperately searching for the secret of immortality, so the dark ones could consume their addictive elixir of death forever.

"About seven million years ago, they managed to build a portal between the two realms of dark and light so they could invade planet Earth. They had to take a body in our three-dimensional universe, so each Archon was to be fitted with a type of technically created pseudospirit or soul-circuit embedded in the back of their neck. The

Archons would be controlled, sustained, and powered by negative energy from all the dark entities of the Hive.

"However, as hard as they tried, every portal they made was so unstable that it collapsed almost immediately as it opened.

"One day, an unusual glitch occurred within the portal, and somehow, the Hive managed to send through twelve of their most advanced Archons. These beings were trained in occult knowledge, science, and technology, through the portal, to land on Earth. Then it collapsed forever."

In their vision, Will and Mica saw the air near them start spinning and swirling into a vast roaring, howling pitch-black sphere. It spun faster and faster, almost to the speed of light, emitting high-velocity winds and ejecting intense electromagnetic pulses that ripped the vegetation from the ground with such intensity it flung the torn plants, splintered trees, crushed rocks, and broken bodies of animals over several devastated miles.

Suddenly, twelve peculiar, cocoon-like black pods came flying out of the portal and bounced on the ground in all directions, eventually settling among the debris. They were still smoking. The portal vanished in a microsecond. Then there was a strange stillness. The whole process had taken just one single Earth second, and yet that one second would change the planet forever.

"On their arrival, the cold, slow Archons were unprepared and found Earth to be a vivid, bright, alien world that overloaded and overwhelmed their minimal senses.

"They were all stranded on this terrible planet. For the first time, the dark ones were filled with an intense, crushing terror. The twelve Archons had never felt so alone and individual before because they were now permanently disconnected from their collective Hive.

"Immediately after arriving, all the Archons uncoiled and burst from their cocoons and dropped to their knees, paralyzed and howling with fear. It was a strange and terrible noise after the blissful silence of the Void. Their lamentations shook planet Earth, causing earthquakes, landslides, and volcanic eruptions."

Will and Mica covered their ears as the Archons howled. Then they just watched these beings with a strange, morbid fascination.

They looked just like Malus. Will and Mica had never seen Malus without his cloak. They wondered what these alien beings would do next.

Anna continued her story.

"The Archons felt loose and unfettered, as if their whole body might just float away forever and be lost in the eternity of space. A strange misconception, considering the incredible power of Earth's gravity. For many centuries, they would only move while they were physically attached to one another via long twisted vines.

"In the Void, the Archons had formed dense clusters of nanoparticles made of dark matter that could change form at will. On Earth, the Archons finally bore a solid form that felt heavy and contorted, and the air felt like a thick and sticky liquid that was hard to breathe.

"The Archons had no real names and referred to one another as 1 of 12, 2 of 12, and so on. They had translucent black skin, and underneath their skin were strange gold symbols, but they weren't static because they could morph and change according to their owner's mood. They were about seven feet tall, gaunt and androgynous-looking, with no visible reproductive organs.

"The Archons had no body hair at all, and their enormous eyes were solid black, and their pupils were gold and vertical, like a snake's. Their noses looked like three vertical slits that moved independently as they breathed the harsh, potent air into their parched lungs. They had no outer ears, just three small jagged holes in each side of their head that could clench shut in the water or dust storms. Their double lips were thick, rough, and raspy.

"They had elongated skulls with a narrow chin and broad forehead. Their jaw muscles were enormous and could dislocate at will. Like a snake, they could feed on much larger prey. They had double rows of sharp white teeth and a long reptilian tongue that they would flick out continuously to taste the air. They were perfectly designed predators. They were stronger, far more intelligent, and many eons ahead of the simple Earth creatures.

"They had to learn to move all their limbs in a coordinated fashion, but due to the thick air and disabling gravity, they invariably collapsed. They began to walk like babies on all fours at first, but gradually they became used to standing on two feet. Their legs locked backward at the knee yet still bent forward.

"The Archons did not understand physical pain and all sensations felt by the mortal body. Eating, digesting, and then passing food was a bizarre experience for them. At first, they thought they were losing vital body parts. The Archons eventually realized that they were expelling water and waste products through one small orifice at the bottom of their left foot, which remained tightly closed when not being used. The bottom of their right foot was sacred and produced DNA at certain times for breeding purposes."

While Anna was talking, the Archons moved perpetually in slow motion, seemingly to barely move at all. Will and Mica were walking around the Archons and staring at their ugly forms. As Mica peered into the face of one of them, it seemed to blink deliberately at her, which terrified her, and she immediately ran back to stand with Anna. Will, too, was unnerved by these strange creatures.

"Although they could absorb some nutrients through their skin, over time, they all became weak, so some decided to eat plants and fruit. The three Archons who preferred the more familiar, darker realms lived in deep, dark caves, only coming out at night to catch and devour small prey alive.

"Trying to communicate and form verbal language was very hard for the Archons, so in the beginning, they spoke to one another telepathically. While speaking in a language, the Archons had a tendency to hiss, spit, and growl when pronouncing words. So they learned to speak slowly and carefully.

"It took them many years to try to recognize and operate all the five senses relative to the Earth.

"Because the light on our planet was brighter than anything they had ever seen in the Void, their eyes could only function properly in the dark, or with thick black goggles they had brought with them through the portal. They wore them during the daytime.

"Initially, the heat was oppressive to them, and early on, their skin frequently blistered in the sun. It was also sensitive to the touch, and even a simple breeze blowing on their bodies was excruciatingly painful. It took many long years for their skin to adapt to the sun before they could even try to clothe themselves.

"Earth was too bright, vivid, and overwhelmingly chaotic to their dark Archonic senses. It was so brilliant and pure on Earth that eventually, nine of their hearts changed, and they began to embrace the light and find acceptance of their new lives. As they physically evolved and adapted to planet Earth, the actual structure of their DNA was changed by particles from the sun, and some of the darkness in their hearts was replaced by light.

"The three remaining Archons, 7 of 12, 8 of 12, and 9 of 12, rejected the light realm. They were terrified of how it might intrinsically change them. They wanted to remain the dark overlords and wait for the return of the Hive of Archon. So naturally, they sought the darkness underground, and as time passed, they became more paranoid and convinced the hive could come back any day. So they practiced only the darkest of arts.

"It took all the Archons a millennium to adjust to their new life, which initially they had all believed was temporary, until the Hive of Archon could create another portal. What the stranded Archons did not realize was that the Hive would take millions of years before they were able to acquire and perfect the technology and knowledge to stabilize the portal.

"In this beautiful and wild garden called Earth, there was no technology, and the Earth creatures were not typically aggressive toward the Archons. One of the small beings was a primitive type of homind. It was a strange, new life-form for them to observe. The creatures amused the Archons, some of whom had even learned to laugh at their antics, which the Graecopthicus Freybergi performed quite happily for various treats and interactions.

"One summer night, many millennia after the Archons' arrival, they summoned all twelve members of the group to a meeting under a glorious red apple tree.

"The leader, 1 of 12, said, 'We have been trapped here for an extended time. We may even expire before the Hive of Archon finds a way to bring us back or open another portal.'

"'They will find us soon,' insisted 8 of 12 confidently. The others ignored him.

"Then 3 of 12, the lead scientist, spoke. 'We have been controlled by the Hive long enough. Here we could be masters of our destiny.'

"'When the Hive finds us," remarked 8 of 12, shocked by these words of treason, 'then we will be annihilated. I will not do this, because I am a loyal and obedient Archon. I will have no part of this insurrection. I want to prepare for my master's return.'

"And then 7 of 12 and 9 of 12 agreed with 8 of 12, but they were torn between loyalty to the Hive and a better life on Earth. So they grudgingly went along with the group's plans.

"'Doesn't a master have slaves?' responded 5 of 12 as he glared at 8 of 12.

"'I am tired of living in the dirt and catching my food,' agreed 5 of 12 wearily.

"And 8 of 12 shot him a caustic look. 'We are still Archons,' he growled. 'What has this cursed light realm done to some of you?'

"'Well,' retorted 12 of 12 sarcastically, 'perhaps it has changed us for the better.'

"'No, it has not!' replied 8 of 12 emphatically. 'It has made you weak. The predator has become the prey. You should feel great shame.'

"'Ridiculous!' replied 2 of 12, irritated at 8 of 12's ignorance. 'You are missing the point, you know,' said 2 of 12 to the others. 'We can all become gods in this light realm.'

"'Indeed,' agreed 6 of 12, relishing the thought. 'It is a good plan. Slaves would make our lives much better.'

"'Yes. It is hard work to survive here on this strange, primitive planet,' complained 4 of 12 as a shiny red apple dropped from the tree above directly into his lap.

"And then 3 of 12 spoke again. 'We could genetically modify some of the species here. Perhaps we could make the little hairy ones a fraction smarter so they could follow our orders and walk upright like us and use their hands to carry, lift, and dig. They need some strength, but they cannot be allowed to overpower us.'

"'Let's make lots of slaves who can look after our every need,' agreed 6 of 12 enthusiastically.

"The majority decided to follow the plan and were all in agreement, except for 8 of 12, who slithered back underground to sulk in his damp, dark cave.

"Ignoring the dark one, the remaining Archons set up a makeshift laboratory using what little technology and equipment they had brought with them. It took a series of experiments with many of the creatures that walked the Earth, but all the hybrids they created died.

"Finally, 3 of 12 told the others, 'I think we will have to mix a small amount of our DNA with the little hairy ones to get the right combination for intelligent life to exist.'

"This decision caused much dissent among the group of twelve. As the apex predators in their realm, the use of Archonic DNA for any purpose was forbidden because they wanted to keep their genetic line pure and uncontaminated. It was a belief all the Archons shared.

"Still, 2 of 12 and 3 of 12 decided to defy the rest of the group. They added a tiny amount of their DNA to the little hairy ones. The hybrids that resulted were big furry giants who were somewhat stupid but placid and agreeable.

"For many years, the giants built some enormous, tall, and amazingly complex structures around the Earth using their tremendous strength. It took eons to create all the monuments because the giants had to be continuously monitored for every single action they undertook, which was very exhausting and time-consuming for the Archons.

"Unfortunately, the Archons got braver and began experimenting recklessly, trying to create a more self-reliant and intelligent giant. They must have inserted too much of the Archonic aggression gene into the beings, because the monsters they made were vicious and predatory and began terrorizing the rest of the creatures on Earth. They wiped out many species native to the planet until, at last, they were all destroyed in a worldwide flood deliberately created by the Archons to kill them. The whole episode was a complete disaster.

"Deciding that the problematic giant era was behind them, the Archon scientists, 2 of 12 and 3 of 12, believed they had no choice but to insert some special genes from their DNA into a unique hybrid. They had to create beings that would be both compliant and intelligent enough to suit their needs.

"After the fiasco with the giants, the other ten Archons did not want to create any more hybrids, but they still wanted slaves to feed them, clothe them, and build them a society. Most of them ignored all the genetic engineering and cloning, except 7 of 12 and 9 of 12. They both finally broke from the rest of the group permanently and joined 8 of 12 in the caves, horrified at what the others had done.

"Then 2 of 12 and 3 of 12 produced the first batch of humanoids. There were several pairs of males and females. They were all slightly different in appearance. Some were short and stocky with massive jaws. Others were taller and thinner, with less defined features. They were all about equal in the intelligence department.

"Finally, having found the right DNA combinations, which included using a primitive hominds, wild pigs, and their own DNA, the Archons made more and adapted these beings to grow quickly, mature fast, and breed continuously to increase the slave population. But like worker bees, they made their life span very short, to prevent them from accumulating wisdom and overpopulating the Earth.

"The Yellow Eyes were created by the surface Archons after the creation of the humans. The Archons had wanted to produce a more intelligent species than the humans in the hope that they could possibly help them close the portal permanently."

"However, the Yellow Eyes did not live up to the Archons' expectations, and 8 of 12 believed they should have been destroyed and not allowed to breed. In his opinion, the creatures had too much Archon DNA in them, but he had been overruled by the rest of the group.

"Originally, the Yellow Eyes were not as malleable or as passive as the humans. They also lived longer, were more warlike and devious, and although surprisingly, not more intelligent than the humans.

"They also had a very dark side. Once thousands of years ago, they became almost powerful enough to rise up against the Archons. They had demanded a higher status than the humans and wanted to be free and rule their own city. The Archons believed it was wise to keep them content since mind-altering chemicals did not affect them at all.

"This was a wise decision agreed upon by the Archons, because, over time, the Yellow Eyes lost their superior strength, their powerful warriors, and their wise elders. Hundreds of years of comfortable living, self-indulgence, and their pampered lifestyle had made them lazy, unfit, and emotionally weak. They were no longer a threat to anyone. They acted like a herd of cattle, and the humans…well, they were merely the sheep.

"Eventually, over time, only three distinct races remained: the humans, the Yellow Eyes, and eventually, the Archa."

Will and Mica were spellbound and in shock, realizing that all humans had been created by these hideous alien beings and were related to them. Now they knew the truth that the Yellow Eyes had come after the humans.

"The remainder of the Archons feigned anger at first, because 2 of 12 and 3 of 12 had committed a great wrong. They feared the wrath of the Hive if they ever found them again.

"Their created beings were trained to worship their creators like gods and learned to build cities and monuments to honor and serve the Archons. The Archons became accustomed to such deference and a comfortable life. They, in time, believed themselves to be gods too.

"They said to one another, 'We are no longer members of the Hive of Archon. We have evolved and created life, so we have become a new race of gods in this light realm.'

"They accepted the humanoids as their subjects and ruled over them for millions of years. The system worked, and there was relative peace on Earth.

"The members of the Hive who had chosen to live above the ground in the light with their creations, humanity and the Yellow Eyes, those Archons had started to develop some religious beliefs since they had been on planet Earth. They had begun to worship the sun as an all-powerful creator. They believed that the light particles had changed their DNA and created a type of spirit or soul because they did not want to accept the emptiness of annihilation at death.

They didn't realize that members of the Hive of Archon could never have an afterlife because they were not created that way.

"Eventually, the ancient Archons expired one by one. They were not immortal, as the humanoids believed. Several devastating Earth cataclysms occurred. Some were caused by the dark Archons and others by nature, and the endless cycles and unpredictability of the natural universe.

"Gradually, over time, all the technology the surface Archons had once created was erased. Their vast knowledge was lost, buried beneath new seas, frozen under miles of ice, or crushed under the new landmasses that rose up to meet the sky.

"Eventually, the history of planet Earth became confused, reduced to barely remembered fables and myths across the world. The few fragments of knowledge that remained were bound into different religious books, often rewritten, altered, and adapted by the dark priests for their personal agendas. Still, these books were worshiped by the peoples of the planet, who still mourned the loss of their seemingly wise and benevolent gods.

"As to the creation story of the Archa, the three dark Archons, 7 of 12, 8 of 12, and 9 of 12, who had separated from the others long ago, they had chosen to remain hidden in underground caves. They were protected by the Earth's crust and fared better than their surface counterparts, whom they despised. They believed, as loyal and obedient Archons, that they existed primarily to continue to try to aid the Hive of Archon to open a portal into the realm of light and achieve immortality.

"Surprisingly, through persistence and hard work, the three remaining Archons eventually discovered that different harmonics, tones, vibrations and certain combinations, would allow the portal to open for a nanosecond. Sometimes just long enough to let one dark entity through.

"No one knew where they came from, not even the beings themselves. Most came through the portal from a different universe or dimension to the Void, and they were unable to speak or think properly for themselves. They seemed to act merely on instinct. They were, however, flawless in following orders and killing. They became known as the black-eyed hunters, and they were used for protection and for hunting food for the three Archons who hated the light and despised leaving the darkness of their caves.

"Unfortunately, these black-eyed beings had to use a live humanoid body to have a form. Very much like a demonic possession. They were able to inhabit the bodies, but not the spirits, of the unfortunate humanoids they inhabited, because that required light, and they were all created from darkness, so they were only vaguely human in appearance. If you stared into their empty, entirely black eyes, they had no soul. They were very much like bio-robotic entities and functioned much in the same way, and they had very unpleasant pale, clammy gray skin and smelled of mildew and wet dogs.

"Maintaining control of the portal due to the instability of the vibrations was complicated. Sometimes the portal would refuse to open or just collapse during the transition. It was a delicate operation, so 7 of 12 abducted twelve humans and started to train a few of them in this ability. The Yellow Eyes were unable to perform at all. They, as a race, were tone-deaf. But some of the humans were magnificent at producing the exact sounds, tones, and harmonics needed.

"So 7 of 12, 8 of 12, and 9 of 12 decided to genetically modify their captive humans. They inserted specifically chosen genes to ensure they had no compassion or love in their hearts, so they would be easier to manipulate and corrupt. These new dark priests had been well trained by the cave-dwelling Archons to become a new breed of psychopathic hybrid humans, and trained to manipulate others, compulsively lie, hypnotize, and charm others of their species. They were taught that by using nefarious practices against their fellow beings, such as mass human sacrifice, war, genocide, and other atrocities, they could keep the rest of the population in constant stress and terror, thus making them much easier to control.

"These hybrid beings became priests of the dark arts and were named the Archa by the three remaining Archons. In actuality, the hybrids were learning the purest, earliest, and most primitive form of the dark arts. They practiced all the rites and rituals with great enthusiasm. The transformation of their DNA had destroyed any vestiges of humanity in these malevolent beings. They started wars and terrorized the Earth.

"They hoped there was also a small chance that the trail of terror pheromones emanating from the Earth's wars and strife would allow the Hive to track them through the ether.

"The Archa were taught how to consume pheromones of fear as an elixir. The Archons explained that the younger the victim was and the more intense terror it suffered, then the elixir would be much more powerful.

"The Archons didn't understand why once humanoids hit puberty, their composition changed, and the purity and power of the elixir were diminished by half. By the time humans were adults only 0.3 percent of this remained. For some unknown reason, the Yellow Eyes had a purer elixir than the humans, so they were preferred as victims.

"Elixirs could be gained by dark and sinister practices that became referred to as Satanism in later ages. The best elixir was produced during a humanoid sacrifice, a process that consisted of four steps on a single individual included:

1. Capture a very young humanoid, preferably a Yellow Eyes, and then spend thirty days just sleeping with and holding the victim to absorb their life energy.
2. Terrorize or torture said individual by letting them know they are going to die.
3. Follow with a violent sex act, during which the individual meets its demise in a very traumatic way, often skinned alive.
4. Elixir must be consumed while still physically connected to the victim, precisely at the point of death, just as the spirit leaves the body." The elixir is called adrenochrome.

Although Will and Mica had known many of the terrible things the Archa had done, the torturing and murder were always done behind closed doors. As watchers, they had known it happened, of course, but it was very different having every grisly detail revealed in a full-color vision. The vivid description of the Archa's perverted rituals caused both Will and Mica to run outside and vomit uncontrollably. It took time for them to calm down. After they had some fresh air and water, they returned to their hut and back to Anna's story.

"Every day the three Archons fed their pet Archa red wine and manna bread that was made from a special white powder acquired from the burning of gold.

"They showed the Archa the secrets of alchemy and how to change gold into powder by burning it at the temperature of the sun for seventy seconds. If the gold were thicker than usual, then the temperature had to be maintained for three hundred seconds. At a seventy-second burn, there was suddenly a vivid, bright flash, like a thousand suns, and all that remained was a residue of a strange white powder while the gold itself had vanished. Strangely, at that time, both the container and the powder became very light. Removing the said powder out of its container allowed the vessel to return to its normal weight.

"This process was called making monoatomic gold. The Archons told the Archa it would make them smarter, healthier, and live longer. They explained that humanoids had a similar white substance in their brains that allowed electronic impulses to pass through as thoughts because the white stuff was superconductive. They told them that gold was the best conductor of electricity.

"The Archons also taught the Archa that consuming the white powder, sometimes made from rhodium and iridium, accelerated the process of visions and spiritual expansion into the dark realms, where the ultimate power lay.

"They explained to their Archa that the chromosomes in their bodies continually divided themselves and caused their telomeres, the piece attached to the end, to get shorter and shorter. This caused aging and final death of the mortal body. The monatomic gold prevented the telomeres at the end of their chromosomes from shrinking so quickly. With this valuable information, they could live much longer than other humanoids and become superior to them intellectually, physically, and mentally. The Archons told the Archa that gold was the secret of power and life and to collect and hoard as much gold as possible. The other solution to longevity was constant blood transfusions from babies because their bodies contained stem cells which could also help with vitality and cure diseases.

"Predictably, the chosen Archa soon rose to unbridled power under the rigid guidance of their puppet masters and believed they were superior to others of their kind in value, intelligence, and bloodline.

"In the early centuries, the Archa ruled the world with iron fists and hearts of stone. They brought themselves vast mighty armies from coffers filled with stolen gold. They rewarded pirates, thieves, murderers, and the church with great riches. Many atrocities at that time were done under the guise of religion.

"By the end of the Chaos Era 1964–2029, the Archa families had been secretly in power for a very long time. Although there were not many of them, their insidious deceit through their secret societies contrived wars where the Archa financially backed both sides. Therefore making enormous profits and their daily manipulation of the monetary system and the subtle management of the masses via society and the media. The deliberate use of the Archa's silent weapons had won their silent wars. Life for the masses became a revolving cycle of war, peace, prosperity, and destitution that they purposefully maintained for their financial benefit.

"By the time 70 percent of the people had woken up to reality, it was too late. Society had become a tangled web of deception. It had become a restricted and a tightly controlled nightmare. The technology was now so far advanced it was possible to chip, track, control, and eventually, round up all the poor, dejected masses.

"Some people escaped to the land, foraging and hiding, but there were constant raids, and the majority were killed or died of disease and starvation because they had lost the skills to live off the land. The remainder of the public was broken by war, religious genocide, and firing squads.

"As planned so many years ago by the Archa, the masses willingly submitted to the Eco-Charter by begging on their knees for food, medicine, and mercy. Old memories of the freedom the people once held were erased by dogma, education, law, and the fact that no one lived past the age of sixty-five.

"The people were now indentured slaves who believed they were safe and protected while living a peaceful, meaningful life and believed they were content, but not as happy as the Archa, who owned them, and considered them property.

"The Archa would never let their secret knowledge or power fall into the hands of the uneducated, impoverished, and unwashed masses over which they ruled. These beasts, who lurked in the secretive, hallowed halls of real power, gleefully whispered to one throughout the ages, another 'mission accomplished.'

"Malus, formerly 8 of 12, was the last living Archon and had absolute power over everything that lived and breathed on planet Earth."

Anna said she believed he was breeding hatchlings somewhere on the planet to take over from him when he finally expired.

"One day, the Hive of Archon will achieve their goal and open the portal," said Anna very chillingly, "and we will see worldwide destruction on a scale that Earth has never seen."

Will and Mica had remained silent throughout her story. Finally, Anna paused for the first time since she began; she sipped some water and took a deep breath. Both Will and Mica were astounded by Anna's depth of knowledge about the history of planet Earth.

"Do you have any questions?" asked Anna.

"Why do darkness and evil have to exist at all?" Mica asked, frustrated by the supreme power of the Archons and the Archa.

"Planet Earth is the only place of free choice in the universe," replied Anna. "We are sent here to experience complicated lives so we advance spiritually. One lifetime on earth accelerates our spiritual growth as much as a hundred thousand years on another planet. Think on this: if life were always safe and comfortable, we would not be challenged at all. We would not progress at all. How would we recognize the light without the contrast of darkness? They balance each other."

"What happens if the Archa don't get their elixir?" asked Will, curiously.

"Like a rabid dog, there is no cure for the affliction they carry," replied Anna sadly.

"Can they ever be destroyed?" Mica asked.

"Everything that exists has a weakness. You just must find it," replied Anna thoughtfully.

"Where did the light realm come from?" questioned Will.

Anna smiled. "A good question, Will," she said. "In a hidden dimension, the light was born. It is believed that a life-form evolved that was so pure in spirit it developed a consciousness of only love and empathy."

Then she continued, "In the beginning, although still curled and small, it was filled with magical, harmonic tones and hues. As it grew, it was surrounded by a glorious, sparkling violet aura that shone like a beacon in the universe. So the whole entity glowed with eternal and ethereal beauty. This being was called the One. It was alone because it was the only light being in existence.

"The One wanted to learn about itself and share its light and love everywhere. It understood it could not know itself by just looking into the universe from its own lonely perspective. To ultimately share its love and light with other beings in space and time, the One had to sacrifice itself.

"So the One fragmented itself in a massive galactic explosion. This ultimate sacrifice of love shook the universe to its very core and filled it with light, stars, planets, and eventually, over billions of years, incredible new life-forms evolved. This sacrifice gave us immortality through our soul or spirit.

"Each fragment of light became a conscious being somewhere in the vast expanse of space and time. After each fragment had completed its journey of knowledge and experience, its material form, which is called the body, would die and disintegrate to be absorbed back into the material world. Then the tiny sparks of consciousness would, eventually, over millions of lifetimes, return to the One."

Anna continued, "It is prophesied that in the future, there would be a time when the One would be whole and complete again. At that time, each fragment will have returned back to the collective consciousness. They would be filled with ultimate wisdom, light, love and finally become integrated back into the beauty of the One."

"So we are all part of the One?" concluded Will correctly.

"We are all created as part of the One," explained Anna. "We choose by our life choices to remain connected to the One, or we sever that connection and sink into dark realms for things that are tempting at the time but, in the long term, bring much regret.

"Some beings only turn to the darkness for just a moment, but the evil drags them down to places where there is no escape. Because then their souls are pursued by the hounds of hell, who weave in and out of other dimensions, realities, and different universes, they move faster than the speed of light and they track you by your scent.

"Once they find you and consume you, they are then freed from their bond. It is the only way to earn their freedom, so they will never give up on a pursuit. Not ever. The consumed fragment caught by the hounds will eventually be reborn over and over until they finally turn to the light. This can take many lifetimes of intense suffering."

"What bond? Where do the hounds come from? Who holds their bonds?" asked Mica.

"No one knows," replied Anna, sighing, "but we should not speak of the hounds because they may hear us, and that could be dangerous."

"Anna, do you think the Hive of Archon could come back again in our lifetime?" asked Mica, terrified after what she had seen in the vision that they had shared.

"Perhaps, when they understand the concept of free will. It is an idea they cannot even conceive, let alone solve," replied Anna solemnly. "However, one day the Hive of Archon may achieve their goal and open the portal. On that day, we will certainly see the destruction of most of the human race."

Anna's words terrified both the watchers.

Then Anna paused and drank some more water and ate some food that Rayna had just served them. They ate in silence, all three of them deep in thought.

"Where did the Terranze come from?" asked Will, breaking the silence.

Anna smiled at Will. "That is the third story I need to tell you, the history of the Terranze, and it is sad and complicated. Although we have always existed, in one form or another, since our creation at the very beginning of the humanoid timeline. Long before the New Eco-Charter, but after the Archa changed our society and destroyed all individualism, until few remained.

"Those that survived lived in fear of persecution, torture, and death on a daily basis. While the religious genocide was happening, thousands escaped to the forest, but there were constant raids, and many people were either taken away or slaughtered, if they resisted.

"The Archa despised the wild ones because they could not control their behaviour or beliefs. So they began to dehumanize them via the media. They began to call them the Nahu, not animal and not human. Those people in charge of New Eco Charter made them targets. They were hated for refusing to comply. Several times they would arrange to kill their own hunters and then tear them to pieces. They would parade their mutilated corpses through the streets, where all citizens could see them. Predictably, the rest of the population began to hate the escaped ones and believed they were diseased and demented wild beasts. Bounties were placed on their heads. The Archa paid well for their capture—dead or alive.

"The tribe we were part of managed to survive undetected for some time, and we became very experienced at hiding. Many years ago, in 2147 during a bounty raid, I lost my husband, Herka, who was killed trying to defend our village. My brother Barga, my daughter Fina, and her son Kiron were all taken away.

"I will never forget that day! I had been alone collecting herbs when I heard a commotion coming from the village. Although I ran back as quickly as I could, it was too late. I realized that I could do nothing of value, and I could not save my child or friends.

"I was watching helplessly, hiding in the undergrowth, when I saw my beloved daughter on the ground, wrapped tightly in one of the nets, just a few feet from my hiding place. When our eyes met, I knew I wanted to be taken too and was about to move when she put her finger to her lips and tried to shake her head. Then, in an instant, she was gone, dragged away while screaming. I remember whispering, 'Fina, I love you,' to the empty air, and I remembered the words of Many Fires." Anna's voice faltered as tears streamed down her face. "That day haunts me," she whispered. "Her screams are burned into my soul forever."

Then she continued, "For a long time afterward, I was racked with survivor's guilt, but Fina was right. I couldn't have saved her, and I would have died too. She knew of the prophecy I had been given by Many Fires and that I had to wait for you to come here so I could tell you these stories. What you do with this knowledge is your choice. I cannot tell you what to do. Your future is written in the stars. Right or wrong, I have lived to fulfill my destiny, as painful as it has been. Will you live to fulfill yours?"

Will was so moved by Anna's story he had tears in his eyes. Slowly he spoke to Anna. "I need time to think about everything that you have told me today. I understand so much more than I did before."

Then Will cleared his throat and held Anna's small time-worn hands in his own, and then he said to her, "I am humbled by your stories. I owe it to you and all the people who have sacrificed themselves so I could live long enough to bring change to this world. I will follow my destiny. I will be the changer."

Anna smiled, still holding Will's hands, and said, "All is well."

The stories had taken most of the day to tell, and everybody was exhausted from the intense experience they had just gone through together. For Will and Mica, there was a lot of new knowledge to process.

Anna told Will and Mica it was time to rest, and tomorrow they would meet the rest of the tribe. Then she left on her cloud of familiar lavender scent.

Rayna came in with more food and water for them. While they ate another bowl of steaming stew, Will and Mica talked about the incredible day they had just experienced.

"We knew nothing about this reality while living in First City, did we?" remarked Mica sadly.

"No, we didn't," replied Will slowly. "Anna certainly explained why Malus and his Archa are so evil. They were genetically bred to be exactly what they are. They can never change—they can only be," he remarked thoughtfully.

After Will and Mica had finished eating and Rayna came to collect their dishes, they realized they were both drained, and they fell asleep dreaming of strange worlds and alien beings.

The next day, Anna came to Will and Mica's hut about midday. She walked in and announced, "It is now the time for you to meet the rest of your people."

"*My* people?" asked Will, surprised. "I don't understand."

"Will, you are my daughter's son. You are my child's child who was taken so long ago," revealed Anna.

"How can you be so sure?" asked Will, shocked at Anna's words.

"You have a birthmark, a small teardrop, at the base of your neck, as did your father. I am sure it is you. You have the same features as him. You are his living image. Welcome home, my child's child, where you belong. Kiron…you bring my joy to my heart."

"Kiron was my birth name?" Will asked slowly, trying to comprehend the enormity of this revelation.

Anna nodded with tears of joy, unable to speak for a moment.

"Do you know what happened to my mother and the remainder of the family after the raid?" asked Will.

Anna replied sadly, "We think your mother, Fina, and my brother Barga died in the FEMA camp and were used for their organs. The Terranze are healthy and robust. We make good replacement parts for the Yellow Eyes.

"Your father, Herka, fought bravely until the end. He was our chief and the leader of our people, and so it was his duty to protect the tribe and die on our land. Barga's wife and child took poison. All the others from our tribe were taken and never returned, like Fina and Barga."

"I am not ready to lead the Terranze," replied Will, feeling suddenly proud to be a member of the Terranze tribe but still overwhelmed with grief and sadness for his parents, whom he had lost forever and yet he had never even known.

"Yes, you are," responded Anna firmly. "You have lived in First City. You understand the people there and the laws. You have spent time with the Archa. You know their strengths and weaknesses. And now you will spend many moons learning the ways of the Terranze. In time, you will be very ready to lead our people."

"The Archa will look for us," said Will, concerned. "They know we escaped."

"We left traces of your blood and clothing where the strange wolves live. They will think you have perished," replied Anna.

"Are we far away from where you found us?" questioned Will.

"About four days, but our village is very well hidden. We have managed to survive here peacefully for many years," replied Anna.

"But," replied Will, "they weren't looking for you, were they?"

"They will believe you are dead," insisted Anna.

"What about Mica?" asked Will.

"She is your companion, so she is part of you and your tribe," replied Anna warmly.

"Now," said Anna, "it is time to meet your people. They have been waiting a long time for your return."

As the watchers stepped out into the warm pale-yellow sunlight, they could see all the villagers had gathered for the occasion.

Anna addressed the people loudly, raising her arms and holding her palms open to the sky. "I give thanks to the One. Today, after thirty-three years, the leader of the Terranze, Kiron, has finally returned home to his tribe."

Led by Tiern, a wise and stoic leader, the warriors, who were in full camouflage and pointing their spears to the sky, let out the victory war cry, while the women and children stomped their feet and whooped. For the prophecy had been told long, long ago, that when the lost son of the last living chief returned, he would be a changer and finally a new era of peace would reign over the Earth and her children, the Terranze.

Everyone was happy, and a big celebration meal had been made. An enormous wild boar was roasting on a spit over the village campfire, and everywhere there were baskets of fresh fruit, baked bread, platters of goat cheese, and boiled eggs. Pottery jugs were filled with an elderberry and raspberry wine, which was delicious and left a warm glow in your body after it was drunk. Anna told Will and

Mica to be careful; it was potent, and they were not used to drinking alcohol.

After the meal, ceremonial dances were performed first by the warriors, then the women and children. After the tribal dances, everyone just danced to the beat of the drums during the village celebration dance.

Will and Mica danced awkwardly for the first time in their lives. It was disconcerting to both of them when the villagers came up and just hugged them, because such spontaneity and physical closeness to other people had never been part of their culture before.

Will now understood what love was. It was the complete acceptance of another being that came from the heart, and he was surrounded by it. Will had never felt so loved, and impulsively he bent down and kissed Mica softly on her cheek. She turned her face toward his, and they shared their first real kiss. About a hundred people, who had become their family overnight, all cheered, and the celebration continued until the early hours of the morning.

As the sun rose at dawn, lighting the sky with shades of rose and gold, Will and Mica sat on a small hilltop overlooking the village. They sat there for a while, just drinking in the glory of the sunrise and watching the smoke from the village fire as it twirled into feathery waves beneath them.

Will told Mica, "I don't think I was ever truly happy with myself until today. I always felt there was something inexplicable missing from my life, and no amount of medication stopped that feeling of emptiness. I believed that was how life was and accepted it, but you are part of all this, Mica, and I want you to be with me for always."

Mica leaned into Will, rested her head on his shoulder, and smiled. She murmured, "Yes, Will, I truly understand. I feel the same way, and I cannot imagine life without you."

They walked back to their hut, still holding hands, and closed the door. As their clothes slipped silently to the floor, they stood naked in the pale pink light, which was now stretching across the painted skies. Will took Mica's hand and pulled her down slowly to their bed.

For just a moment, they just stared at each other so intensely they could see into each other's soul. They started kissing, and sensations of desire snaked up their spines. For the first time, they touched each other's soft, naked skin with long and slow strokes, exploring, caressing, and kissing each other. Will began to kiss Mica's neck and breasts, sucking and licking each one, igniting a burning desire that glowed profound and primal in their bellies.

From their lips came words of love. Will leaned down to Mica, down to where her flesh was as soft as silk, tasting her. She was filled with glorious waves of burning, sensual heat rippling across her entire body. As Mica felt Will slip inside her, their bodies entwined together. They were slick with sweat, moved slowly and rhythmically, then faster and faster, until they spiraled higher and higher together and they exploded into brilliant violet-purple light. Kaleidoscope of colors flew around them as they were connected, not merely to each other, but to the entire universe. Their spirits were spinning and spiraling in harmony, and around them, stars burned brightly.

"We are you, we are me, we are one," whispered Will breathlessly, and each breath was a cosmic connection to everything that had ever existed or would exist. Will and Mica were in a place somewhere in space and time that the liquid purity of their love had created. Afterward, they were quiet and still, lying in each other's arms, lost in the beauty and intensity of the love they had just shared.

Much later, they arose and went to the shower rooms. There were little cubicles in two different huts, one for men and one for women. The water pressure wasn't that powerful, but the water was warm, and there were fragrant-smelling soap and clean, handwoven towels. They dressed in their uniforms and boots, complete with their various weapons. They wanted to be ready for anything. Mica rubbed her ragged hair, glad that it was finally growing again. She wanted it to become really long, like those of the other women in the village. They all had such beautiful hair.

Will and Mica ate some fruit, cheese, eggs, and bread for breakfast. They fed each other, teasing, laughing, and joking with each other as lovers do. After eating their morning meal, Will became serious. "Mica, I want to think how to plan a coup. I want to destroy the Archa and give the people on Earth back their freedom."

Mica said very carefully, "I agree. Destroying the Archa is a service to mankind. They are not human, they are evil and corrupt. But I wonder, Do you really think that all the people in the cities wish to know the truth?"

"At first, I didn't believe that, but that was back at the Compound. Now I feel different. All the people of First City deserve the ability to live and love as they wish," replied Will.

"But it was so hard for us. It will be more difficult for those who are old and very young," answered Mica slowly.

"Why?" asked Will, surprised. "Don't you think they want to be free to learn to love and feel and live like us?"

"I think many people might agree, but there will be some that won't because they are either too old or afraid," replied Mica.

"Destroying Malus and the Archa will be a difficult task, but not impossible. Not now. We have the support of the Terranze, who are remarkable warriors. I was thinking about asking the animal hybrids for their help too, because they despise the Archa," remarked Will.

"Yes," agreed Mica, "that's an excellent idea. I wonder where they went."

"I don't know," replied Will, "but I hope they made it to somewhere safe, after all the abuse they suffered. They were held captive in those caves for such a long time. If they were all Terranze originally, technically, they are still our people too, and we should help one another."

"We shall find them, Will, in the early spring. I believe they will make valuable friends and allies," replied Mica. "However, first we must learn to become warriors of the Terranze, and we have much to learn." She smiled at Will.

"That is very true, my wise and wonderful woman," replied Will, smiling back at her.

CHAPTER 18

Living Wild

During the remainder of the summer and then into the fall, Will and Mica learned many things from the Terranze. How to be so still that even their breath wouldn't stir a cobweb, and the ability to camouflage themselves in the woodlands. What they could eat from the land and which herbs cured illnesses. Will and Mica helped hunt and watched the village women tan hides, make candles and soap, weave fabric and wool, and cook. They worked together, learning everything they could, because the Terranze knowledge was critical to everybody's survival. Will and Mica were healthy and happy, embracing each day that they lived with the remarkable Terranze.

Tiern had accepted Mica as a warrior for the Terranze, which she learned was a great honor. She was the first woman warrior in the history of the Terranze tribe. Mica loved the life of a warrior, working alongside Will. Tiern was a remarkable leader and always calm and patient. He was tall, about six foot, and had long black hair and brown eyes, and every muscle on his body was defined. He rarely smiled because he lived to protect and serve the Terranze, and Tiern took his oath to his people seriously.

In the late fall, when the chill winds came and the nights became longer and darker, Anna told them it was time to move to the winter settlement in the caves beyond the enormous mountain.

The Terranze dismantled the village. The round houses were carefully put away in some small caves near the village site. When the Terranze had finished packing their winter supplies, the burnished leaves of autumn were starting to fall rapidly as the bare branches reached up to steely skies. Their happy home for so many months now looked like an abandoned village.

"How long is the journey to the caves?" asked Mica.

Will told her that Anna had said it was short, primarily because there was a secret passage that connected the summer village with the winter caves. They could relocate everything they needed through this tunnel without being seen. It took about two full days to move everyone and everything that they needed, including the animals. Will realized this was the secret to the Terranze longevity and survival. Only the hunters ever strayed far from their village, and they were almost impossible to track.

There was one of the Terranze who adored Will and followed him everywhere he went. She was young, about sixteen years old, and petite. She had a cascade of long silky dark hair that reached her waist and big greenish-yellow eyes (a very unusual color) fringed with very long black lashes. She looked like a porcelain doll. She flirted shamelessly with Will at every opportunity, making no effort to hide it. She was always shaking her rear end or leaning over him, exposing her ample cleavage. In Mica's opinion, she was devious and full of silly giggles.

She intensely irritated Mica, who wanted to swat her like a bug. Her name was Neyra, and she had many admirers, but unfortunately for Mica, she only had eyes for Will.

One day, Mica, fed up with Neyra's increasingly erratic behavior, broached the subject with Will.

She asked Will calmly, "Did you notice Neyra flirting with you today?"

"With me?" replied Will incredulously. "What reason would she do this? She is just a child."

"She thinks of you as a potential life partner," retorted Mica icily.

"But you are my life partner," replied Will, confused.

"Not in her opinion," Mica snapped uncharacteristically. "Will, if you haven't noticed by now—which you should have—she is extremely forward toward you and she completely ignores me."

"Oh," replied Will uncomfortably, not knowing what to say. "I didn't realize. I will speak to Neyra the very next time I see her and address this issue," he promised.

"Thank you," said Mica, feeling relieved.

The Terranze began walking slowly and steadily, heavily laden with their equipment, up to the tunnel entrance, toward the mountains and their new winter home.

Very shortly, Neyra bounced along next to Will and Mica. "It is a good day, Will, is it not?" chirped Neyra, smiling her big phony smile while pointedly ignoring Mica.

"Did you see how pretty the light of the dawn was this morning? How it shone on my hair and made my skin glow like the flesh of a ripened pear?" She flirted with Will by batting her eyelashes and giggling at him.

"A ripe pear. Oh my stars, that must be the most ridiculous metaphor I have ever heard. I hope the flies eat you alive," murmured Mica incredulously under her breath while shooting Will an irritated look.

"Neyra, I need to talk to you for a moment," replied Will awkwardly.

"In private?" She smirked hopefully, sneering at Mica, and then pouted her lips.

"No," replied Will uncomfortably. "I think well of you, Neyra, like a daughter. Mica is my life partner, and one day you, too, will find your life partner and be very content."

Neyra's beautiful face twisted in rage. "What good is she to you? She is old, big as a man, and it looks like rats have eaten her hair. I think you do not like a beautiful woman who would bear you many strong warriors. She cannot even give you a child. She is not like other women. She is like a dried leaf!" To emphasize her point, she crushed a dead leaf in her hands and blew the dried dust toward Mica's stunned face.

Then she ran ahead, fast, to join the front of the line, afraid that Mica might break her neck in one smooth move. Mica was seriously considering the option.

"May Gaia keep me sane," mumbled Will, shocked by what he had just witnessed. "That is too much emotion for me. I should order her back to apologize to you. She was very disrespectful and cruel."

"No!" Mica replied sharply, then she was silent for a moment. "Neyra is right. I cannot bear you warriors," she said sadly.

"I have a whole tribe of warriors right here," replied Will, "and we have important missions to plan. We are Terranze, but we will not follow all their ways. I need a warrior woman by my side, not a foolish child like Neyra. We have much to do, and I do not have time for this stupidity."

Mica smiled at Will. "Yes, we do," she said, "and many long winter nights to fill our time."

"Indeed," replied Will, catching her drift. He smiled back.

Neyra was not who she appeared to be. She was not born a Terranze, but she had been adopted by the tribe a long time ago when she was a small child. She had been found alone and orphaned near the Compound one summer. Somehow, she escaped a grisly death at the hands of Malus and the Archa, and she did not remember her past. Mica thought she looked like a hybrid between a Terranze and a Yellow Eyes. She said nothing to anyone about her suspicions but watched Neyra very carefully.

For the Terranze, it was a day of uneventful traveling through a long tunnel system up toward the winter cave. After they had exited the tunnel, the cave was relatively close, probably less than a mile away. They arrived at the winter cave just as it had started to snow. Big soggy flakes were falling from icy white skies, and from the north came a bitter, howling wind, announcing that winter had begun her reign.

The warriors quickly moved a few big rocks that blocked the cave entrance; they were used to prevent bears and other animals from hibernating or sheltering in there.

The cave entrance was about five feet high and about six feet wide. The Terranze began filing into the cave passage. The passage was relatively narrow for the first ten feet, and then it opened out into a vast cathedral-size hall, with many shelves and ledges. There was a rock room, as it was called, immediately to the right.

The Terranze used the rock room as a latrine. It was similar to an old medieval midden. Inside the room were woven screens separating different holes in the ground. Each hole was a deep pit. When a people used the bathroom, they threw a bucketful of "mix" into the pit. The Terranze made the mix of lime, charcoal, ashes, and dirt then stored it in huge wooden barrels. For toilet paper, they used dried mosses and scraps of cotton soaked in a tub of wild rosewater. Every winter the Terranze dug new holes, and at the end of the winter, the old holes were sealed up and left untouched for a couple of years.

Further on, past the cathedral room, there was a cave to the left that contained several small rooms separated by short passages. The tribe used these caverns as storerooms for clothing, soap, fragrant herbs, dried meats, and rows of fish, dried fruits, wine, and cheeses. Pats of butter were wrapped in cotton cloth and put in snow-filled wooden buckets. Root vegetables were stored in a sand pit and potatoes sat in a dark, dry corner.

The goats and chickens were put into their enclosures, built many winters ago. The women dried grasses throughout the summer to use as hay for the goats, and the chickens would eat corn and wild grains harvested every year from their crops.

The Terranze women had made hundreds of tallow candles from animal fat and used wooden sticks dipped in birch tar that they positioned throughout the cave for lighting. The Terranze warriors collected the snow in large oak barrels for fresh drinking water.

To the right, there was another small cave passage, and behind that a hot mineral water spring and pool, where everyone bathed and used it for relaxation and hygiene. The spring's properties helped relieve winter aches and pains that lurked deep in the tribe's elders' joints and bones.

Will and Mica were amazed at how comfortable and beautiful the caves were. Outside the winter nights grew colder, but the caves maintained a reasonably even temperature of about seventy degrees Fahrenheit all year round.

Winter in the caves was usually peaceful. The cave had a cheerful, bright fire in the center of the cathedral room, and over this was an enormous metal stewpot that was refilled by the women. So the air was filled with fragrant stew that simmered all the time. The Terranze sewed skins, wove and sewed, chatted, made bows and arrows and poison darts, and carved pipes, bowls, spoons, and simple furniture. On mild days, the warriors went hunting for fresh meat.

Will and Mica still had their Eco-blankets and mattresses, so they didn't need to be close to the central fire for warmth. They selected their ledge high in the main cathedral, as far away from everyone else as possible, to have some privacy. The tribe had tanned many hides over the spring, summer, and fall. Anna gave them some animal skins for comfort.

On days when blizzards raged, the elders would tell incredible stories, teaching the tribe history as well as entertaining them. Anna was the best storyteller, and when she spoke, her audience could barely take a breath until she had finished.

Will and Mica talked and planned for hours, high on their secluded ledge. They spent many nights making love. They were so infatuated with each other that they did not notice that Neyra spied on them continuously and eavesdropped on most of their conversations and most private moments.

As the winter grew cold and bitter, so did Neyra's heart. She was the most beautiful woman in her tribe, and no man had ever refused her before. Neyra learned how to hate that first winter when the watchers came to stay. She had plans to destroy Mica and claim Will for herself. She was so busily spying on the couple that she did not realize Anna was also watching her carefully.

There was much ongoing drama in the cave, caused by Neyra. She continued to stalk Will relentlessly despite being told not to. One day, Will and Mica came back from the bathing cave and found her naked in their bed. Mica was furious and was ready to throw her out into the blizzard and leave her there. Will was uncomfortable and infuriated with Neyra but didn't have a clue how to stop her peculiar behavior.

Neyra started to steal Mica's and Will's possessions. She would hoard them for a while and then return them. Sometimes she would creep up silently behind them to listen to their private conversations. Then Neyra started sitting a short distance away from Will and Mica, staring at them for hours on end. Will and Mica felt like they were being monitored again, which brought back a lot of unpleasant memories.

Finally, a frustrated Mica spoke to Anna and told her she would make Neyra disappear if Anna didn't stop the harassment.

To maintain harmony in the caves, Anna made a public announcement that Neyra was to be married to Argan in the spring. Argan was a tall, handsome, accomplished young warrior who was eighteen and known for his calm manner. He was about six feet tall with long dark hair, his skin still tanned from the sun, and he had a disarming smile. His mother had died many years ago in childbirth while giving birth to his younger sister, Syra, who luckily survived. Argan took responsibility for her, after his father, a great warrior, was killed several months previously in a tragic hunting accident.

Syra was now fourteen. She was beautiful and as accomplished as Argan, with her long dark hair, big brown eyes, and oval-shaped face. Syra was slim and lithe with a good character and genial disposition.

Anna believed that Neyra would not have time for causing any more problems with the two capable siblings watching over her. Anna had been planning to announce their betrothal anyway in the coming spring. In her opinion, Neyra needed to be safely married anyway, as too many male eyes watched her sashay around the camp. Soon she would cause further trouble to someone else and undermine the harmony of the tribe.

When a woman became engaged in the Terranze tribe, it was customary that the men begin avoiding eye contact and not directly look at her. When the young woman was married, all the male members of the tribe were already trained to avert their eyes. Divorce was rare, and affairs were discouraged to prevent the warriors from arguing among themselves and losing their fighting edge. Discord among the women caused the whole system to collapse. For this reason, drama among the Terranze was strictly discouraged.

After Anna announced their upcoming marriage, Neyra became mean and hateful to Argan, but since Anna had made the decision, it could not be changed. Neyra still refused to leave Will and Mica alone. Finally, Argan decided to tie Neyra to Syra so she could not cause any more misery by sneaking off and spying on Will and Mica. Argan hoped she would forget her infatuation with Will, especially once their children started to be born.

Argan had been in love with Neyra since they were children, and he thought patience and kindness would eventually win back her heart. She had flirted with him all the time before the watchers came to live with them, and he had always believed they would marry one day. However, he did not blame either Will or Mica for the current situation.

Sadly, instead of marriage to a great young man who would one day replace Tiern as leader of the warriors, Neyra chose another path. One sunny morning, the poor, confused Neyra cut off her ropes with a sharp stone and escaped from the cave, intending to make her way to the Archa Compound, looking for a better life and riches. She was going to betray Mica and Will's location for a hefty price.

Only Anna had watched her go; she knew the outcome of Neyra's fate, which had already been revealed to her in a dream. Neyra had been born with a dark heart. One day, that darkness inside her could erupt and cost the tribe their very existence. Anna did not try to stop her from leaving. Sometimes, free will was the best way of sorting the wheat from the chaff.

Unfortunately for Neyra, the best-laid plans often go awry, and although she had left on a bright and sunny morning, by the afternoon, a severe and unexpected storm rolled in. Quickly she became lost as the storm raged into a blizzard. Neyra wandered around disorientated and almost frozen for a couple of hours, desperately trying to find shelter.

Relieved, she finally stumbled on a small cave, and as she crawled in, she saw two golden eyes shining in the dim light. A fierce growl came from inside the cave. Her beauty, ambition, and charm did not affect the hungry mountain lion that found her, and in an instant, the predator had become the prey. As Neyra was torn to pieces and eaten alive, her last screams were for Will.

Nobody went to look for Neyra in the blizzard because it was far too dangerous. The Terranze thought the foolish girl had run away for attention and must have been consumed by madness to leave the warmth and safety of the cave. Most of the tribe believed she had frozen to death somewhere and that they would eventually find her body in the spring, once the snow had thawed.

Argan was the only person that mourned her loss. When the spring came, he searched for many weeks, trying to find Neyra's remains, but it seemed she had disappeared forever.

Anna kept the terrible secret of Neyra's demise to herself. Anna did not want the Terranze to relive her tragic death, which would be seared forever into their minds and their hearts. Anna knew that Neyra was not worthy of so much potential grief. To everyone's relief, the remainder of the winter passed as it always had, peacefully and slowly.

Will and Mica, relieved by the disappearance of their stalker, turned their attention to the matters at hand. They both believed they needed to find the human-animal hybrids and persuade them to help with their mission. The Terranze were divided on this issue. So Mica and Will planned to go alone, hoping for the chance of an alliance.

One sunny day, they climbed to the top of the mountain. About seven miles to the west, Will and Mica saw the tiny wisps and curls of smoke, barely visible to the untrained eye, which was significant of a possible camp. Knowing the Archa might still be looking for them was only a mild concern now because most of them lived in the warmer south. For some unknown reason, unlike the Archon, the Archa did not like the cold weather. Spring was on its way, and Will and Mica's plans that were made in the dead of winter now had to be brought to fruition.

CHAPTER 19

The Taming of the Beasts

The winter had finally passed. It was officially spring, and the Terranze were preparing to return to their summer village. Will and Mica were getting ready to leave on a journey, hoping they would locate the animal hybrids. Anna wished them fare-well and said she would pray for their safe return.

Will and Mica made their way west, listening and watching for the wild animals that were now coming out of hibernation. Will and Mica were happy to be alone together and out in the fresh, sweet air once again. The forest began to come alive; the wildflowers were blooming, and beautiful bluebells carpeted the fragrant woods. They had heard wolves howling at night, but they sounded miles away, so Will and Mica weren't concerned about them.

The days were incredible, with crystal clear blue skies. The birds were chirping, and little creatures rustled about in the undergrowth. Will and Mica were only three days into their journey when they heard tiny bells tinkling in the silence. It was obviously an alert system to warn somebody somewhere.

Will and Mica looked at each other in alarm and slowly took a few steps back, treading on camouflaged strings that curled across the forest floor. Instantly, they were jerked up into the air, about twenty feet from the ground. They were suspended by thick, hairy ropes that were tightly wound around their ankles. Will and Mica swung wildly for a few seconds and then just hung there, humiliated that they had been caught so easily.

The squirrels seemed highly amused by the whole incident and chattered to one another while they watched from the safety of the neighboring trees. The squirrels were not brave enough to fully explore these strange humans, dangling helplessly from their nesting trees.

"Oh no, we are captured!" said Mica irritably

"It might be a good thing," replied Will. "If the traps belong to the hybrids and not the Archa." He wriggled and tried to stare at his ankles, which was difficult to accomplish while hanging upside down. "I think these ropes look crafted by hand. The Archa use man-ufactured rope."

"Perhaps there is another group of creatures that we know noth-ing about," replied Mica dismally.

"No, Mica, I am sure this is a hybrid trap," Will replied confidently.

"Mica, swing hard," he suggested, "and I will too. Perhaps we can grab on to each other's arms."

"I will try," replied Mica half-heartedly.

They swung to and fro until they were able to grab each other. At that moment, there was a loud, dull banging through the woods. It sounded as if something or somebody was deliberately banging on trees, using a communication system.

Then something huge came crashing through the woods, tear-ing toward them, growling and roaring. It leaped up to where Mica was hanging, and a large claw sliced through the rope like it was silk. Instantly Mica fell into the piles of dead old leaves that littered the forest floor, breaking her fall. She was stunned for a second but immediately jumped up to her feet while holding a large jagged knife she had ripped from her right boot. She roared like a beast, and the creature jumped up away from her and then released Will the same way. It jumped to the ground, and Mica instantly dropped her knife

"It's you!" she gasped, relieved. "From the caverns."

The strange and agile cat-man purred and rubbed against her side.

214

Will, not realizing what had just happened, ran toward Mica, thinking she was being attacked, and in a flash the cat-man leaped toward him on all fours, hissing and growling.

"Will, NO!" screamed Mica. "He is our friend."

Will instantly dropped his knife and raised his arms above his head. The cat-man relaxed and backed away from Will until he was standing next to Mica again. He stared at her inexplicably for an instant with his huge orange eyes.

"He wants us to follow him," said Mica confidently as the cat-man took his massive paw and gently patted her face.

"How do you know this?" Will asked.

"I just do. Trust me." She said it so convincingly that he believed her.

They followed the cat-man for about two miles when he seemed to disappear. They realized he had walked behind a mighty waterfall. The noise was deafening as the icy water crashed against the rocks below. They continued to walk on the ledge behind the waterfall, which turned slightly left, and back toward an old lava tube. As they walked into the long tube, the sunlight became dimmer. Burning birch torches were attached to the walls, lighting the way into a wide junction made up of several tunnels. Mica hesitated for a moment then caught sight of the cat-man's tail disappearing into the dark.

"This way, Will!" she shouted, choosing the second tunnel and running fast to keep up with the cat-man.

Finally, they arrived in a large room where a number of creatures were sitting and standing in rows. At the front, facing them, was the ape-man, who had helped them leave the Nightmare Caverns the day they had all escaped.

Some of the creatures were unsettled by the sight of two humans and broke into a frenzy of noise. The old ape-man bellowed louder than all of them, and the room fell silent. The ape-man walked toward them and said one word, "Friend," then began grasping them to his scarred and massive chest. He smelled musty and terrible, but Will and Mica returned his greeting with enthusiasm. "Friend," they both said, hugging the monstrous beast.

"Happy see friend," said the ape-man. He pointed to both of them and then addressed the crowd. "Freedom," he said, and all the creatures bounced and jiggled around in a crazy menagerie, making trumpeting, hissing, and all sorts of guttural and growling noises.

The ape-man bellowed again and beat his chest. The room became silent. He was signing something to the other creatures. "I tell them we free only by you, or many die in cave a bad death."

He started to speak and sign at the same time. "Some my people," he said slowly, "hear words, but not speak. All people here sign."

"Will you teach us how to sign?" asked Mica, and the ape-man translated her words to everybody.

The whole room stomped their feet with a thundering applause, approving of Mica's request.

"Stay here, I teach," said the ape-man.

Mica and Will nodded. "It would be a great honor," replied Mica.

The ape-man immediately signed her reply, which brought more foot stomping—the noise was deafening. Mica wondered what would happen if they disapproved of something that she said or did. She quickly realized she didn't want to find out.

The ape-man signed for the others to leave; only the cat-man stayed behind with them.

"Why you here?" asked the ape-man.

"I wanted to see you and your people and ask for your help," replied Will.

"I give my life for you," said the ape-man sincerely.

Will was touched deeply, amazed that these creatures were capable of such love and loyalty to humans.

The cat-man seemed to agree, as he moved forward, purring loudly.

"We want to find the Archa and kill them. The Terranze from the forest, the people who live in the cities, and your people, we all wish to live in harmony, each in our own way. We all want peace, no more cruelty, no more murder, and no more suffering," stated Will firmly.

The ape-man looked thoughtful and spoke with slow, lilting words. "We fill others with fear, we do not look like you."

"A dog or a horse does not look like us, but they become our friends," said Mica insensitively.

"We not pets," replied the ape-man harshly. The cat-man hissed.

Will quickly interrupted. "Whose law says that all beings cannot be friends and help one another?"

"Archa make all laws," replied the ape-man bitterly.

"Not anymore," said Mica quietly. "These are not your laws, these are not our laws. We must make better laws."

The ape-man nodded. "You speak wise words, small one," he said.

"What do you call your people?" asked Mica.

"We called the Mongollons," replied the ape-man. "I am Ape-Man, this Cat-Man."

"How many are in your tribe, Ape-Man?" asked Will.

"About this many." He indicated about a hundred by opening and closing his massive fists ten times. "The others went back to Earth, in bad place, where caves are," he said sadly. There was a respectful pause, and then Ape-Man spoke again.

"Not all Archa dead," stated Ape-Man correctly.

"No, they are not all dead," replied Will. "Malus, Morus, Metus, Desi, and all the Yellow Eyes are still alive."

"They look like you, but Yellow Eyes very bad," said Ape-Man, narrowing his eyes. He continued, "Some Yellow Eyes came to cave, kill Mongollons, hurt Mongollons!" growled Ape-Man angrily. "We must send them back to the Earth, but they many and we few," he added sadly.

"There are others like us," said Mica, pointing to herself. "But their minds are asleep. We have to wake them, and then there will be many of us."

"Why do they sleep?" asked Ape-Man, looking and sounding confused.

"The Archa put bad things into their water and food," replied Mica. "They do not know about the Archa. They do not know the truth about this world."

"We will wake them up, and then we can send the Archa back to the Earth" added Will.

"How you wake them?" asked Ape-Man curiously.

"It will not be easy," replied Mica. "Some people may want to stay asleep because it is less painful."

"Pain not good," agreed Ape-Man. "Pain not our friend." As Cat-man swished his tail from side to side.

Will and Mica wanted to stay with the Mongollons, to understand them, to learn their strengths and weaknesses, so when it was time to put a rebellion together, they could make the most effective battle plans.

Mica asked Ape-Man, "We wish to learn the ways of the Mongollons. Will you teach us?"

"Yes," replied Ape-Man directly, "but now we eat."

Will and Mica quickly realized some of the tribe ate raw meat but others ate only fruit or grass. They were as diverse in their habits as they were in their appearance.

The Mongollons looked at Mica as if the Archa had taken human and animal genes and fused them into various hybrids. Cat-Man had obviously been an experiment of several types of both large and domestic cats, mixed with human DNA. Some of the creatures were more human-looking, but others more animal, and a few were so bizarre it was impossible to tell what species had been used in their creation.

One creature was dark blue and had eight arms or legs, with one large eye surrounded by several smaller ones. The large eye was definitely human, but the others looked like spider's eyes. The blue creature seemed like an impossible mix between a spider, an octopus, a crab, and a human. It scuttled sideways when it moved and made tiny barking noises. It could also jump and hang in the trees like a monkey, and it had a small mouth full of razor-sharp teeth. Mica carefully scanned and recorded all the different creatures because she wanted to show the Terranze what they looked like so they wouldn't be so afraid when they first saw them.

Mica showed some images of the Terranze to Ape-Man. He pointed to one person and said, "Anna," and then bellowed in grief.

"Do you know Anna?" asked Mica gently.

"She my sister, long time ago," choked Ape-Man, with tears rolling down his cheeks. "When family went back to the Earth, Archa took them." He banged his fist into the rock, and a cloud of dust rose around him while the huge hole gaped at them from the rocky wall.

"Ape-Man, I am Kiron, Fina's son," announced Will, suddenly aware that Ape-Man was his relative. "And you are my family." Will turned around and showed him his teardrop-shaped birthmark on his neck.

Ape-Man suddenly grabbed Will and almost crushed him in a tight embrace. "I can now find peace," he said, "because I find family, once I…" He had trouble speaking the words. "Man, like you. Archa make me monster, but I lucky to live. Now I have great strength, we have much power. We kill the Archa. The Mongollons help you."

"You must reunite with Anna," suggested Mica.

"No!" yelled Ape-Man fiercely. "I not want her see brother as monster. Better she remember Ape-Man when young."

Mica disagreed but said nothing. She knew Anna wouldn't care how he looked; she would just be glad he was still alive.

Later, after the tribe had retired, Will and Mica stayed awake, talking into the night.

"We need to do a reconnaissance mission on Ninth City. It is supposed to be a war city, full of warriors that serve the Archa, but nobody has ever seen them, which is strange. It is many miles from here," said Will. "But we can use the map, and we may need a MECA to get there."

"Malus is still alive," remarked Mica. "He will want revenge."

"Perhaps we will burn down the Big White House when it is time," replied Will icily.

"Does anyone really know of Malus's actual powers?" asked Mica.

"He is so evil and rules by fear. Who could stand against him?" Will wondered out loud.

Mica suddenly grabbed Will's arm excitedly. "I know! Boy 01 could," she said.

"The boy?" questioned Will, surprised.

"Yes," replied Mica, "the one in the ORRC building. He is of pure light and spirit."

"The filthy boy who wrote on the wall with his own feces?" asked Will, shocked with a disgusted look on his face.

"Yes," replied Mica, "but when our fingers touched, I could see everything, the past, present, and future. I could see the entire universe and how everything is connected. He carries the light within him. They think he is just insane, but I know what he showed me. He is not who they think he is. He has never shown them his powers."

"How do you know for sure?" asked Will, wondering how she managed to touch the dirty, foul-smelling boy.

"I am a seer," replied Mica, "and you are a changer." She paused. "I don't know how the power works. I just know it does."

"I think you are right," said Will. "And I trust you."

With that thought, they fell asleep to the crackling, spitting warmth of the fire.

In the next two weeks, they both learned to sign with the Mongollons, and being able to sign made communication much easier. They were able to understand the tragic stories of these tortured beings.

Before they left, Mica and Will spoke with Ape-Man alone. "Do you know the source of Malus's powers?" Will asked.

"Fear," replied Ape-Man. "I watch him, many times. He feed on it like we feed on food."

"Does Malus have any other hidden powers?" asked Will.

"He climb in your head and know your thoughts. Must think good thoughts if he does this," said Ape-Man, shaking his head.

"Can he do other things?" asked Will.

"No, only your mind. He make you bad, want to kill, or give you pain. He stronger, faster than human," replied Ape-Man very seriously.

"Does he show any weaknesses that you have seen?" asked Mica.

"No see weakness, but all beings have weakness. Go to his lair and look. It tell you things I cannot," replied Ape-Man wisely.

"Fare-well, Ape-Man. We will visit you again when the time is right," said Mica.

"I wait for your visit," he replied and bowed his enormous scarred head. "Fare-well, friends." As Cat-man purred.

"Fare-well, Ape-Man, my relative. We will see you again soon," said Will.

Mica and Will made their way through the forest, intending to go back to the Terranze village. They had plenty of supplies given to them by the Mongollons.

CHAPTER 20

Ninth City. The Hatchery

As they walked, Will and Mica discussed their options.

"Do you want to return to the Archa Compound? We need to find out where the Archa disappeared to and try to discover Malus's weakness," said Will.

"No!" replied Mica honestly. "I dread the idea."

"It is a fearful place to go, but we must do this soon. It may give us the answers that we need," said Will. He thought for a moment. "With most of the twelve Archa dead, do you believe that Malus is at the Big White House?"

Mica replied, "Even if he isn't, the staff will be. If we go there, anyone of them could turn us in. How do we get in and out without being seen? If we get caught, we are dead. Then we cannot help anyone."

"If we had the equipment, we could just hack into their feed. We wouldn't need to enter the house," said Will thoughtfully.

"Where could we get the equipment? We need an expert in communications. I don't know where we could find one that we could trust," replied Mica.

"Something may turn up," suggested Will, "but our next mission should be to go to Ninth City and see if we can find out what type of military force is there. If we steal a MECA, we could be tracked, but it is a very long way to hike through the woods."

"It's risky," replied Mica, "but I think we have to hike. It's about a hundred miles away. What if we traveled at night along the highway and slept during the day in the woods?"

"That is a good idea. There is virtually no traffic at night, and the wild animals are fenced off from the highway. We are fit and healthy and could easily cover twenty miles every night on a straight path," agreed Will.

"Let's start tonight," suggested Mica. So they made their way toward the main highway, climbed into a large oak tree, and tied themselves to the branches to sleep for a few hours.

Soon the sun began to sink below the horizon, and as the darkness spread across the Earth, Will and Mica emerged from the forest and started to jog down the highway. The first night they didn't see a single vehicle, and right before sunrise, they slipped back into the woods and slept in another tree.

When they woke up a couple of hours before dusk, Mica said, "I hear water." They looked and found a small flowing stream nearby. They washed up and filled their water holders. They both ate some food and headed back to the highway and began jogging and walking all through the night.

When they saw a couple of black cars with tinted windows speeding along the road, Will and Mica lay facedown and flat in the long grass that grew along the side of the highway. The vehicles swooshed by, never noticing the two watchers hidden in the long green grass. It only took them five nights to reach Ninth City.

Will and Mica saw the sign for Ninth City. It read, "Private Troop Installation: Do not enter without authorized passes. Unauthorized intruders will be shot."

The entranceway was barricaded by green steel gates and with a guard post on either side. Concertina and the barbed wire ran along the perimeter of the whole compound, and there were also periodic signs that read, "Warning: Active Electric Fence."

The whole compound looked run-down and unkempt. The vegetation was overgrown, and the only area adequately cleared was around the front of the buildings. The silence there was overwhelming. Something odd was going on in this dilapidated place.

"How do we get in?" Mica wondered out loud, confused by what she saw.

"I don't know. We have to watch what happens during the next two days," replied Will.

While Will and Mica watched the compound, they noticed that a truck entered each day at dawn, and another at dusk. They appeared to be supply trucks. The driver stopped the vehicle, then he jumped out and brought the paperwork to the guard's tiny shack. The two men seemed to know each other and exchanged a few words for a minute or two. Then the driver walked back to his truck, waited for the guard to open the gate, and drove through. After they had watched for two days, it seemed to be the only routine where vehicles went in and out on a regular basis.

"I have an idea," suggested Will. "While the driver and guard are talking, we could slip under the bottom of the truck, hold on underneath, and pass through unseen. We can get out the same way. We should take the dusk truck in and the dawn truck out. It is such a vast compound we should be able to explore when it is dark and minimally staffed."

Mica thought it was a good plan.

So at dusk, when the big truck rolled up to the gate, Will and Mica slipped out of the shrubs and clung on to the bottom of the vehicle as it went through the gates. It moved a few hundred yards and stopped. Then the driver got out and walked into the main building.

Mica and Will slipped into the shadows and hid in the overgrown vegetation nearby. Mica watched the driver key in the code with her night vision goggles. "He typed in 3, 4, 1, 2, I think," she whispered to Will.

Several people came out, dressed in red tunics, and unloaded the truck of laundry, food, and other supplies. Then they refilled the empty truck with dirty laundry and some large containers.

"Fare-Well," said the driver, apparently speaking to someone. "I will see you the next day at dusk with the breeders. I have to return to Eighth City now."

The truck drove away, and the door to the building slammed shut. The whole compound was eerily silent.

"This is not a warrior post," whispered Will. "It is an illusion. I wonder what they actually do here."

"I don't know," replied Mica. "Let's search these outer buildings now and check the main building before dawn."

They agreed and slowly started to move deeper through the undergrowth. There was one main building, which was dark, except for one room on the ground floor, where the light was still burning. There were four other buildings, separated from one another by about a hundred feet. Other than the front guard, the compound seemed deserted.

They crept toward one building, labeled 4. The window was wide open, and a single light shone from inside the room. Two Yellow Eyes scientists appeared to be discussing something important; their tone was intense and harried.

"Obviously, with most of the Archons long dead, we can't clone them anymore. We need all the twelve DNA strands. But we can still clone the Archa," suggested the first scientist. His tag and number read S 1.

"I don't think Malus cares about replacing the Archa," replied the second scientist quickly; his tag and number read S 2.

"He has much bigger plans. He wants to resurrect the Archons," stated S 1 fearfully, "which will bring madness and havoc to this planet. His orders have kept me awake for weeks. It could be the end of the human race, except for a few thousand slavs, if he succeeds. Luckily, we Yellow Eyes will still survive."

"I know. I feel the same way. We have many Archon embryos in cryogenic storage. Malus wants us to thaw them all out and implant them immediately," replied scientist S 2.

"I don't see what we can do to stop this. There are only two of us. How can we defy Malus? He will tear us to shreds—after all, we are just scientists," said S 1, becoming very agitated at the thought of Malus and his displeasure.

"Do we have hosts already selected to incubate the embryos yet?" asked a concerned S 2, trying to change the subject.

"Yes, yes, that will not be a problem," replied S 1. "They are bringing in twenty-four lower-echelon breeders tomorrow at dawn."

"Do they know it is a one-way sacrifice?" asked S 2.

"No, of course not," replied S 1. "They think they have been chosen to bear the purebred golden ones. Can you believe it? They were fighting one another for the opportunity."

Both scientists shook their heads in disbelief.

"The opportunity for a slow and horrific death." S 1 shuddered.

"I wonder why they won't grow in human hosts. There seems to be no substantial scientific reason that the embryos shouldn't implant in humans too," commented S 2.

"It is a mystery," agreed S 1, baffled. "Although the Yellow Eyes do have some different DNA strands from the humans."

"It must be the gene differences. We should have the opportunity to study this phenomenon, although I don't think we will have time," remarked S 2.

"It's bizarre how those alien embryos take a full twelve months to develop while gradually absorbing the nutrients of their breeding host. By the time they hatch, their host is an empty, dry husk. It's very creepy," commented S 1.

"I hate the sound of the pupas chewing their way out of their host husk with those double sets of teeth. They crunch and munch for hours," agreed S 2 with disgust.

"And they are dangerous and vicious," remarked S 1. "You can never be too careful around the beasts, even when they are hatchlings."

S 2 agreed with him. "They bite and eat anything alive, like a pack of piranhas. I am glad we just throw chunks of meat into the pens for the first nineteen years."

"It's nauseating when we have to give them solid food. I hate throwing the live animals and poor Yellow Eyes babies into their pens. I must admit, it still really bothers me, even after all these years," lamented S 1.

"Why do you think they grow so slowly, S 1? They take a hundred years, our whole lifetime, just to reach maturity. It's ironic, twelve different DNA donors are used to create one single Archon offspring," commented S 2

"Well, they say it takes a village to raise a child. Here it takes a village to make a child, literally," joked S 1.

Then they both started laughing hysterically at their feeble joke.

"Malus wants us to try to speed up the maturing process without harming any of his precious embryos. We will have to experiment with Yellow Eyes embryos to get the procedures correct. However, it's going to be very difficult, perhaps impossible, because they are not the same genetically. We need to experiment on the Archon embryos, but Malus would never allow that," replied S 1, very concerned.

"I know," said S 2, agreeing with him. "I dare not displease Malus. He has unpleasant endings for those who anger him. Do remember that scientist who accidentally destroyed one of his embryos? Malus went crazy and threw him into a vat of liquid nitrogen. When we pulled him out, he shattered into a million pieces of bloody ice all over the floor. It was a horrible mess, but that wasn't as bad as the time when…"

At this point, Will and Mica believed they had heard all they needed to know. They slipped away back into the darkness, leaving the two Yellow Eyes scientists to reminisce about their most terrifying moments with Malus.

"Oh my stars," gasped Mica, "this is an Archon hatchery, and they have convinced everybody this is a warrior facility! If we can destroy those embryos, they cannot produce more, and we could eliminate future generations of these parasites forever."

Will nodded in agreement. He was angry at the weak scientists who would not disobey orders. They could quickly destroy the Archon embryos and prevent the deaths of millions of beings. They cared only about their own lives. Will was disgusted by their cowardice.

Will and Mica decided to try to slip into the main building. Mica punched in the code, and the door opened silently. They walked through the long hall, looking left and right into all the rooms. It appeared that nurseries were being set up and prepared.

The cryogenic lab was at the end of the corridor, protected by a massive steel door with codes and biometric readers. It was doubtful any of the scientists but the most senior ones would have access to that room. Unable to destroy the embryos, they left the building.

"I don't think these fences are working," remarked Mica, staring at the wire fence. She threw a rock at it. Nothing happened. Then she touched it with a stick. Still, no reaction.

"I don't think they will electrify it until they have the breeding hosts here tomorrow," Mica concluded.

Before Will could stop her, Mica threw her jacket over the wire and climbed up and over the fence, so he followed suit.

They retreated into the shadows to plan their next move. They decided to return to the Terranze village.

Their return journey was as uneventful as their journey there. Will and Mica took their time talking and planning. Within seven days, they had returned to the summer village.

The little birds were busy building nests. Flowers were blooming everywhere, bees were buzzing, little chipmunks and rabbits scurried underfoot, while the squirrels were chattering and jumping from tree to tree above them.

Anna was relieved they had made it back safely. They returned after almost a whole month, and the villagers celebrated their return with a great feast.

Later on, Will and Mica retired to their newly reconstructed hut to talk with Anna. They explained that the Mongollons were with them, and showed her the images they captured. Very gently they broke the news to Anna that her brother had survived the death camp and was now Ape-Man.

She was so shocked when she saw his image that she wept openly. "I don't care about his appearance. I want to see him," she said at last.

Mica replied softly, "Anna, he believes that he is a monster now and not worthy of your love. The years of abuse and the genetic engineering have changed him into someone that you may not recognize anymore."

Anna said fiercely, "His appearance does not matter to me. I wish to see him and to make peace with both his spirit and mine. I must do this because the balance of the universe must be restored."

"I understand," Mica said. "We will arrange it."

Will and Mica told Anna what they had found at Ninth City.

Anna was surprised that the military site was a new hatching facility for the Archons.

"I think, at one time, the city was a military facility. Over the years, Malus and the Archa were so sure of their power and superiority they became complacent and didn't maintain any security besides their black-eyed hunters, whom they trust implicitly. They didn't believe anyone would ever dare try to destroy them," concluded Mica.

"We must destroy Archa while they are still weak," said Anna thoughtfully. "They may never be this vulnerable again for millennia."

"We have to go to First City and awaken the people so that we can build a stronger force," suggested Will.

"How will you do that?" asked Anna.

"First, we must remove the fluoride and lithium from the water," replied Will.

"What are lithium and fluoride?" asked Anna.

"Lithium is medicine that was once used to treat mental illness in the Chaos Era," explained Will. "It was put in the water in 2020 because the government believed it would lower crime levels, particularly the rape, murder, and suicide rates. For many people, it has a lobotomizing effect on their brain and creates a dull haze in which they live. Surprisingly, in First City, the people have taken it all their lives and function quite well on it."

Will continued to explain, "Fluoride is a toxic chemical that is a by-product of aluminum production. It causes the deterioration of cognitive functions when ingested. It also causes the pineal gland in the brain to crystallize."

He saw the confused look on Anna's face and said, "Basically, fluoride causes people to be compliant, complacent, dumber, and spiritually disconnected."

"We have to stop the contamination of the water," insisted Will, "and then destroy the Vitalift."

"Will the people become sick if they don't take all medicine anymore?" asked Anna thoughtfully.

"Yes," replied Will. "It will be very painful to detoxify, and some citizens may even die."

"Should we not let the people decide if they wish to consume this medicine or not? I do not believe it is our place to make life-and-death choices for them," stated Anna firmly.

Mica agreed with Anna. "If we do this without their consent, we are no better than the Archa," she remarked sharply.

"But it will be better for them," argued Will, "so they can wake up and experience reality."

"That would be your choice," replied Anna patiently. "You cannot make such a life-changing choice for another that could result in their death."

"But aren't I the changer?" asked Will. "Isn't this what I am supposed to do, change things?"

"Yes," replied Anna, "but you must find another way."

"What other way?" asked Will, now exasperated.

"The truth is always the best way," suggested Mica wisely.

Anna nodded in agreement. "Yes, that is the right way."

"But what if they won't listen to me?" remarked Will, upset that his plans were falling apart.

"A changer must change things with skill and not use force against the innocent," stated Anna forcefully.

"We must go to First City, speak to the Council of Twelve, and prevent them from contacting the Archa," suggested Mica.

"That is using force," retorted Will childishly.

"But we will not kill them," explained Mica patiently, "only restrain them while we speak the truth to them. Then we must talk to all the people in First City."

"What if they won't believe us?" asked Will doubtfully.

Anna spoke. "We must take some Terranze and some Mongollons with us, show them images of the water and trees everywhere, and tell our stories. They will believe us then."

Mica nodded in agreement, and Will saw the wisdom in Anna's words. "This will be our new plan," he said.

"First," suggested Mica, "we must get Boy 01. He is from the light, and he is the only one that can stand against such darkness."

"Where is he?" asked Anna. "I know of him. He is Ewan, the boy who is home."

"He is a prisoner at ORRC," replied Mica, amazed that Anna knew of Boy 01. "We must rescue him and bring him here."

"Oh, Anna," said Mica casually, "Will has arranged a meeting between you and Ape-Man in two days, in the morning before dawn, at the hidden pond."

"Thank you," replied Anna with gratitude.

CHAPTER 21

Anna's Reunion

Will had banged on the trees, spelling out a unique code to the Mongollon camp, asking Ape-Man to come to the hidden pool to see Anna.

Two days later, Anna was sitting alone by the pool of the secret cave. The sun was beginning to rise, and golden yellow, pale pink, and vibrant red hues streamed across the sky while she was trailing her hand through the calm crystal waters of the pond.

She heard Ape-Man, Mica, and Will approaching behind her. She dared not turn around and continued to trail her hand in the water; it was trembling as she moved it back and forth.

Soon a monstrous beast sat next to her. "Annie," it said very gently. Her hand stopped moving as they both stared at each other in the reflection of the water.

"Barga," she whispered, "is it you?"

"What they left," Ape-Man mumbled.

"Why is the sky blue?" she asked him quietly.

"Because you not tell me what color to paint it, sister," replied Ape-Man.

Anna suddenly brought her hand from the water and clasped his big ugly, rough one. Slowly she raised her eyes to his. "Oh, Barga, it is you! I thought I had lost you forever."

She began to cry as he held her tightly to his enormous scarred chest.

"They make me monster, Annie," said Ape-Man, crying too.

Anna put her hand to his lips. "Never say that again. I am happy to see you. I don't just see your face, but your beautiful heart and spirit. My face is not beautiful anymore either," she said, smiling. "I have become an old woman, but I am happy to see my brother. Not everyone returns from war, Barga. Those that survive are all strong spirits and noble warriors."

They together sat in silence for a long time, until the sun rose above the horizon, casting hazy shadows in the forest. The sky filled with hues of rose, gold, and red. As the sunrise lit up the trees, life began to stir. Rabbits came out to eat the sweet grass. Metallic pink, blue, and red dragonflies fluttered around the pond. Frogs croaked, birds fluttered in the breeze, and the squirrels scurried around the forest floor.

"Let us walk, my dear brother. We have much to discuss," suggested Anna.

Ape-Man nodded, unable to speak, and they walked alone into the woods.

Will and Mica stood by the pool, overjoyed to see that Anna and her brother had found each other and were together again after some thirty years. Mica and Will slipped away, returning to the secret cave, leaving Ape-Man and Anna alone with their bittersweet memories.

"What happened after they took you away?" asked Anna.

"They took me to FEMA," replied Ape-Man.

"Was my daughter, Fina, with you?" she asked hopefully.

"No," said Ape-Man, staring ahead. "He took her."

"Who took her?" Anna asked, already knowing the answer in her heart.

"Malus," replied Ape-Man, still not looking at her. They both knew what that meant. "Archa put Kiron in ORRC. Never see again, until now," said Ape-Man.

"Did you stay at FEMA?" asked Anna.

"No, take Ape-Man level 3 ORRC," replied Ape-Man.

"Oh my stars, what happened to you, Barga?" Anna asked gently.

Ape-Man nodded and began to tell Anna his story.

"Got genes from ape and monkey and put into Barga to make big bad warrior. Took many years. Sometimes it go wrong. Ape-Man have many treatments until they make Ape-Man monster. I there, I don't know, maybe ten winters. I have to learn speak again because I not remember how. Then they send Ape-Man to cage in cave—bad place, Annie," he said, reliving the pain of those lost and tortured years. His face contorted, and it was hard for him to speak.

Ape-Man took a deep breath and continued his story.

"Archa tell Ape-Man must kill other creatures, make lots of pain. Ape-Man say no. So Archa do bad things to Ape-Man, give Ape-Man much pain. Still, Ape-Man say no kill. So Archa begin to kill Ape-Man friends. Kill friends every day, until Ape-Man say yes. So Ape-Man learn to kill fast, so no pain to friends. Ape-Man clever, make Archa think that Ape-Man take a long time to kill. They like Ape-Man.

"Malus know the truth, but he angry. Say he kill Ape-Man slowly. Ape-Man laugh, say he happy to die, but if Ape-Man dead, Malus dead too. Malus laugh now. He say Ape-Man strong, he respect Ape-Man, but Ape-Man no fun. So Ape-Man spared to do other work. Malus say Ape-Man be guard in cave. Ape-Man in charge of all creatures, so no Archa or Yellow Eyes die. Ape-Man see many friends have bad pain and die.

"Archa and Yellow Eyes do bad things to friends. Cut them in pieces, eat them alive, play bad games, hunt them, make them kill other…some things so bad Ape-Man not speak of them."

Ape-Man shook his head in disgust.

"Ape-Man say to Malus he want special plants to eat. If Archa want Ape-Man be guard, then Ape-Man want better food. Ape-Man drew picture of healing plants and plants to stop pain and plants that kill fast. Ape-Man get plants and make medicine to help friends die quicker and heal faster. Help bad pain of friends. Ape-Man stop suffering of others. Ape-Man hate pain. No one know about his medicine. Malus think Ape-Man big and dumb.

"One day, after twenty winters in cage, two strange humans come to cave, not happy like Archa, not excited like Yellow Eyes. They sad to see caves. They cry, they say no more creatures hurt, no more creatures die. They let us out. I tell all creatures not hurt them, they save us."

He paused.

"Now I see you, Annie, many bad things go away," said Ape-Man quietly. "Annie, tell Ape-Man your story after bad raid."

Anna had been crying throughout Ape-Man's story.

"Oh, Barga, you have suffered so much my heart feels broken," sobbed Anna so hard that her shoulders shook.

"No cry, Anna. Ape-Man now strong. Archa made me monster. Now Ape-Man give back pain. Ape-Man give back death, for relatives, friends, and companion and child. Then Ape-Man find peace. Ape-Man become warrior again like young." Then he said insistently, "Ape-Man need hear Anna's story."

"After Fern Point, do you remember that?" asked Anna.

"Ape-Man forget nothing," he replied sadly.

Anna continued, "Do you remember the village we built in the north, where we all lived so happily until that fateful day?"

Ape-Man nodded.

She continued, "That day when you, Kiron, and Fina were taken and my husband, Herka, was killed, it was a tragic time in my life. I thought I would die from grief, and I thought of death every day. One day, as I mixed many herbs because I was getting ready to go back to the Earth, Many Fires came to me in a vision. He said, 'No, Anna, you must wait for Will 4523.'

"'I cannot,' I told him. 'The pain is too great.'

"Many Fires told me that Will 4523 must change our society. 'If he dies, all hope dies for this world. Too many will die if you do not live.'

"Then Many Fires said, 'You are strong, Anna, and have much to do. It is not your time yet. I told you that your life plan was going to be a hard and challenging journey. It will be full of loss and tragedies. But when you are an old woman, you will understand how everything I am telling you fits together.'

"'Why did you not come to me before, Many Fires? You said you would watch over me. Where were you?' I asked him angrily.

"'I was always there,' replied Many Fires sadly. 'You just couldn't see me. You were so blind with anger, hate, and pain you forgot to look at me with your heart and spirit, not just your eyes. When your path seems too hard, know I am always there for you. You will see me as a golden butterfly.'

"'You must stay, Anna,' Many Fires said, and then he faded away.

"I never saw him again in a vision. When the pain of grief wanted to consume me in those early days, a golden butterfly would land near me, and then I would know it was Many Fires watching over me, giving me the strength to continue.

"So I started to meditate again and work on my spiritual growth, and in time I came to understand and see so much more. Many Fires was right.

"I never found another companion, although there were offers, because my heart still belonged to Herka, and it still does," she whispered shyly.

Anna said very quietly, "I buried your companion and your baby son that day. They took poison. The Archa did not kill them. They went to the One. They did not suffer like the others."

"I am glad they not suffer," agreed Ape-Man, nodding. "Ape-Man never forget. I see raid every day in head, never go away."

Anna was still holding Ape-Man's hand, and she squeezed it tightly. "We will see all of them again when it is our time to go back to the One. There will be many of our loved ones waiting for our return," said Anna, smiling.

"Ahhh, yes," replied Ape-Man, agreeing with her. "That day a good day."

"After the raid, there were only a few of us left, so we went even farther north and found an immense cave. A golden butterfly showed me the way," Anna said, continuing her story. "So I filled my life with helping and teaching the people of our tribe. We all lived in our winter cave for about two winters. Our hunters would find more people and bring them to us. Our numbers grew, but sadly, there were other tribes or small family groups who refused to join us. Many were killed or kidnaped in raids.

"One day, when I was walking, looking for some special herbs, I found an unknown passage that had been partially covered with a rockfall a long time ago. While I was staring at it, I saw a golden butterfly land on the rocks. I knew it was a sign from Many Fires, so I called all the tribe, and we spent days unblocking the secret tunnel. It led all the way down the mountain into a beautiful, deep, hidden valley that was not passable by any other way.

"The valley was full of fruit trees and vegetables, so it must have been a farm once a long time ago. A few wild chickens, goats, and sheep were also still living there, so we made it our safe summer camp. During the summer, we filled the cave with supplies for the winter, making pens for the animals and filling them with hay. There is even a warm spring in the cave to bathe in, and much snow gave us water to drink. This system saved our tribe, so unlike other Terranze, we were not seen moving around with our old and the young slowing us down and allowing us to evade capture.

"Our warriors, now safe, became very well trained and learned to be invisible to people and animals. They are now the ghosts of the forest. We are safe because of them. Our tribe is well-versed in healing. We have saved many lives, as you have, Barga. We managed well, and our life was simple and good for a long time. As the years passed, I slowly forgot the vision that Many Fires had shown me. Then I started to dream of Will 4523, and I knew things were going to change for the better.

"My dreams became stronger and more intense. Until the day my warriors brought him to me, and when I realized he was Fina's child, Kiron, I knew life would be better. It was a sign for all of us to find each other again and take back our planet.

"It has been a hard life, Barga, so full of sorrow and loss, as Many Fires told me it would be, but know this: we chose this mission. We are old souls, and our lives were never to be ours in this lifetime. It was not our time to enjoy but to grow and expand our consciousness. As an old woman, I now understand we are only here to sacrifice and to help the others with this mission of change," said Anna wisely.

Ape-Man nodded slowly. "Yes," he replied sadly. "Annie...I know."

They sat in the woods, still holding hands. They sat in silence, each grateful for the chance to see each other again here on Gaia.

"I am not afraid anymore," said Anna at last.

"Ape-Man have no fear," he replied, and they both smiled at each other.

Anna and Ape-Man stayed there talking until noon and then strolled back to the pond. They said Fare-well to each other, hugged, and then went their separate ways, each having significant responsibilities for the mission.

The balance was restored, because their spirits were at peace with each other and, even more importantly, with themselves and the One.

PART 4

The Revolution

Never doubt that a small group of thoughtful, committed citizens can change the world. Indeed, it is the only thing that ever has.

—Margaret Mead

CHAPTER 22

Return to First City

On return to First City, the warriors were aware that the remaining Archa could track and find them, but the journey, although long, was uneventful.

The leaders agreed that the Archa were hidden somewhere and trying to reconstruct the portal, which would be their ultimate objective

When the group arrived at First City, the Council of Twelve was shocked to see Will and Mica armed, leading Anna and the Terranze warriors. They were horrified at the sight of Ape-Man, Cat-man and some of the Mongollons; clearly terrified, they didn't want to let them into the city. However, they relented since the whole of First City was overwhelmed by curiosity at this unexpected crisis.

"We must speak in private first before you can address the people," demanded Ed 456, who was the most senior councilman. The four leaders agreed, and the promise of a peaceful and private first meeting seemed to put the Council's frayed nerves to rest. So the strange convoy was allowed to enter First City.

All the citizens had gathered and were just staring at them as they filed into the Council of Twelve's decision-making room. The rest of the convoy remained outside, silent and motionless, as the people in First City continued to stare at them (from a safe distance, of course) in disbelief and wonder.

Anna began with a shortened version of the Terranze history and the dark origins of the Archons and the creation of the Archa.

Then Will and Mica told them of all that they had seen and heard during their assignment as watchers, followed by the horrors endured by Ape-Man and the Mongollons. The Council of Twelve was transfixed. When they heard that nobody had to die at the age of sixty-five, they were very disturbed, because they had been willingly murdering their citizens regularly for decades. The council members couldn't believe that the lithium and fluoride in the water were put there to drug the people, and aghast at the actual purpose of the Vitalift pill.

Mica showed them many images she had taken since she and Will had left First City. They were amazed at the pictures showing abundant food and water sources everywhere. The Council couldn't believe that the Archa flew in Skybirds, in Hoppers, and drove vehicles every day and had advanced science and technology.

The Council was disgusted at the Archa, who had enforced their barbaric laws on all the humans in First City and the other cities, for making humans into to disposable slaves and forcing them to use limited and primitive technology.

The Council was incredulous that Eighth City and the deviant and corrupt Yellow Eyes existed at all, because they had never heard of another humanoid species living on Earth.

"We want to speak to the people as we have spoken to you," requested Will.

The Council of Twelve wearily nodded, realizing that this information could not be hidden from the citizens any longer. The Council of Twelve called an emergency city meeting. Every citizen in First City was required to attend this unprecedented event.

Then the leaders explained the same information to the citizens as they had to the Council of Twelve. Anna's story of the Hive of Archon, her people, and the creation of the Archa mesmerized the crowd. Nobody moved or spoke a word while she was talking.

After Anna, Mica stood up, recounting everything she and Will had seen and done while they had been away.

Next, Ape-Man told his story of the Mongollons and all their suffering.

Finally, Will got up to speak; he took a deep breath and addressed the citizens of First City.

"You must not be afraid of this knowledge we have given you. You must find the courage in your hearts to survive in this world that you didn't know existed.

"You must understand that evil lurks in the dark shadows—it always has and it always will. Without evil, there would be no measure of goodness. Always remember it only takes one drop of light to chase away the dark.

"There is a place where these parasites feed on our fear and terror. It is not our reality, but a shadowy, dark one, from another dimension in space and time, but like a tick on a dog, they can be removed by a lighted match. We must let the light shine everywhere so there is no place they can find to hide. We must slay these beasts of darkness.

"These beings, from the Hive of Archon, are so old and very spiritually dark. They have been in existence before the Earth was born, created before dirt itself. This evil has been beating time without a heart or spirit. It is a temple of terror. A symbol held for eons to enslave and create pain, fear, and suffering, with the purpose to impart negativity and to fill the human race with despair and hopelessness. It is the black net that catches all the golden butterflies.

"To break through this illusion, you must learn to stand still, be humbled, know that you are part of the One and, therefore, part of everything. Show no fear that the dark forces can feed upon. Always know that you, the people, are worthy and are the beacons of light in this reality.

"The ancient ones knew words held great power in their harmonics, light, and vibrations, which make up the fabric of the entire universe. We have lost this great wisdom, but we will learn again.

"It is only after the death of the selfish one, which is the one that serves the self, the ego, that there is a new birth process that evolves in each one of us, thus coming to a new understanding of our entire human evolution.

"We must tear down the dark old fibers, the old web of opaque strands that tunnel into our vision. Destroy this old way of thinking—it is old energy. If we don't, we will only ever see the matrix they want us to see. It is a slow and torturous process, but this is a paradigm of all carbon life-forms.

"We are all part of this together, so let's walk into the light and the beauty. Our ancestors are waiting for us because we are the ones we have been waiting for.

"We must all join to build a new society, by the people, for the people. We must take all the lessons we have learned throughout history. A great society must be built on wisdom, fairness, compassion, and selflessness, to be able to provide for everybody's needs, but not necessarily their wants. Sometimes what people want is not always what they need. We must remember this.

"We must live in harmony with the planet and all its life-forms. Our footprints on the land must be light. We believe humans are not a plague or disease that needs destroying. Moderation in everything will be the key to our success as a species.

"Although we must provide for everybody's needs, we must make our primary purpose here on this Earth, evolution, both spiritually and intellectually for all people. Nothing will change until we grow up as a species. Spiritually, we are like stunted three-year-olds. Our technology has far surpassed our spiritual growth, to the detriment of our species.

"The Terranze and the Mongollons will live according to their traditions. There will be opportunities for knowledge and culture sharing for those that wish it.

"Citizens in all the cities will still receive the same amount of tokens for whatever assignment they perform, and they will all work the same hours.

"However, people may now request certain assignments, and the guardians will evaluate all your requests. Only if that citizen is able or talented enough to perform their dream duty will they receive it. Everybody may now create things and trade or barter their goods with the cities. In all the cities, citizens will also be able to use their tokens or barter goods.

"Citizens will be allowed to grow their hair and adorn themselves with items like shells, beads, or whatever they wish. Uniforms will still be worn at work. Leisure clothing may be altered but will include vestiges of modesty. Your body is precious and not an object for trivial purposes.

"Long-term partnerships will be allowed again, by permission and license.

"The population must remain controlled, and the ability to bear a child must continue via the existing lottery in the cities. People who wish can participate and will be allowed one live child per person. There will be no more breeders and breeding centers.

"Children in First City will stay in the education centers, but parents may be more interactive and visit every six and seventh day if they wish to.

"The current Council of Twelve will be dismantled, but twelve citizens will be voted into power by their peers every four years. The current council members may run for a new election.

"Food should be shared equally among the people, and a new menu will be introduced into the CFF. Meat shall be eaten more than once or twice a year.

"Travel will be allowed, but controlled, and each citizen will receive the same opportunities to travel. Engineers will work on a solution—maybe underground tunnels could be built and used as a connection between cities.

"Currently we will maintain the same living spaces in each city. Those in long-term partnerships will now receive a combined six hundred square feet of living space.

"Music and dancing will become part of First City's culture. Exercise and community service will continue, as will activities like swimming will now be allowed, and there will be one large concrete pond per quadrant in each city.

"Fluoride and lithium will be removed from the water supplies. The choice to remain on Vitalift, lithium, or fluoride will be given to the older citizens, as detoxing might kill them, but all young citizens will undergo detoxification.

"Citizens will live according to their natural lifespans. Each life will be valued—there will not be one life worth more than another. The Terranze will not be hunted or used for cloning or replacement parts. Medical research and technology will be furthered in our FEMA centers, but in both humane and respectful ways. There will be no more involuntary experiments on any living being.

"Those citizens with mental disorders will be sent to rehabilitation centers, to be helped and educated. Those who show cruelty, anger, or act with hatred towards others will also be receiving treatment.

"New ideas will not be considered a mental illness anymore, and there will be an office created to look at your ideas. They will be judged by the Council of Twelve, which will vote on them. The great Council must have nine of the twelve votes to pass any changes.

"The Yellow Eyes in Eighth City will be captured and sent to rehabilitation centers for treatment for up to one year. If they respond to their treatment, they will be integrated into our society, because they have many skills and knowledge of science and technology that will benefit all the cities.

"MAMM will be eliminated.

"The remainder of the Archa and Malus's embryos and hatchlings must be destroyed. We must ensure they cannot survive and open a portal between their reality and ours ever again.

"In our World Charter, all choices must be balanced by responsibility and integrity."

Will, still standing, finally took a breath, and everybody rose to their feet and clapped their hands.

The noise was deafening.

The citizens that had chosen to "awaken" had been fearful about going through detoxification, but most people came through the process well, and there was only about a 1 percent fatality rate. None of the children died.

Will, Mica, Anna, Ape-Man, and the others were excellent teachers. They held classes to educate the people. Naturally, many citizens in First City were angry that they had been lied to and deceived. Some were devastated, and others went into temporary shock, and some accepted the new reality well. Probably due to the enormous support system that was there to help the people understand their new reality.

It had now been four weeks since many of the people had taken Vitalift, lithium, and fluoride. Everybody in First City seemed to be functioning well, and there was no increase in violence or crime. In fact, people were working together with excitement, enthusiasm, and a great deal of compassion. Laughter filled the streets, and First City seemed to come alive for the first time since its founding.

Those who were sixty-five and ready for the Final Journey were still there and confused, not quite knowing what they were supposed to do. They had not planned anything after their sixty-fifth Birthtime. Mica organized many of them to help the others through the changes. So they were kept busy, felt needed, and were still active in the community. The elders became a valuable resource of knowledge, experience, and wisdom, as it had always been.

The newly elected Council of Twelve was having their first meeting with Anna, Ape-Man, Will, and Mica. Each council person would run their Skyline in First City. They were in charge of and attended meetings on a weekly basis.

First City would eventually become the headquarters of the judicial system once the Archa and Malus had been dealt with permanently.

The Council was discussing the fact that many citizens wanted to exact revenge and form a hunting party to hunt down all the Archa and kill them, including all the Yellow Eyes living in Eighth City.

"No," said Will forcefully. "This is not the way. We would be no better than the Archa were. We would start another cycle of violence on Earth. Once the killing starts, it will never end. Revenge begins feuds that last for years, and once you take a life, it changes you forever."

"What should we do, then?" asked the new Council of Twelve, who consisted of six females and six males.

The most senior member was Mary, a tall woman who was levelheaded, experienced, and well respected by many citizens. She now ran Skyline 1 and was considered the leader of the Council of Twelve.

Jane was a mathematical genius; she could calculate figures in her mind so fast and accurately that she amazed the other citizens.

Jane was in charge of Skyline 2: Financial Credits, Housing, and Tetchas (tokens).

Jean was a guardian and a remarkably intelligent person with the capability to multitask. Jean handled Skyline 3: The Good Citizen Enhancement Facility. It was still the government's education system from age three months to sixteen years. This agency would assign jobs to citizens.

Fiona was an experienced ORRC officer and was responsible for Skyline 4: The Obedience Reinforcement and Rehabilitation Center.

Karon was a renowned healer in charge of Skyline 5: The Full Emergency Medical Assessment Center. Primarily it was used for medical advancement, and genetic testing, although the primary facility was in Sixth City. Here in First City, Karon would be coordinating all the organ transplant waiting lists and working with FEMA, once it was restored to the people.

Roger was an experienced Eco-Enforcement officer with twenty years' experience and was now in charge of Skyline 6: The Eco-Enforcement Unit.

Tony was a great athlete and organizer and was now the director of Skyline 7: The Community Services, Entertainment, and Sports Facility.

Steven was a very competent and diligent multitasker and was now running Skyline 8, which was the Government Center for Power, Transportation, Heating, and Thermostat Control. It also dealt with grid passes, monitoring Relay Systems, RFID tracking, travel, movement, and location. He also interacted and coordinated with the Cultural Enforcement Office. He was given two assistants to help manage this facility since it was an inordinate and time-consuming responsibility.

Tyra was an excellent chef and nutritionist. She was the new director of Skyline 9: The Central Food Facility, and she handled the planning of balanced meals and providing new nutritional menus for all the citizens that ate at the CFF. She also supervised the rations system and Vitalift-lithium-fluoride combination for those who still wished to take it.

Richard was now managing Skyline 10: The Hygiene Department, concerned with water rationing, waste recycling, and processing of waste into protein. The massive lithium and fluoride program was in the process of being dismantled. The protein issue had to be dealt with too. Meat would not be eaten three times a day, of course, and all the details had to be managed and coordinated with Tyra and Skyline 9 team.

Eric was the new director of Skyline 11: The Healing Facility, which provided medical care for the citizens of First City, including births, deaths, and now hospice treatment, which would replace the mandatory death sentence of the Last Journey Ceremony.

Jon was sagacious and had trained and worked on the Farm, growing crops for many years. He was now in charge of Skyline 12: The Farming and Fauna Facility, which was going to be coordinating with the farm and orchards at the Archa Compound once it was under human control again.

Mary thought for a moment. "In Eighth City, the Yellow Eyes live much longer than us," she stated in a matter-of-fact tone.

"Not anymore," replied Will. "Not without constant transplants and other surgeries. They will now be on the official waiting list, which is fair to all the citizens."

"Perhaps those in Eighth City could be given a choice. They can either self-destruct by choosing to go on their Last Journey or be rehabilitated and assimilated into our new society," suggested Karon.

A sensible option, remarked some of the others.

"I think we should vote on this issue," announced Mary.

Sixteen hands went up in agreement—all the Council of Twelve plus Will, Mica, Anna, and Ape-Man.

"Agreed," said Mary, satisfied with the solution to a very complicated problem.

"The next issue we have to decide on is what to do about Malus, the remaining Archa, and the Archon embryos in Ninth City," declared Mary.

"We must terminate them. There are no other options for those evil creatures," remarked Will.

"The remaining members of the Archa could be put in the rehabilitation system and eventually undergo retraining," suggested Karon naively.

"It will not work, because they are beyond repair. I imagine Malus and Archa would need to be restrained indefinitely," responded Will, "and that is not a viable option."

"They could be useful. I would like to study them," reiterated Karon stubbornly.

"You do not have to understand evil to recognize and defeat it," commented Anna wisely.

"But If the Hive of Archon is ever able to send more Archons through or find a way to open that portal again, it would be catastrophic for all our people. We must always prepare for the possibility that one day they may break through the portal. It is not fair to our generations to come to leave them defenseless and unprepared," retorted Jean.

"But what if one of them was to escape?" asked Roger. "They would unleash mayhem upon the world. They would be even more vengeful and cruel."

"An excellent point," agreed all the others.

"There is wisdom in your words, Roger, and yours too, Jean," replied Fiona. "These beings remain a threat here, today, as well as in the future."

"So it seems the remaining members of the Archa will be captured and then exterminated. Is that correct?" asked Mary.

"Well, that sounds so cold and cruel," replied Karon. "Instead of killing them, could we cryogenically freeze them?"

"For what purpose?" asked Will sharply.

"Well, if we ever find a cure for their condition, they could be thawed and cured," suggested Karon stubbornly.

"Nice idea," interjected Mica sarcastically. "What if they accidentally thaw out? We don't know what will happen if we expose them to those types of low temperatures. Who knows, they may be able to transform themselves into something even worse. Remember, they were first created in the icy Void."

The Council of Twelve looked around at one another. They were scared when they heard Mica's words.

"A remarkably good point," agreed Mary.

Mica took a breath. "Look, many of you simply haven't seen the amount of torture, suffering, and murder we have. Trust me when we say we must destroy Malus and the others."

"It still sounds too harsh," repeated Karon defiantly.

"Well, so is ripping a small child apart and eating her alive using your bare hands!" yelled Mica, incensed by Karon's compassion for Malus. "I don't think she stopped screaming until he ripped her head from her poor, broken torso."

"Stop it, stop it!" screamed Karon. "I don't want to hear of such evil things anymore!" She covered her ears with her hands and then burst into tears. Mica noticed some of the other members of the Council were crying in horror too.

Mica took a deep breath. "I am sorry I have upset you today. It was not my purpose in coming here. Will, Anna, Ape-Man, and I have witnessed horrors that no human should ever have to see. Please try to understand what these creatures have done since they began their reign of terror long ago. They are sick and depraved. There was no mercy for thousands, even millions of their victims. They have drenched our Earth in our blood and undertaken crimes so vile that a quick death is kind—a kindness greater than any of their victims ever received."

Mica continued, "It is not logical to let a top-apex predator from another dimension free. Or confine him inside a place where he could escape and murder you." She stared at Karon, who shifted uncomfortably in her seat. "Or you," Mica said, looking at Mary. "Or even me." She pointed to herself. She paused and looked around the room. "Well, is it?" She sat down to a silent and stunned audience.

Will spoke to the Council. "Mica is right. She is a seer, and I have never known her judgment to be wrong on an important issue like this. She has my vote."

Anna spoke. "Compassion is a worthy virtue. I believe all beings deserve love." She paused. "Unless they want to kill you, destroy your people, and decimate your culture, to impose their own beliefs. Allowing them do so, is societal suicide, which is not logical. Sometimes hard decisions must be made. It must be the way of this world until those with blackened hearts are removed."

Many heads nodded, agreeing with Anna. Karon still refused to see common sense.

Mary took charge immediately. "All in favor of extermination, raise your hands."

Everyone in the room, except Karon, raised their hands. "The motion is carried, fifteen to one, for the extermination of Malus and the remaining Archa and any of their offspring," stated Mary with authority. "This meeting is now over."

Will and Mica spent several weeks in First City overseeing the detox program, getting the newly elected Council of Twelve settled. Then Will and Mica gratefully returned to the Terranze summer camp to join Ape-Man and Anna and discuss their plans.

The new laws in First City were called the World Charter and had been written down and signed by the Council of Twelve, plus Anna for the Terranze and Ape-Man for the Mongollons. Will and Mica also signed the World Charter since they created it. First City was doing well, and word had spread to Second City, the manufacturing plant, and they had adopted the Charter too.

Seventh City, the biggest of all the cities, which grew food, was also in the process of adopting the Charter. First City had sent out a trained Charter team to help them implement the new changes smoothly since they had had barely any dealings with the Archa, only with their subordinates. It was not difficult for them to change. Eventually, they would be maintaining herds of cows, pigs, goats, and flocks of chickens at their facility to increase meat allowances for all the cities.

Third City, the reproduction center, nicknamed the Farm, was still functioning and could not be closed down until they could find Malus and the remaining Archa. The same applied to Fourth City, the Obedience Reinforcement and Rehabilitation Center. Fifth City, the Technology and Science Center, and Sixth City, the FEMA Center, were all continuing the programs of the Archa.

Of course, Eighth City, where the Yellow Eyes lived, was proving to be an enormous headache. There were so many people living there who did not want to change their lifestyle one iota. They would have to detain them forcibly during a massive and coordinated operation.

So far, it had been reported from the nervous and misguided chatter in Eighth City, who issued a foolish statement, saying, the ugly humans had better stay away from their city because Malus would always protect them because they were part of the Archa too.

Mica laughed at their naïveté, wondering if these beings honestly knew they had been eaten alive and sometimes barbecued regularly at the Compound by Malus and the purebred Archa. They had even said that the Yellow Eyes tasted much better than humans. They were much more tender and juicy, with a purer elixir and not contaminated by all the drugs, which was why they were allowed to breed so much.

The humans were the Archa's slavs. The Terranze were for sport and spare parts. The Yellow Eyes were kept around solely for food, for sex, and as useful breeding vessels for the Archon embryos. The Mongollons were seen as the equivalent of pets, although the Archa treated them abhorrently.

First City would need to train some more rounders to help round up the Yellow Eyes. They weren't perceived as much of a threat because they were unarmed and tottered around in funny shoes, elaborate clothes, and tall wigs.

They shouldn't be too hard to capture, thought Will, and he remarked to Mica, "The Yellow Eyes should be easily subdued"

Mica agreed. "But they could surprise us, so we must prepare. We should leave nothing to chance, we cannot afford for things to go wrong," she told Will.

Ninth City, the breeding and hatching site for the Archons, had to be destroyed, and soon.

They knew for a fact that the remains of Lucas, Lustria, Invedia, Ira, Ava, Huber, Gula, Connie, Crudelis, and Gerald were all found in the caverns. There were also several Yellow Eyes whose identities were still unknown. Their priority was to locate Malus, Metus, Morus, and Desi, who seemed to have disappeared off the face of the Earth.

They had no reports coming through about Skybirds or Hoppers flying. They had no information about them or their whereabouts at all.

Will believed Desi might have stayed at the Compound in his nursery. Possibly Morus, Malus, and Metus had been on their way to the caverns a little later than the others, when the massacre occurred. They must have heard the mayhem and fled quickly back to the Big White House for safety, where Will and Mica had last seen them, and after that, the Archa had utterly disappeared.

"Haven't nearly all their staff gone too?" asked Anna.

"Yes," replied Will, "I think so, but it is a major compound, and it has plenty of supplies. A couple of people could live well there for at least a year. Desi is not like the rest of them. His mental damage is very different to the others, and he is unable to defend himself or run away due to his enormous weight."

"If we want to find the others, the Archa Compound is where we need to start, although to be honest, I am afraid to go back there," stated Mica.

"You are right," replied Will. "We must begin there, but we must prepare for anything, including the Archa returning. We must have an expert team, high-tech equipment, and several backup plans in case something goes wrong. It could be a life-and-death situation."

Mica nodded in agreement, so did Anna and Ape-Man.

"I will give you my best warriors," said Anna.

"Thank you," replied Will.

Then Ape-Man spoke. "I come with best warriors too."

"Thank you," replied Mica. "We will go as well and bring our finest equipment." She continued, "This may be a trap, so I think we should carry some poison, just in case we get caught. I would not give Malus the satisfaction of being able to torture us. I would like to spit in his face with my last breath."

They all looked at Mica uncomfortably, but they knew she was right.

"I will prepare you something," replied Anna quickly. "It will be instant and painless."

"Thank you, Anna," said Mica, grateful.

As they held each other's gaze for a moment, a small tear slid down Anna's face. "My family is together again," she said, taking Ape-Man's huge hand in one of hers and Will's hand in her other one. "I will not lose it." Anna took a deep breath. "I must be alone now and speak to the universe. It is time for all to rest. Tomorrow we will make more plans."

Everyone agreed and went their separate ways. Will and Mica went to their hut and lay naked in their bed and slept in each other's arms until dawn. In the early morning, they made love under the luminous pink light that filled the horizon. Then they took showers and ate a hearty breakfast.

"We should make a list of the equipment we have and a list of equipment we need," suggested Will

"Good idea," replied Mica.

They still had the foil map and a collection of weapons: shooters, bangers, cutters, stunners, and talkers.

The Terranze had poison darts and arrows. They could also use a thing called a slingshot, which threw rocks at high speed and killed on impact with the head or, at the very least, caused the enemy to sustain severe injuries like smashed and broken bones.

The Mongollons had their sheer, brute strength and were able to grab weapons of opportunity. Some could fly, climb walls and ceilings, or hang motionless for hours. All in all, they had a mighty army.

CHAPTER 23

Falling from the Sky

Will and Mica heard a small Skybird in the distance; it was in the sky about six miles away. Suddenly it spluttered, spiraling to the ground, and crashed, bursting into flames close to the Mongollon camp.

The watchers got up, immediately on alert. The Mongollons sent a message by banging on the trees to say that they were investigating the crashed Skybird.

About an hour or so later, they could hear a familiar voice. "Be careful with me. Yes, I am truly Will and Mica's friend, and they will be angry if you hurt me."

Suddenly, Ape-Man appeared and dumped a familiar but bleeding Robert very unceremoniously at their feet.

"Greetings," said a ragged, singed, and still-smoking Robert. "I am here to help."

Ape-Man grunted.

"It is okay, Ape-Man. This is Robert, our friend," replied Mica calmly.

"Ape-Man just checking," he said, still grumbling.

Robert stood up and hugged Will and Mica. "What have you watchers gone and done? You were supposed to protect the Archa, not kill them," he said, smiling.

Ape-Man roared.

"It is all right, Ape-Man. It is just a joke," responded Will quickly.

"Not like Robert jokes," snarled Ape-Man.

"Ape-Man, thank you for bringing Robert here, but we must prepare for our mission. Can you return to your camp and see if your warriors are ready? We will all meet here in a few hours," advised Mica gently.

Ape-Man grunted again. He pointedly stared at Robert for a moment, as if he was warning him, and then shuffled off toward his camp.

"Greetings, Robert," said Will. "You just met Ape-Man, the leader of the Mongollons."

"The who?" asked Robert, apparently confused.

"It is a long and complicated story," replied Will.

"What are you doing here?" asked Mica. She couldn't stop the sense of suspicion she was feeling.

"I heard on the radio when the massacre happened that all pilots were to be looking for both of you. They offered a great reward for your capture alive, and a much lesser one for you dead," Robert explained.

"Who issued the order?" asked Mica.

"Malus did, on the night of the massacre. Since then, we have not heard from or seen any of the surviving Archa. Then it was announced last year that you both died, supposedly killed by a pack of hybrid wolves, and the search was called off. I didn't believe that. I trained you both too well. I have been looking for you both ever since you went into hiding," replied Robert.

"How did you find us?" asked Will.

"By accident," explained Robert. "My Skybird had a mechanical problem and crashed. The terrifying Ape-Man pulled me out of the burning wreck. He saved my life, and when he asked who I was, I told him I was Robert, the friend of Will and Mica, and then he dragged me to your feet, and here I am!"

"It is so good to see you both again," claimed Robert. "I was beginning to think you were both dead."

"We are glad to see you too," replied Will, somewhat reticently.

"Do you know where the Archa are?" asked Mica.

"No," answered Robert. "It seems they have just disappeared into thin air."

"Robert, you said you wanted to help us…?" Mica asked cautiously.

"Yes," he replied too fast, interrupting Mica and avoiding eye contact with either one of them.

"Why?" questioned Mica, determined to get to the truth of his story.

"How can you ask me that question?" replied Robert. His smile had now gone. "I am your friend. We spent a year together."

"Robert, this is not about our friendship," interrupted Mica harshly. "This is about a very vital mission that affects all beings living on Mother Earth."

"Why?" persisted Mica, more gently this time, "do you wish to help?"

"Because you need me," Robert replied very feebly.

"We have managed well without you," remarked Will, who was just as suspicious as Mica about Robert's motives.

"Try again. Why do you want to help?" said Will more forcefully.

"Is there a right or wrong answer?" Robert asked nervously.

"Yes," said Mica, but at the same time, Will said no.

Will explained, "There isn't a right or wrong answer if it is the truth."

Mica nodded in agreement.

Robert sighed and sat on a rock. "I can't do this," he said. "The truth is, they are going to kill you, all of you. They know where you are, the Mongollons and the Terranze. We had better win this fight, or they are going to kill me too."

"If this is the truth, then why are you here?" asked Mica.

"My mission was to pinpoint your location by GPS and send them the exact coordinates," confessed Robert.

"Have you sent them any coordinates?" Mica asked, now very concerned.

"No," replied Robert. "The fire destroyed my equipment." Then he said honestly, "I did crash."

"Where are the Archa now?" asked Will.

"I don't know," replied Robert. "They spoke to me on my talker, gave me orders, and told me if I didn't do this mission, Malus would take care of me personally. Then they sent me out here to this general location, where they thought you were."

"Are you RFID chipped?" asked Mica, worried.

"I was, of course," replied Robert, "but not anymore. In the crash, my arm was cut open from my wrist to elbow. I felt for the chip, but it must have fallen out and burned in the explosion." He held up his bleeding and bandaged arm as proof.

"So naturally, they know your last known location, where your Skybird crashed? Robert, is that correct?" stated Mica thoughtfully.

"Yes," said Robert sadly. "I am sorry if I have put you all in danger."

"They think you are dead now, I would assume," replied Will.

"Yes," said Robert. "It is a good thing, though, unless they check the Skybird for a body. However, it does buy us some time."

"I wonder if the Archa have gone to some caves somewhere and are trying to open the portal," suggested Mica.

"What portal?" asked Robert, confused.

"You need to meet Anna from the Terranze. She will help you understand some things you need to know," suggested Will.

"Who are the Terranze?" asked Robert. He was looking pale and clammy and was going into shock; he needed medical treatment immediately.

"They were called the Nahu by the Archa," explained Mica patiently.

"We lived with them for a while," added Will.

Will summoned a runner who was standing nearby and watching the whole scene intensely. "Take Robert to Anna, tell her he is our friend, and see that his injuries are attended to. Tell her 'code 1' and send another runner," ordered Will.

The runner nodded, picked up Robert over one shoulder like he weighed nothing, and started to carry the now very dazed Robert deep into the woods.

"Do you trust him?" asked Will.

"I am not sure," answered Mica, then she paused. "But I would like to. He used to be a good friend to us."

"That's why I sent him to Anna, because the Terranze will observe him," replied Will.

"We must warn the Mongollons," announced Will, picking up a large rock and pounding out the code 1 onto the nearest big tree.

The Mongollons replied immediately.

What Robert didn't know was that anyone who wasn't participating in the mission were hiding in their secret locations. The Terranze were hiding in their winter cave, and the Mongollons were safe, buried, and invisible in an underground bunker they had constructed deep in the woods; while all the leaders had been in First City, the other members of the tribes had been hard at work too.

In about two hours, twenty of the group's most prominent warriors, both Terranze and Mongollons, had assembled with Will, Mica, Robert, Anna, and Ape-Man.

Robert was still pale, but thanks to Anna's expert care and magical herbs, he was feeling much better, because his arm had been cleaned, stitched, and bandaged properly. She confirmed his RFID chip was indeed missing.

"We should all go to the secret cave," suggested Will. "Do you remember where it is?"

"Yes," replied Anna, "by the ruins of the old village, Fern Point."

"Will, the Mongollons will not fit through the entrance," warned Mica. "It is too small."

"I remember this," replied Anna slowly. "But there is another entrance, and it is not through the water or the small rocks. It is through an old stone door. Ape-Man should be able to open it. The Terranze can all swim and will go with you. I will lead the Mongollons and Robert. We will meet in the little cave."

"We will be safe there. The Archa cannot track our heat signatures through the rock," said Will, relieved. "But we must leave now before more Skybirds come. Robert, you will go with Anna."

They all set off to meet in the hidden cave.

Mica, Will, and some of the warriors arrived safely at the big pool, just as they heard the Skybirds take to the skies. They jumped into the water one by one, emerging on the other side just as the Skybirds flew over their location. The Mongollons were already stomping down the tunnel, carrying supplies of wood and food, with Anna leading the way. Just as a Hopper whirred over Robert's crashed Skybird, the group began to settle in for the night.

CHAPTER 24

Malus and the Archa

"Headquarters, come in, this is Pilot 2. It appears Pilot 1 crashed and his Skybird exploded into flames. Pilot 1 is presumed dead on impact," reported Pilot 2.

"Pilot 2, retrieve the black box and search for the remains," ordered Headquarters.

"Affirmative," replied Pilot 2 and prepared his Hopper to land.

Pilot 2 was walking around on the ground, surveying the still-burning and blackened wreckage. "It's getting dark," he said, "but I have found the black box." Which he put into his Hopper.

Headquarters replied, "Splendid, Pilot 2. Now try to look for the body in the wreckage."

"Affirmative," said Pilot 2 as he walked back to the crash site. "It is difficult to tell. The Skybird is still smoking and burning. I see something that could be the remains of a charred body, but I am not sure. This plane virtually exploded on impact, and I don't believe this crash was survivable."

Headquarters replied, "Repeat, Pilot 2, load any possible human remains onto your Hopper for further identification and then return to Headquarters."

"Affirmative," said Pilot 2. "I am on my way back to my Hopper to get a body bag." Then he was suddenly startled. "Oh my stars!" He gulped. "They are surrounding me." To the pilot's horror, he could see the hybrid wolves, snarling all around him. Their pale yellow eyes glowing in the flames from the burning wreckage. There was nowhere to escape. "Gaia, help me," he whimpered as the wolves closed in.

Then Headquarters heard his haunting screams, which seemed to last forever, as the hybrid wolf pack tore him apart. The alpha male was triumphant to have found some human prey at last. He made sure Pilot 2's death was excruciating and devoured him one limb at a time.

"This is Headquarters. Are you there, Pilot 2? Where are you, Pilot 2?" The talker started to crackle as the wolves growled and gnawed on it; they hated humanoid voices. Then there was nothing, just complete silence.

"For Gaia's sake," complained Operator 1 at Headquarters. "Now we can't get the black box until it is light, because of the wretched wolves."

"Well, it's obvious both pilots are dead," concluded Operator 2 over the radio from another location.

"That is not your call," snarled Malus as he walked into the cave room headquarters.

"I am sorry, your lordship, I didn't realize you were there. I… er…spoke out of turn," stuttered Operator 1.

"Indeed you did," replied Malus icily. "Maybe, Operator 1, I should send you to get the black box right now."

"If that is your lordship's wish." Operator 1 trembled.

"Not this time, but I don't want to hear your opinions again, understood?" snapped Malus.

"Yes, your lordship," replied Operator 1, relieved, wiping the sweat from his brow.

Operator 1 was shaking but recovered and continued his dialogue. "This is Headquarters. Come in, Pilots 3 and 4. Do you detect any form of heat signatures on the ground?"

"Negative," responded Pilot 3. "No humans."

"Negative," repeated Pilot 4. "No humans detected."

"Nothing!" screamed Malus, frustrated. "They are supposed to be there, all of them. The hybrids look like big animals. Aren't there any heat signatures at all?"

Pilot 3 repeated, "No, your lordship, just a few rabbits and squirrels."

Pilot 4 echoed Pilot 3. "No, your lordship. I can see the pack of wolves that killed Pilot 2, nothing else."

"Continue searching," ordered Malus, "until you need to refuel, and then return to Headquarters."

"Yes, your lordship," replied Pilot 3. "Over and out."

"Yes, your lordship," parroted Pilot 4. "Over and out."

Malus was furious. "Where can the humans and hybrids be? I wonder if Robert's crash alerted them and then they all evacuated the area. It makes no sense. They could not have evacuated so many individuals so quickly."

Morus casually interjected, "If I were them, I would hide the rest of the tribes and only keep an extremely qualified fighting team available."

Malus was about to fly into another one of his rages, and then he changed his mind. The humans were not that smart; they thought more like Morus, so he was probably right.

"Good assessment, Morus," Malus quickly replied. "I do believe you are correct. What would you do next if you were them?"

"I would hunt us down and kill us," replied Morus with no emotion.

Malus exploded, "How dare they try to kill us! We are gods!"

"Not anymore," said Morus. "We are the prey now, and once you kill all the alphas, it is all over."

Malus was furious; he couldn't believe the stupid beasts of the Earth had risen in revolt and were trying to exterminate him. "We need to open the portal!" he bellowed. "And attempt to bring some of the Hive in."

"Don't we need Ira for that?" asked Metus calmly.

"Ira, if you hadn't forgotten, is dead. He does not exist anymore!" exploded Malus, appalled at Metus's stupidity. He continued, "Are you happy this happened, Morus and Metus? Because you don't seem the least bit agitated at this disaster," snapped Malus.

"I am a hunter now being hunted," Morus replied sinisterly. "If I am going to stay alive, my mind must be calm. I must think like a hunter and not the prey."

"Unbelievably, Morus is right," commented Metus, astounded on his insight into the humans. "So what exactly would your plan be, Morus, if you were them?"

Malus spoke before Morus could reply. "We are going to open the portal and then kill all of the vermin, but I want those two watchers left alive."

Morus nodded. "You deal with the portal, I will plan an attack on the humans and the hybrids."

Metus agreed. "It sounds like a solid plan to me. After all, what damage can a few puny humans and some freaks do in the meantime?"

Morus stared at Metus in disbelief. "Never underestimate your enemy," he said seriously. "We would not be in this situation if we hadn't become complacent."

Malus narrowed his eyes at both of them and swept out of the room, realizing if the Hive of Archon came through the portal, they would punish him for his incompetence, in losing control on Earth. But at least the Archons would destroy all the humanoids in just a few hours.

CHAPTER 25

Fern Point

Safe in their little cave, the Mongollons, the Terranze, and the watchers were preparing to rest. They had built a fire and finished eating when Mica asked Anna what happened at Fern Point all those years ago.

"Was it a massacre?" she asked.

"Indeed, it was," replied Anna sadly. "I was there."

"Really?" Mica asked, amazed. "Will you tell us the story?"

Anna began to tell the story. "Well, the story originally starts around 2030, when the Eco-Charter began. Some people ran to safety into the woods when the religious persecution began. Those were dangerous times. Most people didn't know much about survival skills because they had never lived outside the domed cities. Life was harsh and filled with danger, but at least the people were free. In 2130, when I was only 20, we still hid in the woods and I always traveled with a small tribe, it was safer and we tried to move around frequently so we didn't get caught.

"One day, a few months later, we came upon an elder—he was a Native American medicine man—and a few of his people, most of them young children. None was older than sixteen. They lived deep in the woods, near the mountains.

"The medicine man greeted us and said his name was Many Fires. I thought it an unusual name, and he turned to me and said, 'Why is my name any stranger than yours?' I couldn't believe he had just read my thoughts. Then I realized I hadn't spoken a word either. I had heard him inside my head.

"'You have a rare gift, Anna,' he said. 'I can teach you much, although there is not much time left. Perhaps your people and mine can survive together. We have both lost so many.'" So in 2130 we set up a village together called Fern Point, more people joined us, and our numbers started growing.

"Then he told me, 'Death is coming for us. I will die soon, but you must live on so you can teach the people how to survive. It is the songs, the stories, and the ceremonies that you must learn first. When the people lose their first words spoken by their ancestors, forgetting their songs and stories, they are like trees with no roots. They are blown around like tumbleweeds, with no direction or purpose, and they become lost forever.'

"I sat with Many Fires for several months, and he told me the creation story I have told you. He explained that everything has a life force, even a rock, a tree, or a flower. As well as all animals and people. He wanted me to go through a ceremony with him so I could see the world as it truly was. He gave me some Paiute—that is a plant to help you see and understand reality. When we had completed the ceremony, I was finally able to see the life force of everything he had spoken of.

"All things were alive and were able to communicate through vibrations and harmonics. Sometimes, through chemicals, things that are not visible to us humans, with our limited vision, in our ordinary, everyday lives.

"In the ceremony, the trees talked to us, and they were sagacious because many had stood for hundreds of years or more, and they had watched all the changes on the Earth.

"The rocks were even older and wiser. They told us all life came from the One. They said we were all related because we were all from the same source and we were here to learn aspects of ourselves and one another.

"Once I had seen the real beauty of Gaia, it changed me forever. Many Fires and I spent every day together, from dawn to dusk, and sometimes talked all night. I began to find it difficult to determine where he ended and I began." Her voice trembled. "I have never been so close to another human being in such a spiritual way.

"Soon word spread, and people began to hear of the wisdom of Many Fires and learned that a strange young woman with green eyes and long black hair was his shadow and his spiritual partner. After some time, our village was up and running. The Native American children taught us so much about survival, and we all worked together.

"One young Native American girl knew much about healing and herbs. Her name was Wildflower. Many Fires had shown her over several years all the different plants and their uses. She taught me everything I know about healing. She and I worked together for many years, teaching others until she returned to the One about six years ago. Wildflower was an amazing woman I was blessed to know her.

"We had been together about eighteen months when Many Fires came to me and told me he was going to join the Great Spirit, which was what he called the One. When I asked him when this would be, he replied, 'Tomorrow, there will be a raid and many of us will die, including myself.' But he said a few of us would survive. I, Wildflower, and he named ten others, including my brother Barga.

"I begged him to leave and go somewhere else. Many Fires said firmly, 'No, this is what is supposed to happen. We will not change it. Everything happens for a reason, although we don't understand it at the time. Not until we return to the One and then we understand everything. Anna, he said wearily I am old, tired, and I am ready to join my ancestors. My work here on this Earth is complete.

"'Tomorrow, you must leave at dawn and take those people with you. I will tell Wildflower. I need you all to go far away to pick some particular herbs that I need. Anna, only you will know they will be for a death ceremony. I will teach you now. It is a particular one, which you must conduct for me after I am dead. It is essential that you do this for me or they will use my bones for their evil rituals."

"'How can I agree to do this?' I asked him, shocked.

"'Doing the right thing is not always an easy thing,' he replied. 'You must survive because later in your life, you will experience another time like this. You must live long enough to meet a man called Will 4523. He is a changer, and you must meet him. Do you understand?'

"As we sat talking, Many Fires said to me, 'Your life will be a difficult one, full of many tragedies and losses. At the end of your life, when you are an elder, you will understand everything I am telling you. Fare-well, my dear Anna. Remember, I will always watch over you, like your grandfather.'

"When I awoke, I took the people with me to collect the herbs, as he had asked me to do. I knew when Many Fires died, because he appeared in front of me, smiling, and then he disappeared. I felt the vibrations of all those that left that day.

"Wildflower saw the smoke first, and we ran back to the village. We saw on our return that everything we loved was gone. Our homes burned down, and our adoptive family lay dead, massacred. My beloved Many Fires lay lifeless. The animals were taken away, because we never found them.

"I took the herbs we had collected, and we sang a song and made the ceremony that Many Fires had taught me. Then we buried all the bodies, left the village, and made our way north to start again. I learned many years later that the Archa were on one of their hunting sprees for wild boar when they found our village.

"Malus had said it tasted bitter and vile and that he wanted to destroy everything in it and burn it to the ground. They all had a taste for killing, they liked it, beacuse they fed off the elixir of fear and felt like gods again.

"Many Fires had terrified him because he showed no fear of death, or of Malus, and asked for no mercy. Malus ordered the rest of the hunters to hack the villagers' bodies to pieces after death. Malus was so afraid that they might rise in the afterlife and come after him. The hunters were too fearful and lazy to destroy all the bodies entirely, but they did hack each one with sharp blades to make sure they were dead.

"Malus left before any of the victims were desecrated. Our spirituality terrified him, and he vowed to wipe all Nahus off the face of the Earth. Malus said, 'These Nahu know too much about things they should not understand, and they are the only ones left who could destroy the darkness.'

"Malus sent hunters back a year later to count the bodies, to make sure they had not left Fern Point. Malus was horrified when he found out that all the people were under the dirt. He believed they had buried themselves, using light magic, as he called it.

"Malus ordered all the bodies to be dug up and counted again. One body was missing. An old man wearing a medicine bag. The hunters looked everywhere, but they could not find his bones.

"After a week, the hunters gave up the search and never returned to Fern Point. The bones were never found, and even today, it is still a mystery how the remains of Many Fires just disappeared."

Everyone was silent after Anna's story.

Mica was too tired to ask questions, she fell asleep, staring at imaginary armies marching inside the roaring fire; wishing all the Archa were already dead. In the morning, everybody woke up early and decided on a plan of action.

The group began planning the raid on the Archa Compound. If Malus or the Archa were not there now, they would surely come.

"Robert, how well do you know the layout of the Big White House?" asked Will.

"Not very well," he replied. "I have only been in a couple of rooms." Robert thought for a moment. "Do you still have the metallic map?" he asked.

"Yes, I do," replied Mica.

"Well, one side shows the grounds, but the reverse should show the interior of the house. I know they give them to new staff so they don't get lost," Robert said excitedly.

Mica flipped the map over, touched it with the clicker, and one by one the rooms appeared like magic. They were able to see the layout of the entire house. Nineteen of the bedrooms were on the second floor and numerically placed either side of a long hallway. Each bedroom had an en-suite bathroom. At the end of the hall was a great bedchamber that took up the entire corner of the east wing of the second floor.

"That is probably Malus's room," suggested Robert, and they all agreed.

The other room at the other end of the corridor was the nursery, complete with the nanny's quarters. To the left was a learning area, and to the right an eating area for children. The nursery suite covered the west corner of the second floor.

The first floor of the house was simple. It had a typical mudroom, scullery, kitchen with pantry, dining room, living room, parlor, music room, ballroom, full bathroom, and trophy room. Underneath the house were several wine cellars, two root cellars, a cheese room, and a meat room to hang smoked meats or fish. Next to these rooms were a coal scuttle and a wood cellar. All the rooms were standard for an old mansion.

The attic was a maze of little rooms that served as storage rooms and staff bedrooms, and finally, two bathrooms used by the male and female staff.

Everybody memorized the house plan, looking at windows and doors for any available exits. There also appeared to be an escape passage in Malus's room that led to the Skybird hangar, and another one that led from the nursery to the terrain vehicle hangar.

There was a third passage that led from Malus's room through the cellars all the way to the coal scuttle. Nobody could work out why, since none of them had ever lived in such a big old house.

Anna solved the puzzle. "It is simple," she said. "The two doors lie upon the ground, both bolted from the inside and outside. They opened when the coal was delivered and poured into the room. The wood cellar is the same way."

"We have two crucial missions," announced Will. "We must kill the Archa before they find us. And we must take a Skybird to bomb Ninth City and destroy their hatchery."

Everyone nodded in solemn agreement.

"I should be the bait," suggested Mica. "Malus has a sincere curiosity about me."

"No," said Will immediately.

"Are you speaking from a lover's point of view or a mission point of view?" asked Robert icily while staring hard at Will.

"He could rip her to pieces in seconds," replied Will fiercely while staring back at Robert.

"Not if I cloak myself with pure white light. He cannot touch me then. He can only feed off my fears. If I have none, he has no superior strength against me. He would be like an ordinary man. I have been preparing for this confrontation with Malus for months now. Anna, please tell him I am ready."

"Mica is ready, Will. You must accept this, and I can help her," explained Anna. "We can enter each other's minds. We both might be able to access his."

"When were you going to tell me about this, Mica? Why have you kept secrets from me?" asked Will, surprised that he knew nothing about this.

Mica spoke. "This was between me, my ancestors, and the One. Will, this was not about you and me. It was about me learning and becoming a better seer. I am ready," she said. "Trust me."

Will merely nodded, understanding her explanation. Whenever she said "Trust me," she was always right; he had learned that much about her.

"I need the boy," Mica said. "Ewan is held in the Obedience, Reinforcement, and Rehabilitation Center in Fifth City. He is in a cage on level 2, beneath the facility. I want to get him out and bring him with us. He is a seer who is already with the One. His body is here, but his spirit is not. He is a child born of pure light."

Robert told them that they did not guard the center very well at night. He believed that there was only one ORRC officer on duty at night, who sat at the front desk, and sometimes a skeleton crew after lights-out. "They do not expect someone to break in. Their security system is designed to stop the patients from getting out," he explained.

"We could dart the guards," suggested Tiern, the chief of the Terranze warriors. "Do you know how to find him, Mica?"

"Yes," she replied and drew a quick map in the dirt with a stick. "The elevator has a code that I remember, and I believe the room with the cage in it is opened by a slip-key."

"The cage," asked Will, "was it locked?"

"Yes," said Mica. "It had a bolt but also a lock because, I think, at some point the boy figured out how to get out."

"Could bars pull apart?" asked Ape-Man.

"Yes," replied Mica. "The boy is gaunt. He could slip through the bars if they were moved just a little."

"Do you think he will agree to come with you?" asked Will.

"I think so, but he is filthy and covered in feces," replied Mica. "We need to bring a cotton sheet to wrap him in and rosewater to clean him."

"We should dart him. It would be safer, in case he panics and starts screaming or biting," advised Tiern. The others agreed.

"Then Mica, Robert, Ape-Man, Tiern, some of his warriors, and I should make this trip to get Boy 01," ordered Will, "and we need the MECAs for this mission. It is too far to walk, and we can hide the MECAs in the undergrowth. If we were to be chased by anyone, we could all take different directions back to the hidden cave."

"Do you know the location of any available MECAs?" asked Mica calmly, looking at Robert.

"I do, indeed," replied Robert, smiling. "There are several back at the training camp."

"How far is that from here?" asked Mica.

"Only about an hour's walk, if you know the trail, which I do," said Robert confidently, smiling again. "We should go tonight," he suggested excitedly.

They all followed Robert on foot as he zigzagged through the forest like a deer. He knew exactly how to find the little-known trails.

"I cut these trails out myself over the years," he said. "Sometimes it tricks the Archa into thinking the Terranze have been through here when they haven't."

Ape-Man said, "Good joke, Robert." And everybody started laughing.

They came upon the training area, which was silent and dark.

"Are you sure it is safe here?" asked Mica. She felt somewhat hesitant, still not trusting Robert entirely.

Robert passed her his night vision goggles. She took them and scanned the area. "It seems empty," she said, agreeing.

"It is," replied Robert. "Nobody comes here except me, and I haven't been training lately. I have been flying for the last few months."

He went to a metal shed and opened it with a slip-key. Inside were four MECAs with solar battery packs, some extra fuel containers, cans of oil, four pairs of night vision goggles, four sets of waterproof clothing, and a few miscellaneous tools.

"We should take these too," commented Mica, pointing to the fuel cans and other items. She moved the flashlight around the shed for one last look, and lying in the corner were eight dusty grenades.

"Oh my stars!" shouted Mica excitedly. She couldn't believe they had stumbled upon such treasure. "Do they still work, Robert?" she asked, staring at them in disbelief.

"Yes, they do," replied Robert, smiling. "We used some a few years ago to clear some land. I had forgotten they were there. I didn't turn them in like I was supposed to. I figured one day I might need them for something important."

"Well," said Mica happily, "that day is here."

"We should come back for the grenades at another time, and for the other supplies. Other sheds house the two Skybirds. They have additional equipment in them that could be useful for our future missions," replied Robert, "but leave the grenades until next time, because you have to handle them carefully."

They removed the four MECAs and shut the shed. Then Robert started the MECAs and showed Ape-Man and Tiern how to use them.

"Easy," explained Robert. "Push the pedal to the left to go and on the right to stop. Tilt the wheel to turn which way you want to go, up, down, left, or right."

They practiced on the MECAs for a minute or two, and then everybody piled into them. With Robert leading the way, they slipped off into the purple haze of dusk as the MECAs whirred silently through the forest toward Fifth City. Everybody was glancing above at the sky, looking for the dreaded Skybirds.

CHAPTER 26

The Rescue of Boy 01

When the warriors arrived at Fifth City, it was dark. There was only one guard on the gate, who was sleeping and snoring loudly. As the MECAs could hover up to about seven or eight feet off the ground, they slipped silently over the guard shack. The guard was still snoring as they passed him.

They parked the MECAs on both sides of the main building in the bushes and shrubs. One of Tiern's warriors could see the officer at the main desk, and from the shadows, he threw a tiny pebble at the door, which made a slight clunking sound. The officer got up to investigate and looked outside for a moment. She saw nothing unusual; she was about to turn around and walk back into the building when suddenly a red-feather-tipped dart shot through the air and hit the officer on the side of her neck. The officer didn't have time to respond before she collapsed to the floor.

While she was unconscious, they removed the dart and dragged her back into her seat and propped her up on her arms with her face lying on her desk. Anyone looking at her position would assume she had fallen asleep.

Mica took her keys and looked down the corridors. She couldn't see anyone, and the whole area was strangely silent, so they walked to the elevator. Mica keyed in the code, and they went down to the second floor, to the end of the corridor, where the Boy 01's room was.

Mica tried the first slip-key, which didn't work. She was starting to worry, but luckily, the fifth and final key worked.

Boy 01 was sleeping on the floor of his filthy cage. Tiern darted him quickly—he didn't even stir—then Ape-Man pulled the cage bars apart just enough to be able to grab his foot and pull him through. He was filthy, so they wrapped him up in the sheet. Ape-Man slung the boy over his shoulder. Suddenly, the Terranze heard someone walking down the corridor. Everyone froze as the footsteps came closer. The Warriors assumed their positions, and as soon as the door opened, Zeta 25 was struck with a red-feather-tipped dart, and she went down instantly.

As Tiern retrieved his dart, Mica wondered why the woman had come to Boy 01's room. The unconscious Zeta was holding some papers when she fell, so Mica picked them up and slipped them into her own pockets.

The intrepid group quietly made their way back to the elevator. Mica pressed button 1 while the armed Terranze were fully prepared to dart anyone in their way. They all held their breath when the doors pinged open, but there was nothing but hollow silence, so they slipped out of the building, climbed into the MECAs, and whirred away into the darkness.

As they passed by the still-sleeping guard, he murmured, "I despise mosquitos," under his breath and continued to snore. The MECAs sped through the forest, with Robert leading, and very soon they found themselves back at their camp.

Anna was waiting for them by the secret cave. They quickly cleaned the stinking boy with soap, rosewater, and soft cotton towels. Then they rinsed him off in the pool, pouring the remainder of the rosewater all over him. They dressed Boy 01 in a soft cotton tunic and pants. He was still fast asleep and wrapped in a warm pelt when Ape-Man carried him through the stone door and down the tunnel that led into their cave.

The Terranze drove the MECAs through the tunnel, ahead of Ape-Man, and parked them a short distance from the main cave.

"How long will the Boy 01 sleep?" Mica asked Tiern.

"Maybe twelve hours," Tiern said.

"Good," replied Mica. "We all need to rest."

The small band of exhausted warriors huddled around the campfire and slept well until after dawn.

When Mica woke up, the first thing she did was look for Boy 01. He was sitting quietly with Anna. Both seemed deep in thought as they carved strange and exotic symbols into the dirt with sticks. Mica believed they were having a cosmic conversation. The boy looked different; now that he was so clean, his skin was glowing, and his eyes were luminous.

Everyone was waking up hungry and began to eat. The mood in the camp was serene, and everybody was happy that the previous night's mission had gone so smoothly.

Mica suddenly remembered the papers she had stuffed into her pockets, so she took them out, smoothed them flat, and started to read them. It was an order signed by Malus requesting the termination of Boy 01. She shared that information with the rest of the group.

"Ewan must be significant to the Archa. They must know that he isn't just an average boy. He was considered a serious threat to their empire," remarked Mica. "We saved his life last night."

The others agreed.

"I wonder what mischief they are doing in that Obedience Reinforcement and Rehabilitation Center," Mica said. "The director told me that she did not have access to floor number 3, where several scientists are working on classified projects." Ape man knew what evil was done on floor three of the ORRC center, but he said nothing because it was over twenty years ago when he was there. Ape man really didn't want to know what inhuman projects they were working on currently.

"There are still so many mysteries that we still have yet to discover, but we must focus on one mission at a time," replied Will. He continued, "Our next mission must be to bomb Ninth City and destroy their hatchery."

Robert suggested that they pick up the rest of the equipment from the training center.

"I have two Skybirds left, since I crashed the third one. I think two should be enough for our mission," Robert said.

"Do we have any other explosives except for the eight grenades?" asked Will.

"No," replied Robert, "but we can make our own using the fuel cans and oil."

"Perhaps we should drive the MECAs and throw the grenades into the Compound," suggested Mica.

"No!" replied Will decisively. "We need to crash one of the Skybirds into that compound."

Everyone was trying to imagine the carnage that would follow such an explosion.

"That is a one-way trip," remarked Mica.

"Not with a parachute," replied Robert quickly. "In fact, I do have one of those. Actually, I think there is two of them."

"We should load one of the Skybirds with whatever flammable materials we have, crash it into the hatching facility, and parachute out. I think we should take the other Skybird and hide it. We are bound to need it for another mission," suggested Will.

Everybody agreed that Will's idea, while undoubtedly dangerous, would thoroughly destroy the hatchery.

"We need to get the Skybirds tonight, before dusk, and camouflage them," suggested Robert. "We should take all the MECAs and bring back all the supplies we can carry from the training center." When he had finished speaking, everyone was happy with the plans they had made.

"So today, we need four drivers for the MECAs and two pilots for the Skybirds." Will continued with his orders. "Mica and I will fly the Skybirds, and, Robert, you will lead the MECAs since you know all the trails well, especially at night. Robert, can you also make a list of equipment we will take from the training site? We need to be efficient. It's unknown if anybody has noticed that the MECAs are missing. I believe the Terranze should do a reconnaissance mission first, because to raid the training center twice is dangerous."

"We should rest today and prepare for our mission tonight. We will send the warriors in on foot first, followed by us on the MECAs," agreed Robert. "It will be a long night."

Mica walked over to where Anna and Ewan were sitting. She sat down next to them on the floor of the cave, immediately breaking their concentration.

Anna smiled at Mica. "Ewan is indeed a pure spirit. We have shared much knowledge today."

Ewan leaned over to Mica slowly and patted the side of her face. "Seer," he said gently and returned to his drawings. The drawings made no sense to Mica, there where spirals, herring bone lines, wavy lines, circles and weird shapes she had never seen before.

Mica asked Anna what the drawings meant. "They are the answers to everything," she replied cryptically.

"Can Ewan help us defeat Malus and the rest of the Archa?" asked Mica.

"Yes, I believe so," replied Anna. "See, in your mind, a piece of glass over dry tinder on a hot sunny day. Ewan can reflect the light onto the darkest of the dark."

Anna continued, "After we have killed Malus and the Archa, there is a special ceremony that Ewan, you, the Terranze, and I will perform. We will close the portal forever, and the dark spirits will come no more."

"I understand," replied Mica, "but now I am wondering if we need Malus alive to study him."

"Mica, why do you need to study evil?" asked Anna, genuinely surprised by her question. "You know what it is. You have seen so much of it that your sleeping hours are full of dreams of terror."

"He has answers to things in the universe we don't understand. Maybe he has been able to contact the Hive of Archon," Mica retorted.

"What does a fly learn from a spider?" asked Anna. "Are the things Malus has learned the things you want to learn?"

"No, of course not," replied Mica indignantly.

"If you lie with beasts, you stand up with fleas," stated Anna in a matter-of-fact tone. "Mica, you cannot study this creature. If you do, he will destroy you. He was created in the Void for the sole purpose of destruction. He can do nothing else. Simply, it is his nature to be this way, as it is for a bird to fly, or a frog to croak, or the sun to shine.

It just is. Accept this fact and understand, without darkness, there would be no light. Without wickedness, there is no way to recognize the goodness. It is about balance. It is how it is supposed to be. There isn't why—there just is. Do you understand?"

"I do," replied Mica humbly. "I will not ask this question again."

"If we seal the portal, it matters not about the Hive," replied Anna wisely.

Anna smiled at Mica. "You must rest. You have much to do tonight." Then she turned her attention back to Ewan.

"Thank you, Anna. You are wise, kind, and patient," replied Mica gratefully.

She went to the pool and swam for a while then took a nap. Mica slept far better than she had in months. She usually had night terrors every time she closed her eyes, but somehow, Ewan being there with Anna made her feel safe.

Later on, when it was dusk, everyone got up and prepared for their mission. Tiern and the warriors left first, together with a runner. After a couple of hours, the runner came back to report.

"There is no movement at the place where we went to look," stated the runner.

"Good," replied Will. He turned to the rest of the crew. "Let's go," he said.

CHAPTER 27

Raiding the Training Area

The enigmatic group set off toward the training area on the MECAs. The runner sat with Will. When they got to the site, Tiern came to greet them. "All is silent," he said, and then he quickly returned to the shadows and climbed on a MECA, heading east to meet up later with Will and Mica.

Will, Robert, and Mica surveyed the site with night vision goggles. Nothing looked disturbed. "I don't believe anyone has been here since we were here last," remarked Mica, relieved.

"There is not much here the Archa would want," remarked Robert logically.

"Just all of us," replied Mica nervously.

Robert ignored Mica's comment and spoke, saying, "We need to hurry."

They all worked quickly in the dark. Luckily, the moon was full and bright, hanging like a giant lantern in the sky. They picked up everything they could carry and then prepared to return to their camp, with the MECAs streaming back through the trees and the Terranze running on foot.

Mica and Will quickly took off from the airstrip and flew low, without lights, past their base camp and landed about two miles to the east. Tiern was already waiting for them in a MECA. Some of the Mongollons were there too and had brought massive branches with them and had collected piles of leaves, ready to quickly camouflage the Skybirds.

Everybody returned to their camp, unaware that they had missed a hunting party that was searching the training area by a little less than two hours. While they lay sleeping in the safety of their secret cave, the hunting party was reporting back to Headquarters.

"Attention, Headquarters. This is Hunting Party 5, or HP5. We are now at the training site. Someone has been here recently, within the past two hours, and removed anything of any value."

"What was removed from the training site?" asked Operator 1.

"Headquarters, it appears two Skybirds, four MECAs, some solar batteries, fuel, ropes, night vision goggles, waterproof clothing, some tools, and various other smaller supplies are missing. This site has been cleaned out," replied HP5. (Luckily, no one at Headquarters knew of the existence of the grenades.)

"HP5, can you see tracks anywhere?" asked Operator 1.

"Affirmative, Headquarters. There are tracks everywhere, but some are recent," reported HP5.

"HP5, how many people do you estimate have been to that site?" asked Operator 1.

"Headquarters," replied HP5, "I can see as many as ten different prints."

"HP5, can you follow any of the prints?" inquired Operator 1.

"Yes, we can, Headquarters," replied HP5, somewhat hesitantly. "But not easily. There are a lot of Nahu prints. They just disappear after about ten feet into the forest. There are some big ape-like prints and combat boots, at least three sets of those prints, but all the prints have been disturbed and brushed over by branches and leaves. The tracks are too difficult to read at night. We will have to track them when it becomes light."

"HP5, stay on the site and track at first light," ordered Operator 1.

"Headquarters, copy. Over and out," replied HP5.

Malus, who had been listening in on the conversation, was furious that the humans stole his supplies. He wondered why Morus or Metus hadn't thought about putting guards on that site, knowing it contained essential items for the resistance. Malus couldn't believe such incompetence. Ira would never have allowed this to happen.

Malus was frustrated that he was stuck with the most stupid and ignorant of the Archa. He wondered why all the smart ones died. Perhaps this was an omen for the future, which made him beside himself with rage, which, as usual, he took out on his minions.

Malus screamed at Operator 1, "Get every pilot we have into the sky right now and search for the stolen Skybirds and MECAs and any heat signatures bigger than a squirrel! Immediately!"

"Yes, my lord," replied Operator 1 in a trembling voice, clearly terrified. He managed to collect himself together. "All operators report to Headquarters immediately. Code red, code red," he announced loud and clear.

"I want those humans found today!" yelled Malus. "Morus, Metus, both of you get in here now!" thundered Malus.

Morus and Metus exchanged looks, raising their eyebrows, and went running through the cave to see why Malus was so angry.

"Why didn't you idiots secure the training camp?" Malus screamed.

Morus looked indignant. "You didn't tell us to," he said sarcastically.

Malus looked like he was going to tear Morus limb from limb.

Metus quickly intervened. "Malus, how are a couple of Skybirds and four MECAs going to change anything? At least we have a way to track them now, which we didn't before."

Morus chimed in, agreeing with Metus, "It will be much simpler to find and kill them now. I see this turn of events to be positive."

Malus calmed down, hoping they were right in their assessment of the current situation. The three of them began to formulate a plan.

Will heard them first: Hoppers and Skybirds flying across the moonlit skies, like raptors hunting for mice.

"Mica, do you hear them all in the sky?" whispered Will.

"Yes," she replied. "I think they have just discovered our mission at the training site. They are looking for us now. Perhaps we should stay here for a couple of days. Flying now is far too dangerous."

"Maybe not," said Will thoughtfully. "Think about it, Mica. We can blend into the sky. There are so many Skybirds up there, and almost all the Skybirds look identical to one another. We will be hiding in plain sight, and we can complete our mission to bomb the hatchery. The most dangerous part won't be flying in—it will be parachuting out and down. Hopefully, they will all be panicking and too busy responding to the hatchery explosion to notice one person parachuting into the forest, especially at night. I am sure they will be searching the skies all night. Tomorrow night too."

"I agree. We should talk to the others in the morning," replied Mica. "Will," she asked softly, "can you hold me for a while?"

"Of course," he replied. "I would never deny all my love to the most amazing woman that ever lived."

She moved back toward him, snuggling into his warm body. Will wrapped his arms around Mica while she fell asleep, feeling warm, comfortable, and calm in the arms of the man she loved.

CHAPTER 28

The Bombing of Ninth City

Will and Mica discussed their new plans the following morning while eating breakfast with the rest of the group.

"I agree," stated Robert. "With one condition: I am the one that will fly this mission. I am the most experienced pilot here. I am familiar with the pilot protocol, and I have made many jumps. You and Mica can fly, but neither of you has my experience or has jumped from a Skybird before."

Will was going to argue with him, but Robert's logic was sound.

"Very well," decided Will. "We will wait for you on the ground and get you out of there before the hunters have a chance to respond."

"Thank you," replied Robert sincerely. "This is an important mission. I will not fail you, and I will destroy the hatchery."

"I know you will be successful," agreed Will, believing in him 100 percent.

Then Mica added, "We trust you."

Everyone was very solemn at the meeting. When the group dispersed, the mood in the camp was somber. Everybody swam, napped, rested, and ate until just before dusk. Then Mica, Will, and Robert prepared to go and get one of the camouflaged Skybirds. The Mongollons had it ready and loaded with fuel, three grenades, and various other combustibles—it would make an enormous explosion.

It was too dangerous to use the MECAs, so they went on foot and used wool blankets to avoid detection from all the infrared cameras that were hovering in the dark and cloudy skies. Whenever they heard or saw the Skybirds or Hoppers, they stopped and lay on the ground, motionless, covering themselves with the blankets. The blankets prevented the heat from their from bodies escaping into the air, substantially lowering their heat signatures. They had to hide behind thick and cumbersome objects, like rocks and fallen trees, but ensure that they didn't physically touch them, because that could easily transfer their body heat onto the objects and give away their position.

When the three of them finally reached the Skybird, Will and Mica hugged Robert and said to him. "May the stars protect you."

He replied, smiling, "I have always loved flying with the stars. It is my true calling. Fare-well, my dear friends. I will see you on my return, and we shall celebrate our victory."

Mica and Will hid under several dead and fallen tree trunks as Robert took off in a small clearing. He flew high into the night sky then put his lights on. He circled once and began flying toward the hatchery.

When Robert switched his radio on, he could hear the communications between Headquarters and all the individual pilots.

"Headquarters, this is Pilot 1. Nothing to report so far."

"This is Headquarters. Operator 1 speaking. Come in, Pilot 2.'"

"Headquarters, this is Pilot 2. Nothing to report either."

"This is Headquarters, Pilot 12. You are veering off course. Your sector is not toward the east. Pilot 12, do you read me?" repeated Operator 1, sounding concerned.

Robert quickly realized he was Pilot 12 and clicked his radio on and off. He made crackling sounds and then used intermittent speech, trying to sound as if he was having radio trouble. "Head… trouble…interim…compass not func…cannot read you…" Robert was getting closer to Ninth City, and he would be there in less than five minutes.

"This is Headquarters, Pilot 12. Can you read me? You are way off course. Make a course correction immediately," ordered Operator 1.

Robert dropped in altitude and crackled another message back to Headquarters. "More…losing altitude…emergency landing."

Malus, who had been monitoring the communications, suddenly grabbed the communicator from Operator 1.

"All pilots, this is Malus," he hissed. "We only have eleven Skybirds in the air. Pilot 12 is a rogue pilot. Repeat, Pilot 12 is a rogue pilot. Take him out now! Whoever is closest, destroy him now!" Malus screamed, realizing that Pilot 12 was heading toward his precious hatchery at Ninth City.

Operator 1 froze, realizing his colossal mistake. He knew he was going to die. He hoped it would be fast.

Robert was only two minutes from his target.

"My lordship, this is Pilot 5. I have Pilot 12 in view. Commencing fire." And he fired at Robert, but luckily, the rounds just clipped the edge of Robert's wing. By now, all the small Skybirds had turned and were heading toward Robert from all directions.

Robert felt several rounds whizzing all around his Skybird. Luckily, most of the ammunition missed because the flyers were not professionally trained fighter pilots.

Suddenly, a stray round ricocheted into his left door. The door splintered, and the bullet slammed into his side, and a piece of shrapnel pierced his thigh. Robert knew if he tried to pull the metal sliver out of his leg, he would bleed to death, because it had cut his femoral artery. Within seconds, Robert became soaked in blood from his injuries. He knew he was fatally injured, and one of his Skybird engines was trying to cut out.

Robert realized his heavily laden Skybird could explode at any second. He was now about thirty seconds away from his target, and the other Skybirds were getting closer and closer.

He suddenly felt weak from the loss of blood, but he knew he could not fail, with his friends counting on him. Somehow his adrenaline kicked in long enough for him to put himself on his target.

While the other Skybirds were still firing at him, Robert put his Skybird into a nosedive right above Ninth City. The machine began to spiral into a death spin, hurtling downward, turning faster and faster.

Robert's last thought as he pulled the grenade pins was, *I will fly among the stars, forever.*

The Skybird crashed into the hatchery and exploded into a massive red fireball that was several hundred feet high, and it lit up the night sky for miles around. Then thick black smoke rose in a vast cloud that consumed everything, even temporarily blocking out the stars and the moon.

Robert had succeeded; the hatchery was destroyed beyond recognition, and the whole complex was a burning, flaming, towering inferno.

Malus screamed, "Noooooooo!" His eyes went as black as pitch, and his fury knew no bounds. All his precious embryos were dead and gone forever. He leaped across the room like a Tasmanian devil, slashing everything in his wake, including Operator 1. The pilots and everyone at Headquarters heard Operator 1 being eviscerated. He screamed piteously over the crackling talker for a long time, and then there was a deafening silence.

Eventually, Malus stated very calmly, "Cleanup crew needed in Headquarters. And send in another operator to replace Operator 1."

Malus stormed out of the blood-splattered cave room, determined he was going to find all the humans responsible and kill them very, very slowly.

Meanwhile, on the ground, Will and Mica realized what had happened to Robert. Shock and sadness filled their hearts.

Will tried to get Mica's attention, but she seemed frozen to the spot and in severe shock.

"Mica!" he shouted at her. "We must get back to the safety of the cave now. Look at me! Do you understand? Do you hear me?" Then he shook her shoulders hard.

Mica stared at him blankly, and then her survival instincts kicked in. She nodded briefly and followed Will, running at full speed into the quiet forest.

The Skybirds were all clustered around Ninth City, trying to understand what had just happened. The pilots were wondering if there were going to be any more attacks.

Meanwhile, Anna was sitting in their cave with Ewan and the rest of the group.

"Anna," said Ewan quietly.

"What is it, my child?" she asked.

"Robert just went home," he said sadly.

Anna clutched Ewan to her tightly.

"He is flying with the stars," whispered Ewan into her ear.

Anna smiled despite her tears.

Then he spoke again. "Anna, the dark one with the black heart wants to kill us," said Ewan quietly.

"Yes, Ewan," she replied calmly, "this is true, but you know the light is always stronger than the dark."

"I know, Anna, but this is different darkness," replied Ewan slowly.

"Ewan, how is it different?" Anna asked carefully.

"Like a black hole, where nothing ever escapes," replied Ewan ominously, and then he returned to his drawings.

Will and Mica arrived at the little cave system quickly, with their adrenaline hypercharged. They had managed to run the whole distance because all the Skybirds were clustered around Ninth City. At this point, no one was scanning the ground for their heat signatures. When they got to the cave entrance, Mica burst into tears and threw herself into Will's arms. Will himself was in shock too, devastated by the loss of Robert.

"He gave his life for our mission. We must continue and conquer the Archa in honor of his memory. We must not fail," Will said to Mica gravely.

Mica nodded, unable to speak.

Hot, tired, and grieving, Will suggested that he and Mica dive into the soothing pool. The water felt calming and healing. They swam for a little while then silently floated upon the surface of the pond, each consumed with their thoughts as they listened to the frogs croak and the crickets chirp, while a wise owl stared at them from the tree with huge amber eyes. After about an hour, they surfaced into the cave and talked to Anna.

"Oh, Anna," said Mica tearfully, running to her. "Robert is gone. He went back to the Earth."

Anna nodded. "I know, my child. He has shown true courage and died as he lived. He was a brave warrior, and his death was a noble one."

Ewan went to Mica and tugged at her dripping pant legs. "Don't cry, Seer. Robert is home, and he is flying with the stars," he whispered to her. Then Ewan went back and sat down next to Anna, putting his head on her lap.

Will and Mica dried off and got ready to rest.

The mood in the little cave was full of loss. The demise of Robert confirmed that death is the reality of war. Everybody became silent in their shared grief.

Will said to Mica, "Other parts of the country, or even this world, may have more hatcheries. At least we have prevented the Archons from reproducing here. Malus will not stop until he has destroyed everything and everyone he believes to be responsible. We must face him soon while he is at his weakest."

"How do you suggest we do that?" replied Mica. She had stopped crying and was now focusing on the mission, determined that Robert's great sacrifice would not be in vain.

"We must think hard on this. We have lost not just Robert, whom we loved, but also vital intelligence died with him. We will have a meeting tomorrow with all the key leaders and decide on a plan, but now we need to rest."

Unfortunately, sleep did not come quickly to anybody that night.

CHAPTER 29

Recon the Archa Compound

In the morning, after breakfast, Anna and the Terranze conducted a death ceremony for Robert. Everybody attended from all the tribes. After they had finished honoring Robert, the leaders sat down for a serious discussion concerning their plans to confront and destroy Malus and the remainder of the Archa.

Anna and the Terranze wanted to meditate on the problem. The Mongollons wanted to talk among themselves first, and Mica and Will sat down to discuss their ideas. After everyone had thought about the situation, they came back together to decide on their options.

Will stood up first and spoke. "I see no alternative but to go to the Archa Compound. It will be dangerous for us, but we need to know where the Archa may have gone. Of course, we may walk into a trap and face an ambush.

"They will know we are there," agreed Mica, "or at least I believe Malus will."

"Then we must take everybody we can," suggested Will. "Of course, Mica and I will go, but we need Ewan and Anna for spiritual help, the Mongollons for their strength, and the Terranze for their stealth and speed."

Mica intervened. "Firstly, we should decide whether we want to attack during the day or at night," she said. "Regarding positive elements, we have weapons. We have a map of the house. We have the element of surprise. We have strength in numbers, and we have Ewan, the child of light."

"Malus has been gone for a long time now," stated Anna, "and I believe he is doing everything possible to try to open the portal. We must stop him."

Everyone nodded in agreement.

Will replied, "However, since we don't know what we are facing, we should send a reconnaissance mission to the Compound for at least two whole days. We need to learn as much as possible about the daily routine there. Tiern and the Terranze should do the recon mission," suggested Will.

Everyone agreed that was the best idea.

Will continued, "On the third night, Mica and I will go with Tiern and his warriors, Anna, Ewan, Ape-man, Cat-man and some of the Mongollons. Everybody must learn the layout of the Compound during the next two days."

"We should not bring Ewan until the actual mission, because Malus could sense him," said Mica, worried about Ewan's safety.

Anna agreed with Mica. "Yes, indeed," she said.

Ewan spoke, surprising the group. "The dark one is a long way away right now."

"Do you know where he is, Ewan?" asked Anna gently.

Ewan didn't reply, having retreated into his private world again.

Tiern and the Terranze went to recon the Compound. They were away for two days and nights, sending a runner back periodically every six hours. The area seemed deserted, and no lights shone at night. There appeared to be just two household slavs maintaining the property during the day. Plus a couple of men taking care of the animals and the orchard.

The Big White House was locked up at six o'clock sharp every evening. Everybody left, probably too afraid to stay there after dark. The slavs were sleeping, huddled together, in the watcher's old cottage. They would go in, lock the doors behind them, and did not emerge until morning. A few Terranze stayed behind to continue to monitor the Compound for any activity.

After the recon mission, they all agreed that it would be safer at night since the house was empty and the staff was safely locked away.

The eclectic group of warriors arrived at the Compound the following evening around 9:00 p.m. The Big White House was eerily quiet and very clean and tidy. On the first floor were the kitchen, the parlor, and the ballroom, and they looked very ordinary.

The warriors crept to the second floor, where all the bedchambers were. They looked through the rooms, which were very grand and royal, with beautiful eighteenth-century furnishings. It looked more like the luxurious Palace of Versailles before the beheading of Marie Antoinette. It was easy to recognize which rooms had been used by whom, but there were two areas they were most interested in, the nursery and Malus's bedchamber.

When they crept into the nursery, they saw a bizarre sight. Desi's enormous crib, changing table, and the playpen were entirely out of proportion to the room. Oversize bottles of sour, congealed human milk were lying on the table next to the monstrous rocking chair. There was no sign of Desi.

The small army entered Malus's room. Cat-man suddenly hissed startling everyone. It was pitch-black without the lights on because the floor, the walls, and the ceiling were painted black. Strange symbols had been carefully hand-painted in gold leaf and some ancient language scribbled all over the entire room. A map of the universe seemed partially illustrated on one of the walls.

They were possibly mathematical equations, thought Will, looking at the writing on all the walls.

Malus had a large bed, but it looked unused. He had two large hooks that were attached to the ceiling, that looked like perches for birds.

"Oh my stars," remarked Mica, shocked. "He hangs upside down at night like a bat."

Malus's closet contained several black cloaks and clothing, nothing of apparent interest.

There was a desk against the wall, beneath the heavy brocade curtains. It was the only place in the room that was in disarray. There were small scraps of paper that were scattered, covering the entire surface of the desk. Some had formulas written on them; others were indecipherable.

"I think he was trying to make calculations to open the portal," remarked Will as he studied the scribbles.

"Look, Will," said Mica excitedly, "there are some notes here that are in ancient writing. Although I don't understand the language, it looks similar to Sumerian. I remember learning about it in the museum."

"Here are some interesting numbers," stated Anna. "Possibly, these could reveal where he is."

Will stared at them for a minute. "Mica, look at these," he said. "I think they are longitude and latitude. I believe they are coordinates on a map."

Mica agreed. "Let's plot them and see what we find," she suggested. Mica began to plot out the longitude and latitude on the metallic map.

"The first one is here at the Big White House. These other ones correspond to the other cities. I think these two coordinates are hunting grounds," Mica explained excitedly. "These three, I do not recognize. This site here is to the east and has a circle of red ink, like Ninth City."

"There is a blue circle around this point. It is located farther north in the mountains. It might be a cave," suggested Will.

"This coordinate is unique," remarked Will while studying it. "I believe it may be a coordinate in space."

There was a significant star map on the wall, where most of the stars had been mapped by hand a long time ago. There was also a coordinate at the very edge of the known universe, near a massive black hole. Anna continued staring at it. "It is the Void," she murmured to herself.

"Mica, what do you think the red circle means? Could it be another hatching ground?" asked Will.

"Yes, I do," replied Mica. "I believe that they would have more than one hatchery."

"The cave in the north—I think that's where the original 7 of 12 and 8 of 12 and 12 of 12 were working on opening a portal. We need to look at these places," suggested Anna.

Ewan suddenly spoke. "The dark one, he knows we are here."

"Is he still far away?" asked Anna.

"Yes," replied Ewan. He pointed on the map. "Here," he said and touched the blue circle.

"Did he go here too?" asked Mica, pointing to the red circle.

"Yes, he did," replied Ewan.

"When did he go there?" Mica asked.

"Four days ago," he replied.

"Do you know what is there, Ewan?" she asked.

"The hatchery," he said, staring at the ceiling. "And this," he said, suddenly pointing to the blue circle, "is a dark portal to the other world."

"Ewan, why did you not tell us this before?" asked Will, a little frustrated.

"You did not ask me," replied Ewan, calmly tracing the strange symbols on the wall with his finger.

"Do you understand those symbols?" asked Mica.

"Yes, I do," replied Ewan. "They are trying to open a passage between the two dimensions, but their symbols aren't quite right. They have forgotten about free will. That's why it won't stay open. The Hive has waited since the universe began to come here and claim Earth." Ewan was silent again and disappeared back into the ether again.

The group went up to the attic, but there wasn't anything of interest, just clean, sparsely furnished rooms for the house staff.

They decided to check the cellars, just to make sure they hadn't missed anything. Afterward, they wished they hadn't.

Two wine cellars had been converted into torture/dismember room, complete with steel tables, various devices, and a lot of surgical equipment. There were ancient, rusty meat hooks dangling from the ceiling, thickly coated with layers and layers of dried old blood. There were machetes, an electric chainsaw, and in one corner, piles of empty body bags.

A large glass display case held trophies from the wretched victims who had lost their lives in these chambers of horror. There were hundreds of hair clips, all kinds of jewelry, silk scarves, feathers, single shoes, and thousands of used RFID chips in a dirty, bloodstained metal box.

"May the Earth Mother have mercy. There was much killing done down here," remarked Mica, shocked and disgusted.

"So many tortured spirits that cannot rest because of the evil they suffered, and they cannot find the light because they feel lost in all the darkness," remarked Anna sadly.

There was a long whitewashed wall at the back of the room. It was a trophy wall used by hunters. The heads mounted along the whole length of that wall were horrific. Apparently, someone was very proficient at taxidermy, because they had caught the grisly death masks on every one of the wretched victims. Hundreds of humanoid faces stared out, frozen in terror, for all eternity. It was a grotesque wall of death.

Anna was looking at the wall of death when she suddenly went very pale and gasped. "We need to leave right now," she said firmly. "We have what we need. I will never return here again."

"What have you just seen, Anna? Tell me!" demanded Will.

"I can't...," replied Anna, all choked up.

"Ewan, what did Anna see?" asked Will desperately.

"Her daughter's face," replied Ewan without emotion.

"My mother?" Will said in a strangled voice.

"Yes," replied Ewan. "Right there." And he pointed to her face on the wall.

Will stared at his beloved mother's face, which was hanging on the wall. The macabre mask of her last moments on Earth. Her face was contorted in pain, her eyes were wide open in terror and her jaw hung loosely to left if it had been broken, most of her teeth were missing. That shocking image would haunt him for the remainder of his life.

"There are some things, once seen or done, that can never be forgotten. That is why I did not want you to see your mother like that," stated Anna sadly.

Mica walked over and held Will's hand. "I am so sorry about your mother, Will," said Mica tearfully, "but we must stop another life from ever being taken by these sadistic monsters."

Some of the Terranze recognized their relatives too. Everyone was silent for a moment, standing in a type of collective shock. While Cat-man paced up and down, swishing his tail obviously agitated.

Ewan broke the silence and said, "The dark one is sending his black-eyed hunters to kill us."

"We must leave now," said Anna urgently, agreeing.

That woke everyone up, and they immediately went into mission mode and left as soon as possible. The warriors barely made it back to the safety of the cave when they heard the hunters. A shot rang out, loud and clear, echoing across the valley.

As soon as they were safely inside their cave, Will exploded.

"We are going to the blue circle. We will find the Archa, Malus, and his offspring and destroy them. We will obliterate their molecules, and they will not kill or torture any more people," he ranted.

"What about us destroying their other hatchery?" asked Mica.

"That will be next," said Will with great determination. "We will wipe this pestilence off the face of the Earth."

Will wanted to sit alone for a while; he felt very traumatized. As he knelt down in the dirt, with his head in his hands, Anna walked over to talk to him, and she sat down next to him.

"How can you accept all this death, Anna, and not disintegrate?" asked Will, obviously distraught.

"We are all here on the path of change," replied Anna. "That is a difficult journey filled with so much pain and loss. Change does not come without the price of sacrifice. It is the way of this third dimension energy. We can either fall to our knees and give up or get back up onto our feet and fight with every breath we have. It is not how we fall that matters, it is how we rise back up again after each fall and whether or not we finish the mission that counts," she replied. "I will always see your beautiful and brave mother as she once was, and I know when I see her again, all this pain will heal. Whatever we suffer here on Earth is only temporary, because the ONE is love and light, and that is what we will return to one day, when we have finished with our missions on Earth."

Will looked at Anna and nodded. He rose from his knees and walked over to Mica with his back straight and his head held high.

Anna smiled and returned to Ewan, who was fast asleep, despite the evening's turmoil.

"Are you all right?" asked Mica, concerned.

"No," said Will sadly, "but I will be, because I have no choice."

Mica just nodded and then hugged him tightly as they lay down to sleep. Will tossed and turned the whole night, still haunted by the faces in the trophy room.

CHAPTER 30

The Blue Cave

While the majority of the crew prepared for the mission they were undertaking the next day in the Blue Cave, Mica, Ewan, and Anna were simultaneously filling their bodies and spirits with pure violet light, which cleansed and healed them by strengthening them spiritually, both as individuals and as a team. The three of them would have to be very resilient to overcome Malus.

Everybody seemed tired by dusk. It had been a painful and challenging day, full of traumatic memories. Many in the group were reliving the loss of loved ones. People were silent, lost in their thoughts, although they ate some food and slept a little. The night seemed to be endless.

When dawn finally broke, Tiern and some of the Terranze went ahead to recon the area. They sent a runner back, telling them it was safe to embark on the mission.

The team had to travel about eight miles, but they couldn't take the MECAs because the hunters could track them. The group made it to the site of the Blue Cave by nightfall. The Terranze did not detect anything suspicious and didn't believe anybody followed them, because the Terranze deftly wiped all the footprints away with branches and leaves.

While a few Terranze continued monitoring the Blue Cave during the night, the rest of the team settled into an empty cave a mile away from their target. They didn't build a fire and were silent, just in case black-eyed hunters were roaming the area. The warriors took turns guarding the front of this cave all through the night.

At first light, the leaders went over their plan of attack on Malus and the Archa. "We need to dart Morus, Metus, and Desi with a full and lethal dose, Malus too, although I don't know if the poison will work on him," advised Tiern.

"We also have shooters and stingers that we can set on kill. Grenades too. When they fall, don't assume they are dead. They could be stunned or pretending to be dead, so make sure you tie them up very tightly, and then we will reshoot them in the head," ordered Will coldly, without any compassion.

The team made their way silently to the Blue Cave, with the Terranze going on ahead as usual. Tiern came back to report that close to the cave, several bio-hunters were guarding the area. He said he couldn't see from their position if there was another entrance to the cave, but the front was covered with a large rock, camouflaged with vegetation, and a few bio-hunters had spread around the Blue Cave and had positioned themselves in ideal sniper positions.

"Take out everyone you see, Tiern, and then wait. We will be following you," ordered Will.

Tiern returned and ordered all the Terranze to dart the hunters simultaneously.

As Will, Mica, and the Mongollons arrived, they heard the fallen talkers crackle next to the evaporating bodies of the bio-hunters.

"Hunter 1, this is Operator 3. Check in, please."

Will hesitated and then picked up the talker. "Operator 3, this is Hunter 1."

"Is everywhere clear?" asked Headquarters.

"Affirmative," replied Will. He was hoping nobody in the Blue Cave would notice a different-sounding voice.

"Hunter 1, this is Headquarters. Check back in fifteen minutes." The talker crackled and then was silent.

"Affirmative," replied Will. "Over and out."

Will did not realize that none of the hunters could speak; they just punched in response codes or grunted. Unwittingly, Will had just alerted the Archa that they were there.

The Mongollons had come from the rear of the Blue Cave area and had found another exit or entrance, so they rolled a large rock blocking the way for a possible escape by the Archa.

When Will gave the signal, the Mongollons rolled the massive rock from the entrance of the Blue Cave, smoothly and silently, and then they filed into the long rock tunnel. They came to a crossroads, where there was a choice of two different lava tubes.

They all froze as somebody came down tunnel 1 toward them. It was Morus, his face a picture of momentary confusion and shock. He tried to make a sound, but the only thing he heard was Tiern's dart whizzing through the air and slapping into his neck. Before he could even move his hand, he fell to the ground with a loud crash.

The remaining black-eyed bio-hunters must have heard the noise, because they all came spilling out of the tunnels at once. *Zap zap.* They all fell, one by one, and then Metus came tearing toward them, roaring like a wild beast. Ape-Man lurched toward him, bellowing, and ripped him apart in seconds. He wanted revenge, and he got it. The rest of the group were in awe of Ape-Man's strength and fury as parts of Metus's body landed on the cave floor and hung on the rocks. Then Ape-Man stopped and slowed his breathing, trying to hear any more movement.

For a brief moment, there was silence, except for a strange, scurrying sound as something scratched and moved around in one of the tunnels.

The team stayed in place for a full minute, but nobody else appeared. The noise might have come from the first tunnel; it was difficult to tell. So very carefully the Terranze warriors were making their way down tunnel 1 when, suddenly, all the lights went out. Four of the members of the group had night vision goggles on and led the way. They could see something moving down the tunnel, but it wasn't clear what it was.

The group was distracted by the glowing blue light in the distance. As they got closer, it undulated and shimmered. Blue-silver threads rippled across the viscous surface. Suddenly, the plasmic force field emitted a high-pitched whine that made all of them fall to their knees in agonizing pain. They had found the portal.

"I am going to destroy it!" yelled Will, on his knees. He screamed, "Incoming!" and, with all his strength, managed to throw two grenades toward the portal. Within three seconds, the whole thing exploded with incredible force. Hundreds of thin cobalt blue light lasers suddenly crisscrossed, like a giant spiderweb, and struck rocks everywhere, which caused some to burn, evaporate, or tumble to the ground. Part of the ceiling began to collapse, and rocks were falling all around them. Then there was silence. Everywhere was gray and hazy, until the dust started to settle.

The Mongollons began pulling rocks off everyone. Luckily, no one had been killed. But one warrior suffered a broken leg, and another a broken arm. The third casualty had a head wound that was not fatal, but bleeding profusely.

Luckily, everybody else was just scratched and bruised. Will looked for Mica and found her coughing in the dust. She had a nasty graze over her left cheekbone and was covered in dirt and debris, like everyone else, but at least she wasn't seriously hurt. She was looking frantically for Anna and Ewan.

"I can't find Anna and Ewan in all the chaos!" she yelled at Will while trying desperately to scrabble at piles of rock.

"Are you all right?" asked Will, grabbing her and holding her tight for a moment. Mica nodded. Will said, "You and I need to cover the Mongollons while they move the rocks. I promise you, we will find them."

Mica nodded and took her position, with her weapon covering the Mongollons while they worked.

In about an hour, they had moved tons of rock. The grenades had utterly destroyed the gateway to the dark realm.

Anna and Ewan were safe and alive farther back in the tunnel. They had been hiding under a ledge when the explosion occurred, and although the rocks had piled all around them, neither of them was injured, just dusty and scared.

"Ewan," asked Mica, "is the dark one here?"

He nodded.

"Where is he?" she asked.

Ewan pointed. "Up there," he said.

Mica looked up, but she couldn't see anything.

"Is he still in these caves?" asked Mica.

Ewan nodded but said nothing else.

The team went back to ensure anyone darted was dead. Will and Mica shot the fallen in the head. They realized the hunters just wore the body of a human because they were without a spirit. They had big black eyes, and their skin was strange, pale-colored, and clammy. When they were dead, they seemed to evaporate, leaving behind a bizarre human carcass that collapsed like a suit, without any bones in it. It was very peculiar and eerie to see.

As the group explored the second tunnel, they saw the enormous bulk of Desi lumbering away from them as fast as his fat legs would carry him, still wearing his diaper and dirty sun hat. They shot Desi several times in the back. He fell with such force it started another small landslide, and the remaining loose rocks fell. The Mongollons cleaned up again and then continued down the tunnel, but they couldn't find any trace of Malus.

"Is the dark one still here, Ewan?" asked Anna.

"No, he has gone," replied Ewan.

They searched every inch of the caves. It was apparent the Archa had used the Blue Cave as their headquarters. But somehow, Malus had escaped when the first rockslide occurred. The explosion had opened up a hole near where Desi's body lay, which had allowed him to slip away and climb upward to the surface and escape.

The team left the cave system and blew it up, setting up a grenade at the entrance of the Blue Cave. Malus would never use the Blue Cave again to try to open the portal.

The group left the cave system dirty, dusty, tired, and concerned. They had many confirmed kills, but their prize had slipped away in the mayhem, and they only had two grenades left.

Tiern wanted to return to their camp and send some runners back to bring the MECAs to carry the wounded. On their way back, the runners were still trying to track Malus, but there was no sign of him, and Ewan could not seem to sense him at all.

Everybody was glad to see their pool and their familiar little cave system, which had become their home in the last few weeks.

While Anna treated all the wounded, the others washed off in the pool, which was cleansing and cooling. They ate some food beside a roaring fire and went to bed exhausted.

Luckily, the rest of the Mongollon tribe and Terranze women kept bringing down food, wood, and clean clothing to their cave every couple of days.

In the morning, the principal leaders had a meeting and decided to try to find the other hatchery. They believed it was now safe to take the MECAs. Malus's private little army of hybrid hunters was now gone, or at least diminished, and the rest of the Archa were dead.

Although Malus was still a formidable enemy, and with his whereabouts unknown, there was still a significant danger lurking behind every tree, bush, or rock.

Will, Mica, Anna, Ewan, some of the Terranze, and the Mongollons took the MECAs and went toward the east, where they believed they might find the other hatchery.

At the Compound, there was a rusty old metal hangar standing, surrounded by trees. Inside the hangar was a floor covered with old straw, dirt, and cobwebs.

The Mongollons brushed the straw away and found a rickety trapdoor, which they opened. Underneath was a maze of rooms that had been empty for a very long time. Whoever had worked down here had gone a long time ago. There wasn't even any trash left behind, just a tiny scrap of paper that read, "Genetic Project." The rest of the page was missing.

Will suddenly had a revelation. Could the hatchery be on the third floor of the ORRC building? Perhaps it was a classified project that even the director, Zeta 25, didn't know about. He asked Mica what she thought.

"I don't know," replied Mica, "because Zeta 25 could have lied."

"Even if she did, it doesn't mean the project isn't there. There was a third-floor option on the elevator," continued Will.

"I am just not convinced," said Mica. "I think they probably conduct experimentation there, but I don't believe it is where the hatchery is. I think Malus would hide his creations in a very safe and fortified place, away from prying eyes. I bet the Archa didn't even know about the hatcheries."

Will sighed. "I think you are right. Where do we look now?"

Mica went over to where Ewan was standing; he seemed to be in deep meditation.

"Ewan, do you know where the dark one is?" asked Mica gently.

"Yes." He nodded

"Where is he, Ewan?" she asked patiently.

"He is in Eighth City," Ewan replied.

"Where in Eighth City?" asked Mica, surprised.

"Beneath," replied Ewan.

And that was all he would say. He went back to drawing in the dirt with his favorite stick.

CHAPTER 31

Malus's Final Journey

Malus fully realized his dire situation as he watched the Blue Cave go up in smoke. All the remaining Archa were dead. He wasn't too concerned that they were gone, though; they were worthless in his opinion. Far below the Archons in intelligence and breeding. But the precious fourth batch of hatchlings had been implanted in the Yellow Eyed breeders and were now dead, disintegrated, and buried under the rubble of Ninth City with their hosts.

Malus had to find a replacement leader before his ultimate annihilation. He was now seven million years old. Eventually, an Archon would painfully disintegrate slowly, molecule by molecule, until they were gone. This was Malus's destiny. He would have to find a safe, dark place to hide in when the process began.

When they first arrived on planet Earth, the Archons had all put samples of their DNA into cryogenic storage to preserve it for later use. In due time, the majority of the Archons had voted not to reproduce. Primarily so that the remaining Hive of Archon would not locate their creations, the humans and the Yellow Eyes, and possibly annihilate them and destroy the surface Archons' legacy as gods in this world. They had ordered Malus to incinerate all their DNA, but he did not comply and hid it instead. Malus conducted a false Ceremony of Destruction to deceive the remainder of the group.

Secretly, Malus had used the remaining hidden, precious DNA to breed a new batch of Archon hatchlings. His first and second attempts were a disaster, and they did not survive. After many decades of research, and with the help of two brilliant Yellow Eyes scientists, the trio had managed to perfect the process, so the third and final batch was successful, but it had used the last of the Archon DNA.

Malus and the scientists had finally managed to achieve a group more synchronized in thought and action, like the Hive. They were indeed a collective. If Malus could save the remaining hatchlings and take them to safety, they could hide for a hundred years and be able to breed again. A hundred years to a creature that lived for millions was just a moment in time. The Hive had a longer life span. Somehow the light deteriorated their DNA faster on Earth than it did in the Void.

Malus had bred twenty-four hatchlings. Twelve hatchlings made up one breeding colony. Eventually, he would have two functioning, breeding colonies in about a hundred years. They were the last of their kind. The hatchlings would remain safely hidden until they reached maturity. The Archa had known nothing about the hatchlings, for an excellent reason. Eventually, the hatchlings were to be their replacements, and the Archa were destined to be their first adult meal.

There were some cryogenically frozen, pure Archon embryos at this hatchery, and they must be taken to safety with the live hatchlings and implanted into hosts immediately. Then Malus could restore the world to its former glory, with the Archons back at the helm again, where they belonged.

There would be no more hybrids tainting the bloodlines of the Hive of Archon's pure, dark DNA. It was vital that he start to rebuild the portal—he would do this a long way away, hidden, but close to a small or medium population for an accessible food and an entertainment source. Gradually they would breed more and more colonies until just enough human slavs remained to serve them and some Yellow Eyes to host and feed them.

Malus had to get to the hatchlings before the watchers did. They were smart for humans, which was a matter of concern. Perhaps the humans were self-evolving. A sample of their DNA would be interesting to analyze, he thought. The hatchlings were hidden in plain sight, in an underground facility at Eighth City, with the entrance to their nest about five miles outside the city walls. It was a vast breeding site, much bigger than the one at Ninth City.

Malus decided it would be better to divide the hatchlings into two separate entities; then if one group was caught or destroyed, there would still be a full breeding colony of twelve left.

Malus made his way to Eighth City on a MECA. He drove to the colony, which was hidden by brush and large rocks. The entrance was the beginning of an unused old lava tube that ran underneath Eighth City. The tunnel was more than large enough to drive through it not only a MECA but a Heavy One too.

Malus reached the nest without incident, and he drove through the security gate. Finally, in the middle of the colony, he went to inspect his hatchlings. High-caste Yellow Eyes maintained the hatchlings and were trained to serve their every need.

First, Malus checked the twelve closest to him. They were beautiful specimens, with translucent black skin, big golden eyes, with vertical pupils. They had similar facial features to him, with two sets of teeth and a jaw that dislocated at will. They were perfect. The instant he walked in, they all sensed him, turned, and spoke in unison.

"Greetings, Father of Twelve," they chanted. They looked like clones of one another, tall and androgynous. Because they were young, they were considered very immature by Malus. Not even eating proper prey yet, they were still hand-fed.

"We must move immediately to a safer place," he told them.

"Can we finish eating, Father of Twelve?" they said as one unit.

Hatchlings had tremendous appetites, had to eat constantly, and they only ate raw meat. They ate voraciously like predators, tearing at their food, with blood and bits of flesh dribbling down their chins. When they were a little older, about twenty years of age, they would eat live meat, as Gula had done.

"Yes," replied Malus quickly. "Then we will leave. We must travel a long way. Maintainers, you will accompany us."

The Yellow Eyes said nothing, remaining bowed, with their eyes downcast, too afraid to do anything else.

"Scientists S 1 and S 2 will go too," ordered Malus.

There was a Skybird waiting farther away from the lava tube, hidden behind a sizable rocky outcrop. Five MECAs full of Yellow Eyes, hatchlings, and cryogenically frozen embryos drove out to meet the Skybird, and Malus quickly boarded its precious cargo.

Malus gave the two pilots a set of coordinates. "Take them to their safe place and then return here for a second pickup," he ordered.

The two pilots looked at the coordinates. "Your lordship, it will take us a day to return," they said. "This is a twelve-hour flight each way."

"I am aware of this fact," snapped Malus. "Leave now!"

"Yes, your lordship," replied the obedient and well-trained pilots. They immediately fired up the engines and started to taxi down the small runway. Soon the Skybird was just a dot in the sky.

Malus was driven back to the nest by one of the Yellow Eyes and went to sit with the other hatchlings to wait for the Skybird to return.

Back at the empty tunnels, Will, Mica, and the others tried to figure out where the hatchlings could be hiding.

"Beneath," repeated Mica, confused. "Surely, Ewan must mean beneath Eighth City."

Anna had been silent for a few moments. "I believe there is an old lava tube beneath Eighth City. The Terranze hid there many generations ago when a mountain of flaming fire crashed into the land and everything burned for many weeks. It was a story passed to me from a long time ago."

"Anna, do you remember where the entrance to the tube is?" asked Mica urgently.

"No," replied Anna, "I don't, but the story says, when the mountain of fire hit the Earth, the Terranze sought refuge from the burning heat in the safety of the rocks. The rocks hid a long secret place beneath the Earth where the Terranze—"

Will interrupted excitedly. "I think I know where it is. It's a rocky outcrop about five miles outside of Eighth City. I saw it when we flew over once before, when we were in flight training."

"We should load up a convoy and take all our warriors and weapons to this place," suggested Tiern.

So the group started to load up the convoy and headed out to the outcrop. As they came closer, the Terranze began to walk so they could look for any tracks that were around the site. It wasn't long before they found fresh MECA tracks, one going in, and five coming out, and then returning.

"We must follow these tracks," said Tiern. "They will lead us to the dark one. I can smell him already," he said, his face wrinkling in disgust.

The convoy followed the tracks, then parked, and everybody continued on foot. The Terranze sent a couple of trackers to run ahead. They darted the guard before he even saw them, and luckily, no warning was sent to the nest.

As they followed the tracks inside, Ewan flinched. "The dark one knows we are here," he said.

Everyone froze and began to prepare for the upcoming battle.

Some black-eyed bio-hunters then came pouring out of the tunnel. The Terranze darted as many hunters as possible, but still they kept coming, like ants from an anthill, so everyone began firing at them.

Will shouted, "Grenade!" pulled the pin, and threw one at the entrance of the lava tube. There was a gargantuan explosion, followed by flying shrapnel, debris, and finally, the sight of many dead or immobilized black-eyed hunters silently deflating.

There was a brief reprieve, and then the second batch of black-eyed hunters stormed them. Will threw the last grenade, which caused some of the tunnel to collapse in places. Dust was everywhere. Smoke plumes drifted, and more debris flew across the air.

Suddenly, out of the billowing smoke came these shrieking sirens, streaking across the ground and cutting through the air. They looked like ancient ghosts screeching from the bowels of the Earth, their bald heads and hairless bodies coated with dirt and debris.

Long dusty cobwebs spread around their demonic faces, and their cotton shifts, which were gray and laden with dust, looked like burial shrouds. Their raspy lips were pulled back in a snarl, and they were showing their double rows of pointed teeth. They tried to attack the warriors by biting, tearing, and clawing at them, like a pack of ravenous velociraptors.

Ape-Man picked one up that tried to attack him and threw the hatchling at the Terranze, who speared them like lightning, one by one. They howled and wailed, writhing and dying, still impaled on the long poisoned spears.

Will was shouting, "We have to find Malus!" The noise was incredible, but Mica heard him just as she spotted Ewan standing off to the side. As the smoke and dust cleared, he appeared frozen, just staring straight ahead.

"Will!" Mica shouted and pointed to Ewan. They both rushed toward him. Anna was farther behind than the two warriors, but she realized what was going on immediately.

Mica and Will reached Ewan, who was looking down the tunnel at a raging and maniacal Malus, who spiraled forward, intending on ripping Ewan apart. Ewan stood still and held his right hand up with his arm straight out; he didn't even flinch at what was hurtling toward him. He seemed to be in a trance. Mica stood next to him and held her left hand out while holding Ewan's hand. Malus came faster and faster toward them, spinning like a top. Ewan and Mica kept their hands up, and Malus came within a mere six inches of their hands. It was as if he hit a force field of golden light, which sent him flying backward and crashing into a rock wall.

Immediately, Malus got back up and came forward again. By this time Anna had joined Mica and Ewan, with her hand outstretched. Malus zoomed toward them at an even higher velocity of speed. He was a spiraling arrow, but this time he hit their barrier of golden light at least three feet away. Mica, Ewan, and Anna all had their eyes closed and were chanting together.

Will could not hear what they were chanting, but suddenly, an enormous golden glow filled the tunnel. The golden light began to spin and become brighter and brighter and turned from gold to an iridescent violet.

The warriors shielded their eyes from the searing light as Malus began to burn. Tiny violet flames appeared everywhere all over his body, growing whiter and hotter. He started to smoke and melt while still screaming his hatred for the humans. Soon he disappeared into a mass of dark molecules that swarmed for a moment and dropped as black ashes. Then a gust of wind blew through the tunnel, and the ashes of darkness were gone, Malus now consumed by the fire and power of light.

Everyone was yelling the war cry of victory. Mica, Will, and Anna hugged one another and grabbed Ewan.

Somewhere across the Pacific Ocean, the Skybird had already dropped off its precious cargo, which had quickly slipped under the safety of the Earth to wait and mature. As the Skybird was on its return journey, it was struck by lightning and exploded over the ocean, sinking quickly into its watery grave, where it would remain forever, lost at the bottom of the sea. The two pilots were dead, leaving no witnesses behind.

"Ewan, do you think they are all dead?" asked Anna.

"I don't know," he said solemnly, "but I cannot feel them anymore."

Just as a precaution, the peoples around the planet looked for more hatchlings.

Ewan insisted many times he could not sense their vibrations anymore.

So Will, Mica, Anna, Tiern, the Terranze, Ape-Man, and the Mongollons all believed they had finally destroyed Malus and the Archa.

CHAPTER 32

The Surrender of Eighth City

There was one way in and one way out of Eighth City. The walls had been built to stop people from coming in. There were no steps on the inside of the walls or any ladders tall enough to scale the walls of the city.

Majority of the Yellow Eyes were not fit and healthy; they did not exercise or perform any physical labor. Their society was all about appearance, excess, and pleasure. They had no weapons or military training. All they had for defense was their arrogance, pride, selfishness, and the false belief that Eighth City was so valuable that Malus wouldn't let it fall. Once they knew that Malus and the remaining purebred Archa were dead, they felt defeated and afraid.

The gate of the city had been torn off by the mile-long convoy that was invading it.

The Yellow Eyes tried to use their tiny cars to escape, but the vehicles only had a forty-five-minute charge, and once they stalled, they were able to be rounded up quickly as they wilted in the hot sun.

The sight of the Mongollons petrified the Yellow Eyes, which was not surprising at all, since many of the wealthiest ones had been willing and participating guests at Nightmare Caverns.

The Mongollons jumped off the front of the convoy, roaring at the terrified Yellow Eyes, who immediately lined up in single file, sobbing and clutching their most expensive and precious possessions while their poor, panicked children clung to the edge of their parents' clothing.

Once they were all rounded up and accounted for, Will stood up to speak to them.

"Yellow Eyes, you are now our prisoners, but we are not inhumane. We will give you options for your future and allow you to choose your fate."

Will continued, "You may choose between self-destruction, called the Last Journey, which is a painless procedure used to end life in the Healing Centers, or you can choose life and attend rehabilitation and training, eventually assimilating into our new society. You will be assigned jobs suited to your abilities and intelligence. We do not have slavs in New City.

"If you want to eat, you must participate. It is your choice, so make it now. Husbands and fathers, your wives and children over the age of sixteen will make their choices. Children under sixteen will not take their Last Journey, they will undergo rehabilitation. Those who wish to make the Last Journey, file to the left, and those who choose rehabilitation, file to the right. You have exactly five minutes to decide."

The lower-caste Yellow Eyes immediately chose the rehabilitation option, figuring life wouldn't be that much different from Eighth City even under some new rules. Children under sixteen automatically moved into the rehabilitation line.

Some of the higher-caste males and their wives chose the Last Journey line, ignoring their crying offspring in the rehabilitation line. Other males tried to drag their reluctant women to the death line. The Mongollons soon stopped that and roared while physically separating the couples, throwing the men several feet in the air and dropping them loudly at the end of the death line.

Many females, after watching this incident, quickly switched lines and stood by their children. With the Mongollons patrolling between the two lines, no other husbands tried to influence their wives, at least physically— although some attempted to argue, they were quickly silenced by the wrath of the Mongollons. Some males even changed lines too.

Will spoke to the Yellow Eyes again. "Your five minutes are up. Those of you who have chosen the Final Journey will be loaded into the vehicles and taken under guard to the Healing Centers. You will return to the Earth within about four hours."

Will then stated, "Those who have chosen the rehabilitation will be divided by gender. You will receive the sterilization chip, unable to reproduce unless you win the lottery. Females already with child will be allowed to birth them. Then they, too, will receive the sterilization chip.

"Everybody will be RFID-chipped so that we can track your movements. You must attend rehabilitation for up to one year, during which time your case will come under review periodically. If, at one of the reviews, you are deemed ready, you will be assigned a work placement and integrate into your new community. We have no castes in First City, which will be a relief for some and difficult for others. Welcome to your new city and your new life."

At that point, the Yellow Eyes were loaded into vehicles and driven away, to begin their new lives or deaths.

The Yellow Eyes went to Fourth City's Obedience Reinforcement and Rehabilitation Center in First City. The first thing they had to do on their arrival was to record their names and ages.

Then they were sent for a medical review and RFID chipping. The females had to take pregnancy tests. The pregnant Yellow Eyes went to the birthing center in Third City, which had been renovated and reopened after the Farm had closed down.

Some of the birthers wanted to stay as midwives. Dr. Linvo from First City replaced Dr. Orrow. The once high and mighty and disturbed Dr. Orrow was in rehabilitation, which was not going well at all. Megalomania was not a curable disease, and his being a psychopathic sadist did not help his case for mercy. Eventually, within two years, he was ordered to take his Last Journey after being deemed a danger to society by the Council. He underwent cremation, and his ashes lay unclaimed and discarded, blowing in the wind and sinking into the Earth. Unlike Dr. Orrow's victims, who received a beautiful service and whose ashes were returned to the forests from whence they came.

Third City was now a legitimate birthing center. The sorting room and the deadly research room had been closed down, repainted, and turned into a proper nursery complete with a surgical emergency room and a newborn intensive care center.

The remainder of the Yellow Eyes settled in at the Obedience Reinforcement and Rehabilitation Center. First, they had to scrub their faces clean and remove their wigs and expensive clothes, which were replaced by white cotton shifts and canvas shoes. The women were sobbing and suddenly looked like little broken birds, with all their plumage gone, and the remnants of their sparse yellow hair were falling to the floor as the dressers shaved their heads.

Mica went to see how the recruits were adapting. One female grabbed her arm. "Why do you hate us so much? We never did anything to you! Why do you torture us so?"

Mica responded, "Never touch me again. I am trained to fight in hand-to-hand combat, and I could react and hurt you without meaning to."

Some of the women immediately cowered back from her.

"I am not here to hurt you," Mica said slowly. "You are undergoing your transformation. To complete this change, first, you must return to nothing, to be nothing, to know nothing, to expect nothing. Then in time you will be reborn and find out who you were meant to be. It is a long and painful journey. I have done this, and like you, I didn't know my potential either. You must have the courage. If you don't have it now, you will find it. Our program here is to help you become your own person."

"What if I don't want to change?" remarked an older woman, stepping forward. She was arrogant, and Mica could tell she was once one of the highest-caste Yellow Eyes, and she was challenging Mica with her haughty stare.

"You were given a choice, death or change. If you don't wish to change, then you chose the wrong line," replied Mica drily.

The female stepped back into line with the others.

"One other comment I have," continued Mica, "is that you are all now equal, not just regarding castes, but also gender. Now you belong to no one but yourselves, and for this reason, you are all the masters of your fates."

Many of the Yellow Eyes from the lowest castes adapted very well, and within six months, most were integrated into their new city and became valued members of society.

The younger high-caste children also adapted reasonably well, usually retrained within six months to a year.

The higher, upper-caste males were a different story; they were problematic from the beginning, and they became even worse as time passed. They remained a constant problem because they seemed unable to assimilate and often became violent and aggressive in rehabilitation.

Some of the male Yellow Eyes had to be put on medication to keep them from fantasizing about some of the more-devious habits that they had enjoyed in the old days in Eighth City. Some of the men who couldn't rehabilitate at all faced execution because they were deemed to be too dangerous to let loose in the community.

The problem was, their society had spoiled them and allowed them to be dominant from the age of two over others—particularly ultimate power over women—and that, combined with too much money and power, had made them into monsters. They seemed to be incapable of empathy for anyone but themselves. Most had to remain sterile because their genes were too contaminated to pass on. This shortage of male Yellow Eyes caused a lot of intermarriage between the female Yellow Eyes and the different tribes, making everybody almost related to one another. In retrospect, that was a good thing.

CHAPTER 33

Lyra's Story

There were some problems with the older high-caste women. One woman in particular could not adapt. Mica went to see her while she was still in the rehabilitation center. Her head was shaved, and she was wearing white shift and black canvas shoes. Mica recognized her immediately from the previous year; she was the haughty woman who had spoken to her the day of their admission.

Mica walked in and sat down opposite her and said nothing. There was silence, until the woman spoke. "You were right, I chose the wrong line. I would like to request to undertake the Last Journey."

Mica asked her, "What is your name?"

"Lyra," she replied. "Why does it matter who I am?"

"Are you ill, Lyra?" questioned Mica, ignoring her comment.

"No," she replied sharply. Then she paused. "Perhaps I am," she said slowly.

"What is it that you can't adapt to?" asked Mica curiously.

"Myself," Lyra whispered.

Lyra explained, "I am who I was meant to be. I realize I cannot be anything else, and there is no place in this society for an old woman like me."

"And who are you?" Mica asked directly.

"I am a person who believes in castes, a person that wants my freedom and solitude back. My culture is so ingrained in me that I cannot change. I am old, tired, and I do not want to be around other people. I want to return to the Earth."

"Lyra, why are you giving up on life?" Mica asked sharply.

Lyra replied, "Mica, you were right. Self-discovery is a long and painful journey, but I took that one many years ago. What I learned is, I was, and am, who I was meant to be. It doesn't matter whether society sees me as right or wrong. As the master of my fate, I wish to take the Final Journey Ceremony."

Mica looked at her and demanded, "I want you to tell me a story first."

"I have no happy stories," said Lyra, shaking her bald head.

"Everybody has a story," replied Mica, "and I want to hear yours."

Lyra was surprised. "Why does it matter?" she asked.

Mica replied evasively, "You will see. Just tell me your story."

"Very well," replied Lyra irritably, "but it won't change my mind."

Lyra began her story. "I was born into a very wealthy and prominent family. My father was from the highest caste, and he was the director of Eighth City.

"I was his first child, and I was born with pale golden eyes and darker, thicker hair than the rest of the people. I wasn't a pureblood, but I was the best female specimen ever produced in the city in many generations.

"My father was very protective of me. My mother had died while birthing my younger brother, who did not survive either. My father told me to never, ever go to the Archa Compound and that he knew some things that others did not about that place. He warned me, if I ever went there, I would not return.

"I listened to him, as I always did. Several of my friends had gone to the Compound over the years, trying to conceive a pureblood child. My father was right—they never came back. I asked him what happened to those that never returned, but all he would tell me was it was not something that young girls needed to hear.

"I remember, when I was older and married, I asked him again. He ordered that under no circumstances should I attend the quarterly parties or let my children go there, because it was an evil place. It seemed odd to me because there were so many friends and neighbors who begged him to get their tickets. Sometimes he did, but he always told them, 'Once you go there, you will be changed forever, and not for the better.'

"I often wondered why my father never remarried. He told me he didn't have time, which seemed strange, because he spent a lot of time with me. A few years later, he said my mother still held his heart, and always would.

"As I was growing up, I had whatever I wished, whenever I wanted it. I learned how to play music, read, sing, paint, cook. I was educated in history and current events by an educator who came to the house daily. I learned how to manage the slavs and supervise a large household, all in preparation for my only purpose in life: being a wife. Only lower-caste women could work if they were past child-bearing years or they were ugly or too poor for marriage.

"In my youth, I was considered the most desirable woman in the city. Many men offered my father vast amounts of silver for my hand in marriage, but he did not need the silver—he had so much of it.

"What he wanted to be was the grandfather of the firstborn purebred in Eighth City. So he found a young man who was a little older than me. His name was Tarfor. His family was not quite as famous or wealthy as ours, so of course, they happily agreed to the marriage, because it would raise their standing in the community, and I believe my father paid them a handsome dowry, although we never talked about such things.

"What was so special about Tarfor was that he was young and had a coloring almost identical to mine. We looked almost like twins. We were both happy about our forthcoming marriage. We were married when I was fourteen and he was sixteen. We did not know each other very well until after we wed. We were young, but we became good friends very quickly, and then after a short time together, we fell deeply in love.

"Falling in love was very unusual for the way of our people. Most marriages are merely business arrangements. It was very traditional for young girls to be married to old men. So I was fortunate.

"Just a year later, our first child was born. Her name was Caya. I loved her so, but she was not the golden purebred everybody expected. However, she looked like us, and so she was a revered child. Our families were satisfied, but not well pleased. She was such a brilliant ray of sunshine in my life. I was so happy—I had a wonderful husband and a beautiful child, whom I adored.

"Two years later, when I was almost eighteen, we had a son, Faron, who was born with pale yellow eyes and had sparse yellow hair. We loved him regardless, but although born to a high-status family, he had the appearance of a very low-caste citizen. Our specialist healer believed that he must have been a genetic throwback.

"Our parents wanted us to drown him as soon as he was born. They told me he would only bring trouble and disgrace to our whole family. I refused to listen to them. I was very young and foolish. My existence was perfect; and I didn't believe anything could ever go wrong in my life. Faron was my child, and I loved him very much. I wished I had listened to them all those years ago. They knew so much more than I.

"Our third child, who was born two years later, was another golden-eyed child who looked like me, but with slightly darker hair. If you were to glance at her, she could have passed for a pureblood. Although up close you could tell she wasn't. Her name was Kariina, and people sometimes mistakenly bowed before her, believing she was a pureblood Archa.

"My father was triumphant, and so was Tarfor's family. We had produced two good specimens and one genetic throwback. When Faron was barely six, I became pregnant with my fourth child. Something went wrong, and my child perished. I also lost the ability to bear any more children. I almost died myself, and my body was fragile. It took several months to recover my health, and I was sad, grieving for my departed child.

"As my health improved, I began to notice that Faron was being treated differently by everybody, from the people in the city to even the slavs, who adored taking care of Caya and Kariina. They seemed as if they resented looking after him because he was lighter than them. They would pretend not to hear his requests and mostly ignored him. I was outraged when I learned this. I had a meeting with the slavs and told them, if they didn't respect my son, then they didn't respect me either and they could leave my household.

"Things were better after that, and I watched over him carefully. He would ask me why his sisters were so adored and why everyone looked at him like he was poison. I tried to explain to Faron, but he didn't understand. I told him, 'People are envious of you, you have light eyes and hair, and most people with these colorings do not have the fortune to be born into such a wealthy family.' I said that he was lucky, but my words did not soothe him.

"As he grew to adulthood, he changed from a bright, inquisitive little boy to an angry young man. Neither Tarfor nor I could reach him. We had spent many years searching for a decent bride for him, but unfortunately, his appearance and his reputation of being a bitter man did not bide well for him. The only brides available were very pale Yellow Eyes, but they were from the slav caste, and they were not educated to his standard. He refused all offers of marriage over the years.

"He grew angrier and more bitter the older he got. People still admired and honored his sisters while dismissing him. As a male in our society, it was very insulting for him that the women in his family were superior and more successful than him. He was always humiliated by his lack of status. If he walked alone through the city, he suffered from harassment. Men, and even women, treated him like the lowest caste and asked him why he wasn't at work. Where did he get those fine clothes that he was wearing? Did he steal them? Because his clothes were inappropriate for a mere slav.

"The public enforcement officers often detained him on suspicion of stealing or not being in his appointed place of duty or trying to impersonate a higher caste. Eventually, he refused to leave our dwelling unless it was dark.

"The only place he felt accepted at was the House of Dreams. They did not care for his coloring either since their patrons were the high-caste rich, but they did love his silver, and he spent vast sums there. He had a special entrance and exit at the back of that house that consisted of a large bedchamber and bathroom. Faron turned it into his main living space, rarely coming home for days on end.

"Eventually, my husband, Tarfor, went to this place to find out why he was spending so much money. Unlike other husbands, he had never frequented the House of Dreams, preferring to spend time with our children and me.

"Tarfor was pale and shaken when he returned home, and he told me that he had spoken to the director of the establishment. She was an old woman who always wore silk poppies on her clothing. She said that Faron had graduated from merely being serviced by the women there into much darker sexual arenas. No longer satisfied with the rooms of chains and bondage, Faron had become obsessed with the Snuff Salon, where he would take the most beautiful girls and spend days slowly torturing and eventually killing them.

"Often he did not return the bodies for cremation for several days after they were dead. The director informed Tarfor they could not keep up with his appetites. He had murdered nine women in the last six months. Of course, none of this was a moral issue for her, but it was now becoming a problem due to supply and demand.

"Her other patrons were becoming upset, not just at the stench that permeated from the back of the house, but because he took many of the most beautiful women for himself. He had been in altercations with some of the higher-caste members, and they wanted him gone. Therefore, he was no longer welcome there anymore.

"I was horrified by the things Tarfor told me, and I couldn't believe that this type of establishment was even allowed in our society. With me as an upper-caste wife and mother, these sorts of things weren't discussed around women in polite society. We were so naive. I, myself, had thought the House of Dreams was a respectable venue, where men went to carry out business transactions and maybe served a meal or a drink by a pretty server.

"No woman ever asked her husband if he went there, or anywhere else, for that matter. Women were not allowed to question their husbands' comings and goings. But I do know the other wives believed it was a place where legitimate business was conducted. They certainly didn't understand it was a house of depravity. The secret was well kept by the men who frequented it. I was the only wife to know this because Tarfor and I had no secrets from each other.

"I had no idea of such dark evil that existed in the minds of some men. The prominent men of the city did not want me to socialize with their wives anymore. I think they were afraid that I knew too many secrets of the House of Dreams and might betray them. They merely tolerated Tarfor for his wealth, but none of the men trusted him because he had told me the truth about the House of Dreams.

"We immediately cut Faron off from all our silver. With nowhere else to go, he returned to our home and stayed in his quarters alone all the time, refusing to come out. When I tried to connect with him, he would just turn his face toward the wall and refuse to speak to his father or me. The following day, we discussed having him taken to see a specialist healer who understood such disorders. We contacted the healer, who agreed to see Faron. He suggested we put him in a rehabilitation center until he was cured, and we acquiesced. Faron was supposed to leave two days later.

"Caya had been married happily for two years but had returned home to spend the night with her sister, Kariina, who was getting married the next day. We had found an excellent husband for her, and I believed she was going to be as happy as Tarfor and I were.

"Faron might have overheard our conversation, because the next morning, both our beautiful and beloved daughters were found slaughtered in their beds, with their throats cut. Kariina never got the chance to marry her handsome young man, and Faron was sitting in his room, silent and soaked in his sisters' blood.

"As he was taken away, he hissed at Tarfor and me, 'Now you have what I have—nothing. You will be stared at every day in the streets as I was. Your reputation is ruined. My pain has become your pain.' And then he laughed hysterically, like a man with no mind left, as they led him away.

"That day was a nightmare. Kariina was cremated with her sister on her wedding day. Caya's husband was anguished about her death. She had been about to tell us she was with her first child. In private he blamed us for not protecting them against a deviant, low-caste, and known murderer.

"All our families were angry with us and shunned us. It was a terrible scandal, and we were almost put before the justice system ourselves, but because we had contacted this healer and my father had such good standing in the community, we were spared. It didn't matter, because our guilt would haunt us, punishing us for eternity.

"My father blamed me because he had warned me many years ago, and he shunned me. My husband's family blamed me too and shunned me. Only Tarfor was by my side as we had our daughters cremated, and when we released their ashes to the gentle breeze, Tarfor was beside himself with grief, and so was I.

"We never saw our son again. After his execution, they asked us if we wanted his ashes. Tarfor said, 'No, feed them to the pigs. He is not my son anymore.' He looked sternly at me, and I dared not disobey him. So I shook my head in agreement, even though I wanted them. I wished to release the pain of the little boy born to the wrong caste.

"Three months later, my beloved husband died. They said his heart had stopped from all the grief. I was left alone, shunned by the people as a cursed woman who brought death to all those who were around her. I never spoke to my father again. I had heard that he had died a few years after my beloved husband. I knew him to be a proud man, and the news did not surprise me. He had left instructions that I should not receive his ashes. So even in death, he shunned me. My heart was already broken into tiny pieces, so his death was just another ripple on the pond of grief. It didn't hurt much anymore.

"I lived alone for many years. I was a woman worth a lot of silver, so I had offers of marriage, but I could see that evil look in their eyes, and I knew they were not good men. They probably wanted to squander my silver at the House of Dreams. Since I did not remarry, I was considered a dark witch. I spent time writing, playing music, painting, and later, a few years after the tragedies, I would relive the laughter and love that had once filled my house. I had no friends. It would be unseemly for any society woman to be seen with me. I had several slavs to attend to the house and garden.

"When my family died, I had a twenty-foot wall built around my home so I could grieve in peace without strange people screaming insults and throwing eggs and dead animals into my beautiful gardens. I never left the house. The slavs did all the shopping and cooking. I never even spoke to them—I just wrote notes for them, and they left notes for me. As I grew older and finally entered old age, the solitude didn't bother me anymore. I liked being alone. It was quiet and peaceful, with no surprises. That made me feel safe.

"One frigid evening some years ago, I was walking alone. I liked to walk alone in the cold, when the city was almost deserted. I was just a heavily clothed old woman by then, and the young people didn't recognize me anymore. It made me feel good to walk alone around the city. Suddenly, I heard a very tiny sound coming from inside the nearby bushes. I looked down among the bushes, and there was a small hybrid cat, very young, with big golden eyes that reminded me of my daughters'. She was looking up at me. She had long golden fur and an injury to her leg that had healed but left her with a minor limp. She had been discarded, left to die because she wasn't perfect, and for this reason only, nobody would buy her or want her.

"Somehow, the ice in my heart thawed, and I picked this tiny, little creature up and held her in my warm coat. She was freezing, and she made a chi-chi sound. I brought her home and gave her milk and mashed up some raw meat. I knew how to do this because a friend of mine had owned such a creature once, a long time ago, in the good days of my life. I had wanted a hybrid cat too, but Tarfor was concerned that one might hurt the children when they were young. Such irony, knowing what happened in our lives."

Lyra gave an ironic smile.

"Well, Chi-Chi and I became close. She became my only friend. She slept on my bed at night, much to the disgust of the slavs. She always traveled everywhere with me. She was my shadow and my best friend. Chi-Chi never judged me, and she loved me for who I was. I loved her for the same reason. Loving and caring for her made me want to live. We spent many happy years together. I lost her when I came here, and I don't want to live anymore. I want to go too."

"Did Chi-Chi die before you came here?" asked Mica.

"No," said Lyra. "She was at home the day we were captured."

"We did not kill any of the creatures," replied Mica. "That is not our way. We set up enclosures for them, and some of the Yellow Eyes take care and feed them. They are teaching First City how to look after such creatures. Your Chi-Chi could be there. Would you like to go and see if we can find her?"

"Oh my stars, can it be? Is my Chi-Chi still alive?" Lyra's whole face lit up with joy.

Mica signed Lyra out of Fourth City Rehabilitation Center, and they walked out into the sunshine. Mica took her to and showed her where the pet enclosures were. Lyra ran to them, calling, "Chi-Chi!" and she heard a faint reply coming from a cage in the bottom left corner. Lyra called louder, "Chi-Chi, Chi-Chi," and heard an answer. Lyra swung open the cage and threw herself on the old hybrid cat, who suddenly was infused with life and purred and rubbed her head against Lyra's while she chi-chi-chied.

Lyra cried into her golden fur, and they sat together for a few minutes, so glad to have found each other again. "Chi-Chi, why are you so thin?" Lyra asked.

"She was sad. She wouldn't eat much. I even hand-fed her so she wouldn't die. I talked to her every day. I told her that you would come back to find her. I told her, 'Don't give up yet,'" said the female called Yaza, who had just spoken to Lyra. She had very pale yellow eyes and once was a very low-caste citizen in Eighth City. Yaza had spent months trying to keep Chi-Chi alive.

Lyra placed the woman's hands in her own. "Thank you," she said humbly and sincerely.

Mica smiled. "Would you like to run the animal enclosure, Lyra? The only reason we don't have a director here is that nobody wants to live here full-time. There is a small living space at the back of the enclosures, and I think you and Chi-Chi would be very comfortable in there together."

"Yes, yes, thank you!" cried Lyra, tears rolling down her cheeks.

"Why did you ask me to tell my story?" she asked Mica in between sobs of joy. "Right now, I could be back in the Earth, and Chi-Chi would have known that and died too."

"I am a seer," replied Mica. "Sometimes I just have to let people see themselves as I do. Your eyes were not those of a murderer. Your aura was of sadness. You believed in the caste system. You think your daughters would still be alive today if you had drowned your son, as custom dictated. You hated the pale Yellow Eyes, like your son, because you believed he must have been inferior genetically because he was an unstable murderer and was the cause of all your pain and tragedy.

"But think of this. Perhaps If you had all lived in a place where the color of your eyes and hair didn't matter, all your family would be alive today. Don't you see? It was the system that was wrong, not your family. Your story is one that is very powerful, one that many children can learn from and understand how sometimes traditions and culture can destroy people.

"I would like you to come in and share your story with the children at the Good Citizens Enhancement Facility. Remember, your beloved Chi-Chi was saved by a pale Yellow Eyes, like your son. In each of us, there is a good beast and a bad beast. They fight each other constantly, and the one that wins is the one you feed the most.

"You must forgive yourself and forgive your son and forgive your father and all those who judged you. What happened was meant to be. Why is not always understood at the time. Only when you return to the One will you ever understand everything."

"Thank you, Mica. You have saved two sad old creatures today," said Lyra happily.

Lyra and Chi-Chi lived for another four more beautiful years together, working at the animal enclosures and speaking to classes of children in the center. Somebody found them one day seemingly just curled asleep together, but neither could be woken. They had died together as they lived together.

Of course, they were cremated together, and Mica took their ashes to their favorite place—a beautiful hill filled with flowers where Lyra and Chi-Chi would sit for hours, side by side. Mica watched the ashes swirl together in the sudden breeze that appeared, and then Mica thought she saw both of them for an instant. The breeze dropped, and their ashes settled into the Earth.

Mica said a prayer. "The One, they have returned to you and all their relations. May they find peace in the beauty of your love and light."

Then she walked down the hill and made her way back to the new city. She would always miss the old woman and her beloved Chi-Chi. To Mica, they had always been a symbol of enduring hope and love.

PART 5

The Future

What the future holds for you depends on your state of consciousness now.

—Eckhart Tolle

CHAPTER 34

Life under the New Earth Charter: 2183

Life was busy for Will and Mica over the next four years. With the help of both the citizens and the Council of Twelve, the cities were organized to run relatively smoothly. Mica and Will set up their primary home in First City but often spent time with the Terranze and the Mongollons. They felt they belonged to all the people and loved them all.

Will and Mica chose to be life partners in September 2182, just as the autumn leaves were starting to turn red and gold. A few months later, in February of 2183, they entered the birth lottery and won a golden ticket. Mica was now pregnant with their child, who was due to be born in late fall.

They still had much work to do; the cities were a big responsibility, and the people were still becoming accustomed to their new lives. They kept Eighth City mostly intact, although the House of Dreams had been torn down. In its place was a meditation park. In the middle of the park stood the statues of a beautiful young woman and man holding an armful of flowers together. The sculptures stood as a monument to all those who had been tortured and murdered there. No such deviant place would ever be allowed to exist again.

Eighth City had become a type of resort, and every year the workers could choose to take a month off work and sign up to spend some vacation time being pampered in Eighth City. They had demolished the large homes that the Yellow Eyes had once lived in but had recycled the materials and built smaller vacation homes.

It was too hard for those who had been members of the higher-caste Yellow Eyes to come back to their beloved Eighth City. Most of them chose to visit the Archa Compound instead, which was now a museum, standing as a testament to the endurance of the human race.

Little cottages had been built around the Big White House so that people could vacation there. They conducted wildlife tours, where people were forbidden to kill but could watch the animals in their natural habitat. Some citizens chose a cultural exchange with the Terranze or the Mongollons.

Malus was dead, and the twelve Archa families who had terrorized and dictated the lives of millions of people had finally gone too. The remainder of the Archa families were eventually rounded up and sentenced to death for crimes against humanity. The whole world had searched for them, and there was nowhere they could hide anymore. They had been executed shortly after Malus and the hatchlings had been destroyed.

A new type of society was in play. A much kinder one— a new world of service to others. Will and Mica did not know how the future would unfold, but they did know training the children to be good people was the key. Once your youth lost their way, so did the future of society. The other thing they had learned was that one person should not own too much money or have too much power because human beings were still awkward three-year-olds when it came to their spiritual and emotional growth.

The Terranze had kept their spiritual ways in spite of the immense persecution and genocide that they had suffered for almost 150 years. They taught the people many stories. The Terranze were the roots of all the people because they had clung, despite everything, to their teachings and their beliefs.

Society was now training talented seers in a new program devised by Anna and Mica. Education focused on spirituality, self-improvement, and intellectual brilliance instead of obedience. Small businesses sprung up everywhere, where people bartered and exchanged goods. Food in First City improved, and there were menus now in the Central Dining Facility. The meat was still rationed, but it was available four times a week.

People were healthier and had longer life spans. Music, dancing, and laughter echoed across the globe. People of Earth were happy, content, and industrious. The population was still constrained by the lottery, and since the Terranze were no longer losing vast numbers of their tribe, they also adopted the lottery system.

Travel was easy now. There was a type of solar train that ran between cities and, eventually, in time, to other cities across the land. Wildlife corridors and forbidden areas were now gone. It wasn't necessary to protect animals and plants because as long as human population remained controlled, nature was automatically protected.

The Mongollons were sterile, so eventually they would die out. Mica felt sad about their prognosis, but Ape-Man ensured her this was the best thing for his people. He said, for them to continue, it would require ordinary people being turned into monsters, and he couldn't accept that. Mica did ask the scientists if the infertility problem of the Mongollons could be solved, but the scientists said because so many of the creatures had fragmented or confused DNA, it was not possible without a great deal of experimentation, and Ape-Man and the Mongollons flatly refused to entertain this option.

One summer evening, a week after Lyra and Chi-Chi's death, Will and Mica sat on the same hill that Lyra and Chi-Chi had loved. The flowers were in bloom, and the hilltop was serene and beautiful.

Will and Mica were sitting together, thinking how very wonderful their lives were when a golden butterfly landed on Mica's shoulder. "I was just thinking of you, Lyra and Chi-Chi," said Mica gently. The butterfly moved its wings a little and then alighted onto Mica's hand. Suddenly, six more golden butterflies arrived and flew around them, their soft wings brushing against their cheeks, and then they suddenly flew away. "Fare-well, Lyra and your family. I see you are all together again." Mica then smiled.

Mica turned to look at Will. She smiled at him and said, "I love you very much."

Will turned to her and said, "*Love* is such a small word. I feel so much more than just love for you." Then he laid his hand on her pregnant belly, feeling the faint fluttering of his son's movements beneath his hand.

Will looked into her eyes while speaking from his heart:

> When there is no time or space,
> Still, we will exist together,
> In our sacred place, as one.
> We are forever linked by spirit;
> Our connection is from the cosmos,
> Destined by those who have gone before us
> And remembered by those who will follow us.

Mica looked at Will and spoke words of love:

> It is in the deep, dark silence of the moment
> That I think of you,
> It is where
> I hear the music of your voice,
> Echoing throughout time and space.
> When I touch your face,
> I see the strength of your spirit,
> The wisdom that you are.
> I know your kindness,
> And I wonder at each moment we have shared.
> For all these things,
> You are beautiful to me,
> And with each breath
> Comes the understanding that I will always love you.

They smiled at each other and lazily watched the golden sun sink beneath the painted horizon.

CHAPTER 35

The Sacred Hill of Golden Butterflies: 2238

Will and Mica spent the remaining decades of their lives running the cities and shaping their new society.

They had a son, Miron, whom they showered with love, and he grew up to be a wise man, a philosopher and scientist. He looked very much like his father. Will/Kiron died at the age of ninety. Mica, his mother, the Seer of Truth, lived another five years.

After Will's return to the One, in 2234 Mica had adopted an old hybrid cat for company, whom she named Li-Li, and over the next few years, they became inseparable.

Mica was still an adviser to the Council, and she was the most respected woman in their society. She had trained many gifted others in the art of seeing.

It was about five years after Will's death when Mica suddenly stopped being very active in the community and went to sit silently on her favorite hill with Li-Li. She stayed there, praying, for two whole days.

When she was younger, Mica had once watched Lyra and Chi-Chi sit together on this very hill. She and Will had sat there for many hours during some of their most happy years, when they needed some much-valued privacy.

This magical place had always been a beautiful and spiritual place for Mica; she had scattered so many ashes here over the years—

that of dear Lyra, Chi-Chi, Anna, Ape-Man, Cat-Man, Tiern, and her beloved Will.

Mica was still there on the third day. Her son, Miron, was concerned about her, and he walked slowly up to the hill. As he reached the top, where Mica was standing, Miron took a deep breath. His mother was a vision to behold, with her arms, palms, and face stretched upward to the warm sun and silent skies. He stopped and watched her in awe. Even at her advanced age of ninety-five, she was still magnificent and graceful.

Mica was standing barefoot in the soft green grass and wearing a long white shift and Anna's wooden carved jewelry at her throat and wrists. The breeze was gently blowing her long gray hair away from her face, and he could hear her speaking clearly with both strength and dignity. Mica was reciting the prayer by chief Yellow Lark from 1887, that Many Fires had taught her.

O great One,
Whose voice I hear in the winds,
And whose breath gives life to all the world, hear me.
I am small and weak.
I need your strength and wisdom.
Let me walk in beauty, and make my eyes
Ever behold the red-and-purple sunset.
Make my hands respect the things you have made,
And my ears sharp to hear your voice.
Make me wise so that I may understand
The things you have taught my people.
Let me learn the lessons you have hidden
In every leaf and rock.
I seek strength, not to be superior to my brother,
But to fight my greatest enemy—myself.
Make me always ready to come to you
With clean hands and straight eyes,
So when life fades as the fading sunset,
My spirit will come to you
Without shame.

Miron stood motionless behind Mica until she had finished praying.

"Ah, Miron, you are here," she said without turning around. "You look so much like your father. You always bring me such joy whenever I see you. I have been waiting for you," she said, finally turning toward him with a smile.

Miron looked confused. "If you wanted to see me, why didn't you send for me?"

Mica replied, "I did. You are here, are you not?"

"Why do you stay alone on this hill?" Miron asked her gently.

"How do you judge a good society, Miron?" she asked, surprising him.

Caught a little off guard, he stammered, "I suppose there are six things I would consider important in a society:

1. The equality by which people are treated in that society
2. The respect that elders are shown by the community
3. The love and attention that must be showered upon the children so they grow and thrive
4. The kindness held for those who are much less fortunate
5. The deep compassion for the four-legged creatures that cannot speak for themselves"

Miron paused, and then he added, "Of course, the most important rule is number 6, which is the respect that you show your mother, Gaia."

"Excellent!" beamed Mira. "I have taught you well."

"Thank you," replied Miron, bowing slightly to his beloved mother.

"I called you here for a reason, Miron," said Mica softly.

"For what reason?" asked Miron, fearful of what she was going to reveal.

"It is my time. I am preparing to return to the One," replied Mica serenely.

"When?" asked Miron, suddenly filled with dread and panic, although his voice sounded relatively calm.

"Soon enough," Mica replied evasively. "Miron, I am surrounded by spirits. Can you see them? Because they are so beautiful," she murmured.

Miron stared out across the valley. "There are lots of flowers and golden butterflies, but I see nothing else," he said, perplexed. "Other than a lovely view."

"When are you going back to the One?" Miron asked again, desperately wanting an answer from his mother.

Ignoring his question, Mica replied, "Then you are not looking properly. You must see things not just with your eyes but with your heart and spirit too."

"I want my ashes scattered here when my body returns to my mother, the Earth," Mica continued, "Miron, please take great care of Li-Li, because she will suffer when I return to the One. Scatter her ashes here with mine when the time comes."

She then told him, "These golden butterflies are sacred. They are the spirits of all those who have returned to the One." She paused. "I am filled with beauty here. I can see all of them." Her eyes were shining brightly. "Will, Anna, Robert, Tiern, Ape-Man, Cat-Man, and so many others that I have loved."

"Sit with me a minute, Miron," asked Mica.

They both sat down together, and Li-Li quickly snuggled onto Mica's lap.

"You have always been my great strength and my rock," said Miron, his voice quivering with emotion. "I know this must happen, but I consider life without you a desolate wasteland. You are my light. I know I am a philosopher and scientist, but still, your death feels like my death too. I am not ashamed that I feel this way." Miron fell silent as a trail of tears began to drop into Mica's hand.

"Miron," replied Mica sadly as she began touching his face and wiping away his tears with both hands. "My time is done. I have walked my path and fulfilled my destiny. You must fulfill yours. It is why you are here. Remember, time is only an illusion. What is a human lifetime compared with the eternity of the spirit? It is merely a single drop in an unending ocean."

She paused.

"Here," Mica said and held her finger up. "Touch the tip of my finger with yours. I give this vision to you so that you will see me again. I will give you my life force, but it must be my last gift to you," she whispered.

Miron was confused, and before he could stop her, she touched his finger for just a moment. In that instant, he saw the past, the present, and the future all at once. Everything was bathed in golden light; there was no time or place. He could see all the faces, from his childhood, he had loved, now long gone. Miron was spellbound by his vision. His father was smiling at him. Miron reached out to touch Will's face, but the images faded and Miron was left reaching out toward a golden butterfly that he had believed was his father.

Mica spoke her last words. "You see, my child, I was not alone. I have always been surrounded by such love, and you will be too." She closed her eyes and said to him, "Remember that I love you with all my heart and soul." She paused for a moment and then murmured something softly to Li-Li with her last words. She took her final breath while lying cradled in her son's arms, still clutching Li-Li to her heart.

Li-Li stood up and held her face to the sky and howled as hundreds of golden butterflies appeared from everywhere, the swarm completely engulfing them.

One golden butterfly fluttered and brushed Miron's lips, and it was like a gentle kiss. As he looked up into the sky, still holding the body of his beloved mother, he could now see with both his heart and spirit. It was an incredibly beautiful vision. She was next to his father, so happy and smiling.

"When you want to visit us, we will be here for you, and when it is your time, you will fly among the stars with us," Mica said joyfully. Then the vision gradually faded, and all Miron could see was the beautiful valley.

Miron sat for a long time on the hill with Li-Li by his side, still holding his dead mother. He didn't want to leave her sacred place.

Eventually, she grew cold in his arms, and the sun began to set. Colors blazed across the horizon—golds, reds, pinks, with streaks of purples and blues. The sky was a mirage of color; it was the most vibrant sunset Miron had ever seen in his entire life. It was a fitting tribute to Mica's life and her death. She had always loved sunrises and sunsets.

Miron got up and made his way back to First City, carrying Mica's frail, lifeless body in his arms. Li-Li followed him, wailing and howling.

All the people mourned. Mica was the last icon of the past, except for Ewan, who had withdrawn many years ago into a hermit-like existence. Ewan had stayed with Anna as a child. When he became an adult, he chose to live with the Terranze, but several miles away from their settlement, because he liked his privacy and Ewan found it spiritually exhausting being around too many humans at once. His heightened senses picked up anyone's distress or sadness, and he found small talk difficult. Alone he could talk to the universe and he could hear the trees whispering to him and the water babbling. All of nature spoke to him, and it filled him with peace and wisdom.

The people understood Mica was with the One, and now she was home. Mica's life was celebrated with feasts and joy for a whole week. Mica had given so much of her life to the people and society, and it was only right that the people honored her.

Mica was cremated, and her ashes returned to her beloved hill. Li-Li died about three weeks after Mica, and Miron sincerely believed that she died of a broken heart. Her ashes were scattered with Mica's.

To celebrate the life of both of his parents, Miron erected a memorial. A long wall was built surrounding the back of the hill. The hill was officially named the Sacred Hill of the Golden Butterflies. Each person who had gone back to the One had a golden butterfly placed on the wall in remembrance of that person's life.

Miron, the son of Mica and Will, wrote of his mother:

> *It is not easy to live a life of courage and wisdom with beauty and grace. Seers see the truth, not just with their eyes, but their hearts and spirits. They see that everything is connected, and always has been. We are stardust, all part of the One. The rock and*

tree are part of your families. So are all those that fly, walk on the ground, or swim in the ocean. It is prophesied that one day we will all return to the One, to infinite light and beauty. So your future is already written in the stars, my mother lived to fulfill her destiny. Will you live to fulfill yours? In your life walk in beauty, and you will always see the light as my mother did. She was the beauty of this world.

Miron wrote of his father:

It seems humans are always looking for a changer to start and guide change. Instead of looking out there for a leader, look inside yourself. We are all born changers because we are human. It takes one brave person to say, "No more," then another to hear this and stand by their side. Until one by one, we all stand side by side and say a collective "No more!" This voice will then be heard, and change will follow. There are sacrifices to be made to enable change, and above all, the end goal should be service to others. Not service to self. This was what my father did to change the world, and it made him a wise and a great man. He was the changer.

Mica's favorite prayer was included on the sacred wall. The prayer Miron had heard on the hill was learned by all the tribes on Earth and hung on the wall outside every learning facility, replacing the tired old mantra that Mica and Will had to learn as children.

Miron became a famous and revered philosopher in his lifetime, and he eventually entered into a lifetime relationship with Kira, who was a talented seer, like his mother. She was twenty years younger than him, but it was a good match. After several years of trying, they finally won the lottery and were able to have a child, a beautiful little girl named Mira, who would grow up to be a wise warrior herself. She was destined for greatness, said Kira. Miron knew she was special because he saw many traits of both his mother and father in her. Miron knew that somehow she would play an essential role to humanity in the future. Miron didn't understand what would happen, but he had a dark feeling that terrible times were ahead.

CHAPTER 36

The Rising: 2272

Since so much time had passed since the famous battle of good and evil, between the people of Earth and Malus and the Archa, they didn't think about the Hive of Archon and its dangers anymore. The tales of that time had become favorite scary stories and celebrated plays while the people of Earth focused on their new, bright future.

The thing about dark forces is, they show their hand when people become complacent about their fate. When things go well for so long, the intuition for recognizing impending doom goes dormant. As the monsters grow, the people continue to smile and go about their business until one day, there is the realization that things have changed and life will never be the same again. Then which they once cherished the most is sadly lost forever. In other words, complacency is a recipe for extinction. One should always be on guard to understand the past and the present and to prevent the future from disintegrating into a full-blown nightmare.

The Hive of Archon was preparing for their final act of conquering Earth and her people. At the bottom of the ocean, in a rusted plane, still lay the last secret of the dark one, and somewhere far away, the hatchlings were getting prepared for their return to power. Nobody was alive from that epic battle, but Ewan, the child of light, who was now a timeworn man—he was a hundred years old—had just started to dream about the Archons. At first, he thought he was dreaming of them because he was coming closer to death.

Ewan realized, to his horror, that he was only able to sense the Archon hatchlings when they were geographically close. Now they had matured and were growing stronger daily—he could detect them. His nights were filled with terrors where the Archons collectively whispered to him in the dark.

"We are coming," they said to Ewan in his dreams.

The Hive wanted to avenge their Archon deaths, and they mocked Ewan by foretelling the deaths of millions on planet Earth, knowing he was now too weak and old to stop them. Everyone that knew how to fight them had gone, and he was dying himself. *As one tyrant falls, there is always another waiting in the shadows, ready to slither into that dark place,* he thought.

Ewan sensed that these newly created Archons would be like Malus, but stronger, smarter, and would be almost impossible to destroy. He knew by 2282 that the Archons would rule the Earth again. Soon they would be able to breed. He believed they would find a way to open a new portal from the Void and let the Hive of Archon finally conquer the Earth, a prize they had waited billions of years to claim.

How could they be stopped? Ewan wondered.

There was no one to tell. It was too late. He must warn somebody, and he started to write on a piece of paper, "The Archons are back." Then the pen slipped from his trembling hand, and a fresh breeze blew the precious scrap of paper from his table onto the floor and settled into a dusty corner of his hut. He knew it might not be found for years.

Ewan focused on the light that tightly spiraled around him and had come to bring him home. He closed his eyes, relaxing. He was not afraid, because he could feel the arms of loving warmth and pure violet light of the One that was coming over him in ecstatic waves, each one stronger than the last. He felt incredible happiness and peace. His final thought was, *I am going home.*

Thousands of miles away, the hatchlings, now mature, began to crawl out, naked, from the bowels of the Earth and into the moonlit night. Silently they crawled through the dunes and the windswept grass, their handler's blood still drying on their mottled skin.

When they reached the edge of the silver ocean, they all rose to their feet and raised their collective heads to the starlit skies, uttering a powerful, primitive, low, vibrational scream that shook the planet to its very core. Humans around the world covered their ears in excruciating pain, terrified, they believed the apocalypse was coming as enormous earthquakes rocked the Earth and tidal waves drenched the land. Somewhere deep in space and time, the Hive heard them loud and clear.

The invasion had begun.

ABOUT THE AUTHOR

Julie Vigil was born and grew up in Britain and has lived in America for over thirty years. She is fascinated by science fiction, visions of possible futures, and forbidden history. Julie is a disabled US Army veteran, breast cancer survivor, and world traveler with a thirst for knowledge. Julie lives with her husband and two teenage children in New Mexico.

CPSIA information can be obtained
at www.ICGtesting.com
Printed in the USA
LVHW021508111119
637002LV00001B/133/P